A miracle drug, thought to cure turns out not only to destroy, but transform those who were once human into something far more deadly. Now, lovers bound by hope, passion and faith must face the ultimate test.

Can their love surpass a transformation of the most horrific kind?

Will survival be worth it, if they aren't together?

"Full of juicy zombie action meshed with romance to make your heart break. The pace is thrilling and the action doesn't stop!" Author of *"The Guardian"*, CJ Gosling

"I was completely blindsided by events in this story. Even now, I can't stop thinking about it." Author of *"Until Dawn: Last Light"*, Jennifer Simas

". . .an apocalyptic world that immediately feels plausible in these days of pharmaceutical "miracles" and quick cures gone wrong. . . .a fearless and unflinching launch into darker issues and terrible choices. There is great depth in this author's work . .." Author of *" Brilliant Prey"*, Brenda Wallace

THE NEVERMORE TRILOGY

SHANNON MAYER

HiJinks

The Nevermore Trilogy

ISBN-10: 1490564624
ISBN-13: 9781490564623

Published by HiJinks Ink
www.shannonmayer.com

Cover art by Damon Za
www.damonza.com

Mayer, Shannon

ACKNOWLEDGEMENTS

I've been blessed to work with a fabulous team that has helped me reach this point of seeing *Sundered* published. To my Beta readers, Sandy Hunter, Jean Faganello and Joanne Ferreiro for taking the time to go through the rough draft, thank you, thank you, thank you!

To my editor, Jessica Klassen, copy editors Kelly Berthelot and Melissa Breau, proof reader Dr. Kathie M. Black, without you, I would not be able to have such a high quality product to put out to the world. I will be forever grateful for your time, knowledge and skill.

My lovely writers group (WIP), you are all an integral part of my writers journey. Your love and unwavering support has been what's kept me going when the days got rough.

Finally, but far from least, to my husband Terry. If you hadn't pushed me to chase my dreams and pursue my writing, *Sundered* never would have seen the light of day. Thank you for loving me enough to challenge me to reach for the stars.

PART I

SUNDERED

Love is something eternal; the aspect may change,
but not the essence.
—Vincent Van Gogh

1

I walked slowly, my hands above my head to keep from touching the scotch broom. My eyes watered, my throat and nose itched, and the patches of bare skin the plant leaned in to kiss were bright red and swelling. Fanny Bay was famous for a lot of things, but when we moved here three months ago I didn't realize it was a breeding ground for my most hated nemesis.

"You coming, babe? I really am sorry; I didn't know the trail was full of broom." Sebastian, my sweet and usually thoughtful husband yelled back to me. He wasn't allergic to the brilliant yellow plant, so he didn't have to worry about the branches that hung on all sides, and he made good time on the trail. I could just make out his broad back and dark brown hair over the tops of the broom ahead of me. At 6'4" he towered over most people and living things, noxious weeds included.

I grunted a reply, not wanting to take in any more air than I had to. The walk through the tunnel of broom wouldn't kill me—it wasn't that bad an allergy—but hell, it wasn't something I was enjoying either. Breaking out in a rash and blowing my nose continually for the next few hours would be what I had to look forward to after this little excursion. But the bottom line was, and even I could admit it, I needed to get out of the house and get some fresh air. I'd been holed up for far too long grieving, and this little hike and visit with the neighbours would get me moving. God love the man, Sebastian knew me better than I knew myself sometimes and this excursion had been his idea.

"Mara?"

"I'm coming, Bastian, don't expect me to run through this crap," I said, shifting sideways to slip between two over-hanging branches.

A stick jabbed me in the belly and I snapped it off with a quick twist. "Stupid plant," I muttered thinking of all the things that had been jabbed into me of late; it was the least painful, both to my body and my heart.

I blinked away tears that threatened, and wiped my hands across my eyes to my immediate regret: they were covered in pollen from pushing the broom out of my way.

"Son of a bitch, I'm an idiot," I muttered, blinking furiously, trying to keep the tears flowing to rinse my eyes out.

The doctors didn't know why we were having such a hard time getting pregnant, and the miscarriage only confirmed that it was something wrong with me. I sneezed and rubbed my nose with the back of my hand, the minor explosion jarring me out of my depressing thoughts.

"Hurry up woman, I told Dan we'd be there ten minutes ago. Last thing I want to do is upset the new neighbours." Sebastian's voice was even further ahead of me now.

"Yeah, I'm coming O white knight of mine who considers a walk in the broom a nice time out for his highly allergic wife!" I yelled back. I wasn't angry with him; this was part of the way he dealt with his grief. It was the same when his father and brother died in the boating accident; at least, that was what his mother had shared with me. His motto was buckle down and move on; push forward and don't look back. Although even with that attitude he sweated the whole way across the Georgia Strait, despite the fact that the ferry we were on was the size of a cruise liner.

A rustle in the bush stopped my feet before I thought about what I was doing. "Sebastian?" He had a nasty habit of scaring me; jumping out from the place I least expected him. The rustling drew closer and I pulled away, pressing my back against a wall of yellow and green, my heart picking up speed. I didn't think it was Sebastian. A musky odour floated past my nose, and whatever was making the noise, it was an animal. A flash of black in the bush across from me and I nearly wet my pants. Bears were more than common on this part of Vancouver Island; they were considered pretty much part of the neighbourhood and one of the few things I was truly terrified of.

Crap. Mouth dry, I tried again, whispering as loud as I dared. "Sebastian!"

The black thing in the bush that I was sure was a bear, grunted and shuffled closer and I slid my way towards the spot where I'd last seen my husband. Maybe the bear wouldn't attack us if we were together? Sweat popped out on my forehead and I no longer cared how much the broom brushed against me, I just didn't want to be eaten. I pushed my back against the wall of plants, not caring as they scratched across my bare skin as I slid sideways up the trail keeping my eyes trained on the rustling behind me.

One step forward and something grabbed me from behind sending me into a flailing mass of arms, legs, and grunts as my heart threatened to burst out of my throat.

"Whoa, whoa babe, settle down," Sebastian said, laughing at me, his blue eyes dancing, his hands resting on my shoulders. I didn't care he'd scared me. Not this time.

I gulped in a breath. "Bear," I said, pointing down the trail, my hand shaking.

"Really?"

I nodded. Then the stupidest thing I've ever seen that man do happened right in front of my disbelieving eyes. Sebastian started back the way we'd come, towards the bear.

"What are you doing?" I hissed, my fear turning to anger as I thought of myself widowed before I'd even turned thirty.

"I just want to see it. I've never seen a bear up close before," he said.

"There's a first and a last time for everything," I snapped and then contrite at the thought of my last words to him being snotty I changed tactics. "Please come back, we need to keep going, I thought you said we were almost there."

Sebastian didn't answer me except to wave backwards. As if I was going to get any closer to the bear, yeah right. He kept moving forward, his movements slow and steady as if he was afraid to spook the animal. I didn't think that was going to be a problem.

I wanted to scrub my hands over my face with frustration but had to settle for gripping the edges of my shorts. There had to be a way to get him to come back.

"Sebastian, I'll divorce you if you keep looking for the bear." Maybe that would work.

"You're too poor to pay a lawyer."

I snorted. "So are you." I thought a moment more, knowing I had the answer.

"I'll tell your Gran on you."

He stopped and turned to face me. "You wouldn't." The look on his face said it all and a twitch started in the corner of my lips. I knew I had him. I let out a sigh of relief and put my hands on my hips.

"I would, just you wait and . . ."

A huge black bear burst out of the bush behind Sebastian with a roar and I bit down on a scream, my worst nightmare unfolding before my eyes. Sebastian stumbled back towards me and fell over a rut in the ground. I grabbed a rock and cocked my arm to throw it, when a hand dropped on my shoulder and shoved me to the ground. The smell of cigar smoke curled through the air, slicing through the sweet musk of the broom and the heavier musk of the large predator ready to eat my husband.

"Stay down girl," a throaty voice said and I looked over my shoulder to see our sort-of-crazy neighbour Dan above me, a gun levelled at the bear. "You too boy, stay down." I wasn't sure if he was talking to Sebastian or the bear.

We both stayed low on the ground and Dan walked towards the bear, his gun never wavering.

"Come on Bob, you know you aren't allowed to be eating the locals. Specially these city folk so new here, they're practically a biohazard with all the toxins and chemicals they've been living in."

"Hey, we eat healthy," I said, then thought about the situation and shut my mouth. A crazy man with a gun and a bear in the middle of a forest trail that no one knew we were on. Quiet Mara, you'll live longer.

I watched in disbelief as the bear—Bob, I guess—dropped to all fours and let out a long low snort.

"Yeah," Dan said, "I feel the same about these imports, but we got to give them a chance before we run them off."

The bear grunted and pawed at the ground a mere foot away from Sebastian's bare legs. I whimpered in fear, wishing I had the gun in my hands. Why wasn't Dan shooting the bear? He wasn't truly having a conversation with the animal; he had to know that, didn't he?

"Go on now, Bob. Come around back of the house later tonight and you can have one of the salmon I thawed out this morning." Dan said as he lowered the gun. Bob gave one last snuffle and turned away from us, heading back down the trail towards the ocean.

I scrambled to my feet and ran to Sebastian, catching him in a, dare I say it, bear hug.

"I'm okay babe," he said into my hair.

"No you're not." I stood up and kicked him in the shin, pleased with the wince it produced. "You idiot! I told you not to go back. That bear could have killed you!"

"Lower your voice girl or Bob will come back to see what all the shouting's about and to be honest I'd sooner shoot you than him. He's better company than most people," Dan said.

I turned to face him, our kind-of rescuer, at a loss for words. Did I say thanks for saving us, or thanks for not shooting us, or was I supposed to be mad that he preferred a bear over people? Dan stared at me as he chewed on the stubby cigar clamped between yellowed teeth. His salt and pepper hair was military short and yet still managed to be messy and his army fatigues were rumpled and stained. I didn't know what to make of him.

Was it an act, or were the other locals right and he was off his rocker?

Sebastian took the lead, exaggerating his limp and rubbing at his shin before holding his hand out to the gruff older man. "Thanks Dan, much appreciate the intervention with your friend. We were on our way to your place. You put an ad on the mailbox that you had some old gardening stuff you want to get rid of? I spoke with you this morning about coming by?"

Dan stared at Sebastian for so long I started to get nervous. The man after all had a reputation for eating Crazy Flakes for breakfast and he was packing a large gun. Not really a good combination. I cleared my throat.

"Things like old pots, and maybe even some veggie starts," I said, wanting to break the awkward silence.

Dan took a drag on his cigar and blew out a string of smoke. "Yup, come on then." He turned his back to us, put his gun over his shoulder and led us down the yellow and green tunnel.

We followed, Sebastian taking my hand and giving it a squeeze. "I'm sorry," he mouthed to me.

I smiled and squeezed his hand, mouthing back, "Okay. But I'm still calling your Gran." Sebastian winced again and I nodded. There was always a consequence for being dumb, even if it was just having your Gran rip a strip off you.

As the adrenaline stopped its headlong rush through my body, I became acutely aware of my bare legs and arms—all the parts I'd shoved up against the broom. By the time we reached Dan's, a fortress of a home that looked as if it had once been an army barrack, every visible inch of me was covered in hives. I stared around me, absently scratching at my

9

arms. Dan's yard wasn't fenced, but it didn't really need to be, not with the way his house was built. What looked like steel plate covered the doors. All the windows had rebar grills over them and the exterior of the house seemed to be made of a cement brick mixture. I ran my fingers over the rough texture, my curiosity for a moment overwhelming my itching.

"Make this quick, Bastian. I'm blowing up like a puffer fish," I whispered to him as I deposited myself on the only chair in the yard. Dan brought me a prickly cactus looking plant and stuck it on the ground beside me.

"Aloe Vera. It'll help with the sting till you get home," he said as he broke off a thick green stem and handed the goopy end to me.

Surprised at his kindness, my opinion of him shifting again, I broke off a second piece of the plant and rubbed it onto the worst patch of hives with a sigh. It was cool and soothing. I was going to have to get me an Aloe Vera plant.

It was nice in the shade; this corner of Dan's garden was already up, the bright green shoots sticking through the ground. I didn't recognize any of them. I was still pretty new to the whole concept of gardening. I could see what I thought were peas climbing a section of netting, large rubber tires housing a creeping plant of some sort, and several raised beds with strawberries in them. Those at least I could pick out easily. It was very strange to see such a mixture of old-school gardening life next to the military feel of his home.

Next to the house a battered old radio played while Sebastian talked planting, tools, and seeds with the old nutter.

After a few minutes, Dan walked to the radio and turned it up just as a female announcer came on, her voice breathy and completely unsuited to radio.

"Bet she got the job by doing a few jobs of her own, eh?" Dan gave me a lecherous wink and walked back over to where Sebastian was digging through an old pile of pots.

I grimaced and shook my head. That was an awful thought, no matter that it was probably true. I reached down to rub at a particularly large hive with the Aloe Vera on the back of my calf, when what the announcer was saying sunk in.

"This is a miracle drug boys and girls. Not only can you eat whatever you want and not gain weight, but it does all sorts of great things, but I can't remember all of them. You can't buy it over the counter . . ."

I got up and moved my chair closer to the radio and a second, male, announcer came on, his voice highly animated and almost as feminine as the woman's.

"So Phillipa, you're telling me there's no downside, no side effects to this—what was the drug called again?" he said.

Phillipa's irritating voice came back on. "They're calling it *Nevermore*, as in, *never more* gain weight, *never more* get sick, or disgustingly fat, *never more* get cellulite, or any sort of weight gain." She giggled and the high pitch and redundancy of what she was saying made me shiver. It was a wonder the speakers didn't blow. She took a breath and continued, "It's amazing, one shot is all it takes, and yes, it is expensive, but that's it. One shot and you're good for life. I've lost ten pounds and I've been eating burgers, cake, and totally noshing on chocolate." The male announcer came back on.

"Reportedly this Nevermore truly is a miracle drug as it also prevents Parkinson's disease, works in tandem with heart medications to stop arrhythmias, and has a host of other beneficial side effects. One that will be of interest to many is that

11

helps tremendously with fertility, more so than any of the current fertility drugs, with less side effects. As it's derived from an all-natural source, the body can . . ."

I turned the radio back down and looked over to Sebastian, still deep in conversation with Dan who was nodding and even giving the occasional smile. Sebastian was not only tall, but a little on the large side. Okay, a little more than a little on the large side. Not that I had anything to preen about, I easily had an extra twenty-five pounds on my 5'5 frame. Maybe even thirty, but it was still less than I'd been carrying a year ago when we decided to start our family. That was when we began to realize there was a problem, and that we might not be able to have a baby. I lost weight, ate healthy, took my vitamins, but getting pregnant was nearly impossible and the one time I did, I miscarried.

Scratching at my collarbone I had a sudden urge to get moving. Not only did I need to get a second dose of Benadryl and a shower to wash the broom pollen off, I had to get on the phone to the doctor. What if this Nevermore drug was what the radio said it was? It seemed almost too good to be true: fertility and weight loss, all rolled into a single shot. My heart started to thrum with excitement. This was what we'd been waiting for. I could hardly wait to tell Sebastian what I'd heard; I could hardly wait to finally be a mother.

2

As soon as we got home I ran upstairs to shower, hoping to diffuse the pollen on my skin. We'd bought a rambling two-story farmhouse on three acres that was at least a hundred years old that I was completely in love with, along with all the history it represented. It was heated with a woodstove and even had an old wood-burning cooking stove that was now on the back porch having made room for my new convection oven. The old woman who owned the farmhouse had been on the property her whole life, ninety-eight years, and had not only been raised in the house, but had raised her own children in the house. I'd hoped to raise my own children here.

My hands slowed in the soapy water as my thoughts wound back to the hospital, the nurses and the doctor telling me that I had miscarried. At five weeks, still in my first trimester and within the real danger zone, I'd woken up in the middle of the night to cramping and blood on the sheets. Since then I'd not gone back to my job as a real estate agent, taking a leave of absence to deal with the grief and to give my body time to heal.

Sebastian worked from home as a web designer, something I was intensely grateful for as he was able to help me out of the depression I'd fallen into after the miscarriage, not to mention pay the bills that never stopped coming in.

The bathroom door clicked and I poked my head outside the curtain. "Hand me the new shampoo."

Sebastian held it just out of reach before finally letting me take it, a grin spreading across his face, his gorgeous dimples framing his mouth.

I ducked back in and lathered up, smiling to myself. He might be a little chubby, but my man was good looking and that smile, even now it made me weak in the knees.

"It's probably a hoax, you know that don't you, babe?" Sebastian's voice was muffled as I stuck my head back under the running water, the cool shower sluicing off the last of the pollen. It didn't, however, make the hives go away. I was covered in them from head to toe, the bumps starting to develop even where the plant didn't touch me, its infection of my skin spreading like some horrid disease.

"You don't know that and neither do I," I said, soaping my body up. "You aren't a doctor last time I checked."

"These sorts of things come and go. It's either a hoax or it will turn out to have some horrible side effect. Like, your boobs will shrivel up leaving me nothing to play with, and then I would die."

I laughed, turned the water off and reached for a towel. The shower curtain slid open and Sebastian lifted an eyebrow at me, a smile tugging at the corner of his lips, his clothes having mysteriously disappeared. His eyes roved over my naked and still-wet body. Heat curled in my stomach, still now after four years of marriage he could set my skin on fire and my heart racing with a simple look.

"The towel, please." I held out my hand, trying to look uninterested. He shook his head and stepped into the tub, his bare toes touching the tips of mine. Without a word he started to dry me off, starting with my hair and working his way slowly down my body, his hands massaging as he dried.

I bit back a groan, the moisture from my skin disappearing, the heat intensifying. I closed my eyes and let the sensations wash through me, the scratching of the itch from the hives almost heavenly as he scrubbed the towel over them.

"Stop," I whispered, not really meaning it. Sebastian chuckled and I peeked out from under my eyelashes. With a single, swift movement he scooped me into his arms and took me to the bedroom and our very small bed.

With more gentleness than one would think from a man his size, he laid me on the bed and pressed his body into mine, our hearts beating in time with one another.

"I love you Sebastian," I whispered as he slid into me, completing me, making us one.

"I love you too my bumpy, hive-ridden woman," he whispered into my ear. I slapped him half-heartedly on the shoulder, and the sweet love making quickly turned into a laughing romp that ended as it often did: in each other's arms, tears prickling at the back of my eyes as my emotions filled me up and spilled over in physical release.

"You okay, Mara?"

"Yes," I said curling deeper into his arms, trying to think of something smart to say and coming up empty handed so I settled for the truth. "Sometimes I just love you so much it makes me cry."

"Hmm. I am quite the hunk. Really, you are very lucky to have snagged me. I was planning on playing the field till I was at least sixty before you came along." He spread his big hands over his chest and leaned back against the headboard, a self-satisfied smile across his face. I smiled up at him, laughed, and shook my head. The size of his ego never ceased to amaze me.

Sobering, I sat up, pulling the sheet around me. "I'm going to ask the doctor about that Nevermore shot. I think it's what we've been waiting for. I mean, we could be fit, trim, and then have a baby too. It would be amazing." I stared at him, willing him to catch my excitement.

It didn't work. Sebastian frowned, and then shrugged his big shoulders. "I still think it's some sort of hoax, but you go ask him. See what he has to say, but don't get your hopes up."

I wrapped my arms around him and snuggled into his arms. I could be excited enough for the both of us; in fact, I already was. My eye lids began to droop as the second dose of antihistamines kicked in. I let them close completely, my heart light with the hopes and dreams of a family, already forgetting Sebastian's warning.

3

The doctor's office was full. And I don't mean all the seats were taken, I mean there wasn't even standing room. I ended up halfway down the hall leaning against the cream-coloured wall next to one of the office doors.

"Excuse me, are you Mara Wilson?" a voice behind me asked.

I turned to face a woman who looked vaguely familiar. She was in her late thirties with beautiful blond hair and eyes the colour of the Caribbean ocean. I cocked my head to one side. "Yes, I'm Mara, have we met?"

The woman laughed and patted me on the arm. "Only briefly. I'm Shelly Gartlet, I live on the road above you, and we met at the mailbox when you first moved here."

I smiled and nodded. "That's right. I remember now." Really, how could I forget? The woman had grabbed me in a welcoming hug, spilling all the neighbourhood gossip in less than five minutes, and in a single breath. I'd made a mental note never to confide in her. "Are you here for the Nevermore shot?"

Shelly smiled. "Yes and no. My husband, George, and I got the shot last week, but Jessica here," she half tugged a younger looking clone forward, "wasn't able to get the shot, she was sick with that flu that's been going around."

I put my hand out. She was a very pretty young girl, with the same long blond hair as her mom and the same stunning eyes. She looked to be about sixteen years old, but could have been younger; it was so hard to tell now days. No doubt the boys went crazy for her at school. "Nice to meet you Jessica." She gripped my hand lightly, ducking her head.

Shelly patted her on the arm and gave me a wink. "Jessica weren't you telling me about Mara's husband, and about how good looking he is?"

Jessica flushed from her chin to the roots of her hair, her eyes widening as our gazes connected.

"I didn't mean . . . it's not like . . . mom, how could you say that?" she finally spit out.

I laughed, warmed by the thought, knowing that my husband *was* an attractive man, so much so that even teenagers had crushes on him, despite the extra weight he carried. Tall dark and handsome with confidence and a wicked sense of humour, he'd had women swooning over him in every age bracket. "It's okay Jessica, I'm sure Sebastian would love to know that he had an admirer."

"Please don't tell him," she whispered. We were interrupted by a woman who pushed her way in to our conversation.

"You here for that miracle drug?"

She was a chubby woman in her mid forties standing behind me. A quick glance and from my experience and time in Weight Watchers, I knew she had to be at least eighty pounds overweight.

"Yes. You too?" I asked.

"Hell no. I'm perfect just the way I am." Hands on her hips, her purple and red muumuu fluttered around her thick ankles as she glared at me, daring me to call her out. I smiled and bit my tongue. She continued her rant, "And all you yahoos coming in for some quick-fix are going to get what's coming to you. There's no such thing; it's ridiculous to think one shot can do all that. Fertility, heart stuff, making bones stronger—foolishness that you've all bought into."

Shelly and Jessica backed away from the woman and I gave them a smile as I too gave the riled-up woman some room.

"Come over for coffee," I said over the muumuu woman's head, "and we can get to know each other. Anytime, I would love some company." Shelly and Jessica smiled and they gave me identical thumbs up. This was one of the nice things about where we lived. Yes, we were in the country, but there were still neighbours close enough if you needed some sugar or a helping hand, or maybe just a cup of coffee with the local gals. I smiled to myself. I loved it here; the island was everything I'd hoped for.

"Mara Wilson?" The desk nurse called me and I followed her directions into the doctor's room, happy to get away from the woman on her tirade. I glanced back and she hadn't paused for a second, now laying into a pudgy teenager on the other side of the hall. The doctor's room was close enough that I could still hear her with the door half shut, her voice rising with intensity.

"Exercise and diet. Kids when I was young were outside playing and working. None of this TV and computer crap." There was a pause and I imagined a nurse speaking to her. "No, I will not lower my voice; I think you all have lost your minds.

19

This is some government conspiracy to plug you all full of tracking devices and drugs so they can better control us."

I shook my head, why couldn't she just let us be? It was obvious she was delusional, she could use the shot and lose a few pounds, and she'd probably live longer. There was a large thump that rattled the wall and made me jump. Then came a god-awful screech that sounded like a parrot being strangled, followed by a dull cheer from the crowd. "You can't kick me out!" the woman screamed, "I have an appointment!"

Ejection from a doctor's office, that had to be a first. I laughed at the absurdity of her claims. Health Canada and the FDA wouldn't allow a drug to be given to the masses if it hadn't been tested. They knew it was safe and there was no way it could get to the public unless it was good to go.

"Hello, Mara." Dr. Cooper stepped into the office, his grey hair and stooped shoulders making me wonder how much longer I would be able to go to him.

"Hi, Dr. Cooper." I smiled, unable to suppress my emotions. This was it; this was the moment I'd been waiting for.

"I suppose you're here for the Nevermore shot?" he asked, his face a mask of concentration.

I smiled wider, my excitement spilling over into my words. "Yup. It's perfect! I can lose the last of the weight that you said I should to be at an optimum size for getting pregnant, and the shot will make me more fertile, right? That's what I heard on the radio and when I looked it up on the internet it confirmed that. And then maybe Sebastian should get it too? Because you weren't sure if the fertility issues were with him or me, we could both take it and then we'd be sure to get pregnant, right? I'm so happy; I can't believe this is finally going to happen. I'm going to be able to have a baby."

Dr. Cooper didn't answer me right away; his eyes stared at the screen of his computer as he scrolled through it, page by page.

"Dr. Cooper? This is a good thing, right?" I was starting to get a bad feeling that maybe Sebastian was right; maybe this was all a hoax. No, there were too many people in the waiting room. If it were a hoax, it'd be all over the internet and news.

"Mara, the drug does all that and more. Strengthens bones, prevents skin cancer, and increases fertility. Parkinson's and arrhythmias are virtually wiped out. It truly is a miracle, of that I have no doubt, and I'm encouraging as many patients as possible to take it."

I let out a breath I didn't know I'd been holding in a huge sigh of relief, my heart slowing back to a normal rhythm. I folded my hands on the desk and leaned forward. "You scared me. I thought you were going to tell me it was a hoax. That's what Sebastian thought it was, some scam to get money out of people."

Dr. Cooper shook his head but he still wasn't smiling, and that made me nervous all over again. "It's no hoax, Mara, but my dear, you can't take the shot."

A loud buzzing filled my ears and though Dr. Cooper continued to talk, I couldn't hear a word he said. I blinked once, twice as I grasped what he said. "Why not?" I whispered.

He let out deep sigh and pulled my hands into his, cupping them like a grandfather would. "Nevermore is derived from cystius scoparius."

I stared at him, confusion rushing through me. "I don't know what that is. Is it bad?"

"Scotch broom. The concentrate within the drug would kill you at worst, and at best you would be in a constant state of agony, hives, sinus infections, swollen glands, and hypersensitivity to the mildest of irritations. There have even been some reported cases where people who were allergic to broom took Nevermore and now they've lost their eyesight." He squeezed my suddenly ice-cold hands. "You can't take Nevermore, Mara."

My mind whirled, hopes thrown about in a tornado of emotions before they crashed and burned. I pulled my hands slowly away from him and folded my arms across my breasts, at a loss for words.

Dr. Cooper leaned back in his chair and slid a sheet towards me. "Here's the chemical breakdown, Mara. Every aspect of the broom has been used in this drug, not just part of it."

"Why are you giving this to me?" I asked, trying to keep the venom that was welling up within me out of my voice, my hand gripping the paper.

"Because I know you, Mara. I know how much you want children, and how hard you've worked to lose the weight that was preventing that dream. I know that you're going to try and find a way around this, and I don't want you to die. There is no way around this." His voice was so soft, gentle, that it broke down the last barrier of strength I'd propped up, and a sob slipped out.

"I'm so sorry, Mara," he said, and I bit back the next sob that was bubbling up. I stood and ran to the door, pushing past the horde of people that filled the hallway, running till I reached my car. I leaned against it, head against the hot metal and let my heart slow down. It wasn't the end of the world; it really didn't make it any harder for Sebastian and me to have a baby. At least that's what I told myself.

"Got the shot did you?" a rather familiar voice threw the question at me.

I spun on my heel to face down the chubby woman who'd been tossed out of the clinic. "Not that it's any of your business, but no, I didn't," I snapped at her, forcing back the urge to punch her in her doughy face.

She nodded. "Smart girl. I'll tell you now, it was the best decision you ever made. The government won't get you now." She reached out and patted me on the arm. I shrugged her hand off me and bit my tongue, the four letter words on the tip that would leave me screaming and ranting at the unsuspecting woman.

I unlocked the car, slid into my seat, and started the engine. The rear view mirror gave me a perfect picture of the purple muumuu waddling through the parking lot, the woman on her way to accost another person leaving the clinic.

"It wasn't a choice I made, it was a choice taken from me," I whispered to her retreating figure. I took a deep breath and headed home to Sebastian and the farm.

4

Days turned into weeks and before I knew it, I'd spent the next month alternately hiding in our tiny bedroom, watching daytime talk shows, and, in general, allowing myself to fall back into the depression that had found me after the miscarriage.

I told Sebastian I didn't feel well, had a fever, my joints ached—anything that would give me time to hide from the world for a little longer. The sunlight hurt my eyes on the few days I dared to peek out into the yard, and that became yet another excuse. Sebastian did his best to console me when he wasn't working on his new client's project. He brought me flowers from the fields, told me funny stories, and even baked cookies for me, something he'd never done before.

On the twenty-eighth day of my—self-imposed—confinement, a booming rattle shook me awake, the bedroom door flinging open.

"That's it, I've been patient and done what I could, but you've got to get up," Sebastian barked as he whipped the blankets off me.

"Leave me alone," I grumbled, grabbing at the blankets. He snatched them out of my hands.

"Nope, time to grow up and get with the program."

Bright sunlight streamed into the room as he opened all the curtains. "There's no use crying over something you can't change." He sat down on the bed and pulled me upright to sit beside him.

"It isn't fair," I said, hating how childish I sounded. "Every crack head and addict out there can get pregnant, and they can't even take care of themselves. We would be able to give a child a life, a family, and a home."

Sebastian nodded. "I know babe, but you're not doing yourself any good by wallowing in this."

I frowned at him. "I'm not wallowing."

"Yes, you are. I have something for you; it's down in the garden so you'll have to haul your butt down there. I've got to go into town; I'll be back in a couple of hours."

I stood and stomped my way to the bathroom, brushing past him. "What do you know anyway, you're just a man; you don't have an internal clock like I do," I snapped as I turned on the shower and got in the steaming water.

Stupid male, what did he know about really wanting babies? Or losing weight for that matter? The man thought he was a Greek god with the way he strutted through the house naked, preening in front of mirrors. I snorted to myself. My anger faded as I worked the soap through my hair, the hot water rinsing away the last of the tears. Damn, now I was feeling grateful for his intervention. I'd have to be careful about how I thanked him, or I'd never hear the end of it.

Fifteen minutes later, I was heading out the back door to the garden when a soft woof met my ears. I blinked, stared, and couldn't believe what I was seeing. Sitting next to the freshly dug earth, with a giant red ribbon tied around its neck, was a tiny yellow Labrador Retriever.

I clapped my hands over my mouth and the puppy woofed at me and started to wiggle, his entire body wagging as if his tail alone wasn't enough. I ran and fell to my knees in front of the little guy, scooping him up and holding him close as he licked my face, his still-sweet puppy breath tickling me.

"Oh, you devil of a man," I said as I cuddled the bundle of fur. "What are we going to call you, hmm?" I rubbed his velvety soft ears and he settled down, resting his nose on the crook of my neck. I pressed my cheek against him. "How about Nero?" I'd grown up with a big yellow Lab that my grandparents had rescued and he'd been my companion and best friend for years.

A voice called from the front of the house, "Hello? Mrs. Wilson?"

Standing up, Nero in my arms, I walked around the house to see Jessica carrying a basket filled to the brim. She smiled at me over the basket, her eyes lighting on Nero.

"You've got a puppy? Oh, he's so cute. Can I hold him?" I handed him to her as she handed me the basket of goodies.

"It's a belated welcome-to-our-neighbourhood gift," Jessica said as she snuggled with the wriggling puppy.

"Thank you, that's really sweet," I said, placing the basket on the porch railing. "Do you want to go for a walk with me and Nero?"

Jessica nodded and put him down. We headed out the front drive, past the iron gates that had hung for as long as the property had existed. They were heavy and sturdily built when the farm first was started. Each panel was taller than me, and easily weighed a hundred pounds. The supports were cemented into the ground on either side, and there was a huge rusting metal bar that slipped into place to lock it. Scrolling leaves and grape clusters were welded on in an attempt to soften the hard steel lines, to make it look more artistic than utilitarian. It didn't work that well. At the best of times it was a major effort to close the thing, which is why we left it open, and why the bar was nearly covered in vegetation.

Jessica chatted at me the entire time, her bubbly personality yet another stamp of her mothers. I didn't mind, she was a sweet girl. I wondered several times why she'd taken the Nevermore shot, she didn't seem to need to lose weight, but I didn't think it was a question I could ask her. Maybe when her mother came over for coffee I would broach the subject.

Jessica pointed out the neighbours who were nice, weird, and neutral quite effectively. Though the properties around here ranged in size, they averaged at five acres a piece with a few undeveloped properties scattered around. On our road alone there were only four homes; the roads on either side of us boasted two and three respectively.

The walk took us about an hour, and by the end of it I was packing Nero; I didn't mind, he was tiny and the walk and visit left me feeling invigorated and more alive than I'd felt in weeks.

"Hey, that was fun. Would it be okay if I came and walked with you and Nero again?" Jessica asked as we stood in front of my place.

"Of course, anytime, you don't need to call. I'm not going back to work for a while yet so just pop in."

Jessica waved and jogged off towards home.

The car was back which meant that Sebastian was home. I smiled and headed towards the house. I didn't care how grateful I sounded or how he might try to blackmail me with it later, he was a good man and I was lucky to have him.

"Sebastian?" I called out, Nero sound asleep in my arms. I wanted to apologize for being a jerk.

"Here."

I clutched Nero close and kissed the top of his down-soft head, and made my way to the living room where Sebastian sat glued to the TV.

"Really? After the talk you just gave me about not wallowing and being out in the sunshine?" I said, tapping him on the shoulder. "I can't believe you bought me a—"

"Shhh," he cut me off and pointed to the TV.

On the screen was a reporter standing in front of VGH, Vancouver General Hospital. "It appears that the miracle drug, Nevermore, wasn't such a miracle after all. Early reports are that the toxins thought to be strained out of the main component of the drug—cystius scoparius, better known as scotch broom—were not eliminated." The reporter choked up, her eyes misting over and I wondered if she had taken the drug or knew someone close to her who had. "The toxins attack the part of the brain that makes us human, whole sections of the cerebral cortex are eaten away until there is nothing left but a base animal instinct." Someone stumbled out of the hospital and the reporter turned and ran towards the man who clutched at his stomach. "Sir, can you tell us why you're here today?"

"I'm so hungry, I can't stop eating. Nothing fills me up," He said. His eyes were glazed and his skin had a strong golden yellow hue to it, as if he were jaundiced.

"Sir, did you take the drug Nevermore?" she asked, sticking the microphone close to the man.

He stared at the microphone for a moment, opened his mouth to answer, and chomped his teeth around the fuzzy piece, growling and snarling. The sounds sent chills all over my body. The reporter backed away, the cameraman keeping tabs on the man attempting to devour the microphone. Then he looked up, right into the camera. His pupils twitched as the camera focused in on them, sliding from a perfect, human round, to a horizontal rectangle, reminiscent of a goat's eye.

I gasped and grabbed for Sebastian's hand. He gave it to me and I clung to him. That could have been me if I'd taken the shot—would have been me if not for the main ingredient. I pressed my nose into Nero's fur and breathed in his scent as Sebastian's hand went clammy in mine.

The man stood and opened his mouth. I couldn't tell if he was trying to speak or if he was roaring at the camera. By the cameraman's reaction, he was roaring. The scene jigged and jogged as the cameraman and the reporter fled, but in her heels and tight business skirt, the reporter wasn't fast enough. The camera turned in time to see her get tackled from behind, her body slamming into the ground under the weight of the Nevermore man.

He reared up and slammed his mouth into her back, ripping a chunk of flesh as if she were a loaf of bread. Her screams were audible from whatever mic was left on the camera, then the camera was dropped and the screen scrambled, and then went black.

"That wasn't for real," I said, though I knew already in my gut that it was. It was like watching a hurricane rip apart a house. You didn't think it was possible, didn't think they would air it, but in your heart you knew it wasn't staged.

Sebastian didn't say anything, he just flipped the channel. They were all breaking news and bulletins. The Nevermore drug had been taken by what officials were estimating was close to ninety percent of the North American population over the last two months—street versions and FDA approved versions—both of which were having the same effect.

We watched in stunned silence for over an hour, the reports coming hard and fast at first, but then slowing as people were cautioned to stay within their homes and avoid all contact with the outside world while the outbreak was taken care of.

"I never thought I'd see the day a zombie apocalypse would happen," I said as Sebastian turned the TV off.

"They aren't zombies," he snapped at me as he rubbed his left arm. "They can't bite you and turn you into one of them. The doctors on TV said that already."

"I didn't say that they could bite you, I just said that they were zombies," I said, confused by his sudden turn of mood.

"No, you didn't. I'm sorry; this has just really freaked me out," he said and pulled me into his arms, Nero squirming in between us.

"It'll be okay," I said, "We've got each other and the farm. We should be good for a while, right? It won't take long. Someone will have this straightened out in no time." Sebastian untangled himself from me and strode to the kitchen. "We have to be ready."

I followed him, "For what?"

"I think we're going to be on our own for a while," he said as a loud thumping footstep echoed through our little house.

My adrenaline soared as I thought about the scene on the TV. The reporter hadn't had a chance, the speed of the Nevermore man and the ferocity of his attack were like nothing I'd ever seen before. I swallowed hard and put Nero in the bathroom on a makeshift towel-bed and shut the door and headed back into the kitchen. I didn't want to believe that we were already going to face down one of the Nevermores, but it was all too likely. I stepped to my knife drawer and pulled out the biggest blade I had and gripped it tight. Sebastian nodded and pulled out a knife of his own. Together we crept through the house to the front door, reaching it as another thump rumbled through the floorboards. What the hell was out there? I didn't want to know, really I didn't.

Sebastian held up his hand and with his fingers counted to three. I nodded and he held up one finger, two, and as he held up the third he gripped the doorknob and snapped the door open.

5

We both stumbled back in relief, Dan staring at us with bushy grey eyebrows lifted high. He had his gun slung over his shoulder and a strap across his chest that was full of ammunition, long gold and silver cartridges. They looked big enough to drop an elephant.

"You two need some lessons in surviving. First off, don't go investigating a strange noise without some serious fire-power. This is not a horror movie, there's no hero going to come rescue you. You want to survive this outbreak of idiots who took some new drug and turned into animals, you're gonna have to do it on your own."

He stepped across the threshold and sauntered into our house, casual like, as if he belonged here. I lifted an eyebrow at Sebastian who shrugged and said, "Dan, what're you doing here?"

"Don't you listen boy? You need a lesson or two before I go and lock myself in the bunker." He paced around the living room, peering out the curtains of the bay window.

"Dan, they'll have an antidote in no time and this will go down as one of the greatest blunders in history and everything will go back to normal," I said, desperately wanting to believe my own words.

"You really believe that, girl?" He turned his steely eyes on me and I froze, my mouth dry as he made me face the reality with a single look. I shook my head ever so slowly. He mimicked me. "Didn't think so." Flopping himself onto our couch he motioned for us to come closer. Sebastian obeyed but I stayed where I was, close to the open door.

"Second thing," Dan leaned forward, elbows on his knees and lowered his voice, "food and water. Next is weapons. Then you got to have a way to keep them out."

"Don't be ridiculous," I snapped, my fear making me surly, "There isn't going to be any horde or pack or whatever you think there's going to be." A breeze blew in and I spun to close the door, gasping at the person standing on the edge of the doorstep. I vaguely recognized him as the portly clerk from Tom's Grocery. But he was no longer chubby. He was lean, the excess flesh hanging off his arms and face, the skin a sickly yellow like the man on the TV. Worst was the way his pupils had become a horizontal slit that stole his humanity from him.

"Hungry," was all he said as he launched himself at me. I stumbled backwards with a grunt striking out with my knife and getting nothing but air. We hit the ground and I rolled, trying to remember my distant Judo lessons, failing miserably. The clerk ended up on top of me but didn't pin my knife hand; I suppose he was too focused on eating me. Before I knew what I was doing I had my left hand wrapped around his throat, keeping his snapping teeth off me, and I slammed the knife upwards into his heart, blood spurting out around the blade and down the handle.

Then he was yanked off me and Sebastian was staring down at me with a look of horror across his face. Dan stepped up next to him. "She's got a good survival drive. That'll serve you well. If she were a screamer you'd be dead in no time."

I lay on the floor staring up at them, my brain trying to process what just happened. I'd been attacked, and I'd killed a man. In a less time than it took to take a breath of air, my life had twisted itself inside out. My hands were slick with his blood, and as I stood a wave of vertigo washed over me.

"She's gonna puke."

Hands were suddenly on me, guiding me outside where I did indeed puke, heaving till my stomach was empty and sweat beaded on my forehead. Dan turned the hose on and I washed my hands clean and sprayed the cool water over my face. I had killed a man. My stomach clenched again and I dry heaved.

"Oh shit," Sebastian said, his voice off to my right, his hands tightening on my arms.

"I'll be okay," I said.

"Not you babe," he turned me to the front of our property and the open gate, "them."

Maybe it wasn't a horde, but there was close to twenty people walking our way, the distinct yellow of their skin visible even from here.

Sebastian let me go and ran for the gate.

"Bastian, don't!" I screamed at him and as a unit, every single one of the Nevermore's heads snapped up, their slitted eyes focusing on the source of the scream. Me.

"Damn it girl, I told you no noise," Dan growled as he walked past me, putting his gun to his shoulder and taking aim at the running horde, though he didn't pull the trigger. Sebastian reached the gate the same time as the first of the Nevermores and he flung the heavy panels shut, slamming the lock into place as they hammered their bodies up against it, screaming and howling, their eyes wild and their hands reaching for Sebastian.

I ran down the porch, jumped across the flowerbeds and ran to where Sebastian stood panting, staring at the horde in front of us. "Why aren't they trying to climb the gate?" I whispered.

Sebastian shook his head, breathing hard. That had been a quick sprint for a man of his size, faster than I'd seen him move in years.

Dan strolled up next to us, casually, like he was out for a Sunday visit, and except for the gun slung over his shoulder and the horde of Nevermores at our gate, he could have been. "Interesting, that. They don't seem to be able to figure it out. Like animals penned up." But even as he spoke, one of the Nevermores pushed his way through to the front of the group and began to fiddle with the gate, his fingers clumsy and far from dexterous. He didn't seem to be able to use the finer points of motor skills, which was better for us. All the same, he was still trying to open the gate.

"We've got to get out of here," Sebastian said, pulling me with him as he backed away from the gate. I didn't need a lot of encouragement. I was not interested in facing down that horde anytime soon. Thank God our place was fully fenced.

"We're stuck here for a while, boy. Might as well get used to the idea, unless you've got a tank in that shed over there."

Dan pointed to the dilapidated chicken coop we'd partially knocked down in preparation for a garden.

"We don't need a tank," I surprised myself by speaking my thoughts out loud to a virtual stranger. "We'll just take the car, they can't stop us, and we'll just run them over."

I could barely believe the words that came out of my mouth and apparently neither could Sebastian.

"You're kidding me, right? Those things out there are people underneath it all, and you want to run them over?"

"In case you haven't noticed, they want to EAT us, not play Parcheesi," I said, putting my hands on my hips. A sharp rattle snapped all three of our heads towards the gate in unison. The horde was leaning into the steel gates, the hinges groaning. Every last one of them had their mouths open, teeth showing, saliva dripping and hanging from their loose lips.

"We need to get out of sight," Dan said, walking back towards the house.

"We need to get out of here!" I yelled, hysteria bubbling up. I'd just killed a man and we had a horde of drug-induced zombies on our doorstep. I clapped my hands over my face and tried to block out the moment. The sights were gone, but the groan of the gates the growling of the hoard still reached me, denying me my moment of escape.

A hand on my arm snapped my eyes open. Sebastian started to drag me towards the house. "We'll talk about what we're going to do inside. The last thing we need is to go off half cocked and get ourselves killed."

I let him direct my body, but I couldn't help but stare over my shoulder at the writhing mass of things that had until very recently been human. "This can't be happening."

A sharp shake brought my eyes up to Sebastian, fear and the denial of that fear making his eyes those of a person I barely recognized. "It is happening, Mara, and you need to get used to the idea," he said, his mouth a thing hard line. I jerked my arm out of his hands.

"You're an ass, you know that don't you?" I said as I stomped towards the front door, slamming it behind me. All I wanted was a little comfort, a white lie or two to get me through the initial shock. After that, I could come to terms with what was going on.

The living room was dim, the flickering of the TV the only light, as the curtains and blinds were drawn down. Dan was sitting on the couch, his feet propped up on the hand-carved coffee table we'd bought for our first place.

"Feet off," I said, shoving his feet off before he could remove them himself. "I don't care if this is the end of the world, I don't want your feet on my coffee table."

The door opened behind me and shut with a soft click. I kept my back turned to Sebastian, my spine rigid and my breathing slow and deliberate as I tried to rein my anger in. A whine from the bathroom and I stomped down the hallway and swung the door open. Nero tried to scamper between my legs but I scooped him up and held him tight. A minute passed and the anger started to drain out of me. Taking one last deep breath I carried Nero into the living room. I stared at the TV and came to a sudden stop, unable to take my eyes off the screen.

Dan leaned forward. "I'd hoped they'd have gotten it under control in the bigger cities at least."

"I don't think that's the case," I said, my hands trembling as I stroked Nero. Lists of major cities that had been overrun and were considered uninhabitable flashed on the screen in no particular order: Toronto, Vancouver, Seattle, San Francisco, Los Angeles, Edmonton, Brisbane, New York, Atlanta, Ottawa, London, Perth, Paris, Frankfurt, Berlin, Glasgow, Mexico City, Venice, Lima; the list went on and on, scrolling for a solid two minutes.

"Every continent has been hit by this catastrophe, though some obviously worse than others." The male announcer's voice blared to life on the screen and I jumped involuntarily. Nero gave a squeak and I kissed him on the top of his head.

The camera panned to a reporter in what looked like a bare-bones room, cement walls, and shelves of strange scientific-looking paraphernalia.

"Dr. Josephson, what can you tell us about the events? Will the drug wear off? What can we do about this situation?" the reporter asked, turning to the camera every few words, as if to gain permission from the viewing audience to ask the questions.

"It's simple, even for a nincompoop like you, Blaine," Dr. Josephson said.

"It's Bruce."

"Whatever. The drug was skipped through the FDA testing as well as Health Canada; money greased the wheels to hurry it to market. In the two months since it's been out, it made over 1.6 trillion dollars. You can imagine how that would make a company eager to get it to the public."

Bruce leaned in. "Those numbers can't be right."

Dr. Josephson snorted. "337 million people, give or take a few thousand, get the shot through legal means. That's in North America alone. Five thousand dollars shot, one hundred people a day per clinic. You should do your research before you go on air Bruno."

The doctor sat down on a ratty old stool and looked up into the camera, as if Bruce were no longer worth speaking to.

"There is no cure. There is no chance it will go away. It won't wear off, it is designed to link permanently to the molecular structure of human bones, organs, and most importantly, brain. It cannot be transferred by a bite, as the modern movie culture would have you believe. These are not zombies, these are people gone feral, wild. They are acting as packs, not unlike a pack of wolves with an Alpha male and female, and the rest working as a group for food and protection." His pale blue eyes seemed to bore into me and I shivered with the intensity. "To the public who have not taken Nevermore I will say only one thing," He paused, dropped his head and shook it slightly before looking back up into the camera.

"Survive."

6

With that the TV went blank and the screen turned into a warning system of striped colours. The silence in our little home was overwhelming and I wanted to say something to break it, but didn't. I couldn't think of anything to say that would mean anything, and since screaming hysterically was out of the question, I was out of options.

Dan stood, drawing our attention. "That's it then, I'm headed back to my place."

"What?" Sebastian asked. "You can't get out of here alive, there's no way you'll make it."

He strolled to the back door, ignoring Sebastian's assessment, glancing over his shoulder at us. "There's a back trail, goes up and around, it's a great view of the ocean at the top. I think these things . . . ."

"Nevermores," I said softly.

Dan nodded at me. "These Nevermores seem to be sticking to the main routes right now, so if you come to my place, come the back way. I'll put a red flag next to it. Other than that, plant a garden, grow yourself some food, mend your fences, and keep quiet."

He put his hand on the door and I grabbed the back of his grubby shirt. "Hey, you can't just leave us here."

Dan laughed and half turned back to me. "You city folk are going to be the first to die off—not prepared, no survival instinct." His eyes narrowed as he looked at me. "You might make it; you got some good reflexes on you."

Sebastian stepped up and I didn't let go of Dan. "You could help us. At least we could be working together," I said.

Again Dan laughed. "I don't work with anybody, it ain't my style. Too much drama when you get more than one person in a room."

"So," Sebastian said, "We're supposed to be grateful you showed up for a belated house warming, and you didn't even bring us a gift? You happen to visit in the middle of a crisis where you don't even help? I don't know why you bothered at all."

I let go of Dan's coat, feeling my own anger build. What the hell was Dan's reasoning, or was he truly just as crazy as we'd heard?

Dan straightened his coat and lifted an eyebrow at us then nodded slowly. "If you can make it to my place, I'll let you have a weapon, but this is Mother Nature's way of weeding out the weak. Only the strong will survive this, and that's how it should be. To tell you the truth, I came here to take what you had and add it to my stores. But you were still here, still alive. Mores the pity."

We stared at him in disbelief, the reality of the situation hitting us both at the same time.

The door clicked softly as he left without even saying goodbye, or better, good luck. I wondered if he meant for us to mend our fences around the property, or the proverbial ones between us. I looked over to Sebastian, took in his drawn face and worried eyes. My heart gave a thump and I put Nero down before I all but threw myself into Sebastian's arms.

Between sobs and I'm sorry on both sides, our lips met and we caught the edge of a mania that perhaps other survivors were feeling. Glad to be alive we stripped each other out of our clothes and stumbled upstairs to the bathroom. The water still ran, we hadn't lost power yet, and we drained the hot water tank showering off the sweat and remnants of blood, wrapping ourselves around each other, washing the fear away for a moment or two.

We made love in the shower and then again in the bedroom, our frantic need to touch and feel overwhelming any common sense—like locking the doors.

Lying in each other's arms we dozed off, dreaming perhaps that this was all a nightmare, a shared fear come to life in the night, but gone when the light of day streamed through the windows. Not so much.

The bedroom door creaked, the knob clicking against something; perhaps nails, or perhaps what we later learned was skin hardening into a hide like leather. I woke, chills rippling over my body, the sensation of being watched heightened by a disorientation of time and place.

"Bastian," I whispered, my eyes picking out a figure silhouetted in the doorway.

"Hmm," he grunted.

I place my hand lightly over his lips and whispered into his ear. "We didn't lock the doors."

Sebastian's eyes popped open and he slowly moved my hand from his lips. Keeping as still as possible, I franticly searched the room with my eyes, seeking a weapon of any sort.

"Help me." Her voice was raspy and though she didn't move I knew we didn't have much time.

I jumped up out of bed, recognizing the voice as our neighbour's teenage daughter.

"Jessica?"

"Help me, please," she said, her body twitching. I flicked on the overhead light and Sebastian cursed.

"We're naked here, woman," he said as he yanked on some clothes. I did the same, keeping an eye on Jessica the whole time, her eyes were semi-glazed and she didn't seem to notice that we were naked. Thank goodness for small blessings.

"Honey," I said slipping t-shirt over my head, "Your parents, where are they?"

"Gone, they turned into monsters."

I froze in mid zip.

"Shit."

"My thoughts exactly, wife."

I moved towards Jessica and wondered again why she had taken Nevermore. Thin as a rail, pretty, and yet she'd had the shot, as had her mother and father. Her Caribbean-blue eyes were still human, not yet sliding into the realm of the feral horde outside. How long would it be before they turned colour and she became one of the monsters?

I touched her arm and she flinched. "It's okay, let's go downstairs and see what we can do."

"The TV said there isn't a cure," she said, her voice breaking up with a sob.

I nodded. "I know, but that could change. I'm sure they're working on a cure right now."

Sebastian made a rude noise and I shushed him. I knew when to tell a white lie. This was a teenage girl who was terrified and alone; the least I could do was try and comfort her.

Once downstairs, seated around the kitchen table, a hot tea in front of her, Jessica told us what happened.

"Parkinson's runs strong in our family, so my parents wanted to make sure I never had to deal with it. They insisted I take the shot with them.

I leaned forward and put my hand over hers. It took some effort not to flinch as she twitched underneath my fingers, but I wanted her to be calm so that she would keep talking. "When did your parents . . . ?" I trailed off not sure how to ask when her parents went crazy.

"Today, after I got back from our walk," she whispered staring into her tea. "I don't have very long, do I?"

Tears welled up in my eyes and I blinked them back. I didn't know Jessica well, but it was hard to see someone so young cut down by something that should have helped her live a long and healthy life. It was hard to know there was nothing we could do to help. Nero whined at our feet and I stood and fixed him a bowl of food. I felt bad for ignoring him, but he wagged his tail and seemed to have forgiven me already.

"How long ago did they take the shot?" Sebastian asked, leaning in towards her.

"Five weeks; I was a week later," she said, her eyes flicking up to him twice, maybe intimidated by his size, the way a lot of people were. Then I remembered that she had a crush on him. I could only imagine the embarrassment of finding her crush in bed naked with his wife.

Sebastian stood up and stomped out of the house. I ignored him, knowing that Jessica needed comfort right now. "You can stay here sweetheart, it'll be okay." Then I frowned. "How did you make it past the horde out front?"

She gave me a wobbly, tear filled smile. "They know I'm one of them. They let me pass, I climbed the gate and they," she shrugged, "there's no other way to say it, they cheered for me, like they were happy I could get in here to you." Dropping her head to her arms on the table she let out a sob. I reached over and put a hand on her head, fighting with my own rising emotions: sadness, fear, and then relief. It could have been me waiting to be turned into an animal. If not for the damn scotch broom it would be me. I would have taken the shot in an instant.

I ushered Jessica to the back bedroom and tucked her into bed, giving her three Benadryl, which would knock her out for the night. I took one for myself, not to sleep, but for the reaction I was having to some airborne allergen. My skin tingled all over my body, my eyes were watering, and the back of my throat was itchy, sure signs I'd gotten hit with something I didn't like. Then I went to find Sebastian, Nero at my heels, my fear beginning to turn into resolve. We could survive, we were smart, young, and in love, there wasn't anything we couldn't do.

He was out on the back porch leaning against the railing, staring out at the star encrusted sky. I stepped up beside him slipping my arm around his waist.

"I haven't had the chance yet to thank you," I said.

He gave me a quizzical look and I pointed down at the puppy sitting on my foot. I smiled, "You didn't have to get me a puppy, but I'm glad you did." I gave his waist a squeeze and took a deep breath letting it out slowly.

"We've got to lay out a plan, Bastian. Food, water, fences, weapons. Maybe get some sort of radio up in case there are notices once the electricity is out," I said. I looked up and my breath caught in my throat. Tears streaked his face, dripped off his chin and plunked onto the railing.

He wrapped his arms around me. "It isn't fair, Mara, that girl is losing everything because she wanted to have a life, to not pass on a disease she had no say on in the first place." His voice was thick with emotion and I held on to him as tight as I could, fighting my own tears, shocked at what I was seeing. Sebastian was usually so stoic. In four years this was perhaps the second time I'd seen him shed tears—and the first time I wasn't entirely certain it wasn't just a hard wind causing his eyes to water. "Go to bed, babe. I'll stay up and watch over you two. I don't think I could sleep anyway."

I kissed him softly on his lips, holding his head in my hands.

"I love you Bastian, more than anything."

He kissed me back and swatted me lightly on my butt as I turned to go inside.

I went upstairs to bed, snuggling Nero down in with me. I listened to Sebastian pace on the porch, muttering from time to time. I didn't sleep much either that night, my mind whirling with plans. In my head I sketched out the best place for a garden—the current spot was far too rocky—where the fence needed to be reinforced, and what we could use as protection besides the knives we had. Dan hadn't even left us a single weapon, though he's said he had lots at his place.

I yawned and closed my eyes, Nero snuggling in tight to me, his warmth a steady comfort, then finally drifted off to a fitful sleep.

7

The dreams that haunted what should have been a deep, exhausted sleep left me wishing I'd stayed up with Sebastian. The clerk was attacking me again, but this time I was on my own, Sebastian in a pool of blood beside me, Dan nowhere to be found, Nero barking madly, and I was pregnant. In the dream, when I realized I was with child I snapped, a mother bear's ferocity coming from a place I never knew existed within me.

The clerk never had a chance, his heart once more pierced by my kitchen blade, his eyes glazing over as death settled on him. A boom from the other side of the house and the back porch door was flung open, a wave of Nevermores pouring in. Yanking my blade out of the clerk's chest I reached for the front door and pulled on the handle. It was locked and my hand slid over the mechanism to unlock it over and over, unable to grasp it. I screamed and turned back to the horde. They rushed me and I fought like a mad woman, protecting the child within me, blocking hands and mouths, slicing off finger and stabbing eyes. Nero barked and bit, but his little body was flung aside like a rag doll, disappearing into the maw of one of the Nevermores. The horde howled and swelled, slamming me into the ground, pinning me as they shook me.

I screamed, or tried to, and a hand covered my mouth.

"You're dreaming babe, it's just a dream. You're okay." Sebastian's deep rumble in my ear slowed my heart rate as I came fully awake. "What time is it?" I mumbled.

"What?" He lifted his hand off my mouth.

"Time?"

"It's just after seven. Jessica's still asleep."

I got up, still in my clothes from the day before. "I guess I should shower."

I plucked at my sweat-soaked t-shirt.

"Might as well, at some point we're going to lose electricity, and then no more hot showers." He kissed me on the cheek then bent and scooped up a yawning Nero. "I'm going to make breakfast for us and the little man here." He ruffled the puppy's hair and disappeared into the hallway.

I showered, taking my time in the hot water. It was hard to imagine being without the simple parts of life, the day-to-day luxuries. It looked like we were about to embark on the camping trip from hell that wouldn't ever end. Not really the most pleasant of thoughts for a newly-relocated city girl.

Downstairs Sebastian was indeed making breakfast: waffles, eggs, bacon, hash browns, oatmeal, sausage, and French toast. Nero was munching on a sausage quite happily and I shook my head.

"Holy crap, what are you doing? Shouldn't we be saving the food?" I asked.

Sebastian flicked his head towards the hallway where the guest bedroom was. "She's going to be hungry and, let's be honest; this could be one of her last meals."

I swallowed my irritation. "You're a good man, my love, I hadn't thought of that."

The guest bedroom was painted bright yellow, including the door, something I hadn't gotten around to changing yet, though it seemed fitting that she was there. I knocked three times. "Jessica, are you awake? We've got breakfast ready."

A shuffle, and then a groan. I backed away from the door thinking we'd made a serious mistake in letting her stay with us, even for the night.

The doorknob turned slowly and Jessica peeked out, yawning. "Is that bacon I smell?"

I let out a breath, relief rushing through me. "Yup, Sebastian's been slaving over the stove all morning, just for you." I smiled at her and patted her back as she flushed and ducked her head as she passed me and headed into the kitchen.

What happened next was like nothing I've ever seen before. Jessica, who couldn't have been more than 5'4 and weighed maybe 110 pounds, ate at least as much as Sebastian, who was a full foot in height taller than her and was at least double her weight. To top it all off, it looked as if they were racing, popping sausages and bites of waffle in as fast as they could chew. The whole scene was more than a little disconcerting. It was kind of fun though to watch her face when she peeked under her eyelashes at Bastian, her blushing and head ducking almost comical in their lack of subtlety. The best part was that Sebastian was completely oblivious.

I had a single helping, keeping it to oatmeal and a banana, then splurged and had some bacon with it. What the hell, if it was the end of the world, who cared about counting calories?

"What's the plan today?" Sebastian asked, looking from me to Jessica then back again.

"Oh. Well, I thought that we should make a tally of all the food in the house, plant the garden, and check fences."

"We just had the new page wire fence put up! And haven't even pulled down the old barbed wire on the other side," Sebastian said, his irritation filling the room. Jessica slouched in her seat and stared at her plate.

I rubbed my face with both hands. "I know that. And maybe it's good that we have a double fence line, but the deer can still get in. I know the deer can jump but what if there's a little hole somewhere? One at ground level? The Nevermores maybe can't jump but I bet they can crawl."

At that Sebastian paused, his mouth open to argue and then he snapped it shut and nodded. The thought of a horde of Nevermores pouring through a small hole was all too possible and all too frightening to take the chance that there was even one small opening on our first line of defence.

"We also need to find some way to store water," I said, leaning back in my chair.

Sebastian nodded and leaned back in his chair, mimicking me. "We can draw water from the well even when the power's out, but you're right, we should store some anyway." He stood up. "I'm going to start with the fences and I'm going to throw another chain and padlock on the front gate. Why don't you come with me, Jessica?" He glanced at me and I gave him a slight nod. Neither of us said what we were both thinking. The Nevermores saw her as one of their own and wouldn't hurt her, and it might keep Sebastian safer too, having her at his side. Jessica nodded and took another bite of a sausage, her face glowing with pleasure. I smiled to myself, it would be good to keep her distracted, and having her crush all to herself was a perfect way for a young girl to have her mind taken off the scary parts of life. It didn't bother me, Sebastian was not the type to wander or stray, especially not for a sixteen-year-old girl.

As they headed out the back door I grabbed Sebastian by the hand pulling him back to me and planting a kiss on his lips. "Don't forget to reinforce the gate. I saw some extra bars in the grass beside it."

"Aye, aye, captain." He saluted me sharply and headed out, following Jessica's lithe figure.

After they left, I spent the morning going through all our cupboards, charting out canned food and preserves, cleaners, toiletries, and perishables. Once I had them stacked in order of how fast we needed to use them my heart sank. I'd never really been a person to buy in bulk and it showed. There were three bags of pasta, less than two dozen cans of soup, one large bag of rice, 8 cans of pasta sauce, 7 cans of tuna, fourteen cans of fruit of various kinds, 3 boxes of Jell-O, one bag of flour and sugar each, a small bag of brown sugar, a half box of tea, one of each of my favourite spices, and that was about it for food of the non perishable sort.

I scrubbed my hands over my face. The fridge was full of fresh veggies and fruit, milk, cheese, half a dozen eggs, and two cuts of beef from dinner two nights ago. The freezer was not so full, but there were a few bags of bread, ground beef, one package of bacon, a package of chicken drumsticks, and two frozen pizzas. How the hell were we going to make this stretch?

"We are so screwed," I said softly, needing to break the depressing silence even if it was with a depressing statement. Nero woofed softly in seeming agreement. I laughed and rolled a ball for him across the floor, which he bounded after. I sat on the floor rolling the ball, enjoying the normalcy of the moment. After ten minutes of playing, Nero began to yawn and I scooped him up, grabbed a towel, and made a makeshift bed in the tub. At least there he wouldn't get into trouble if he woke up and I was outside.

A huge rumble reached my ears as I tucked Nero in, a rumble that I recognized and had cursed most mornings as the neighbour and his god-awful diesel minus-a-muffler truck headed to work. Scrambling to my feet I ran to the door, flinging it open in time to see the horde out front of our house get scattered by the black Dodge mowing them down.

Bodies were flung in all directions, screams of pain and rage coming from every side. I shouted and pumped my fist in the air. I knew we could get out with a vehicle, I just knew it.

8

My jubilation was short lived. The Dodge lurched to a stop just past our house and I frowned. Sebastian and Jessica came running in from the far field, tools in their hands, worry written across their faces.

"Mara?" Sebastian yelled.

"I'm here. The guy with the noisy truck!" I hollered back, pointing to the front of the property.

We stared as the truck rumbled, coughed, and fell silent, choosing this moment to protest its rough usage. The horde of Nevermores swarmed around the truck, scratching and screaming, their nails on the metal making my skin jump and twitch.

"What's he doing?" Jessica asked.

"I think his truck stalled out," Sebastian said.

The back window slid open, hands emerged, and our neighbour squeezed himself out into the truck bed.

"Hey!" he yelled, "Little help?" He flapped his arms and pointed around him like we hadn't noticed the Nevermores surrounding him, or like we had some magic wand that would carve a path for him through the horde.

"What are we supposed to do? Walk out there and ask them if they would mind not eating him?" I said, not really expecting an answer.

Jessica was nodding though. "They let me through once; maybe they'll let me through with Tom."

Sebastian and I stared at her. "Jessica," I said, "you don't know that they won't attack you."

"They didn't attack us on the back of your property when I was with Sebastian. They just stared at us, swaying, and kind-of-like singing under their breath," she said, her voice far more confident than I felt.

Chills rippled over me at the picture that came to my mind, the scene I could see in my head even though I hadn't been there. What Dr. Josephson on the TV had said slid into place along with what Jessica had said, and my mind filled in the missing bits. The horde would be working like wolf pack with an Alpha male and female, the rest acting together as hunters and protectors. A final moment of understanding came to me and I sucked in a lungful of air, the simplicity of it making more sense than I would have thought. The pack, or whatever it was, wanted Jessica, if that Dr. Josephson from the TV was right and the Nevermores *were* working like a wolf pack, they'd be looking for females to increase their numbers.

Oh. My. God.

More pieces slipped into place. The drug made people more fertile, made them territorial, ravenous *and* made them disease resistant. The population of Nevermores was going to boom. And if the genetics didn't pass the drug to their young and make new Nevermores, I had no doubt what they would be eating for their next pack meal.

"No," I said, startling both Jessica and Sebastian. "You can't go out there." I was standing in her way, "They want you, the pack—pride, whatever it is, they *want* you." I swallowed hard. Sebastian stood behind Jessica, frowning.

"What are you talking about Mara?"

"Hey, come on guys, don't leave me hanging here!" Tom yelled and the pack went wild with the sound of his voice.

"In a minute," I yelled back, turning only my head to them then focused back on Jessica. "A breeder, that's all you'd be. Something to make babies and those babies will be just like them." I flung my arm out behind me, "And if they aren't, you can guess what's going to happen to the babies."

Jessica paled and Sebastian frowned at me. "They'd eat them," she whispered. I nodded.

"You don't know that Mara," Sebastian snapped at me, "and you're scaring her."

"It's the truth," Jessica said. "I can feel them pulling at me, wanting me to come to them. Especially that one there." She pointed to a big male who stood back from the rest of the pack, overseeing their efforts to pull Tom down who was now on the roof of his truck. The leader stood with his hands on his hips, his eyes narrowed as he grunted and barked what seemed to be orders to the rest of the group. He was taller than the rest but not as big as Sebastian, with light blond hair that had seen better days. He looked to be in his mid-thirties, but it was hard to tell with the changes the drug put them through. The male had a definite air of command around him, and I had no doubt who was in charge of this pack. Trouble, that's what he was.

Jessica stared at him, her eyes not moving away for even a split second, it wasn't a look of fear that washed over her face—but desire. Shit.

She walked past us, heading straight towards the gate. "He won't eat the babies. I'll come back after I get Tom out. I don't have to go with the pack yet," she said certainty strong in her voice as she climbed the fence and dropped lightly on the other side. The pack made room for her, touching her lightly, stroking her hair. She walked straight up to the big male, brushing her fingertips against his. He stared down at her and she shook her head, and then pointed at Tom.

Sebastian shifted on his feet. "Is she negotiating with him?"

"I guess," I said, not sure this was a good idea at all. The big male shook his head, then roared.

The pack scattered, leaving the truck clear.

"Tom! Hurry your ass up, man!" Sebastian yelled when Tom hesitated. Another breath and he jumped down from the truck and started to run towards our gate. "Shit, I forgot my stash," he yelped and turned back towards the truck. He grabbed the handle and I grabbed Sebastian's hand.

"Forget your weed, man! Move it!" Sebastian yelled.

"He's not going to make it," I whispered.

"He'll make it," Sebastian said.

One of the pack members crept forward, sniffing the air. It was too much for the creature's desires. It lunged at Tom and I stifled a scream. Tom screamed for us both. Like unleashing a tidal wave, the pack rushed back in and Tom disappeared under a flurry of bodies and mouths.

SHANNON MAYER

Jessica screamed and tried to run towards Tom, but the big male held her tight against his chest until she stopped squirming, her eyes glazing over with resignation.

"Don't hurt him!" she yelled, but the pack didn't listen to her anymore than they listened to Tom's pleas for mercy.

I buried my head into Sebastian's shoulder.

"Look," Sebastian said.

I turned to see the pack retreating with their prize; none of it even recognizable as human, and Jessica and the Alpha male were walking to the gate.

As if in a dream we met them there, just out of reach.

"Thank you. I wish I could have stayed with you longer," she whispered, silver tears pooling in her quickly shifting eyes. She reached through and though Sebastian grunted at me, I took her hands and held them with my own, rubbing my fingers over her knuckles. If she were my daughter, my child, I would want her to have this last moment of humanity, touching one of her own kind before she forgot everything she was and could have been.

"I wish we could've done more." Sebastian stepped closer and the Alpha male growled, his grip tightening on Jessica. Sebastian held up his hands then slowly lowered them to my shoulders, squeezing me almost painfully tight. I ignored the pissing contest and stared at Jessica. "Be safe, sweetheart," I whispered and lifted her hands to my lips, kissing the back of them.

The skin underneath my lips was spinning into a dusky yellow with faint lines that looked like veins, but weren't. They were images of yellow teardrops like a poorly drawn tattoo of a broom flower. The plant was taking hold of the humans it inhabited like it did all the areas it was introduced.

The Alpha male pulled her away, but not before giving Sebastian one more glare, one filled with hatred so intense that I was surprised he didn't try to come over the gate.

"I don't think he likes me."

"Neither do I," I said. I turned away from the gate, heart heavy at losing Jessica though I'd known it would happen. I just didn't think it would be so soon. I reached up, took Sebastian's hand off my shoulder and wrapped it around me, taking some comfort in the warmth. If only I could so easily ward off the chill in my heart.

9

The next week was spent digging the garden in, watering it daily, checking fences, and drinking lots of water to keep our hunger at bay. Nero romped at our feet oblivious to the danger all around us, though he quickly learned to stay far away from the fence line. Only once did he stray close to the front gate; the growling and fury, along with a set of hands reaching for him, sent him running back to safety.

We phoned family and friends, trying to find out who had taken the shot, and who hadn't. Of them all, only Sebastian's Gran was still answering her phone, and she was in London.

"You two take care of each other. I'll be fine here, I have a flight to . . ." She was cut off, but at least we knew she was still alive and well. It was a small ray of sunshine.

We argued about whether or not to go to Dan's, but I won out.

"Fine, Mara. Fine. We won't go to Dan," Sebastian said, his body slumped on the couch.

"We can't trust him, Sebastian. He came here to raid us, not help us, he said so himself. We're safe here; the Nevermores can't seem to get in. If it comes down to desperation, then yes, maybe then we could go to Dan, but he's a last resort," I said and went back to attempting to hand-stitch a patch on a shirt.

The pack left us alone for the most part, sending out what seemed to be a scout once or twice a day. He was smaller than the rest, and slightly hunched over with angry red slashes on his upper body and face, with one that went right across his forehead. The scout, who we simply started to call Scout, would attempt to rattle the massive gate, give us a growl, and then wander off.

The long hours, hard work, and emotional stress taxed us, making us both edgy and out of sorts, not even leaving us enough energy to make love, unusual for us. The day before the power went out, we checked the TV as we did each morning and each night. For the first time in over a week there was an announcement of sorts.

"Mara, come here, the TV's on," Sebastian called out. I ran downstairs, a towel wrapped around my hair.

There was no announcer, just a single picture like a page out of a book that scrolled up on a continual loop.

I read it out loud as it went. "All areas of North America are now considered dangerous territory, as is the North and West of South America, all of Australia, Europe, and much of Asia."

There was a long stretch of blank screen and then a last warning.

I read it slowly, disbelief and a low thrum of resignation settled over me.

"All remaining residents from these named continents are now considered independent of any government, agency, or military command. We consider . . ."

That's where it ended. The screen blinked and slid into white fuzzy static, reminding me of the twilight zone. I grabbed the remote and turned the TV off.

"What does that mean?" I asked, already suspecting the answer, but wanting Sebastian to say it out loud.

He reached up and took my hand. "We're on our own, babe. That's what it means. No one's going to come help us or try to get us out of here. They're going to let nature take its course, just like Dan said, and hope the Nevermores die off."

I squeezed his hand and slid into his lap. He circled his arms around me and we held each other tight, the fear surrounding us. "We've still got each other," I said.

Sebastian didn't answer me, just laid his head against by breast, his breathing uneven as if he were holding back tears.

The next day, two weeks in, the power finally went and we had to break out the flashlights and candles, hoarding them, using them only when necessary. It was at that point that we realized we needed to dig a latrine of some sort. Shit—in the most literal sense of the word.

Worse than that realization, was the fact that we were through half our food stores—not that we had much to begin with—and our garden was a long way from producing.

"We're just going to have to cut back some more," I said, staring at our already meagre meal of pasta and a half a can of tuna cooked over the barbecue. Come winter we could use the wood stove and the old wood-burning stove I'd thought to replace for heat and cooking. But there were so many things on the list of needed items: candles, seeds for the garden, and canning equipment, just to name a few.

Sebastian scrubbed his hands through his hair, his wedding band catching the last rays of the setting sun. I watched as it slid around, bumping up against his knuckle. The weight we were both losing was a testament to our hard work and lack of nutrition.

I started to laugh at the irony of the situation.

"What's so funny?"

I gulped the laughter down enough to answer him. "We've wanted to lose weight for so long and all it took was for the world to shut down." Another peal of laughter ripped its way out of me, leaving me shaking and gasping for air, tears running down my cheeks. Hilarity rarely gripped me and now I seemed unable to shake its grasp.

He frowned at me, which only made me laugh harder; lack of food, poor sleep, and hard work making me giddy. I sat on the floor and the laughter rolled out of me, Nero dancing around my head woofing and making me howl all the louder. Sebastian got up, left his plate of food and went outside, the back door slamming behind him.

I lay on the cool tile of the kitchen floor till the laughter subsided and the tears threatened to start. I forced them back, refused to let them get a hold of me. I wouldn't let the fear rise again. We weren't going to die here, we were going to live and survive. Nero lay down beside me, ever attentive, the perfect puppy, and I was grateful he took to his sit-stay commands so well. I couldn't have handled an unruly dog with all that had been happening. I let my hand rest on his quickly-growing body for a moment. What were we going to do about him? We could barely feed ourselves and the dog food was diminishing as fast as our own.

I stood slowly, wobbling a little, the distant thud of axe and wood telling me where Sebastian was. I ate half my meal and covered the rest with plastic wrap, something else we were nearly out of.

Crap. I knew I'd made a mess of it with Bastian. I headed outside, Nero at my heels and Sebastian's plate in hand to find him chopping wood, sweat dripping down his rapidly slimming frame. He would always be a big guy, but it was scary to see how fast he, especially, was losing weight.

"I'm sorry. I've pulled it together," I said in between chops. Sebastian lowered the blade and half turned to me.

"It's okay. I suppose from time to time you're going to have breakdowns. It's to be expected. As long as you can always pull yourself up and out of it," he said. I handed him his plate and he sat down on a log to eat.

"Well, it's not like I'm going to be here by myself, right? You're not planning on doing a walk about in the middle of the night, go for some sort of marathon run to see if you can outdistance the pack, are you?" I smiled at him and he gave me a half-hearted smile back.

"No, not planning on it."

I blinked hard, wondering at the sudden fear that gripped me. Was he trying to say something without saying it?

"What's wrong, Bastian? I know this is a crap situation, I know it's not how we planned our lives, but we *are* alive and we still have each other. That's all that matters." I sat down beside him. A rattle drew our attention to the gate, Scout making motions at us, more than usual. He grunted and pointed at the food on the plate.

Sebastian stood and walked to the gate without a word, Nero whining the closer he got to the Nevermore. Scout backed off, obviously intimidated by his size until Sebastian held the plate of food out to him.

"What are you doing?" I asked, the scene before me disturbing me. Why was he showing kindness to the Nevermore? Why would he give him food that we had so little of, which we so desperately needed?

Scout slunk forward cautiously, his eyes downcast until he was right at the gate, Sebastian towering over him. One shaking hand reached out to grab some noodles, streaking back to his mouth so fast I could barely track it with my eyes.

A second time he reached out to grab the food and as his hands grasped noodles, Sebastian's big hand clamped down on his arm. Scout squealed - which set Nero off barking like a mad man - and tried to pull away but couldn't. Sebastian held on to him, not doing anything but holding, Scout squealing and screeching so loud and high pitched I found myself on my feet, heart pumping ready to run.

"Bastian, he's calling the others," I said, fear blooming once more. We'd been almost back to normal; I could almost forget the scene of Tom's death, of the pack surrounding our property, of Jessica going off with the Alpha.

"I know."

Two words, so simple and yet they meant so much. He wanted Scout to call the pack in, but, why?

Rustling in the bushes was the only warning we had before the Nevermores exploded onto the road, screaming and gnashing their teeth. They were thinner than the last time I'd seen them, but they didn't seem worse for the wear, their energy still high.

I searched the group, standing on my tiptoes and finally standing on a log to see if Jessica was with them.

"She's at the back!" I said, "She looks okay." She was thin, her clothes ragged, but unlike some of the others who had scars and missing pieces of hair, she looked . . . like the queen of the pack. The Alpha male stepped out of the bush and put his hand on her shoulder, claiming her while he stared at Sebastian.

"What does he think? That you're going to fight him for her?" I asked more to myself but Sebastian heard me.

"That's exactly what he thinks. I'm bigger, stronger, and younger. A threat to his position in the hierarchy of the pack," he said.

"But you aren't."

Sebastian turned to look at me, his eyes sad; my heart dropped.

"Mara, the results from the fertility tests came back while you were out of it. It wasn't you that had fertility problems, it was me. The day I gave you Nero, when I went into town . . ."

I started to shake my head, backing away, half falling off the log and stumbling over Nero.

"No, no you didn't, you wouldn't have. You said that it was stupid, that there was no way you would ever . . ." The world swayed around me and I fell to my knees, grabbing at the axe for support.

Sebastian walked to me, and turned me so that we both faced the gate and the pack beyond it. His hands were hot on my bare flesh and I began to itch, the concentration of broom in his body coming through in his sweat. It finally made sense and I understood my reactions at strange times, after he kissed me or we made love, my body responded to

the concentrate within his system and I had to take antihistamines. I was allergic to him, to what he was becoming.

I let out a moan and he held me tight.

"I'm sorry Mara, I took the shot." He looked me in the
eye, his own beginning to tint a light yellow that I'd been
telling myself was just the way the light reflected on his iris.

"I took Nevermore."

10

I sobbed into his chest, pounded on it in a fit of rage that he could do this to me, that he would be leaving me, forgetting that if I'd had it my way, it would be the other way around.

The pack dispersed, once more stymied by the gate and their inability to climb it or unlock it, melting back into the bush as if they had never been there.

All that was left was Scout, who stared at us with his slitted eyes and rattled the gate to get our attention. In less than three weeks, that would be Sebastian, outside the property, an animal who no longer loved me, an animal who would as soon eat me as make love to me.

I stood up, pushing away from him, anger and pain at war with one another inside my heart. "I need to be alone."

"You're going to get a lot of that in the not too distant future, probably more than you want. I would take advantage of the time we have."

I spun on my heel, ready to slap him. "You asshole! Why didn't you tell me you'd taken the shot?"

He frowned and shook his head, "I didn't want you to worry."

"It's my right to worry! I'm your wife, if anyone should know that you're going to turn into an animal, it's me!" I yelled at him, Nero whimpered at my feet, upset by the yelling. I bent and scooped him into my arms.

"The right time didn't come up. And I wasn't sure at first, I didn't feel any different, I wasn't losing weight, but at the clinic they said that might not happen as fast to me because of my size," he said, shrugging his shoulder, lowering his eyes.

I stomped off towards the backyard and the garden, the sudden urge to kill something leaving me only one option. Pulling weeds. Over my shoulder I yelled, "The right time was the minute you figured it out."

I froze at the sight in front of me. Three deer stood in my garden neatly pruning every last shoot of a vegetable that had come up in the last week, their ability to jump the fence giving them the edge over the Nevermores who also wanted in. I wanted to cry, I wanted to yell and scream and throw things. I put Nero down, and as I did I scooped up a rock, hurling it at the four-legged interlopers. I missed by an easy mile and had to settle for running at them full speed down a slight slope, Nero woofing and running full tilt which wasn't any faster than me, following them well into the open field. As they scattered, I slipped, tumbling the last of the way down, coming to rest on what had been my pea patch.

"Mara, are you okay?" Sebastian asked as he lifted me gently to a sitting position. I nodded tucked my face into the crook of his neck, breathing in his scent, trying hard not to think about what was coming.

"I'll help you get ready, babe, I won't leave you here without the things you're going to need."

"That gives me little solace when I know that you won't love me anymore," I whispered.

He was silent for so long that I wasn't sure he heard me. It was the shuddering that started deep in his body that made me sit back. Tears streamed down his face, washing lines of dirt and grime away leaving streaks of almost-clean skin.

"I will always love you, no matter how far my mind goes, no matter what I become; my love for you will never change. I couldn't imagine my life with anyone else, Mara, and these last four years have been the best part of my whole life. I wouldn't change a thing." At my raised eyebrow he conceded, "Well, maybe one thing."

He stroked my face with his hands and he whispered against my lips, "I didn't tell you enough how much I love you, didn't always cherish you the way I should have, but I will always, always love you, no matter what comes." He kissed me softly and I leaned into it. If this was all I had left with him, I would take every minute of it; my anger washed away in a wave of love so strong I thought my heart might burst with it. We clung to each other until the tide of emotion that swelled around us receded and we could both breathe a little easier. I leaned back from him to stare into the face that I would love no matter what it looked like.

"What are we waiting for then?" I asked, pulling him to his feet.

He cocked his head and stared at me. I winked and started to slide my shirt over my head. It took him a brief moment, then he was there helping me undress - as I helped him - and we made love in the garden. It wasn't like we were

71

going to be damaging the crops or anything, and we took our time, savouring each touch, each kiss, as if they were our last, breaking up only when Nero came romping back, woofing and leaping at us as we held each other tight.

11

"I'm going, Mara. I have less than a week, a few days maybe, and it's a window of opportunity we can't let pass," Sebastian said as he dressed. It was early, pre-dawn, and we'd been arguing about this subject most of the night.

"Bastian, the Alpha male, if he catches you outside the gate he'll attack you. Maybe he'll even be able to turn the whole pack against you," I said shadowing my husband as he searched our closet for the extra knapsack.

"That's why I'm going so early, you know that Scout's never been here before the sun is up. I'll raid as many of the houses as I can. You need the food, and you can't go. It's like with Jessica, they won't touch me, I'm one of them."

I snorted, "Nobody wants to get laid by you. That's what they wanted from her, and you know that."

"Hey. That's not nice, or true. I can think of at least one person who wants to get laid by me." He bent and kissed me on the lips the tingle not all due to our chemistry. Mostly now it was due to the drug I was so allergic to, rushing through his system.

73

I followed him downstairs where he grabbed the flashlight, a hammer and the big kitchen knife. In the dim light he looked like a burglar, which was appropriate considering what he was going to do.

"Did you write me a list at least? I don't want any complaints that you didn't get everything you wanted." He smiled at me, trying to ease the tension I suppose. I let out a breath, knowing he was going to do this whether I wanted him to or not. I was losing the battle in large part because I knew he was right. I needed him to get food and supplies, and he needed to do this one last thing for me, to be my husband and knight in shining armour.

I sat down and lit a candle so I could see enough to write. The list was simple, any preserves he could carry, batteries, feminine hygiene products, Benadryl or other allergy medicine—any medicine for that matter—bow and arrow set, garden seeds … I tapped the pencil against my teeth. What else was there?

I shrugged. "I can't think of anything else."

Sebastian took the list from me and tucked it into his pocket. "I don't know how long I'll be, babe, but try not to worry." He bent and kissed me goodbye, patted Nero on the head, and then blew out the candle. As he left, the door clicking behind him, a sense of finality settled over me. This was it, in little more than a week I would truly be on my own. This was like a test run on what was about to be the rest of my life.

I sat there till the sun rose, warming the room and forcing me to admit in the light of day that I was on my own.

I cleaned the house, pulled weeds in the defunct garden, checked fences, pulled water from the well, picked rocks out of the lawn and small pasture, and washed the clothes by hand, hanging them to dry on a makeshift clothesline. By late afternoon I had done a lot and was eyeing up the axe and woodpile. Sebastian was right. I was going to have to learn to do this on my own.

Never having chopped wood in my entire life left me wondering if there was a technique or a method to the process. I scratched my head a moment, then pulled out a fir log that needed to be split, standing it up on end as I'd seen Sebastian do. Before my first swing I pulled the tennis ball I kept in my pocket out and threw it into the field for Nero. He blasted off after it and I had my chance to swing without fear of hitting my pup. I held the very end of the axe handle and gripped it like I would a baseball bat, then with one swing I brought it down, missing the log entirely and burying it into the dirt at my feet.

Rough laughter reached my ears and I spun to see Scout watching me, sitting at the gate. The dirty little bastard was laughing at my attempt. I flipped him off and he flapped his hands at me, as if egging me on. It was strange to see glimpses of a human personality inside what I viewed now as a large, predatory animal. They weren't zombies and they weren't mindless. They really did seem to act like a pack of wolves, hunting their food and sharing it amongst them. I'd even seen them eating shrubs and berries, though it didn't seem to satisfy them any more than eating large amounts of meat. I let out a snort and tried again, this time giving the log a glancing blow. That'll teach it. Yeah, right.

I took a deep breath, stared at the log right where I wanted to hit it and brought the axe down for a third time. The axe bit into the center of the fir, dividing it cleanly in half. I dropped the axe in surprise and then did a dance around the two pieces.

Again laughter reached my ears, but I ignored Scout. This was a great moment, one I could be proud of. But with no one to share it with, it was more than a little bittersweet.

I chopped a few more pieces gaining proficiency until my hands began to hurt and blister, then proceeded to stack the wood in with the rest, throwing the ball in between stacking to keep Nero busy. Washing up with the water I'd pulled out of the well earlier, I went inside as the summer sun began to set, catching a glimpse of myself in the hallway mirror. I paused and really looked at myself. A few short weeks ago my life had been about ease and getting pregnant and now, I looked like a . . . I didn't even know what I looked like. I was deeply tanned, something I'd avoided the last few years, my hair had already lightened, the dark brunette getting a good dose of red highlights, and from the mirror it looked as if I'd lost fifteen or twenty pounds. My clothes hung off my frame, no longer fitting me, something I hadn't noticed with all the chaos. Even my face had slimmed, my cheekbones becoming more prominent, the shape of my face more defined.

I shook my head, what did it matter now? It wasn't like we were going to have children or go on vacation somewhere warm where I could show off my body in a two-piece.

Three glasses of water and leftovers from breakfast, cold oatmeal and a half of what was my attempt to make pancakes the day before was what made up my lunch. Yum-my. Exhausted, I dropped onto the couch; fell asleep in minutes. But, not before I made sure my knife was tucked into the cushion beside me, and Nero was curled up behind my knees.

I dreamed about Sebastian, that we were on our long-awaited honeymoon. There was a beautiful blue ocean, clear to the bottom. Maybe the Caribbean or somewhere in Hawaii—I didn't know and didn't care, he wasn't sick. I could see that even though he was down the beach from me. His skin was tanned and healthy, not a single yellow tinge on him.

I looked down at myself in, hell yeah, a two-piece and a white gauzy sarong around my now-slim hips, the kind the super models wear on a beach shoot. I looked up and Sebastian was gone.

"Bastian?" I said, my voice eaten up by the waves and the sound of the crashing surf.

"I'm here, babe." He was behind me, his arms circling around my waist.

I leaned into him. "I thought you were gone."

He kissed my temple and let go of me, I spun in the wet sand but he was already down the beach, walking slowly, bending every now and then to pick up something from the sand. I laughed and ran towards him, sprinting to cover the short distance. But no matter how hard I ran, no matter that he was only walking, I couldn't catch him.

"Sebastian, wait for me," I yelled, out of breath and no longer feeling so sexy.

He didn't turn back, just kept on walking as if he couldn't hear me, his broad back quickly disappearing into the distance.

"Sebastian!" I screamed, throwing myself out of the dream and off the couch, thumping hard on the wooden floorboards, Nero waking up with a snort.

Footsteps pattered on the porch out front, multiple feet running. Shit, shit, shit. I gulped down a breath and slid to the window, peeking up over the sill. There were four of them and one of me. This was not good, not good at all.

12

What felt like an eternity, yet was probably only ten seconds, passed as I tried to come up with a plan. The doors weren't locked and the Nevermores didn't seem to have the fine motor skills it would take to work the handle. But I had no doubt they would break glass trying to get at me.

"Thought you said there were people here."

The man's voice startled me and I nearly popped up and waved at what I realized with great relief were humans, not Nevermores. A tingle in my stomach held me to the ground though, waiting, Nero let out a low growl and I clamped my hand over his nose. "Shhh," I whispered.

"I saw the bitch in my binoculars, she's here somewhere. The big guy left this morning."

A second man with a deeper tone spoke. "Come on, let's get inside, that one at the front gate is staring at me, he's creeping the bejeesus out of me."

"Fine you pansy, in we go."

I slithered along the floor and crawled over the couch to hide behind it, the gap just large enough for me to fit, Nero wiggling in beside me. No doubt he thought this was a new game.

As I slid into my hiding place the front door creaked open.

"Honey, I'm home!" They all laughed at that and I hugged my blade to my chest. I was trapped. As soon as they started looking I had no doubt they'd find me, at least the Nevermores would have just tried to kill me. I wasn't fooling myself about what these men were after.

Footsteps drew closer and I tensed. A body flopped onto the couch and the rank smell of sweat and blood assaulted my nose, Nero started to growl, his wicked sharp puppy teeth showing under a curled up lip. I put my hand over his nose again and he quieted.

"Marty, go see if there's any food in the joint—and make it snappy, I'm famished. Den, you go upstairs and find us our lady friend, and remember, I get first dibs," the one with the deeper voice, the one on the couch, said.

Footsteps and grumbles receded and the leader leaned back resting his head on the well-padded cushions. He let out a fart, a belch, and then another fart, settling himself deeper into his seat. I pinched my nose, the smell was worse than the pig farm I'd visited last year. I held my breath, and then resorted to breathing through my t-shirt till the worst of it had passed.

"Hurry up, boys, I'm getting mighty hungry for dinner and desert. Luscious sweet pie." He laughed and I crouched. I had a chance if I could catch them off guard, and if Scout was still at the gate, maybe I could use him. A plan started to form, and I knew I would have to act fast and use the element of surprise if it was going to work.

I stared up at the longish hair hanging over the back of the couch. Before I thought better of it, I stood, grabbed a handful of the greasy mop, and placed the blade of my knife up against the leader's neck.

"I wouldn't move or say a word unless I tell you. Got it?" I hissed at him, adrenaline pumping, nerves jangling like a trip wire.

He swallowed and his Adam's Apple bobbed against the knife.

"Very slowly get up. Nothing tricky or I'll slam this into you." I leaned forward the same time he did, coming over the back of the couch without losing my grip on him or the knife. I had no intention of actually cutting him; I just wanted to get him close enough to the gate for Scout to grab him. After that, well, it was going to be dicey but I thought it would work.

"Hey boss, found some . . . son of a bitch!" The one I surmised was Marty stood in the doorway between the kitchen and the living room, his hands full of our canned food that was left, his mouth hanging open.

"Don't just stand there, do something!" Leader Boy said.

I yanked his hair, pulling him back towards the front door, glancing at the floor. Thanks be that Nero was a loyal pup; right at my feet, heeling as if he'd already been trained. I laughed, "Really, you think that's a good idea?"

Marty dropped the canned food. "What do you want me to do?"

"Good question," I said, "Follow us outside, nice and slow like."

More footsteps and Den joined his buddies. I shook my head at him as he reached for his belt and what I assumed was a weapon. "Don't," I said. He dropped his hand and I tightened my hand on the knife.

I inched us out the door backwards, drunk on adrenaline. That's my excuse anyway for forgetting the fourth man.

Something hit me from behind, my shoulders and upper back taking the brunt of the blow, but it didn't make me let go. I instinctively tightened my grip, but as I stumbled backwards, the blade pulled through the leader's neck with a clean slice and a low gurgle. I didn't have time to react to the fact that I'd just killed a second man in less than a month.

I wobbled a few feet away, the stunned silence from the other men giving me only split second to make my next move. No doubt the men still standing couldn't believe what had happened anymore than I could and it took them a moment to recover. I spun and ran, blade still in my hands, dripping blood, Nero right beside me.

"Get her!" I don't know which one of them yelled it, doesn't matter, not with what happened next.

I ran to the gate where Scout crouched in the shadows, his eyes glittering at me as I sprinted towards him. The three men were closing in on me, fingertips brushing the back of my shirt as I panted for air, hoping for enough oxygen to make the desperate jump and climb over the metal gate. As I drew close Nero veered off, running to the garden, his fear of the gate the only thing that would drive him from my side.

The gate was cold and I struggled to get my hands on it, the bunches of metal grapes and leaves biting into my flesh. I managed to get half way over before the closest man grabbed my ankle. I pulled hard and tumbled to the ground on the other side of the fence, knocking the wind out of me. Even so, I made myself get to my feet and jogged to the center of the road, the three men following me, cocky, swaggering as if they knew something I didn't.

They had their backs to Scout, but I could still see him and I gave him a slow nod. His eyes widened and then a grin spread across his face. With a blur of speed he hamstrung two of the men with his bare teeth before they knew what hit them. They fell screaming, the sound echoing around us. It wouldn't be long before the pack showed up for this banquet. The last man standing half-turned to see what had happened and I rushed him. With a swift move Scout took him down, snapping his neck in one clean twist.

Marty rolled on the ground, "Bitch!" he screamed as Scout jumped on his chest, ripping at his neck, blood spurting every which way. I gagged at the smell and the sight and forced myself to unfreeze my legs and move. I was horrified by what I'd done, essentially leading the men into the lion's den. Finally my semi-paralysis broke and I jogged to the gate, deliberately not looking at what Scout was doing as he sniffed around the flailing body of the one man that still lived.

"Help me!" he yelled, reaching for me. I avoided his fingers and put my hands on the cold metal piping that made up the gate.

As I climbed back over to my side, I turned back in time to see the pack emerge from the bush around us.

I walked slowly back to the house, the screams of the men only lasting a brief moment before they were cut off. This was a moment I wasn't proud of. I was horrified deep within that I could essentially kill four men and feel nothing. No, that wasn't true. I didn't want to do it, but the world was now literally dog-eat-dog, and I would go down fighting every time.

I climbed the steps to the house and stared at the leader's body, blood pooling around it and slipping through the cracks to the ground below.

It was then that I lost it, the shakes starting deep within my belly and spreading throughout my entire body, forcing me to the ground. I sat, leaning against the house, the body beside me as I waited for the shock to pass. When I was sure I wasn't going to pass out, I let out a whistle. Within a few moments Nero came running up on the porch and leapt into my lap.

"Good dog," I said. When he went to sniff the body I reprimanded him lightly. "Leave it." I stood slowly and with my hand against the house for support I stood over the leader.

"I can't let Sebastian see me like this," I whispered to myself. I bent and picked up the man's feet, dragging him off the porch and towards the gate. It was hard work, the body floppy and uncooperative, and I was sweating hard by the time I was only halfway. I paused and caught my breath, and stared down at the body at my feet, really seeing it, the open gash across the neck; the surprised expression on his face. Emotions started to well up and I pushed them back down. There was no place for that, not anymore.

With a heave I started to drag the body again, this time getting it all the way to the gate before considering a problem I hadn't before considered. How the hell was I going to get it over the gate?

A grunt brought my attention to Scout, crouched back in the shadows. He stood slowly and approached me, his hands outstretched. We were going to have to work together if we were going to get this body over to him.

I lifted the feet up as high as I could; panting and breathing hard, a squirm of fear that Scout might make a grab for me while my hands were occupied. He reached over the fence and grabbed one boot, then the other, and yanked, snapping the body through the air and onto his side.

With a grunt and a smile, he dragged the body behind him to the edge of the bush and started in on it, his back hunched over the chest, and a loud crunching rolled over me followed by a wet ripping sound that I chose to ignore.

I made myself watch as he feasted on the body and thought about Sebastian, how soon it would be him eating whatever he could get his hands on. I hoped he was okay, hoped that he hadn't been hurt. A part of me, though, hoped I didn't ever have to see him shift, turn into a mindless eating machine, see him become like Scout, or Jessica or the Alpha.

Which would be worse, to lose him now and not know what happened, or lose him to the drug and forever have that image of Sebastian as a monster engrained in my mind?

THE NEVERMORE TRILOGY

13

I spent the better part of the morning cleaning up the blood and hiding all evidence that the raiding party had ever been here. I didn't need it as a reminder of what I'd done.

Exhausted from the long night and hard work, I fell asleep around noon on our bed, Nero once more cuddled up behind my legs. It was a heavy sleep, dreamless and surprisingly restful. A light touch on my cheek snapped me awake and I lashed out, reaching for the knife under the pillow before I even opened my eyes.

"Easy, babe, it's me," Sebastian said.

I gasped and let go of the blade and threw myself into his arms. All my thoughts of not telling him what happened broke under his presence and the words tumbled out of me along with the tears that I hadn't been able to shed for the men that died, and the part of me that died along with them.

Sebastian stroked my hair and let me confess to him without a single word. Gulping back a final sob I looked up and had to force myself not to react. His skin had changed in the short time he'd been gone and the patterning under the skin up his neck looked a great deal like a faint tattoo. Exactly as Jessica's had right before she left.

"There's nothing I can say that will make this better for you, babe," Sebastian said. He continued to stroke my hair, never breaking eye contact with me. "You've got to be strong now. There's no guarantee that more raiders won't come, that you won't be attacked again. In the past there was always someone to call for help, the police or neighbours. We have to take care of each other now, whatever that means and whatever that takes."

"It scared me how little I felt," I whispered, "Like their deaths didn't matter, when I knew they should have meant something."

Sebastian frowned and shook his head. "Babe, you are going to have to fight to make it. Don't let your fear stop you from surviving. I think it's just your way of not losing your mind. Bad shit is going to happen, there's nothing you can do about it but be strong."

He pulled me tight into his arms, held me close and I let out a sigh of relief. "I was scared you would think I was an awful person for what I did."

"I'm going to try and eat people soon. I don't think you have to worry about getting that bad," he said. I knew he was trying to lighten the mood but he failed miserably, the shadows of what was coming for him lay heavy on us, a physical weight we both tried to ignore but couldn't. I saw an image of Scout in my mind eating the body and it morphed into Sebastian, feral and nasty.

Sebastian stood up. "Come on; let me show you what I found."

I followed him downstairs, prepared to be dazzled. Boy was I disappointed. The kitchen table was covered, but most of it wasn't food. There were a number of different drugs; he'd found me some allergy medicine, batteries, and then some canned food of miscellaneous types. Nothing that would last much more than a week if I stretched it.

I forced a smile. "Looks good, how far did you have to go for all this?"

"All the way down to Bowser. Most of the homes have been ransacked and I was chased by a few smaller packs, but it was quiet for the most part."

"What about Dan's? Why didn't you go there?" I brushed my fingers across the package of batteries, wishing they were edible.

Sebastian shook his head. "I went there first, but he . . ."

A grimace crossed over his face, twisting it into a parody of the man I loved. I reached out and he pushed my hand away, stumbling towards the front door.

"Bastian."

He didn't turn around, just kept walking, using the furniture for support. I followed, knowing what was about to happen, wishing there was some other way, wishing I could help him. Wishing I could take his place. I let out a sob, it should have been me, I should have been the one to turn, not Sebastian.

He turned at the door, his pupils shifting, sliding into the vertical slit that was becoming so familiar to me. Tears dripped off his chin, the last tears he would cry as a human.

"I love you."

I ran to him; he tried to push me away. I wouldn't let him go that easily. I pulled his head to mine and pressing my lips to his our tears sealed what would be our last kiss.

"Always Bastian, you will always be my love. Forever," I whispered against his mouth and then he jerked himself away from me and ran for the gate, climbing clumsily over it. As his feet touched the other side he let out a roar, guttural and wild. I slid to my knees, tears streaming down my face. The pack emerged from the bush, Scout creeping forward first, the Alpha and Jessica at the back like always.

They milled around him, sniffing and grunting and he pushed them away easily, making them keep their distance. When one got too close, Sebastian snapped his foot forward catching it in the mouth and sent it flying backwards. After that they easily gave him the distance he wanted. As they turned to go, the pack slipping back into the bush, Sebastian stayed, standing in front of the gate like a sentinel.

He turned his head and looked back at me, his now-foreign eyes meeting mine. With a low moan he dropped to the ground, tucking himself into the shadows that Scout had previously occupied. With my own moan my head dropped forward till it touched the wooden railing.

Sebastian wasn't going with the pack. He was staying to guard me. I didn't know what was worse, having him gone completely and knowing he had no memory left of his life before, or knowing that he was trapped inside a body with unnatural desires, and still remembering me and our love.

14

I spent the better part of the next three days hiding inside, sleeping and wishing I had the courage to take my own life, only moving when Nero whined for food or to go out. I dreamed of blood and death and knives, Sebastian making love to me, our child we never had, the men who broke into our house, and Jessica with her sweet smile. The dreams left me moaning and tossing, my own cries waking me up only to let the sadness swallow me down again.

On the third day a rock banged on my bedroom window and I leapt out of bed, half dressed and completely confused, scrambling for a weapon of some sort. Nero was on full alert, his hackles high and a low growl rumbling past his lips.

"What the hell?" I muttered and made my way to the window to peer outside. Sebastian stood at the gate, a rock in his hand, arm cocked back and ready to throw.

I lifted the windowpane and hung my upper body out. "Okay! I'm up, stop throwing rocks, you nut," I shouted at him. He blew a raspberry my way that I could hear even from this distance and sat back down in the cover of the bush, disappearing from view. But he was still there, he hadn't left me, not completely, and he still had some of himself left, enough to still care about me.

Cold water makes a good bracer to wake you up in the morning, and I scrubbed my body clean in the back yard with a bar of soap and two buckets of water. I even found the energy to play with Nero, splashing him with water as he ran around the yard. Clean clothes next, and I felt more awake and ready to face whatever this day would bring me.

Suddenly ravenous, I went to the kitchen and pulled out a can of beans. I cracked it open and ate the whole thing down without a breath. A can of peaches was next, followed by a jar of maraschino cherries. The sweetness of the cherries slowed me down, and I took my time to savour the thick juice they were in, licking every finger to get the most out of the jar. I looked at what I'd done when I had finished, and even though I knew that it was no more than I would have eaten had I been awake the last few days, I still felt bad for eating so much in one sitting.

"Damn," I muttered for no particular reason except to say something, to break the silence. I put away the supplies that Sebastian had brought home, organizing the quickly diminishing stocks. There wasn't much here and soon I'd be the one heading out of the property to get food stuffs. I wasn't sure if it was better to wait or to go right away.

The next few days went like the last few weeks had: water, garden, fence checking, splitting wood, wash some clothes and hope they last a while yet and keep an eye on the gate. Through every chore, every necessary task I wondered what the hell I was going to do with the next fifty years of my life alone on a farm surrounded by a pack of wild humans with nothing more than a yellow Lab for company.

More than a week had passed, maybe even longer since Sebastian had left me, and I found myself talking to Nero, having full conversations with the puppy. He would cock his head and listen, his pink tongue hanging out as he stared up at me. It was in the middle of one of these conversations that our three acres suddenly felt terribly claustrophobic, so much so that I started to tremble.

I scanned the back property for where Dan had gone into the bush. A spring of hope whispered through me. Of course Dan was still alive! He had a freaking bunker full of guns and food, Nero and I could go and get food and a gun. My rational self tried to remind me that Sebastian had gone to Dan's and come away with nothing, that I had convinced Sebastian not to go to Dan's, and that I didn't trust him—but my need to see and speak to another person was driving me beyond what was rational.

"Do you want to go for a walk?" I asked Nero. He gave me what I chose to believe was an affirmative yip. The trek would require me to put my life on the line to reach a man I barely knew and wasn't entirely sure of, yet I was ready to do it if it meant having someone to talk to, even for a just a little while. I justified my idea with the thought that I would be able to get food from him and maybe even a weapon, if he held true to his word.

"It's all I've got," I said.

I went inside, and grabbed the three empty knapsacks tucking them inside one another till there was only the one for me to carry. I couldn't take them all full, but it was a nice thought to think that I would be filling them up.

I wanted to bring my knife so that it was at hand without me holding on to it the whole time. It was a forty-five minute walk, maybe longer if I had to duck for cover. I paused in my preparations; maybe it would be shorter, if I had to run the whole way. I put the backpack on backwards and lifted Nero into it, his head sticking out along with his tongue. I laughed at him and he gave me a doggy grin, licking at my face. He was getting bigger, but I didn't think he could walk the whole way, and I didn't want to leave him here on his own in case I didn't come back. At least out there he might have a chance at finding food and surviving.

An ungodly screech filled the air and the hairs on the back of my neck stood at attention. I ran to the front door, skidding to a stop on the threshold. The pack was in a giant circle on the far side of the gate, screaming, hollering, and otherwise making as much noise as possible. In the centre of the circle was the Alpha male and, I let out a low moan, Sebastian.

Pulling myself together I slid off the pack and put Nero on the ground then ran to the gate, my knife clenched firmly in my hands. What I thought I was going to do about this was anyone's guess; I sure as hell didn't know.

The pack ignored me, focused solely on the two men in the circle as they jabbed and struck at one another. I knew it was a fight for dominance, but it was hard for me to see my usually passive, nonaggressive husband with his lips curled back over his teeth, growls emanating from his mouth.

They rammed each other; grappling for the upper hand, and I found myself yelling along with the pack, screaming at Sebastian to finish the Alpha off, Nero barking and jumping at my feet. The energy around us swirled, bringing us for a

94

moment into their world, swept up in the fight for the stronger leader. If it was a battle to the death, there was no doubt in my mind who I wanted to win, even if Sebastian was no longer himself.

The clash of bodies caused a huge dustbowl, the dry dirt road and wind making perfect conditions for it. The two men were soon caked in a fine dusting of powdered earth, the sweat rolling down their bodies, catching each particle and sticking it to them. Their bodies now a strange shade of yellow highlights and red-brown mud only added to the animalistic surrealism in the scene. I took a step back and really looked at what was going on. The pack was split, half on one side of the circle and half on the other. I had a feeling that Scout would be on Sebastian's side. I scanned the crowd and spotted him on the left, Jessica next to him. I frowned. Wouldn't she want to be on her mate's side? A strange squirming feeling settled in my belly. She would be, unless she saw Sebastian as the better mate for her, stronger, younger and better able to care for her and any babies she had.

"You stay away from him!" I surprised myself by yelling at her. Not that she paid me any attention; she was totally focused on the match, her eyes never leaving the two men.

I took a step back and a deep breath. What did I think was going to happen? I closed my eyes and tried to slow my ever escalating thoughts, tried to banish a sudden image of Jessica and Sebastian rolling on the ground, their bodies naked and intertwined, wrestling in a far different way than he was now entangled with the Alpha. He wouldn't do it. I had to believe there was enough of Sebastian left that he wouldn't have sex with Jessica. My stomach rolled and I swallowed on the bile that rose in my throat, an unexpected burn of anger starting.

He hadn't even done anything and already I was feeling the effects of jealousy and bitterness at the thought of Bastian and Jessica together.

A crack of bone and I opened my eyes to see the Alpha male on the ground, his ankle twisted at the wrong angle. He let out a moan and dropped his head, defeated by his younger opponent. The pack swirled around, hopping and thumping the ground with their hands and feet, some of them diving into their fallen leader and taking pot shots at him.

The pack stepped back; their eager grunts and gestures making it clear even to me that they wanted Sebastian to finish him off. This was the final moment of his humanity and I knew it. The minute he killed the man helpless at his feet would be the minute I had to say goodbye to him forever. If it had been a battle to the end, that would have been different, survival, but not this killing of a defenceless creature at his feet.

Sebastian walked over to the Alpha and stared down at him, not moving, just looking. The Alpha kept his eyes down and held perfectly still. He knew as well as the rest of them what was coming.

"Sebastian." I said, not truly thinking he would heed me. To my disbelief, he turned and looked me in the eye. "Don't do this. Don't let them take the last of what makes you, you."

My eyes filled but I didn't cry. I put every emotion I could into my next words, hoping he would listen.

"Don't kill him."

The pack, perhaps sensing my interference started to grumble. They milled towards the gate and I stepped back out of reach but I never broke eye contact with Sebastian.

Something flickered in those alien eyes—an emotion that was so achingly human—a piece of my husband I thought was gone forever. Compassion.

He stepped away from the Alpha and growled at the pack who then froze in their advance on me and the gate. A second, lower growl and they backed off, slinking into the bush from where they had come. All except for Jessica who hovered close by, her rail thin body swaying to music I couldn't hear, and the previous Alpha who pulled himself to his feet and dragging his broken ankle, limped down the road alone, away from the pack's territory. Jessica didn't even look at her mate as he passed her. She had eyes for only one person.

Sebastian stared at Jessica and I recognized the look, he'd given it to me more than once. His eyes were dark with desire, his lips parted and a steady pulse throbbed at the base of his neck. She preened under his gaze, a noise similar to a purr bubbling out of her as the swaying intensified, her tiny hips rocking faster and faster, side to side.

I didn't want to see this, it was bad enough knowing it would happen right outside the home Sebastian and I had started to make for ourselves. I turned my back and started to walk for the house, feeling like if I ran it would somehow made things worse. A low grumble from Sebastian and an answering purr from Jessica sped my feet up. But I didn't run. Around the back of the house I went, straight to the garden.

I stared at the ground, far enough away that I couldn't hear anything. A girlish shriek made me jump. On second thought, the back fences needed checking. I ran now, Nero right behind me, his panting giving him away, to where they couldn't see me. Through the tall grass that would have one day been pasture for the kid's pony I'd hoped to have, past the tall maple we'd tied a rope to for a tire swing, all the way to the back fence where I collapsed to my knees.

Breathing hard, my blood thumping in my ears, I strained to hear any more while at the same time desperately wishing I wouldn't. My blood slowed, heart rate settling back to a steady beat, and nothing but the birds in the trees and the occasional song of a frog reached me. Nero plunked himself down beside me and rolled on his back, luxuriating in the cool grass. I wish I could be as nonchalant about life, could enjoy even the little moments.

"I can't do this, not on my own; not by myself," I whispered, lying on the ground, staring up at the blue sky with the tall, brilliantly green stalks of grass surrounding me, making me feel like a child again. In a daze with my heart numb I struggled with the jealousy, anger, and pain that warred for my attention. I think in the back of my mind I had thought that he would snap out of the drug's effects, that because he still watched over me, still remembered me, he would come back to himself. That hope was dashed against the reality of what was happening outside the gate.

My head knew that it would be unfair to judge him; he would never have pursued Jessica if he were in his right mind. But that knowledge didn't change how I felt, or how much it hurt me to see him want her.

I closed my eyes and laid down next to Nero, and when I opened them again I knew I was dreaming, knew it wasn't real, but I wanted it to be.

Sebastian stood across the field from me, the summer season having slipped into fall and the grass golden in the fading sunlight. "What are you staring at, babe?"

I laughed and stood, my balance off kilter, and when I looked down I realized why. I was pregnant, and not just a little bit, a lot. I ran my hands over my belly, the babe rolling under my fingertips. "We're pregnant," I said, looking to Sebastian for confirmation of what I felt inside me.

He smiled and started towards me. "Of course we are. That's why I took the shot, remember?"

My elation faded. "No, you didn't take the shot, couldn't have, it turns people into monsters."

Sebastian laughed and then was suddenly at my side his hands on my belly. "No one turns into monsters, babe. We are the future, the others, those who didn't take the shot, they're the past." He held a mirror up to my face and I gasped.

Yellow eyes stared out at me from what looked like my face, a gaunt, emaciated version of me with jaundiced skin pulled tight over the bones. I stared at my arms as the flesh shrunk and the skin stretched showing every sinew and ligament in clear relief. Horror rippled through me, my mouth dry. I clung to my disbelief like a life raft in rough seas.

"No. I can't take the shot, I can't," I said as I backed away from Sebastian. He didn't change, didn't look any different and then he smiled, a big toothy grin that showed me row upon row of shark teeth glinting down on me. He lunged and I gasped as I sat bolt upright in the long grass, my hand going to my stomach.

Sebastian and I had made love several times since he'd taken the shot. Was my subconscious trying to tell me something, or was my mind playing tricks on me?

15

I walked slowly back to the house and peeked around the edge to see the front gate still standing, with no one there, not even Scout.

That was it then, Sebastian was gone with them now, Jessica and him a pair. I let my mind sit on that, accept it for fact, and then slipped into the house going straight to the bathroom. I flipped open the calendar and looked at the little "P" that I'd put on the dates that I had my period and my breath caught in my throat. With all the upheaval, I hadn't noticed that not only was I late, I was almost due for a second period.

I threw myself to my knees and ripped open the bathroom cupboard. Toilet paper, towels and bars of soap went flying out behind me, Nero yelping as something bounced off of him as I searched for the pregnancy test I knew was in there somewhere.

"Where the hell is it?" I yelled just as my fingertips brushed up against a rectangular box that I knew was pale pink before I even pulled it out. I ripped the package open and stared at the instructions. I knew the drill, drop your pants, pee on the stick, and wait for two minutes.

The waiting was the hardest part. I sat on the edge of the tub and stared at the stick resting perfectly flat on the edge of the sink, counting to 120 under my breath.

". . . 115, 116, 117, 118. Close enough." I stood, walked to the sink and looked down to see a perfect pink plus sign.

I didn't know whether to be happy or terrified; both emotions rushed through me, swinging from one to the other and back again. I placed my hand on my stomach. I had to figure out how far along I was. The first time we'd made love after he took the shot was . . . I counted back in my head, using the calendar for a reference. It was six and a half weeks ago.

"I can't go to Dan's. I can't risk you little one." I touched my stomach as a new, and even more terrifying thought assailed me. The baby had been conceived when Sebastian had the Nevermore drug flowing through his system. What would happen to him or her? Would the child be born as a Nevermore or as a human? I shook off the questions that at the moment didn't matter. Until the baby made it here safely, there was no point in borrowing trouble.

I made my way downstairs and counted the food I had. There was no way it was enough to see me through nine months of pregnancy and the first few months of motherhood that I would need it to. If I was careful I could make it stretch for a few more weeks, closer to the end of my first trimester. At that point I would have to make a supply run, several in fact, if I was going to make it.

Resolve filled me as I considered the alternative. A certainty that I could do this, if not for myself then for the child I was carrying, the last connection I had with Sebastian. I sat down and started to make a list of all the things I would need, not just for myself but for the baby too: diapers or cloth to make diapers, bottles, formula, blankets, and clothes. Crap, baby clothes might be hard; we lived in an area of retirees.

"Not that I'm complaining little one, but your entry into my life sure has turned things upside down."

I smiled, thinking about having the baby, tried not to think about all the things that could go wrong or that I would be by myself for the delivery. I scrubbed my hands over my eyes, pooped out despite the nap I had in the field. Climbing the stairs, my legs feeling like lead, I snuggled into bed. Nero curled up beside me as I breathed in the scent of Sebastian's aftershave on his pillow, for the first time in days not feeling completely lost, feeling like there was a purpose to me being here and a reason to fight to stay alive.

16

I spent the next three weeks being careful not to do anything too strenuous while still attempting to keep things going. I hauled water every day, just smaller amounts; I checked fences still, only slower. I even managed to get some carrots to grow. They were a long way from edible, but the piss-poor fencing job I'd put up around the small garden patch was at least keeping the deer and rabbits out. Not to mention Nero ran after everything that moved; rabbits, crows, and deer included in that list, which helped with the critter control.

I looked back on the calendar to see how far along I'd been when I miscarried the first time. Only about five weeks, which I was well past now. There was a small bump by late evenings from the bloat, that if you didn't know me you'd think I'd been slacking on my workouts and had developed a bit of a paunch.

I told stories to the baby every night, mostly about Sebastian and how we'd met, and then I'd sing until I fell asleep, my bedroom window open and the cool summer night air breezing in. The pack was remarkably silent during this time, so much so that it was easy to forget they were even there. Scout only checked on the gate once and I found myself smiling and waving at him, happy to see someone other than the local wildlife. Of course, I suppose he was part of the local wildlife. Even Nero had given up barking at Scout, settling for a minor growl and a lip curl. I didn't correct him for that, as far as I was concerned at some point he would be a big dog and it was good for him to learn now who to mistrust. Everyone but me.

Three weeks and two days into finding out I was pregnant; I was down to the last two cans of food, both beans. It was early in the morning, just as the colour was beginning to change the sky. Today was the day.

"This is it," I said. "Okay, baby, we have to make a hard trip, probably several, and I don't want you to be afraid. I'll protect you, no matter what." I ran my hands over my belly, stroking the hard bump, wishing I could hold the little one.

I took my list and tucked it into the back pocket of my jeans, grateful now more than ever that there was some weight loss before I got pregnant, otherwise I'd be looking for fat clothes for me along with food and clothes for the baby.

My kitchen knife slid into a homemade sheath that went on my belt for easy access, one of those projects I managed to do while essentially waiting for the food to run out. Then the last two cans of beans went into the bag along with a can opener. I was worried I might have to stay in other homes where there was no food. Better to be over-prepared than caught out in the open like a fool.

I peeked out the front bay window before leaving, hoping the pack was there, but not expecting it. If they were at the gate, I was less likely to run into them on the back trail. Movement at the gate surprised me.

Sebastian leapt from the shadows where he'd sat the first few days after he'd removed himself from the farm, his eyes wide as he stared at me. I stepped out onto the front porch, my heart pounding in my throat.

I swallowed hard, aware that my emotions were even closer to the surface with all the hormones rushing through me. I had to stop thinking of him as my husband. Sebastian was gone, even if his body was still here. Even so, I had to say something to him. I had to more for me than for him.

"Sebastian, if you're still in there, it's okay. I don't like that you and Jessica . . ." I had barely said her name when he started to shake his head.

I frowned, wondering if it was just a nervous tick. It had been over four weeks since he had turned; I didn't want to fool myself into believing he was still in there, still Sebastian underneath it all. I didn't want to go through that pain again of losing him.

"Jessica is a good girl, it's okay, I understand." It wasn't okay, and I didn't understand, but I could keep those thoughts to myself. Again though, he shook his head, this time adding a frown for good measure. Did he mean what I think he did? As if to punctuate that he didn't, Jessica took that moment to come screaming out of the bush, half naked, hands flailing as she attacked Sebastian. The ferocity of her attempt shocked me, and Sebastian shoving her hard was even more of a shock. She tumbled to the ground and lay there breathing hard, her bare breasts heaving.

Seeing me, she screeched and snapped her teeth at me, and I gave an involuntary step back. A sly look slid over her face and in a flash she was completely naked, the rest of her clothes strewn about the ground, swinging her hips and touching her own body as she tried to entice Sebastian. He looked at her and shook his head; turning his back on her he faced me, again shaking his head.

When she wouldn't leave, he turned and roared at her, making her cringe away from him as she scooped her clothes and ran back to the bush, snarling and snapping the whole way.

"Bastian?" I said my voice as soft as I could make it without whispering. I don't remember walking to the gate, but suddenly I was there, well within reaching distance. Sebastian stepped close, his eyes strange and yet, somehow, I could see that he was still my husband, the man I loved and the father of our child. Fear tickled at the back of my neck but I pushed it away and focused on the love.

I reached out and he flinched. "Please," I said, "give me your hand."

Sebastian stood still for so long I wasn't sure he understood until ever so slowly he raised his hand, offering it to me. The back of it was covered in the faint lines that shadowed so much of the bodies of those who took the drug, designs that look suspiciously like the flower on the broom plants.

His skin was cool to the touch, far cooler than it should have been, but I revelled in the touch of skin on skin.

With a suddenness that sent me reeling, Sebastian snarled and snatched his hand out of mine, slicing his own arm as he ripped it back through the gate. I stumbled backwards and fell, instinctively rolling to protect my belly.

Tears filled my eyes, not from the pain in my body, but the pain in my heart. "Bastian," I whispered, choking on his name. His eyes softened and he crouched down and reached once more through the gate. As much as I wanted to, I couldn't trust him. With a sob I stood and ran to the back of the house, gave Nero a pat and grabbed my backpacks. I brushed the tears away and took a deep cleansing breath. There was no going back, Sebastian might have been fighting his natural inclinations, but even I could see that the drug was too strong.

17

The broom was mostly out of bloom now, the seed pods hanging heavy on the branches, ready to germinate for next year's crop of hateful plants.

I walked as swiftly as I could, not wanting to run and crash through the bush unless I had too, knowing that every sound I made could draw the pack down on me. Stepping lightly, I avoided twigs and piles of branches, pushed overhanging limbs out of my way, and gently let them go back into place.

Twenty minutes into my hike, a shiver went down my spine and I froze. I'd only felt this way once before, when Sebastian and I had gone to Dan's and the bear had jumped out at us. I turned slowly to see Bob, as Dan had called him, on his hind legs sniffing at the air. Bob was thin, far thinner than he should have been for the middle of the summer season. No doubt the pack was direct competition for him and his regular food sources.

"Now Bob, I know you don't like me, but remember what Dan said?" I hoped I could talk my way out of this, though my body was trembling, the adrenaline coursing through me.

Bob grunted and dropped to all fours, again sniffing the air. Maybe the pack smelled different than regular humans? It would make sense. Bob took one step towards me and I took a step back. He gave a snort and pawed at the ground. With great care and slow movements I took my bag from my back and took out one of my precious cans of beans. The can opener clicked as the lid popped off and the scent of molasses covered legumes filled the air.

"See, Bob, I'm a nice girl. I'm going to give you these beans and then I'm going to leave." I put the open can on the ground. It was a sacrifice, but I had to make it if I wanted even a chance at more food.

Bob sniffed the air and let out a low grunt. As he padded close to the can, I backed up; grateful his attention was solely on the food. I kept backing up till I rounded a corner, then turned and ran. I pushed myself as far as my adrenaline and legs would take me then stopped to listen, my ears straining for any sound. No bear behind me, and the birds were still chirping. That had to be a good sign.

Another five minutes and I came to a six-way intersection, the trail to the right flagged with a red kerchief. "Thank you, Dan, even if you were a miserable old coot," I said and headed down the marked path. What I found though was something less than what I was hoping for.

Dan hadn't made it home from our place, at least that's what it looked like. His army boots, shredded pants, and tattered shirt were spread around a veritable pile of bones. His rifle had been pushed to the side, untouched and unused for fear of drawing more Nevermores. Or maybe he'd been hit from behind and never had a chance. I would never know.

"I'm so sorry, Dan," I whispered as I bent to retrieve the rifle and ammo belt, quickly looking for any other useful things on his body. It wasn't a nice task, but necessary.

In the one intact pocket of his pants was something that let me know I did have guardian angels watching over me. Dan's house key.

Crouched over Dan's bones, I again had a feeling of being watched. "Come on, Bob," I said, "I only have one can left." I turned to see not Bob behind me, but Sebastian.

We stared at one another, no gate between us, nothing to stop him from attacking me, as his pack would do if they found me out in the bush.

I took a deep breath and stood slowly, my one hand still holding the rifle, the other gripping the key. Sebastian watched me, his expression not changing or giving me any hint to what he was thinking. I looked up the trail the way I was headed then back to Sebastian.

I licked my lips. There was nothing between us now, no gate to save me, only the rifle if I dared use it. I set the rifle on the ground and walked slowly towards Sebastian, my heart pounding, my head screaming for me to run. There was one thing that might keep Sebastian from attacking me, but it was a roll of the dice.

I put my hands on my belly and said, "I'm pregnant."

Sebastian blinked, then frowned and stepped towards me. It took everything I had to hold my ground as I thought of his face as he snarled at me at the gate.

With slow, deliberate steps, Sebastian approached me.

I watched his eyes as he reached for me and I held perfectly still. With the softest of touches, his fingertips rested on my bump, the slight frown of confusion swiftly followed by the flush of understanding. His fingers trembled across my belly and I lifted my shirt so he could touch the skin and feel the changes in my body. His hand brushed across my belly button and then cupped the small swell of our child within me. I looked up to see his eyes wide and sparkling with unshed tears. In that moment I knew that Sebastian would never truly lose himself, he was too strong for that and he loved me too much to forget me.

"I love you Sebastian." My words, simple and true as they were, sparked something in him.

He let out a low keening wail as he slid to his knees, pressing his cheek against my stomach. A flash of fear warmed my skin but I put it out. I couldn't truly be afraid of my husband, he didn't have it in him to kill the Alpha, and there was no way he would hurt me or our child.

"I have to go." I pulled away and Sebastian looked up his eyes betraying his every emotion. "I have to get more food, clothes, and things. I'm going to Dan's first." Maybe that was too much hope on my part, thinking he could fully understand, but I had to believe.

I tucked my shirt in and adjusted the backpack. I trailed my fingertips across his face and then stepped back from him. I smiled, then turned and started walking, trusting that my heart was telling me the truth and I was not being another fool in love.

Footsteps from behind sped my pulse, but he wasn't running. He was keeping pace with me. As we walked, twenty feet between us, I thought about what it was that compelled me to trust him. Was it the love we shared? Yes, somewhat, but I think more than that . . . Sebastian growled and the tension around us rose. I glanced over my shoulder to see him snarling at the bush where a bird suddenly took flight. I shook my head and picked up my train of thought again. More than the love, it was that I knew him; I knew the person he was, and how set he was in his own beliefs and standards. He hadn't just been a good man; he'd lived his life as a good man, what he said and what he did always matched up. Even though he was a Nevermore now, I could still see those qualities in him, and they were what allowed me to trust him.

Ten minutes and I pushed my way through a small clump of huckleberries and found myself in Dan's backyard. I pulled back and peeked out through the bush. No need to go running into Nevermores at this point in the game.

For several minutes I waited, breathing in the sweet and intoxicating scent of the flowers on the huckleberry bush. A soft shuffle from behind me and I went very still, a warm breath whispering down the back of my neck. Sebastian's hands circled around me, brushing first my belly, then my waist and sliding up to cup my breasts. I tried to think straight as he pressed his lips to the back of my neck, nuzzling the tender skin behind my ear. He let out a low purr and then pushed me out of the bush and into the garden.

I gasped in a lungful of air and spun to hear a soft chuckle from the huckleberry bush. I couldn't help but smile. Damn, even now, even this way he wanted me and I wanted him. That was love; it had the power to overcome any physical change in each other.

Dan's key was cool in my hand but I didn't need it, the door was unlocked. Stepping into the dim interior, I waited for my eyes to adjust to the low light before going any further. I shut the door behind me, locking it for good measure. It was musty and warm, the windows all shut tight and the air stale from no movement. Eerie, and with more than a measure of feeling haunted, the house echoed my footsteps as I started my search.

The obvious places were first, kitchen and pantry, both of which were full to the brim with food, all preserves, cans of fruit, and pasta. Evaporated milk. My mouth watered at the thought of dairy, and I scrambled to find myself some water to mix it with. I didn't have to look far. Dan had stacks upon stacks of individual-sized bottled water in the pantry. I pulled one out and mixed in the evaporated milk, shaking it for good measure.

I downed every last drop of it, the chalky texture and faint milk flavour heavenly to my deprived taste buds. The stress of the walk, my moment with Sebastian, the fact that I was pregnant and already tired, along with my huge guzzle of milk left me more than a little sleepy. I shook the feeling off though. I couldn't dawdle here, there was too much chance that the pack would come looking for Sebastian—or worse, Jessica would come looking for him.

I climbed the stairs to the upper level, the weight of the air seeming to grow heavier with each step. On the top step a creak sounded from inside the house and it wasn't me.

Frozen to the spot, I strained my ears listening till they were ringing with the silence. After several minutes with no more noise I convinced myself to take another step and that's when the gun was shoved into my face.

"What the hell are you doing breaking into my house, woman?" Dan snarled at me as he stared down his rifle at me.

"Dan. I thought . . . I mean I found . . . bones," I stuttered out.

He lowered the gun. "Well at least you ain't one of them." Dan brushed past me and clomped downstairs. "Come on, woman, I told you I'd give you food and weapons if you made it here and you did."

I followed him, my mouth dry, and my heart not sure if it was going to gallop away with me or stop completely. It seemed to settle on an unsteady rhythm that left me more than a little wobbly of leg.

"I see you've made yourself at home," Dan said as he pointed to the open bag of dried milk.

I shrugged, determined not to feel bad. "I thought you were dead."

He grunted and went to packing my backpacks with food. "This should last you for a while. Come back when you need more." He handed me one pack full, two empty. That wasn't going to be enough, not by a long shot.

"I'm pregnant, Dan. I need to take more than that; I need to stockpile the food at my place. Unless you want me to move in here with you."

"Shit." He spit on the floor. "Why'd you go and get knocked up? I sure as hell hope it ain't by that infected man of yours."

I sucked in a breath. "How do you know about Sebastian?"

"One of those things was following him, a young female. She wasn't interested in eating him. So I shot at him."

"What?" I yelped. That was what Sebastian had been trying to tell me about Dan, that he'd been shooting at him. A tap on one of the windows brought my head around.

117

Sebastian peered in through the dirty glass, his head cocked to one side. Dan snapped his gun up and I pushed it down. "No! Stop, he's not like the rest of them!" Sebastian snarled at Dan and I put my hand up on the window.

The snarl faded and he mimicked me, putting his hand against mine. Dan's eyebrows rose. "Well I'll be buggered."

"He remembers me, Dan, I don't know how or why—but he does. Please don't shoot him."

"For now. But if he shows even the slightest inclination to attack, that's it, he's done." Dan said.

I nodded and let out a breath. "Thank you." I looked around the pantry. "Now, can we please fill the other backpacks?"

"I ain't helping you move this stuff woman. I ain't stepping outside this house except for my own needs, no one else's," Dan said.

I put a can of tomatoes in. "That's fine, Dan. I thank you for the food; I don't expect you to help me pack it."

We filled the packs with the heavier stuff, cans, sauces, and rice. I could make more trips this way, bringing home the lighter loads the more tired and pregnant I got. I stepped outside, one backpack on and one in each hand, and Dan raised his gun, pointing it past me.

"I hope you're right about your man, for your sake, woman," he said as he slowly shut the door in my face. Sebastian's hand came down on mine startling me. I looked up and he motioned at the bag on my back.

"It's all I can take. I'll have to make more trips anyway," I said. He shook his head and pointed to his own back.

"Are you sure?" I asked. Again he nodded and I helped him to position two of the packs on his back, his fingers unable to even tighten or loosen the straps.

The trip back to the farm was uneventful which surprised me. I thought maybe Bob would be waiting for another can of beans at the least. When we got to the back gate, Sebastian twenty feet behind, I slipped through and beckoned him in.

"Come on. You aren't going to hurt me. I know that," I said. He shook his head and shrugged out of the bags before slipping off into the bush, as if he'd never been there.

Maybe I trusted him, but it looked like he didn't trust himself. That was enough to give me pause, to make me consider the fact that even though he was my husband, I'd been truly foolish to let him so close to me, no matter how much I loved him.

If only I'd remembered that a week later, then perhaps things would have turned out differently. Perhaps I wouldn't have had to turn my knife on him and do what no woman should have to.

18

For the next week I made two to three trips a day and the routine was well set. I took three bags, my can opener and a can of beans. Bob would meet me halfway to Dan's, and I would give him the can of beans like some offering a knight errant would give to a bridge troll. Sebastian followed me and packed a bag back so that by the end of the week we'd moved twenty-one backpacks full of food and necessities. Dan even had a good stash of drugs squirreled away: antibiotics, over the counter pain killers, and some pill forms of morphine. I took it all thinking of possible complications and pain during the labour that I would face in a few short months.

Dan grumbled fiercely that I was taking his offer to the extreme, but when I pointed out that I'd barely made a dent in his supplies, he settled down. It didn't hurt that on the third day I managed to bake cookies and I took some to him, though they were burnt around the edges. I was still trying to figure out the ways of baking with a wood burning cook stove. I suppose that even a grizzled old man likes homemade goodies, burnt on the edges or not.

On the seventh day, Sebastian was more than a little edgy, his eyes darting and his mouth clicking from time to time. I'd offered him food as I always did and he pushed it away at first, in the past few days never once taking from the stores we were collecting.

"Eat it," I said, the open can of peaches smelling positively delectable. Sebastian groaned and took the can from me, swallowing the peaches and the juice without a single gulp. I put the can into my bag. I could get rid of it at Dan's.

We walked up the well-worn path, gave Bob his beans, and continued on. As always, I paused at the huckleberry bush and waited. Not just to see if the coast was clear, but to let Sebastian come closer, to touch me, even if it was only for a moment.

This time was different though. His hands went to my belly first as always, but he slid them under the shirt, over my bare skin and up to my suddenly taut nipples. He rubbed the flat of his hand over them, unable to tease them with his fingertips, the lack of dexterity not slowing him down for a moment. I let out a low moan. This was torture of the best kind. He pulled me tight against his him and slid his body up and down mine as he rubbed my breasts, his breath hot against my neck, his teeth grazing the skin. I knew I should be afraid, at least a little bit, but the emotions rocketing through me didn't leave room for fear. Love, desire, skin, hunger. Those three left me trembling and useless in the way of thinking straight.

Sebastian nipped my earlobe and I started to reach back for him. He pushed me forward, knowing better than I did the limits of his control.

I stumbled to the door and let myself in, nearly gasping as I tried to get my hormones and emotions under control. I banged my hand against the door, suddenly angry and embracing the heat that burned off some of the desire.

"It's not fair!" I whispered.

"What's that woman? Not fair that you're stealing all my food from me?" Dan asked.

I turned and leaned against the door. "No. Just, I don't know, everything isn't fair. Nothing is the way it should be."

He grunted and helped me packed my bags, more baking supplies, chocolate chips, raisins, coconuts, walnuts, flour, and sugar. I smiled to myself. Dan surely wanted more cookies; there was no subtlety in his methods.

I gave him a peck on the cheek, "Thanks, Dan, I'll bring more cookies next time."

"Get out of here, woman," he growled at me, waving me off as he tried to hide a smile. I stepped outside with the three bags and started down the slight slope to the edge of Dan's property. I hefted one bag into place and packed the other two to the huckleberry bush where Sebastian was. Except it wasn't Bastian waiting for me.

It was Jessica.

She launched herself at me and I was barely able to step out of the way, stumbling to my knees as I slid in the grass. I dropped the bags of food and slid the bag off my back. I ripped them open and hoped the same trick would work with her as it had with Bob. Marshmallows and chocolate chips sprayed through the air, the scent of sugar drawing Jessica's nose to the food stuff instead of to me.

More members of the pack spilled forward, filling up Dan's garden and forcing me to the front of the house and onto the main road. The backpacks were shredded and the baking supplies were everywhere. I kept backing away; Jessica stared at me, her hatred palatable but the food a stronger pull than killing me, at least for the moment. I knew that as far as she was concerned, I'd stolen her man.

A loud boom rattled the air and the Nevermore closest to me dropped to the ground. I looked up to see Dan shooting at the pack from the top floor of his house.

"You'd better run, woman," he yelled. The pack swarmed through the yard, mostly focused on the food, but some were trying to get into the house, ending any chance I had at getting into safety.

I backed up until the pack was out of sight and then I ran. Okay, jogged, but I knew that I had to move. In my belief that I was safe, and in the concern for how much weight I should carry, I'd been leaving the rifle at home. All that stood between me and the pack was one measly knife. Deep shit did not even cover the depth of trouble I was in. Two more loud booms, then nothing more. Dan was giving me a chance at least.

I ran for fifteen minutes before I got a stitch in my side and had to slow down, but I was getting close to the halfway mark. Next up was the tunnel of broom that had nearly done me in, where we'd first met Dan and Bob.

I pushed my way into the thick greenery and found myself face-to-face with Bob. And I had nothing to give him. Again, shit seemed so understated.

"Bob," I said, "I'll bring you two cans next time, just please let by." I couldn't back up; I didn't dare to with the pack coming my way. Already their voices were screaming and getting closer. A Nevermore hand shot through from behind me and I spun and slashed at it with my knife, opening a deep wound. Bob roared and stood up on his hind feet, even taller than Sebastian.

He roared again and the screaming and hollering stopped. Bob stepped forward and I stepped to the side to let him pass. Apparently beans were the right commodity to keep him friendly to me, and I thanked my lucky stars.

Bob shoved past me, roaring and growling, the scent of his musky coat heavy in my nose. I ran down the trail, so close to home that I could almost taste it. One hand instinctively on my belly, the other hand holding my knife, I ran, pushing through the broom and bush, no longer caring how much noise I made. The pack knew I was there. The only thing I hadn't counted on was Sebastian.

As I hoofed it up the street, our house in view, the gate a blessed sign that I would be safe in a matter of moments, Sebastian burst out of the bushes, breathing hard and eyes wild.

"Bastian!" I said, trying to speak while I was out of breath making his name come out as a whisper.

He snarled, his mouth open wide, his hands clenched in fists and ran at me, all the animalism that the rest of the pack exhibited every day coming home to roost on him finally.

"Please God, no," I said, scrambling backwards, holding my knife out in front of me, my husband advancing faster than I could back up. At the last second I slashed at him, opening the skin of his chest in a scarlet red line from left to right.

It didn't stop him. He slammed into me, taking me to the ground as he howled his body hard and his ferocity terrifying me. If ever I thought I had been safe with him, I knew now I had been wrong. Maybe he'd been slipping slowly, but he'd still been moving away from me, moment by moment, step by step.

"Please don't make me do this," I whispered my knife arm free. Sebastian's body pinned mine to the ground in a mockery of the intimacy we'd once shared. With my left arm I pressed against his throat, keeping his teeth as far away from me as I could. There was no longer any trace of the man I loved left in his eyes. Tears spilled down my cheeks and I felt him pause, felt him muster something from deep inside.

He opened his mouth, I thought at first to growl or bite.

"Do it," he said, his eyes softening for a brief moment as he stared at my hand holding the knife.

I let out a cry of pain, gripped the handle with my right hand, and knew that if it were the last thing I did, I would love him forever.

There was no time; the pack was coming and they would kill me, Sebastian along with them for the ride, if didn't do something—and do it fast. For me, for our child, I had to do it; I had to kill the one man I loved more than any other person in my life.

A deep, gut-wrenching sob ripped out of me. With a last effort I raised the knife, holding it above his back, right over his heart.

"I love you Bastian," I said and brought the blade down.

PART II

BOUND

A man is not where he lives, but where he loves.
— *Latin Proverb*

1

There are moments in time that define you, make you who you are, force you to delve deep within your heart and grasp hold of the person you want to be. They are hard, gut wrenching, soul splitting seconds, that leave us spiritually drained, yet somehow in the end, stronger.

The blade in my hand caught the sunlight as I brought it down, ready to bury it into Sebastian's neck. As hard as it was to trust the monster he'd become, I could never kill him, not even to save myself or our child. My fingers released the smooth wooden handle and the blade fell to the dusty, hard packed ground.

"I can't Sebastian." Calm flooded through me as I accepted that he would kill me. The pack he led would clean my bones, feeding their young and old alike with my flesh.

He let out a groan and his body sagged onto mine, his face pressed against my neck. A low rumble started deep in his belly and his arms circled around me. I clung to him, holding back the sobs that were building in my chest. Before I could react, Sebastian stood, not letting go of me, but pulling me to my feet alongside him.

He stepped back and lifted his hands to my face to wipe away the tears that streaked down and dripped off my chin.

A screech from behind us, from the trail I'd just run out of, brought reality crashing back home. I had to get back on my side of the gate before the rest of the pack showed up.

I started to turn, sliding my hands off Sebastian's hard body. "I have to go," I said. He nodded, lifted his eyes towards the gate and let out a growl, his lips rippling with the noise. I completed the turn as a loud click echoed down the road. A man in an army uniform had a very large gun pointed at us.

"Ma'm, step away from the Nevermore, slowly, no quick movements, it draws their attention," he said, his eyes hidden behind dark sunglasses, a baseball cap pulled down low over his eyebrows.

I put my hand up, "No, you don't understand, he's not like the others."

Sebastian let out a snarl and leapt past me, seeing only a threat to me, a threat that had to be annihilated.

"No!" I shouted, running after him but unable to keep up with his speed. A boom rattled the world around us and Sebastian's body jerked backwards, a bloom of red spreading out behind him, his right shoulder suddenly soaked in blood. I let out a cry of pain as if the bullet had gone through me and not him. This couldn't be happening, not now, not when we were so close to being safe.

Another ungodly howl went up from down the road and I could hear the Nevermores running now, their feet beating a discordant tempo on the hard packed road.

130

"Ma'm, I'm going to need you to get behind the gate, this is not safe," Mr. Army said. I ignored him and dropped to the ground next to Sebastian, who was on his hands and knees, panting, blood dripping from the gunshot wounds as well as his mouth.

"Shut the hell up and help me!" I snapped, trying with little success to lift Sebastian. Even with his diminished weight, his size made it nearly impossible to do so. I looked up at the hard line of Mr. Army's mouth. "I mean it asshole; help me get him up and inside that gate now!"

Sebastian started to growl, I shushed him. "Be quiet, he's going to help." Mr. Army drew closer, his eyebrows raised above his sunglasses.

Sebastian subsided and Mr. Army and I hustled to the gate and pulled Sebastian through just as the pack came thundering up, hollering and screaming, beating their fists on the metal bars. Jessica was the worst of the bunch, yanking her own hair and hitting other pack members around her as they got too close to her.

"We've got to get him inside the house; I have to get that wound clean," I said.

"You're nuts lady; this big bugger's going to tear us all apart," a second voice said.

I looked up and gasped, nearly dropping Sebastian. There was a large dusky green army vehicle in our driveway, guns welded to the front of it. Men surrounded it, all in army fatigues, all with guns levelled at us. Instinctively, I kept my body between the men and Sebastian. There was no way they would give him a chance if he so much as twitched.

"What's going on?" I asked, my grip tightening around Sebastian's waist. His head lolled to my shoulder and he started to slump sideways. I shifted my arms and struggled to hold him upright.

"Our last satellite photos before we lost power showed this region as being one of the least infected areas with the highest possible chance of survivors," Mr. Army said, his voice even, his expression unreadable behind the dark glasses and cap.

Two men rushed forward, guns still trained on us, and a third man in crisp, pressed army fatigues followed more slowly, guns at his waist and a large bobby stick in his right hand. A few more steps and he stood over us, a cruel twist to his thin lips.

"You must be Mara, and I assume this is your Sebastian?" He asked, his voice cold.

"How do you know who I am?" This was freaking me out and I began to shake from exertion, exhaustion and the loss of adrenaline pumping through me.

"We've searched your house, confiscated the food and we found your information. Though Sebastian here looks fairly different from your wedding pictures, it is obviously still him. Amazing that there is somehow a connection between the two of you, despite the Nevermore drug." He leaned down and Sebastian let out a low growl. I put my hand over his mouth. This man standing over us scared me.

I swallowed hard. "Who are you and what do you want from us?"

He answered my question, but then asked his own. "I'm Vincent; these are my men. How is it that he doesn't try to eat you? What training methods did you use? Torture?" Something dark, an emotion I couldn't put my finger on right away, flickered through his eyes as he spoke. He blinked once, twice and then shook himself out of wherever his thoughts had taken him.

He looked at me, his brown eyes empty of emotion. "You're coming with us Mara, you and your monster Sebastian."

That was it, no explanation, nothing. Hands latched on to my arms and dragged me towards the truck. I kicked and screamed, no longer caring if the Nevermores heard me.

The men laughed, making rude gestures at me, pantomiming things I hoped I was misinterpreting. I fought harder, my breath coming in ragged gasps, the skin on my arms burning where the men's fingers dug into my flesh.

Finally they let me go, but it was only to watch me fall to my knees so they could laugh at me. Tears of anger burned at the back of my eyes, but I held them in.

Feet came into view and I looked up. Mr. Army stood in front of me. "You're only making this harder on yourself. And I would think the condition you're in, that's the last thing you'd want to do." He made a small motion towards my baby bump.

His eyes softened only a little, but I realized that he was, in his own way, trying to help me. How he knew I was pregnant I could only guess.

I pulled in a deep breath and the scent of the hard packed earth and the dry air filled my nose, which made me sneeze.

"Oh isn't that cute," one of the men said in a high falsetto, sending the men into another bout of laughter. Mr. Army stepped forward and offered me his hand, well worn and calloused. I stared at it, took stock of the bruises and aches throughout my body and let go of my pride. I took the offered hand and the men around us immediately began to catcall and whistle. As soon as I had my feet under me, I snatched my hand back.

With a single snap of his fingers, Mr. Army silenced the men, his eyes once more hard and in control.

"Get the big bastard loaded up. It's time to leave."

2

Men rushed forward, securing Sebastian's hands behind his back with a large set of handcuffs and then they dragged him to the back of the large truck. He snarled once and one of the men slammed the butt of his gun into his head, silencing him.

"Don't hurt him!" I yelled, the pack howling behind me. Nero came running from around the back of the house with a young army guy, who looked barely able to shave, right behind him.

I whistled and Nero ran straight to me, leaping into my arms. I caught him and held him tight. I wouldn't cry in front of these men, they weren't worth my tears or emotions.

"You can't bring the dog with you; we've got enough trouble feeding ourselves without adding a mutt to the mix," Vincent said.

"I'll feed him off my own plate, but I'm not leaving him behind."

"I'm not giving you a choice," Vincent snapped. He reached out and snatched Nero from my arms by the scruff of his neck.

"Stop! Give him back you ass!" I yelled, lunging for him. Vincent smirked at my attempt, cocked his arm and threw the three-month-old puppy over the gate and into the writhing mass of the starving pack.

I screamed; Nero yelped as he hit the ground and then a blur of yellow streaked out from under the pack's feet and vanished into the bush, three quarters of the Nevermores right behind him. The crashing of underbrush reached our ears, then a high pitched cry, and finally, silence. I spun and punched Vincent as hard as I could, feeling my knuckles pop as my fist connected squarely with his jaw. He stumbled back, tripped on a piece of wood, and fell on his butt.

Silence fell over us for a brief second, the men around us holding their breath in a collective gasp. Vincent stared up at me from the ground, his eyes full of hatred, and then slowly stood, his movements stilted with barely controlled anger.

"Marks," he motioned Mr. Army over. "Get everyone on the truck; we've got to head back with the supplies and the prisoners."

Marks nodded, saluted and started to shout orders.

"You'll pay for that bitch," Vincent said, as he dusted his pants off.

"Bring it," I hissed at him. There was no way Nero would survive out there, not with the pack and Bob on the loose. The desire to hit him a second time reared its head and I tightened my hand into a fist.

"Get her in the truck!" Marks snapped and the men jumped, hustling me to the back of the army vehicle. I pulled my arms free of the men escorting me, though I suppose they let me go. With a flurry of hands I was shoved up next to Sebastian behind the cab of the truck. The other men settled in a few feet away, leaving us to sit by ourselves, which was fine by me. I pulled his head into my lap and pressed my hand against the gunshot wound, applying pressure as best I could. He let out a low moan and I whispered soft nothings to him, the sound of my voice keeping him calm.

Marks jumped into the back of the truck, the flap of material giving me the last glance at our farm. He stared at me and Sebastian, a look of derision evident on his face.

"What's it like having sex with a monster?" He asked, his lips curled with disdain.

"I don't know, why don't you ask your father?" I snapped back.

There was dead silence, then the laughter started as the other men guffawed at Marks' expense, the noise quickly filling the back of the truck.

"She got you there Marks.""Damn that's some sass for a woman this far out. You remember the last gal we brought in? Pulled most of her hair out . . ."

"Not to mention she was a raving lunatic."

"What was it she said was stuck in her head?"

"Bees, she was screaming about bees in her head she couldn't get out." Laughter rippled around the truck again and I ignored it, focusing on the fact that Sebastian was still breathing, slow and steady, the blood clotting on his chest wound.

"Don't worry about him," a new voice said. I glanced over my shoulder; it was the young man who'd been chasing Nero.

"I'm Burns by the way. Sergeant Burns. I was looking after your dog for you," he said, his words sincere, his face open and very honest looking.

"You didn't do a very good job did you?" Burns had the decency to blush and duck his head.

"As soon as he heard your voice he took off on me. I didn't expect it, I'm sorry," he said.

I was surprised by his apology, "Thank you."

"Don't apologize to the prisoners Burns," Marks snapped. Burns retreated and I went back to crooning to Sebastian. I didn't bother to ask where we were going, it didn't really matter. We were captives, trapped and soon to be under lock and key. The only good thing was that Sebastian and I were still together; I wondered how long it would last.

A half hour into our drive the truck began to slow and I thought we'd arrived at our destination. Maybe Comox and the air force bunkers there? That was a possibility. Then hands were reaching into the back of the moving truck, Nevermores running at top speed, howling at us as they tried to drag men from the back. I scrunched up tight against Sebastian; even though we were up against the cab, I still had visions of being pulled out. I didn't think these men would stop to try and help me either.

"Shoot them," Marks said and the men pulled back the flap and open fired on the Nevermores.

Something slammed into the side of the truck and I had no doubt what it was. A pack was trying to get into the truck and all the "food" it carried. A second slam rocked the vehicle and the driver picked up speed again.

"Keep shooting boys," Marks commanded, and they eagerly did as he said.

A hand shot into the back of the truck, fast like lightning, and grasped the leg of the closest soldier, yanking him out with a scream.

I bit the inside of my cheek to keep from screaming myself. The truck never slowed and the other men barely reacted. If they wouldn't look out for their own, I had no doubt that I was going to be in some serious trouble.

Silence surrounded the truck as quickly as the Nevermores had, the pack chasing us obviously given up their quest with the prize they'd managed to snag.

I pressed my face against Sebastian's and took slow even breaths. There was no way I could do this without him, even though so much of who he had been was lost. "Hang on love," I whispered. "Just hang on."

3

"We're here," Marks said as he stood up. We'd been driving for a little over an hour. He pushed the flap cover of the truck back, tying it to the side. The bright sunlight blinded me after the dim grey interior of the truck for so long. Hands grabbed me and pulled me out; Sebastian grunted and then snapped at someone, and the distinct thud of a rifle butt hitting a skull resounded in the truck.

"Stop hitting him!" I said, twisting hard and trying to free myself from the hands that gripped my arms.

"Those bastards heal faster than any human; he won't even have the gunshot wound to worry about in a couple of hours," Vincent said, as he watched us disembark, his gun in his hand.

"Where are we?" I finally asked. I could see trees, a huge tall fence with razor wire around the top and some sort of wooden buildings that could be barracks. On three sides of the fence were packs of Nevermores, keeping their distance but still making sure to be within sight. It was no different than at the farm; they were waiting for their next meal to step outside the fence. I shivered; there had been moments on the ride here I'd convinced myself it would be better, safer, wherever it was the soldiers were taking me.

I turned a full circle and found myself staring out across the water of the Georgia Straight and what was left of Nanaimo, one of the major cities on Vancouver Island. That is if you considered a population of eighty thousand people major.

"The Diefenbaker bunker," Marks said, putting his hand on my arm, his fingers digging into my skin. I didn't understand why until I saw the other men dragging Sebastian away from me, towards a door seemingly in the mound of a hill.

I cradled my belly with one hand and tried to pull myself free. "Don't separate us. Please," I said. "I'm pregnant; I don't want to stress the baby." I looked up into Marks' face and saw the softening I'd hoped for. Maybe he didn't like the fact that Sebastian was a Nevermore, but he didn't seem to be a complete ass.

Vincent frowned, then a slow smile made its way across his face and I had a feeling I was about to pay for humiliating him in front of his men. He motioned to Marks.

"Take her to the upper barracks; we don't have room in the bunker at the moment." Vincent pointed to the wooden structures to the left. Marks let out a low sigh and started towards the buildings.

Marks put me in the first barracks and shut the door, but not before he gave me some advice.

"Don't piss him off. Vincent is not the kind of man you want to take on Mara. He will destroy everything you love just to make a point."

"Thanks for the warning," I said. The door clicked shut and I was alone.

I frowned and rubbed my hands over my face. These men held not only my life in their hands, but Sebastian's too. I would have to do my best to behave, to get close to Bastian again. I looked over the room. Sparse was an understatement. There was a small cot with a thin blanket. That was it. Cement floors, a barred window with no glass and solid wood panelling surrounded me. I walked to the window and stared out just in time to see Sebastian get dragged to a large grassy covered mound. A flurry of activity and then the mound opened up, a doorway leading into what I assumed was the bunker.

"Crap, this is not going to be easy to get out of."

I said the words and then really considered what I was saying. Did I actually think I could get the two of us out of here?

I placed my hands on the bars, the cold and slightly rusted metal a grounding sensation. We were surrounded by armed men who were some sort of militia who had guns and weapons, not to mention an enormous fence, which was in turn monitored by at least three Nevermore packs. And not a single soul to help me.

Tears threatened at the ridiculousness of the situation but I pushed them back, swallowing the thickness that tightened my throat. Poor Nero was dead, Sebastian was locked away from me, wounded and alone, and there wasn't a damn thing I could do about any of it. I hiccupped a sob back. Crying wouldn't do me any good. I blinked away the mist filming over my eyes and stared out the window, not sure if what I was seeing was a hallucination or reality.

From below the army truck we'd come in on, a familiar figure dropped to the ground. He scuttled along the grass, lifting his nose every once in a while to scent the air. Following his nose brought him straight to the window I stared out of. He stood, smiling at me from the other side, his scrawny body battered from the ride he'd endured in the undercarriage of the truck. Apparently Sebastian and I had inspired some serious loyalty in the pack.

I smiled and gripped the bars a little tighter, my nerves good, but I still didn't entirely trust him; he was, after all, a Nevermore.

"Scout, how the hell are we going to get out of this mess?"

4

Scout smiled back, then spun, a noise I couldn't hear alerting him. He tapped on my hand gripping the bar then scurried off around the side of the building to hide. A moment later the mound opened up and people poured out of the bunker.

The men lined up, rifles loose and at the ready; a bound woman was dragged forward and tied to a post against the high fence.

"They wouldn't," I whispered. I couldn't hear the commands given, but as the men raised their rifles I whispered, "Ready." I waited a heartbeat and the tension rose, "Aim." Another heartbeat and the woman began to thrash within her bonds, "Fire."

Even knowing it was going to happen didn't prepare me for the boom of ten rifles going off at one time. The woman's body jerked and jumped, blooms of red spreading from her legs up to her forehead.

I swallowed hard, nausea making me weak at the knees, and I slid down the wall with my head against it. Was that how they made room for the new people? My gorge rose at the thought that my presence had somehow caused the woman's death. I had to get out of here; this was worse than we'd ever had it at the farm. I had Scout now and surely I could use him, if he didn't try and attack me, that is. I backed away from the window and lay down on the cot, my hand over the small bump on my belly. I had to find a way to protect myself, Sebastian, and our child.

"Think girl, you're smarter than a bunch of noodle-headed army brats." I thought about all the possibilities, scenarios that could be, might be, and would never be.

I stood and paced the small room, the air warm and musty despite the perpetually open window, the scents tickling my nose and making me sneeze. Rubbing my face I looked down at my clothes covered in Sebastian's blood. There had to be a way for me to get into the bunker and close to Sebastian. From there we could find our way out. I had to believe the lies I was telling myself.

A knock startled me and I jumped, my heart racing, adrenaline suddenly surging through me.

"Mara, it's Sergeant Burns. I have some water and some bread for you."

My mouth ached at the thought of carby, starchy, white, fluffy bread. "Come in," I said and again looked down at my blood stained clothes. Burns came in, ducking his head and blushing a little. I had an idea, a light bulb moment that might give me a way out of here. If I could manage it.

Seduction was not something that came easy to me, it never had. During our courtship, Sebastian pursued me, not the other way around. Who was I kidding? I was pregnant, at least ten years older than Burn's and to be honest, deception wasn't something I was any better at than seduction.

I took a deep breath and decided the best thing I could do was be his friend and hope I could inspire some pity or compassion.

"Thank you Burns. I'm sorry I snapped at you earlier, Nero was such a sweetie and so well behaved, he wouldn't have been a pain at all," I said, letting emotion colour my words, choking up a little.

Burns nodded and handed me two slices of brown, stale bread and a large tumbler of water. "I know. My family raised yellow labs when I was a kid, they were always good dogs, never had a moment's problem out of them. Vincent can be a real bastard."

I bit into the slightly stale bread and let out a low groan; it wasn't white and fluffy, but it was still damn good. Around my mouthful I said, "This is amazing, I haven't had bread in so long."

He blushed and went to leave.

"Wait." I swallowed the bite. "Please, I haven't spoken to anyone and I just want to know what's going on out there. Is there any news? Has there been any mention of a cure? Is there anyone trying to help the survivors?"

Burns shook his head and folded his arms. "I don't know that I can say anything about anything. As for the outside, the world has pretty much shut down from what we all can tell. There have been transmissions here and there, but nothing for a while now. I think that everyone is pretty much on their own."

I took a sip of the water, my mouth dry and my throat tight. "Is there no where safe?"

Again he shrugged. "Rumours and gossip float around here lots, but far as we can tell it's all false information."

"You aren't even really in the army are you?" I said, remembering the final announcement to come across on the TV, warning survivors to steer clear of men claiming government titles and armies.

Burns unfolded his arms and swallowed hard. "I would have been, but never got the chance."

"These people, this Vincent, they aren't really helping others are they?"

He looked over his shoulder and stepped close to me, completely invading my personal space and making me fight to stand still. Bending close he whispered in my ear, "I know you don't want to be here, but there's no way out and they have some places bugged, they are using everything they can that runs on batteries." He stepped back, the colour on his cheeks high and his eyes bright.

"Thank you," I mouthed at him, giving him a smile. He smiled back and again started to leave. For a second time I stopped him. "Wait, how long are they going to keep me out here? There isn't even a bucket to pee in." The baby was starting to make his or her presence known to me on a regular basis in the form of potty trips.

Burns reached outside the door and pushed a small ice cream pail into the room, shame filling his eyes. "Sorry, you're going to be here a while."

"Will you do one thing for me?"

"I can't promise anything."

"Tell Sebastian I'm okay. That we'll get out of here together."

Burns stared at me as if I'd lost my mind. "I'll try, but I don't think it's a good idea to lie, even to a monster."

I smiled, even though inside I wanted to smack him for calling Sebastian a monster. "Just tell him, that's all I ask."

The door closed behind Burns and I watched the lanky young man walk back to the bunker. I gripped the window bars and swallowed hard. I let out a low whistle and within a few moments gaunt finger tips slid up the edge of the window, yellow veins throbbing on the back of Scout's hand. I ripped my second piece of bread in half and pushed it into his fingers. We were trapped, but that didn't mean we were out of options.

"Our backs are to the wall now Scout. But if they think I'm going to just give up, then they've got another thing coming."

Scout chuckled and tapped the bars with his fingers, then tapped his forehead before slinking away to hide once more. I shook my head and lay down on my cot. It was a bad day, when I considered Scout to be my confidant and ally against other humans.

5

They kept me in the utilitarian barracks for another four days. Burns continued to bring me my food and water ration twice a day and I continued to talk to him, building on our tentative friendship.

"My mother and older sister were all I had left and they both took the shot as soon as they had enough money. They attacked me and I killed my mom and knocked my sister out. I was running down the street when she came screaming out after me and half the neighbourhood packed up with her." His voice was a flat monotone, emotions buried under the necessity of living.

I leaned forward, my elbows on my knees. "How did you get away?"

"Marks came driving down the street and ran the monsters over; I jumped in the back of the truck and we came up here." He shuffled his feet. "I think they're going to bring you into the bunker tomorrow."

My eyes widened. This was what I'd been waiting for. "Really, why?"

"You know that woman they shot?"

I swallowed hard, dread filling me. "I'm next aren't I?"

Burns shook his head. "No, you aren't like her. Fran tried to kill Vincent in his sleep. He caught her with a big kitchen knife held to his throat. She almost did him in."

He didn't sound terribly upset by the whole thing. "So you didn't like her either?"

Burns shrugged. "I didn't really know her. She was only for the officers." Then he blushed, his face going red. "I mean . . . I didn't . . ."

I shushed him. I knew exactly what he meant and I did not need it spelled out for me. But why would she try and kill Vincent? As if reading my thoughts Burns continued.

"I don't know why she would try to kill him, it didn't make sense. She and her daughter were taken in. It's not Vincent's fault Danielle got outside the gates. Ron was on guard that night and fell asleep."

My head snapped up and my eyes narrowed. "The woman had a little girl?"

Burns nodded. "Yeah, she was about ten years old, I guess. I didn't see her much either. She spent most of her time locked in her room." Again Burns flushed as if he'd said too much. He changed the subject back to the original topic.

"Something's inside the compound, something that's been eating Fran at night. We don't have enough power to keep a camera system up and running to catch it and they're afraid it might be one of the Nevermores busted in here somehow."

Heart pounding I licked my lips, knowing full well it was Scout. Though he came for my whistle and ate the bread I offered, I had no doubt he was the culprit responsible. "If it was a Nevermore, why wouldn't it attack you when you walk back and forth?"

Burn's eyes snapped up to meet mine. I let out a breath, knowing why. "That's why you've been sent out here, to draw it out; you're part of the bait, same as me. That's why they left me in here so long."

Burns shook his head, the doubt apparent in his eyes. "No, they wouldn't do that."

"You so sure you'd bet your life on it?"

We stared at each other, neither one of us backing down. I knew I was right and the sudden flicker of his eyelids told me he knew it too. Without another word he took my empty water glass and left, slamming the door behind him.

I stood and walked to the window. As soon as he went into the bunker Scout sidled up to the window and I handed him a half a piece of bread.

"You wait outside when I go in. I'll bring Sebastian out and then we can all go home," I said. I had no idea what we'd do once we got home, but it seemed like the only place to go that might be safe. Scout grunted and slipped back into the shadows around the back side of the barracks. I don't know how he kept out of sight. Then again, there had been no movement outside the bunker other than Burns bringing me my food. Even the other Nevermore packs had gone pretty quiet. If I watched, I could see them moving in the shadows of the bush and trees, but it was faint, like watching for a deer.

The next day came slowly, the heat rising early and the small room quickly becoming a hot box. I lay on my bed, praying Burns would come soon with my rations. At that moment, though my stomach was empty, it was the sweet taste of lukewarm water I craved.

Footsteps thumped towards my room and I stood, wobbling a little as the room spun. Weak from lack of food, as well as the heat, I did my best to stand and face whoever was coming through the door.

Sunlight streamed through the doorway and Vincent peered in, wrinkling his nose. "You need a bath and clean clothes if you are to be any help." He snapped his fingers and Burns strode in looking grim, but gave me a wink as he grabbed my arm and pulled me along beside him.

We got ahead of Vincent and Burns whispered to me, "Stick close, I'll look out for you."

I gave him a small smile. "Thanks." He was nothing more than a tall boy, barely out of childhood. I had a feeling that it would more likely be me looking out for him, when it came right down to the crunch, but that was okay. Stepping quickly we reached the bunker in less than a minute. I glanced back over at Vincent, who was dawdling, crouched over something in the dirt. Maybe a footprint of Scout's? Movement at the edge of the wooden barracks caught my gaze. Scout crept forward and made eye contact with me, pointing at Vincent. We might not have another chance, but I wasn't sure it would help us to kill the leader of the men here.

I took a shallow breath. Like a gun, Scout was waiting on my say so; this death would be on my shoulders just like the raiders that had broken into our home in Fanny Bay.

I closed my eyes and shook my head. Scout paused and stared at me, then began to creep forward, ignoring my command.

"No!" I yelled and twisted out of Burns' hands, running back towards Vincent. His mouth circled into a wide surprised 'O' and he didn't even try to grab me as I rushed past him and put myself between him and Scout. It wasn't that I cared if Vincent lived or died, not really; it was the fact that I needed Scout. If he got himself killed, because he didn't listen to me, it was one less ally for me to count on.

As I drew close to Scout he started to growl but I didn't stop. I squared my shoulders and increased my speed, stopping only when my toes were less than a foot away from his.

"Scout, go. Go back to the barracks." He stared at me, his lips curled back over his teeth. I frowned down at him, clapped my hands and snapped, "Now!" He flinched and I pointed to the back of the barracks again. He grumbled and scratched at his crotch before backing away with his head down. He glanced back at me like a surly child being sent to his room several times, but otherwise did as I told him.

"I have never seen any of them respond to someone like that. How did you train him?" Vincent asked, the awe in his voice not making me feel any better about what I'd just done.

"I don't know." I had an idea about why Scout listened, but I wasn't about to share it with Vincent. He scared me to the core and I didn't trust him any further than I could throw him.

What I figured out in my time alone in the barracks was that I'd seen how the pack worked, how they revered the Alpha's mate. Scout knew I belonged to Sebastian, better than any other Nevermore did. In a strange way, I'd become a member of the pack, a member that was in higher standing than Scout. Which meant that I could push him around, just as a true Alpha's mate would. From his reaction, I wasn't far off the mark in my theory.

Burns grabbed my arm from behind, apologizing to Vincent, "I'm sorry, I wasn't holding her tight enough."

"It's quite alright Burns," Vincent said. "In fact, I think you've done us a service. I think perhaps we can finally begin to make real progress with the monsters."

He stared at me, a slow smile spreading across his angular face, yellowed teeth winking at me. I swallowed hard. I didn't want to become a commodity to them in any way, but if I was going to be valuable, at least it was for my mind and not my body.

They hustled me into the cool of the bunker, the door slamming and locking behind us. Stepping down into the underground safe house I let out a sigh of relief even though it was too dark to see after the bright sunlight, the dank air cool on my skin.

"With your help training the monsters, we can finally take over the city from Donavan. I will make him pay for what he's taken from me." Vincent's voice was right in my ear, the heat from his breath making my skin crawl, the stench one of un-brushed teeth and more than a hint of alcohol.

"Don't touch me," I said, jerking myself away from him. Vincent glared at me and I glared right back.

"You *will* help me Mara," he said as he straightened his shirt, though it didn't seem to need it.

I lifted my chin. "And if I don't?"

"We will both find out just how much pain your big boy can handle." Vincent gave me a sharp nod and stepped out in front of me, leading the way.

I swallowed hard. Vincent had me; he knew my weakness and there was nothing I could do about it.

6

I was pushed through the darkness, low lights along the floor giving us just enough illumination to not run into anyone head on.

"I want to see Sebastian," I said. "I know he's in here and I want to see him. I don't trust you not to have already killed him."

"You will see him when I'm damn good and ready to let you!" Vincent roared back at me, his voice echoing through the halls. The silence after his shout made my ears ring and I fought hard not to cringe. I didn't think that showing him any more weakness would help me. He wasn't sympathetic at all.

Again he straightened his shirt and began to walk. "First you will get clean. You stink. Then we will discuss the training of the Nevermores that you will be doing. Perhaps if you show your usefulness, I will let you see your precious Sebastian."

Burns turned me to the left and then down a flight of stairs. The rest of the barracks were filled with men whispering as we passed in the semi darkness, leaving me feeling as if there were bugs crawling all over my skin buzzing to get in.

One more corner and we were in a huge bath house, the lights brighter, glinting off the pale mauve tiles.

"Here, get clean," Vincent said. "Burns, bring her some fresh clothes. I won't be in a room with a woman who smells of filth and sweat."

Burns handed me a threadbare towel and a small bar of soap and the two men stepped out of the room and shut the door behind me. I waited a full minute then put my hand to the knob, opening the door a crack.

"Is there something you need Ma'am?" A man's voice asked.

"No, thank you," I said, my manners coming into play despite the fact that I was a captive of these men and had even warranted a guard on my bathroom time. I walked to the middle of the room. It was set up like a locker in a men's gym, cubby holes for your stuff and shower heads sticking out every three feet.

I didn't understand what was going on, but at that moment the thought and temptation of hot water overrode any other concerns I had.

I stripped and stepped up to the closest shower head, then turned it on full blast. Ice cold water hit me in the face and I gasped and choked on it, but forced myself to stay under. Scrubbing furiously with the small bar of soap I was able to get at least a couple of layers of dirt off from the last few days.

The cold didn't ease and my skin began to hurt. It was at that point someone hollered, "Hello?"

I turned the water off and grabbed the towel, wrapping it around me as my teeth chattered. "I'm here." The towel

160

barely covered what God gave me and did little to stave off the cold.

Burns stepped into the room and put a pile of clothes on the floor. I imagined he was probably blushing as he stammered out, "Here are some clothes, and I'll just be outside when you're dressed."

"I'll be quick, I'm freezing." The door clicked shut again. I towelled myself off and thought of Sebastian when he'd towelled me dry and we'd made love, laughing and romping together with abandon. That was before Nevermore came into our lives. I didn't realize I was crying until the tears dripped off the end of my chin and onto the floor.

"Stop it Mara," I whispered. "You can't turn back time, now you have to move forward, that's all there is left. You have to be strong and smart for all three of you." I placed my hand lightly on my belly and let out a long slow breath.

Once I was fully dressed and had my emotions pulled together, I opened the door.

Before Burns could say anything, I lifted my hand to stall him. "I want to see my husband; where is he?"

Burns shook his head, "He's down with the others. He's okay, but I can't take you to him. Vincent wants to see you right away; I don't want to get caught disobeying him."

"Please, can we run? I just want to see him." I begged him, putting my hand on his forearm, not caring how little he thought of me. Burns let out a sigh and looked down the hallway. He shook his head and my heart sank.

"If we run, you can maybe see him for 20 seconds at best," Burns said. My head snapped up and I nodded, my mouth unable to even form a thank you past the shock of Burns helping me.

I followed him at a run down three more flights of stairs to what he informed me was the lowest level. The section was split into cells, not unlike a jail, each cell holding at least one Nevermore. As we ran past they reached out but not one of them made a sound. That was unusual; with the pack at home if we were ever this close there was at least a growl or two.

As if reading my mind, Burns began to fill me in on Vincent's "training" methods.

"Vincent wants to show how the Nevermores can be trained and so he had us capture a male and a female—at least that was it to start with. He punished them when they did anything that he didn't think they should. Like making noise when we walked by."

I glanced into a cage as we passed to see a form curled into a tight ball; burn marks oozing and open to infection covered much of the skin I could see.

"He tortured them," I said, no longer feeling smart about the decision to keep Scout from attacking Vincent. The next cage showed a very pregnant woman, her wrists and ankles raw where it was obvious she'd been tied up and struggled, her skin in bloom with faint lines of the broom flower.

"That's Marks wife. Or ex-wife, I guess. They were separated when she took the shot," Burns said.

I looked away. "Please, just take me to Sebastian."

"Here," Burns said, stopping in front of the last cage on the block. He stepped over to let me pass. "Vincent thinks we can use the Nevermores as a trained army to take over Donavan's compound. At least that's what he told us and we believed him."

I stared into the last cage, its gloomy interior not showing me anyone. "Sebastian?" I called out. A shadow shifted and stood tall; in two strides he was at the front of the cage, his hands reaching through for me.

"Wait for me at the other end of the block," I said to Burns as I took Sebastian's hands in my own, my eyes never leaving his.

"I'm not supposed to leave you alone."

"Burns, you gave me 20 seconds, at least let me have those moments alone," I said.

Burns coughed and shuffled back down the way we'd come.

"I'm sorry Bastian."

He grunted and pulled me up against the bars, our bodies separated only by the cold metal. Sebastian pressed his lips to my forehead, his hands roving up and down my back, finally settling on my hips. I pressed a hand against the scar on his shoulder that only days ago had been a bullet hole. "I'm glad you're okay."

He lifted the top of one lip in a half smile, took my hand and slid it down his chest, pressing my palm against the evidence of his arousal. For the first time in a long time, I blushed, a rush of heat firing my blood. He tipped his head and pressed harder against my hand, his eyes softening with desire. I flexed my muscles and he groaned, leaning his head against the bars and grinding his hips into my fingers. I sucked in a deep breath, my body aching to be touched, to feel again his heart beat against my own. Footsteps echoed and we pulled back, both of us trembling and our faces flushed.

"Mara, I need to take you to the war room, Vincent, he's waiting, and he's going to know we took a detour if we put this off any longer. We do not want to piss him off," Burns said.

"Okay." I blew Sebastian a kiss. "I'll be back soon."

He gave me a slow nod and disappeared into the shadows.

I followed Burns as we jogged back the way we'd come, stopping before we reached the floor where the showers were. I did my best to memorize the turns and twists of the tunnels, the stair wells and room numbers—because the minute I got the chance, I was going to bust us out of here.

7

The war room was covered in maps of the area and the world in general; a large table dominated the center and it looked to be mahogany, polished to a brilliant sheen. Sitting at the head of the table was Vincent, his army fatigues neat and tidy, and his face unreadable.

"It took you long enough," he said, standing as he spoke.

I shrugged and tried not to let my exertion show. "I wanted to get clean; you know, getting filth off can take time."

"Don't sass him," Burns whispered to me.

Vincent rolled his shoulders and clasped his hands behind his back. "This is very simple. You are going to help me train the Nevermores. If you don't, I will kill your Sebastian. If you still flaunt my authority you will find yourself in an unfortunate situation where you will no longer be carrying your child. And if you still continue to fight me I will kill you."

The blood fled from my face and pooled somewhere down in my legs. He couldn't be serious; he wasn't so cold as to cause me to miscarry, was he? I stared into his pale gray eyes, searching for a spark of compassion, and found nothing.

He spun on one heel and tapped on the chalkboard, "Perhaps this will help you see reason."

I squinted my eyes. There were six words written in perfect capital letters. I read them out loud. "Control of cure, control of power."

My mouth dropped open and I leapt to my feet, my heart pounding with an unspoken hope. "There's a cure?"

"I thought perhaps that might get your attention. You will see that I can be fair to those who are loyal to me." He gave me a tight-lipped smile and continued. "If you help me take Donavan's compound by way of the Nevermores, I will give to you and your Sebastian whatever cure Donavan has cooked up. It is in his compound on the harbour front where he and his scientists have been working on it night and day. They've produced some phenomenal effects." He paused. "We are starting to see the realities of what Nevermore first promised."

My legs started to tremble and I slowly lowered myself back into my chair, not wanting to show weakness. The door opened and I turned to see Burns bringing in a tray of steaming food. I sniffed, smelling chicken noodle soup and garlic toast. My stomach growled, giving away my hunger.

"Eat. I can't have you falling down while you train the Nevermores."

I sipped at the soup then slurped back a spoonful of noodles, the cheap yellow broth delicious, and the slightly stale garlic bread tickling my nose with its scent as I took a bite.

I swallowed a mouthful and Vincent sat down in his chair again, folding his hands on the table in front of him.

"I want to know how you trained the Nevermores. It is more than apparent that they listen to you."

I took another bite before answering, giving myself more time to come up with an answer that would satisfy him.

I pointed my spoon at Vincent. "How do I know you're telling the truth? Have you seen any Nevermores turned back into humans?"

Vincent's jaw tightened. "Are you calling me a liar?"

"No," I said, feeling the ground start to give way under the conversation. "I'm only asking for a little proof, something that would encourage me, give me hope. It will make my job training them easier if I can see a light at the end of the tunnel." I was talking fast, trying to come up with viable reasons for him to give me proof. We both knew that the death threat hanging over me was enough to ensure I did as he wanted. He didn't need to give me anything else.

Vincent snapped his fingers. "Let me give you a little chemistry lesson. How much do you know about the components of the Nevermore drug?"

Chewing on a bite of garlic bread, I thought back to the sheet my family doctor had given me on the breakdown of the drug.

"It's made from scotch broom and there's dopamine in it. And something called tyramine too I think, but I'm not entirely clear on how that helps the drug work."

He wrote in those perfect capital letters on the board and as he tapped each word with his chalk he explained them to me, like a teacher would instruct a student.

"Genistin increases the calcium content in bones and prevents more bone mass loss. Sparteine and certain flavonoids are what help in dealing with cardiovascular problems like arrhythmias. Dopamine, when released in the proper form, crosses the blood brain barrier and makes immense improvements and even prevents Parkinson's disease." Vincent paused and frowned at me. "Dopamine is also released as a reward when we consume food or have sex."

"What about tyramine?" I asked, caught up in the intricacies of a drug that I had almost taken.

Vincent nodded with a bare twist of his lips. I found myself almost smiling with pleasure that I'd asked a good question. This was dangerous. He was a man who could terrify and yet still make you want to please him.

"Tyramine helps to release the body's stores of dopamine. That only adds to the feel good factor the drug induced."

Another tap on the chalkboard brought my eyes back to center. Vincent continued his explanation. "Tyramine can also affect blood pressure, regulating it, which goes hand in hand with improvements of heart health."

I frowned. "But none of that has anything to do with weight loss."

Again he nodded with that small smile. "You ask good questions Mara. You remind me of . . ." He shook off whatever he was going to say. "That is the incredible part when it comes to this drug. It wasn't designed for weight loss. It was designed for all these other things. But as the test subjects described their experiences of losing weight at a rapid pace, it became evident that the cocktail that damn scientist had mixed up forced the body's metabolism into overdrive."

"But then what happened to make them lose their minds, to go feral?" Despite the fact I should have hated him, I found myself wrapped up in the education he was giving me. I couldn't help but be caught up in wanting to know what exactly had happened to Sebastian and all those people who took the Nevermore shot.

Vincent started to pace in front of the chalkboard, his hands once more clasped behind his back. "There are a great deal of toxins within cystius scoparius that were supposed to be eliminated. They weren't."

"How do you know all this? Are you a scientist?" I asked.

"No, but I was there when the drug was being produced. And I applied myself to learning all I could about it when it was given to someone I cared about and it became apparent the drug was not what it was supposed to be."

He turned to the chalkboard and continued as though I hadn't interrupted him.

"The very things that were meant to help those who took the drug had side effects too. The components, every one of them, had a flip side, a dark side." He made small arrows to and from each component to a big ugly X he slashed onto the board. Again he began to pace the room.

"Genistin stimulates breast cancer; I've not seen too many cases but there are several Nevermores that have been disposed of that had massive tumours hanging off their chests—so large, in fact, that they had difficulty standing upright."

I didn't know what to say; that was an image that came all too easily to my mind.

"The poison within the broom leaves the person with numb hands and feet, and that numbness travels up through their limbs. I believe this is why they are unable to climb, or at least a contributing factor. The fine motor skills also seem to be damaged a great amount; again, I believe this to be some of the toxins causing blockages." He stopped his pacing and leaned against the table to stare at me, his intensity unnerving.

"The flavonoids, they are carcinogenic in the right parameters and some of those seem to be met in certain patients. Again, tumours, skin cancer and the like have been apparent on a number of them."

Sipping at my soup, I tried to process all that he was telling me and I remembered what the early reports had said about the toxins in the brain. I was afraid to ask, afraid of the answer, but I asked it anyway. "Are their brains really being eaten away?"

To my relief, he shook his head. "The initial thought that the brain was actually being attacked by the Nevermore drug and eaten away was incorrect. Parts of the cerebrum are being depressed while other parts are being stimulated. Thus we get the effect of the Nevermores." He put the chalk on the table and placed his hands beside it.

Vincent hit a button on the desk, an intercom of some sort I suppose. "Bring Adam and Eve in."

The door slid and this time only a single guard came in, a woman and man slightly in front of him. I stared hard at them, finally standing and cautiously walking closer to get a better look.

Their eyes were still yellow, but the slit had blended back into a proper human iris. Their skin was still speckled here and there with the bloom flower tattoos so common on the Nevermores, but their skin itself was no longer yellow.

Something was still off though and I finally put my finger on it. It was the flat, dead gaze that stared out of their faces, the vacancy that should have had a sign above their heads. I waved my hand in front of their faces.

"They aren't in there anymore are they?"

"Adam and Eve were injected with one of the earlier formulas of the reversal drug. We broke in to Donavan's compound before he made better arrangements for protection." He came around to my side of the table. "Because the toxin from the cystius scoparius depressed parts of the cerebrum that make us human for so long, it didn't leave any pathways for the brain to re-connect. They no longer know themselves or much of their surroundings for that matter. But they are no longer monsters."

I backed away from them. "That doesn't make me want to give the formula to Sebastian."

Vincent stepped up behind me and put his hands on my shoulders, squeezing the bones until they hurt. "What is better, a man you can trust in your bed—simple, but safe—or an animal who is unpredictable, ready to tear your throat out at the slightest provocation? I saw him attack you outside your home, saw the terror it inspired in you. At least this way, you could have him with you."

I stared at the couple. A thin line of drool formed from the woman's mouth and hung from her bottom lip, dropping until it reached the edge of her breast. Which would be better? A vegetable, unable to communicate in any way? Or a monster, at least still aware of me and the past we shared?

I didn't have a choice but to help Vincent and his men. It was that or get us killed, and I wasn't about to make that mistake. I would do what I had to do to keep Sebastian, our child and myself safe, no matter what. But I knew that I would never let Sebastian take this reversal drug—at least as he was now, he still knew me.

8

Adam and Eve were escorted back out and Vincent pushed a sheet towards me. "This is what I want you to train the Nevermores to do. They must be able to follow these simple commands if we are to take Donavan's compound."

I read the list out loud. "Attack, kill, left, right, forward, back, halt, quiet, loud." I shrugged, "Will you give me what I ask for to train them?"

Vincent frowned. "Won't they just listen to you?" Again I shrugged. "Maybe, but with Scout I used food to gain his trust."

He shook his head, "We can't spare any."

"Then I'm not sure how well this will go," I said, clenching the paper in my fingers.

Vincent snorted and slapped his hand on the table. "Figure it out Mara or I will see you shot, but not before I eviscerate your husband and feed his liver to the crows."

Nausea rolled through me, not just because of his words, but because the food that I'd been without for too long wasn't settling well. "I'm going to puke," I said. Vincent gave me a look of disgust, his lip curling and his eyes half closed.

I lunged for the waste basket and caught the edge of it as the chicken noodle soup was brought back up, most of the noodles still intact. I heaved till my stomach was empty and then some.

"Get her out of here," Vincent snapped. Hands circled around my waist lifting me to my feet. "Stomach, don't squeeze it," I said, as another dry heave wracked my body.

A glance up showed me it was Marks escorting me. That was a surprise; I'd assumed Burns was assigned to me.

We made our way through the bunker to a hallway lined with rooms. The third door on the right opened up into a compact, tidy room with a real bed, small desk and chair, and even a tiny closet.

"Here, this is where you'll stay. I'll come get you in a few hours for your first session training the Nevermores," Marks said. I laid down on the bed, groaning with relief, my head spinning. "Can I have some water?"

"Sure." The door closed behind me and I closed my eyes, putting a hand to my belly. I wasn't cramping so I was pretty sure it wasn't a miscarriage, but the baby was not happy with the soup. Just the thought of the noodles made me gag again.

The door opened and Marks set a large plastic tumbler of water down on my side table. "Here, you can have as much water as you want but everything else is on rations."

"Just bread or crackers, I think, for me for now," I said and then took a sip of water. It washed away the puke taste a little and I lay back down on the bed.

Marks said nothing more, leaving me to my nausea. The door closed and I wondered if I'd be able to fall asleep. It didn't take long for me to find out.

I dreamt of the beach again. But this time it was Marks with me, holding my hand, staring into my face, his eyes soft, a smile at the corner of his lips.

"Stay with me Mara," he whispered into my ear, as he wrapped his arms around my waist.

"I can't," I said, pulling away from him. "I love Sebastian."

"He's a monster, he can't love you."

I shook my head, my hair falling around my face, hiding the scene from me. "No, he does love me, you don't know him!"

Hands touched me and I flinched and found myself looking up into Sebastian's face.

"Baby," he said, his lips in my hair, his words muffled, "I don't know how much longer I can hang on."

"Stay with me Bastian," I begged. "Don't go."

"He's right, I'm afraid to hurt you," Bastian said, letting go of me, pushing me towards Marks.

"No! Please, stop!" I yelled. I fought, but Marks held me tight as again I watched Sebastian disappear from view. "I promise you, I will never stop loving him."

He let me go and I tumbled to the hard-packed sand.

I woke with a start, the blanket tangled around me, soaked through from my sweat. Sitting up, I grabbed for the glass and gulped back the water, easing the dry ache in my throat. "I promise," I whispered into the semi darkness as I clutched the glass. "I promise."

9

Once I'd woken up from the dream I sat thinking over how to train the Nevermores for Vincent. Scout listened to me because he was afraid of Sebastian, but that only worked because they were from the same pack and Scout understood the hierarchy. It was a long shot, but perhaps Sebastian and I working together could do the same with the Nevermores here. It would require me to do something I never thought I would; something that the very idea of gave me shivers of fear and desire equally.

It surprised me when instead of Marks; Burns came to get me to take me down to the Nevermore's cells. I did my best to keep the conversation and contact to a minimum; the dream, still more than fresh, had left me feeling jittery.

"I have to go in to him if I'm to start the training. The others have to see me as his mate," I said. Much as I wanted to be with Sebastian, there was the distinct possibility that he could turn on me. It was a chance I had to take if this was going to work and a part of me wanted to be with him, despite the changes in him. Burns and I were standing at the start of the cell block; the only sound was that of shuffling bodies and the occasional whimper.

"Does that mean what I think it does?" Burns asked me, his eyes wide.

I flushed. "He's my husband."

"I know, but he's not human anymore," Burns said, not making eye contact with me.

"If you knew anything about love, you'd know that it shouldn't matter what he looks like," I said, crossing my arms over my breasts.

"But he's a monster."

"Not to me."

Nothing more was said as we walked the rest of the way to Sebastian's cell.

Burns did as I asked, letting me in and locking the door behind me. Then he surprised me further by handing me the key. At my look he laughed, "Well, it's not like he's got the motor skills to handle the key and get the door open himself."

I smiled. "Thank you. I'm going to need some time alone with him. I don't know how long this will take." I didn't care what Burns thought of me, what any of them thought of me. I loved my husband, loved him deeply with a passion that superseded any condition he might have. Monster or human, he was the man I wanted in my life.

Burns let out a sigh, nodded, and walked back to the end of the cell block. I heard the door open then shut and click as the lock was turned. For the first time, Sebastian and I were truly alone.

"Bastian," I whispered, stepping into the darkened back of the cell. Hands reached out of the shadows and pulled me into the gray gloom. Sebastian sat on the edge of a cot and placed me easily on his lap. I wrapped my arms around him, breathing in the scent that was still him, just wilder, raw and untamed.

He groaned as he pressed his mouth to the hollow of my throat, licking at my skin, pulling at it lightly with his teeth. A shiver of desire rippled through me. I slid my hands up his arms, then up his neck to cup his face and bring his lips to mine. I might try to convince myself that this was so I could train the pack, so that they would see me completely as Sebastian's mate, but in reality, this was for me. I needed to feel connected to him in every way, to remember our love as it had been.

Carefully, I pressed my mouth to his. The memory of the bittersweet taste of tears that our last kiss had given us haunted my heart and I wanted to erase it. A rumble started deep in his belly that vibrated through my body, setting me to squirming in his lap. He grabbed my hips and held me still as he pulled me tight against his arousal, pressing himself against me. It was my turn to groan, but he swallowed the noise down as he kissed me hard, his mouth demanding a surrender that I gave freely.

I struggled out of my shirt and Sebastian slid his hands up my torso to cup my swollen breasts, bending his head to capture a nipple in his mouth, suckling and teasing at it till I cried out. My hands tangled in his hair and I guided him to the other nipple, relishing in the passion behind each touch, each brush of skin against skin. My breasts began to tingle, my allergies reacting to the drug in his saliva, but it only heightened the sensations, leaving me writhing and on the brink of release.

Sebastian growled softly, wrapped one arm around me and stood, holding me easily in the air. A whisper of cloth and he leaned me up against the wall, his palm pushing into the juncture of my thighs, no longer able to tease me as he once could. I arched as he brushed across my sweet spot, back and forth, over and over again, the rough edges of his hand quickly bringing me to a climax. As my breathing increased he slid into me, rock hard and throbbing with desire. A single thrust and he was fully inside of me. I let out a moan that he captured with his mouth, our tongues tangling, breath coming in gasps.

Together we found a rhythm, our bodies remembering each other with ease, rocking hard against the desire that ripped through us. We climbed to the peak, our breath losing sync as our cravings took over, bodies losing any control we might have had until at the final moment we crested together, the climax like nothing I'd ever before experienced. This was different than our love making in the past, more urgent and wild, but it was still him, still my love.

Panting hard, Sebastian held me close and moved us to the cot where he'd been sitting when I'd come in. I didn't want to let go of him, not yet. I wanted this closeness, to feel him in me, his body still throbbing with pent up yearnings. As he sat down I started to move, shifting my hips in a seductive dance, as I brushed my breasts against his chest, letting my nipples tickle along his hardened skin.

He grabbed my waist and helped me find a decadent pace that brought us both near to writhing once more. Sebastian bent his head and pulled a gasp out of me as he suckled my breasts, our hips still dancing. With his touch and tongue, my body constricted, quickly peaking again, the spasms of my muscles bringing him along with me, driving us high and leaving us gasping for air.

Finally exhausted, I leaned my naked and sweating body against his as his hands roved over my skin, settling on my belly bump, cupping it with divine tenderness. A lump rose in my throat and I knew that no matter what, this love could never be taken from us.

"I love you Sebastian, I don't care about the changes in you. Love can make this work. Somehow," I said. I kissed his lips softly, and then rested my head on his shoulder.

"Love too," he whispered into my ear, licking the sweat from my neck and pulling me back under a tidal wave of desire.

10

The next day I stood in front of Vincent while he read the list of things I would need to train the Nevermores.

"You want to set them loose in the rifle range? I don't see how this is going to train them unless we are shooting *at* them. Is that going to be your plan of attack?"

I shook my head and tucked the scarf I'd confiscated around my neck a little tighter to hide Sebastian's love bites. I knew that Burns knew, there was no way he could have ignored the wobble in my step, the flush in my cheeks or the dilation of my pupils as I stumbled out of the cell block. That didn't mean I wanted anyone else to know. It wasn't shame, it was fear. Vincent was already using Sebastian against me. What if he decided if I was willing to sleep with Sebastian, I might make a good playmate for him too? I suppressed a shiver of revulsion. I thought of Fran, a woman who'd been forced into servicing the officers and was killed when she stood up for herself. I couldn't let Vincent think of me in a sexual way.

"I need to set up a simulation of what a real pack would exist like. It's what I think will work the best."

Vincent grunted. "I'll have Marks round up the Nevermores we have and put them all in there."

"Except Sebastian, we have to hold him back till the rest of the males have fought it out," I said.

"Why? You can't protect him forever," he snapped, his eyes narrowed.

I laughed and shook my head. I'd already known that would be Vincent's accusation and I was prepared for it. "No, we need Sebastian to win and to give him the best shot we'll hold him back. He's big, but even a big man can be taken down by three average-sized men."

Vincent leaned over and pushed his intercom button. "Round up the Nevermores and put them in the rifle range. Be sure to catch the one wandering around outside and throw him in there too. Get the big bastard lined up, rope him good, and bring him to the outside of the range. His keeper will meet you there."

He stared at me, a wrinkle in between his eyes that drew tighter the longer he stared. I forced myself to hold still and not fidget under his steady gaze. "What?" I asked.

"You seem to have quite the glow about you. I must assume you truly . . . enjoyed . . . your visit with Sebastian," he said, his tone more than implying that he knew.

A hot flush spread up my neck to my cheeks giving any pretence about me away. I took a deep breath and squared my shoulders. "He's my husband. I love him."

"I have no doubt of that Mara," Vincent said. He let out a sigh. "I can even understand it."

I blinked twice and my brain tried to catch up to what was going on here. "You can?"

Vincent nodded and sat on the edge of the table. "My Juliana, she was forced to take the Nevermore shot. Even as a monster, I would still have her in my life."

Confusion rippled through me. This was a side of Vincent I hadn't expected. "What happened to her?" I asked curiosity and a strange sense of kinship filling me.

Vincent took a deep breath and let it out slowly. "Donavan forced her to take the shot, made her take it and then locked her away in a cage when she became a monster. He's only doing it to hurt me. It's why . . ."

I nodded, understanding. It was why Vincent wanted to take the city from Donavan. For the lost love of a woman. "I'm sorry," I said.

"Don't be." Vincent snapped his hard exterior back in place after that small glimpse of his humanity. "You have a job to do, so do it. Train the Nevermores. Here," he handed me a pad of paper and a pen.

"I have rounds to do. I want a detailed list of how long it will take, how you see this training progressing, as well as any information you can give me on the Nevermores. Observations, abilities, weaknesses."

I sat down as Vincent strode out of the room and quickly scribbled down a few things. But as soon as the door clicked shut, I stood and started to pace. I needed to move, to try and get my thoughts in order. I found myself in front of the single book-shelf in the room. My fingers trailed along the spine of the books. Would they give me insight to the dictator who held my life in his hands? Would they help me figure a way out of this mess?

There was nothing of consequence, just a mixed bag of novels, non-fiction and how-to manuals. My fingers brushed a thin volume that was light pink and I paused, slowly pulling it out from between to heavy books on artillery. It so did not fit in with the rest of the books.

It was a journal and the name on it was Juliana. Unable to restrain myself, I let the book fall open in my hands and started to read. Chills rippled through me as the words painted a very different picture than the one Vincent was trying to feed me.

I didn't hear the door open.

"What the hell are you doing?" Vincent screamed at me.

I dropped the journal and spun to face him. There was nothing to say. I was caught red-handed.

Vincent rushed me and I ran around the large table, keeping distance between us.

"You bitch, I'll kill you!" He snarled.

I did the only thing I could. I lied. "I believe you Vincent. Donavan wasn't the one she loved, it was you."

He stopped at the opposite side of the table from me. "What?"

I was breathing hard, but I forced the words out. "Juliana was in love with you, that's what I saw when I read her words. She didn't want to be with Donavan, but he made her, hurt her."

Vincent stood up, squaring his shoulders. "You should never have read her journal."

I nodded. "I know. I didn't realize what it was. But then I saw that you and I are in the same position really."

Vincent's eyes narrowed and I rushed on, spinning the lies as fast as I dared. "You love Juliana, but she was taken away by the Nevermore shot. We should be working together, to find a cure for her and Sebastian."

His jaw twitched. "The Nevermores have been rounded up and been put in the rifle range. I suggest you leave now and deal with their training."

I backed away from him, my hands finding the doorknob by feel alone.

I turned and walked as fast as I dared in the dim tunnels, getting into dead ends twice before I stumbled into the kitchen, my mind racing with what I'd learned. At the moment though there was nothing I could do about it, I had to focus on keeping myself and Sebastian alive which meant training the Nevermores.

There was no one in the kitchen and I slipped in thinking about Sebastian and Scout, how hungry they must be. It didn't matter that they didn't seem to need the food to survive; I wanted them to have something. It wouldn't hurt with the whole training program either if I provided some food

In the second cupboard I found a loaf of stale bread, faint green mold on the edges. It would have to do and besides, I'd seen Scout eat a human body, I doubted he would mind a little bacterial culture. I tucked the loaf under my arm and continued my search for the stairs, finally reaching the top level and the hatch that would let me outside. A soldier nodded to me and opened the door, but sunlight didn't flood in—rain did. A summer rainstorm filled the morning sky with dark, ominous clouds, a feeling of foreboding hanging over the open door.

"Where's the rifle range?" I asked.

"Follow the fence line North, you can't miss it."

Movement back by my original barracks alerted me to Scout. I ran towards him and he scrambled backwards, falling over himself to keep some distance between us. I pulled a slice of bread out and held it towards him.

"You can have more, but only if you're good," I said, trying to keep my face and voice stern.

He stared at me; eyes squinting as if he was considering the offer, more likely he was trying to figure out how to get the whole loaf and maybe my hand along with it. He lifted his head and sniffed in my direction then froze, a shudder rippling through his body. I smiled to myself. I hadn't showered after I'd made love to Sebastian, I wanted his scent on me and it was working. Scout knew I was Sebastian's mate in every way and that meant I held rank over the lowly Nevermore.

"Be good," I said, and flipped the slice to him. He caught it and swallowed it in two bites. "Come on, we've got to go." I snapped my fingers like I would have for my Nero. Scout, trembling, scuttled to my side. He lowered his head, his spine curved in, completely submissive, not a single trace of predatory hunger. This was a good sign; my plan just might work after all.

We walked north along the fence line, finally coming to the rifle range and a second fence around the edge of it. People, more accurately, Nevermores, milled about inside the range, not making a single sound despite the soldiers that were placed at intervals around the outside edge. I placed a hand on Scout's head.

"No attacking," I said, and patted him for good measure. He sat back on his heels and stared at the ground. Good enough. I did a quick head count; there were at least thirty Nevermores in there. I counted 23 men and 7 women including the heavily pregnant one, Marks' ex-wife.

"Now what Mara?" Marks asked, as he started to walk towards me from the other side. He froze when he saw Scout tucked up against my legs.

"Where's Sebastian?" I asked.

Just then three soldiers came out with Sebastian bound up and walking between them. He was growling and lunging at the end of the catchpoles they directed him with, his face twisted in a snarl of anger.

"Bring him here," I said, my heart trembling. How do you love someone so much and yet still fear them, knowing they could turn on you in an instant? It was a terrible combination of emotions and they warred for my attention within my heart.

Sebastian saw me and his struggling ceased as he got closer to me and Scout, his eyes softening, his growls subsiding completely. It was a good sign and the guards started to relax their grips on the poles.

"Let him go," I said. "He'll be fine if he's right beside me." I pleaded with them, hoping they believed me.

"We can't ma'am. Standard orders when dealing with the big boys." One of the guards said. I let out a sigh. There was no use for it. At least they weren't beating him.

"Now what?" One of the other guards asked.

I stepped up to the fence and threw three quarters of the loaf of bread over the top. The Nevermores inside the range froze in place, noses lifted to the wind in tandem, the rain running down over their skin. Then they broke as a single unit, scrambling over one another as they fought to get to the bread. Mass hysteria broke out, fists and feet flying, and the pack let loose with their unearthly howling and screeching.

From there it seemed to go downhill, but it was what I was counting on. I fed Sebastian a piece of stale (but not moldy) bread as we sat on the wet ground. As the rain poured down around us, the first pair of males squared off. This was going better than I had hoped, better than if I'd planned it myself.

I put my money on the larger of the two Nevermores. His body was tightly coiled and heavily muscled and he outweighed the smaller male by at least fifty pounds. They circled around one another, jabbing and growling as they tested the other's reach and style. In a sudden flurry they launched at one another, screaming their rage. The fight lasted maybe a whole minute, with a surprise victory to the smaller of the two men. He stood over his opponent and crowed to the cloudridden skies before he dropped and ripped the bigger man's throat out, sealing his win in blood. A ripple of chills went through me and I tucked my body tighter against Sebastian's. The soldiers around us didn't make a move, not even a gasp. I wondered how many times they'd seen this sort of thing.

The winner was immediately challenged by a young male who was tall and lean, almost as tall as Sebastian, with a shock of red hair that stood on end as if he'd been electrocuted. Living here with Vincent, the possibility of that kind of torture was all too real. I had to work at putting away my sympathy for him, knowing that he could be the one Sebastian faced off against.

This fight lasted longer, the two combatants wrestled to the ground, mud covering their bodies. It was hard to follow the progress and I had no idea who was winning until the very end. A loud crack followed by a scream signalled the fight was over, this time the young one was the victor. He strutted around the compound, kicking at the limp body of his opponent as he passed, eyeing up the rest of the pack. No one lifted their eyes to his, giving him the submission he was demanding with only his presence. He had no other challengers.

"Now we can put Sebastian in," I said, untying the ropes on his wrist and slipping the catchpole off his neck before Marks or anyone else had time to protest.

"Mara don't! He'll attack us all and that'll force us to shoot him," Marks yelped at me.

"Sebastian," I said, holding his head and pulling his face close to mine. "I need you to go in and take over the pack. We need them to help get us out of here, okay?" I kissed his lips and he nodded, slowly. I pulled the rest of the ropes off of him and he followed me to the gate where the nearest soldier opened the door and stood behind it.

"You're one crazy bitch," the soldier muttered.

"Love will do that to you." I said with a twist of my lips. Sebastian stepped into the rifle range, drawing all the Nevermore's eyes to him. "Scout," I said. He jumped and I pointed in. Slinking along, he did as he was told and the Nevermores saw him listen, saw him obey a human woman.

And then the fight was on, the young buck rushing Sebastian and without realizing it, us too. The soldier slammed the gate shut. There was only one problem; he didn't wait till I was out of the way, and the door hammered my back throwing me into the rifle range with the Nevermores and the raging male.

11

"Get her out of there!" Marks snarled, and I heard the gate start to open, but then slam shut a second time as the rest of the Nevermores surrounded me and Scout, sniffing and touching, Sebastian already battling it out with the young male.

I stood slowly, my heart hammering along at a breakneck speed. Scout stayed at my heels, pressing him up against me, looking to me for leadership in the new pack. Shit. This was not how I'd planned things to go.

I still had three slices of bread and I pulled one out of the bag. A woman made a grab for it and I slapped her hand down and growled at her, doing my best imitation of Sebastian and Scout. She lowered her eyes and withdrew her hand. I split the piece into four and slipped the first to Scout, who took it eagerly, showing him favouritism. Then I handed one to the woman who'd reached out, her eyes filling with a joy so intense it brought a lump to my throat. They were starving, doing their best to live, to exist. Though they weren't human, they still felt emotions, needs and wants. The third piece I handed to a grizzled old male who looked like he'd been in his share of battles. I looked over my shoulder to see Sebastian pounding the living piss out of the young buck.

The last chunk went to Marks' ex-wife. Then I broke my last two slices into as many pieces as I could, handing them out to the rest of the pack.

They took them eagerly and when I growled and shooed them with my hands, they backed off. Maybe it was a good thing I was shoved in here. They weren't attacking me and they were seeing me as the Alpha's mate, higher than them in pack standing.

A roar and I turned to see Sebastian standing over the young buck, his foot on the throat of his opponent. I ran over to him, pushing my way through the pack to put a hand on his arm.

"Don't kill him Sebastian, you don't need to," I said.

I wasn't so sure I'd made the right move when Sebastian turned his eyes to me, rage and a feral hunger flickering through them. I swallowed hard and put my hand on his chest. "Come back to me Bastian."

He shook his head slowly and the air went out of him. He lifted his foot and Buck, as I was already thinking of him, scrambled away with a groan.

Sebastian clamped his hands on my shoulders and let out another roar, his message clear. He was Alpha, I was his mate.

"Well your methods seem to be working. You can stay with them then. I think you should be perfectly safe with your Sebastian looking out for you. Yes?"

I turned to see Vincent at the edge of the rifle range staring in at us. His face was blank, but there was a tiny corner of a pink journal peeking out of his shirt collar. Damn, he was going to punish me for reading the journal.

A crash of thunder made me flinch; it was followed by a brilliant bolt of lightning and a second round of thunder. Sebastian pulled me tight to his side and the rest of the Nevermores circled in close, putting a protective shield around us. Something bumped into my hand and I looked down to see Buck pushing his fire engine red head up into my fingers. Sebastian growled at him, but I gave my man a squeeze, recognizing that Buck only wanted comfort.

The soldiers peeled away with a signal from Vincent, all except Marks.

"Mara, I don't want to leave you in there. It's not safe," he said, his face a full of concern and fear. I smiled at him and stroked Buck's hair while I leaned against Sebastian.

"Marks, in case we don't get a chance to see each other again, I want to thank you. You've been a good friend to me. I think you're a good man; don't let them turn you into anything else."

Marks pressed his lips into a thin line and, even with the distance between us; I could see the indecision warring in his eyes.

"I'll be okay. I've got Sebastian, and apparently, a new family. If I know nothing else, I know that packs look out for one another and for the moment, I'm one of them," I said, certain that the words I spoke were true.

I watched Marks walk away as the rain poured down on us, the lightning outlining everyone in sharp relief. I was standing in the middle of a Nevermore pack, a place that should have me well and truly terrified and yet, for the first time in weeks, I knew I was safe. At least, I thought I was.

12

That night we slept in a huddled bunch underneath the over-hang where the shooters took aim at the targets. Sebastian was in the centre with me curled up beside him, Scout across our legs and every other member of the pack snuggling up as close as they could, not only to conserve warmth, but I think to feel secure and safe.

We were woken by a rattle of the gate and a holler. It was Burns. "Mara, I don't want you to have to fight for your food."

I scrambled to my feet and stared across the range. Burns stood with a basket of food. I thought of the moldy bread and was ashamed that I thought it was okay to feed it to Scout. Of course he'd eat it, he was starving. And now here I was about to get the same treatment as the Nevermores, despite the fact that I was still human. I let out a sneeze, scrubbed my nose and walked to where Burns stood.

"Thanks," I said, as he handed me a basket of stale—but not moldy—bread, and two plastic containers, one full of beans and the other full of creamed corn. Not exactly the breakfast of champions, but it was better than I had expected.

Burns handed me a jug of water and a plastic glass. "Here. Don't share this with them; they'll drink from the puddles."

I took it and shook my head at him. "I know they're wild, but if they were your family, would you expect them to drink muddy rain water?"

Burns ducked his head, but not before I saw the high spots of shame on his cheeks. "No, I wouldn't want that, but I also know that if given the chance they would tear me limb from limb, even your Sebastian."

I stared at him, knowing that what he said was true. They would kill any human they could for food; I managed this integration into the pack only because of Sebastian and our bond. Burns leaned towards me and tucked a hand gun into the waist of my jeans. "Marks asked me to give this to you. Just in case. If Sebastian turns on you, you're going to need this. Here's the safety, just flick it off and you're good to go."

I looked down and stared at the weapon tucked into my jeans. "I can't shoot him."

"You could wound him though, to get away." His eyes stared into mine.

"I know you mean well, and I thank you for your concern, but it won't be necessary. Sebastian will take care of me." I turned and walked back to the pack that'd watched the entire exchange but hadn't approached.

Sebastian had a solid frown on his face as he looked from me to Burns and back again. Oh God, that was the last thing I needed right now, a jealous feral husband trying to protect me from the good intentions of a lonely teenage soldier.

"Food," I hollered; the pack swarmed around me and I doled out the food, keeping the largest amount for myself and Sebastian. I gave him the whole container of beans and I shared it with him, dunking chunks of bread in and sopping up the juices.

My stomach, shrunk as it was from the lack of eating, rebelled when I had only one chunk of bread left. I looked around to see Marks' ex-wife laying with her back to us, shuddering. I headed over that way, stopping only when Sebastian put a hand on my arm. I glanced over my shoulder.

"Something's wrong with Momma," I said, giving her a name impulsively. It was easier to keep track of the pack members this way.

I reached her and bent down, touching her hip as I did so. She flinched and curled up tighter against the blows I think she expected. "Shhh. It's okay," I said softly. She rolled her eyes to see me and I smiled at her. "Come on now, sit up and eat." I moved to the other side and helped her sit up, a low moan slipping past her lips as she shifted her bulk.

I pressed the bread into her hands and she stared at me like I was some heavenly being. It was uncomfortable, especially when I thought back to my first reaction to the Nevermores surrounding our property, suggesting just getting in the car and running them over to get away. She ate the bread slowly between low moans, finishing it off as she let out a keening wail that set the whole pack off howling.

Liquid suddenly pooled out around her and I gasped. "Shit."

I helped Momma lie back down then ran back to Sebastian. "She's having the baby!" I yelled at him, hopping from one foot to the next, not sure if I was excited or terrified. On impulse I ran to the gate, "Burns! Burns! I need your help!"

There was no one up here, what was I thinking, that they would hear me back in the bunker? Even if I fired the gun I didn't think they would hear me that far underground.

I spun and ran back to Momma, shooing away the pack members who had crept close and were sniffing at the fluid. If one of them so much as took a single sip, I would throw up on their heads.

Though I'd read a lot of books in preparation for being a mom myself, I'd never thought I'd be helping someone else give birth. Certainly not in an army camp's rifle range. I knew that walking was good, so that was the first objective. "Sebastian, I need you to help me get her up," I called to him, while I tucked myself under one of her arms. Sebastian approached cautiously.

"I mean it, grab her arm and help me get her up," I said. He took a deep breath and helped Momma stand, where she moaned and wobbled, then tried to lie back down.

"No, not yet. Walking first," I said, encouraging her to step out with me. She took one step, than another and soon we were making our way around the perimeter of the range, her breathing improving and her face relaxing. A contraction would hit and she would pause but then keep going. I smiled at her and made soothing noises, occasionally touching her belly to feel the muscles contract. Sebastian watched all of this from a distance with a very strange look on his face, one I couldn't identify and was too busy to analyze. When the other members of the pack tried to approach me and Momma he growled at them, letting us have our space.

We walked for an hour and I could see that Momma was getting tired. I took her to the back of the overhang and found a relatively clean, dry spot for her to lie down.

It was then that the contractions really started. Her whole body would tense and the muscles across her stomach would ripple and harden. Momma would sit up, her hair plastered to her face with sweat as she bore down.

"That's it sweetheart. You can do it." I looked between her legs, the crown of the baby's head showing clearly.

I smiled up at her. "The baby's almost here, another push." She leaned forward and let out a wail as she screamed along with a contraction and pushed. The baby's head and shoulder slid free; a second push and I caught the babe and helped guide it the rest of the way out as Momma collapsed back to the ground, one more contraction and the placenta came out right after. I used a hair elastic to tie off the umbilical cord. Hardly sanitary, but it was all I had.

"It's a girl!" I shouted and brought the tiny angel child around to show Momma. The little one let out a wail and I laughed, tears of happiness trickling down my face. If Momma could have a baby that was so obviously human, could do this in the wild with no doctor, it gave me hope for the child I carried.

Momma propped herself up on her elbows and reached for the baby, her eyes wide and staring. A cold chill swept over me. The baby was definitely human; would Momma accept her or would she try to eat her? Or was the intensity I saw a look of a mother wanting to hold her firstborn?

Momma's fingertips brushed the baby girl, a look of hunger flashing over her face, a drive so intense that I knew even her own child wouldn't be spared. I wanted to believe that what was human inside Momma would override the animal instinct to eat another species' helpless newborn, but as Momma opened her mouth and snapped at the wailing baby girl, I had to accept this for what it was.

A complete and utter disaster.

13

I jumped clear of Momma's snarling reach and growled back at her, holding the baby close as she wailed, trying to figure out what the hell I was going to do with her. I couldn't keep the child here in the rifle range; I had nothing to wrap her in, no breast milk or formula, and I wasn't entirely sure I could keep her safe from the whole pack.

A hand touched my shoulder and I spun with a gasp. Sebastian stood behind me, a quizzical expression on his face at the squalling babe in my arms. "Momma wants to eat her baby," I said, as if that would explain it all to him. He placed his hand over the still-slick skin and pressed it against her chest.

His big hand covered her entire torso, and the yellow skin against the brilliant pink of the newborns was yet another contrast. Sebastian, still staring at the child, lifted his hand and pressed it against my belly. His understanding went straight through me like a blade; how could I have ever doubted him?

"We have to get her out of here," I said. "She isn't safe."

Sebastian nodded, bent and kissed the crook of my neck, giving me a nuzzle. I leaned into him, his body curling around both me and Momma's little girl.

A hand brushed up against my leg and Sebastian snarled at the one who dared to come too close. I jiggled the baby, putting my pinky finger in her mouth to give her something to suckle. She latched on and quieted down in my arms, in the shadow of Sebastian's protection.

A scuffle and a rattle of the gate turned my head. There stood Burns like an angel come from heaven to rescue the baby. "Supper, Mara." Was it that late already? I'd barely noticed the passage of time with Momma's labour.

"I have to give her to him," I said, as much to convince myself as anyone else. Sebastian gave me a gentle push and I walked to Burns, whose jaw dropped open in surprise as I drew close.

"Holy crap, the pregnant one didn't eat her baby?"

My head snapped up. "What do you mean? Was there another one?"

Burns nodded, opening the gate. "Three weeks ago another of the women gave birth; I think it was that one there." He pointed to a heavy-breasted brunette and I could see that she did indeed have some extra flesh around her middle, not much, but more than any of the others.

"The baby came out, and before we could get in the cell she'd grabbed it and taken a bite out of it. We wrestled her to the ground and took the kid, but he didn't survive."

"Well, you've got chance number two now." I stepped close to him and tried to transfer the baby into his arms. He shook his head. "She won't be any better off with us, Mara. Can't you feed her?" He stared at me, his eyes dipping to my breasts with a blush. I stared back.

"She won't survive out here, I have nothing to wrap her in and I don't know if I can feed her," I whispered, horror filling my heart where hope had only moments before resided. Burns handed me the basket of food.

"I'll get you some blankets and some more food for you. But you can't share it with the rest of them." I nodded slowly as a lump rose in my throat. I'd helped to bring her into this world; I only hoped I hadn't done her a disservice.

"I'll bring up Vincent too," Burns said. "Maybe there's something he can do to help."

"He won't help me or her," I said, my arms tightening around the little girl.

Burns didn't answer me, just slipped off his jacket, handed it to me, and then shut the gate. The baby startled awake at the slam of it and started to wail. The pack, hearing the newborn's cries, rushed the fence, snarling and growling, reaching for her. I snapped, kicking and hitting, screaming at them to get away. They fell back from me and I threw the food on the ground.

"There! You're hungry, go ahead and eat," I screamed at them. I ran across to the farthest point of the compound, holding the little girl close. A glance over my shoulder showed Momma still where we had left her. She glared at me and I glared back. "Bitch," I muttered under my breath. A squirm in my arms and a nuzzle at my breast pulled my attention back to the child I held. I didn't know if I had the milk to give her, but I had to try.

Slipping her under my shirt not only protected her from the breeze, but I was able to hold her to my breast and attempt to get her to latch on. It wasn't easy—she couldn't seem to get it right—but after several tries she latched on and started to suck. I had to hope that my swollen breasts would be able to give her some nourishment in time, that my milk would start with her suckling. It was the only hope she had.

"Love."

I looked up as Sebastian crouched down and slid over to me. I reached out for him with a free hand and pulled him in close. He whispered in my ear, "Love." His voice was rough from disuse. He wrapped his arms around the both of us, sheltering us again; his large hands rubbed my back as he consoled me. Nothing happened, despite how she suckled; there was no milk yet for me to give her. She gave a quiet mewl then snuggled into my arms. The tears started then, dripping down my face. No sobbing or any more scream-ing, just the steady flow of pain escaping me. This could be our child in a few short months; we could be fighting off a Nevermore pack just to keep our baby with us.

I stroked the light blond downy hair, still damp in patches. I wouldn't be able to sleep knowing how close the pack was. But maybe if Sebastian claimed her too, maybe then she would be safe.

A short time passed and there was a commotion at the gate. Sebastian stood and growled. I stood and saw that Burns had come back, Vincent in tow. I made my way over to them, the baby exhausted and asleep in my arms. I had no doubt the lack of nourishment was already affecting her little body.

Burns opened the gate. "You can come out now." He closed the gate behind me, and I was outside of the rifle range. I let out a sigh of relief. I didn't realize until that moment how on edge I'd been, even with Sebastian watching over me.

Vincent snorted. "This is what you brought me up here for?"

With what looked like a casual flick of his hand, Vincent knocked Burns to the ground, stunning both Burns and I alike.

"Now, give me the baby," Vincent demanded, and held his hand out, like he wanted a piece of fruit placed in it. Certainly not how you'd offer to hold a child.

"What are you going to do with her?" I asked, holding her tight to me, my heart racing.

"I don't have to answer to you woman. Now give it to me," Vincent growled, again reaching for the little girl. I side stepped him, keeping just out of reach.

Chills swept through me. "She's human Vincent, she isn't one of them. Look." I tried to hold her so he could see the pink skin and the pale blue eyes that stared up at me.

"It'll turn, just like the rest of them, and I'm not feeding anymore monsters. Give it to me or I will take your Sebastian in its place," Vincent snarled.

I cradled the babe, my hand brushing against the package Burns had given me, the gun he thought I would need against Sebastian and the pack.

"Burns. Hold the baby for me." I handed the little girl to him before he could say no. He held her awkwardly and she squawked at the jiggling.

With my back to Vincent, I slipped the gun out. A single slow breath in and I turned, with the gun coming up as I flicked the safety off. There was no other recourse now, at least not as far as I was concerned.

Letting the breath out, I took aim and fired at Vincent before Burns saw what I was doing, before Vincent could do more than widen his eyes in surprise.

The trigger was easy to pull; the recoil though was not so nice. I wasn't ready for the kick, and it threw my arm up into the air, the bullet hitting Vincent in the throat. He fell over backwards, hands scrabbling at his neck, gurgled air hissing through the bullet-made tracheotomy.

The baby wailed. Shaking, I dropped the gun and held my arms out to Burns. "Give her to me," I said. Eyes seeming to fill his entire blood-drained face, he handed her over to me.

"Mara, I . . ." He stumbled over the words, not even getting a full sentence out.

"This is a dog eat dog world Burns. Vincent was going to kill her, and if not her, then Sebastian. I had the means to stop him," I said, cradling her to my chest. I needed a name for her; I couldn't just keep calling her the baby.

My eyes refused to see the still twitching body in front of us, focusing solely on the child in my arms. I cooed to her, rocking her gently back and forth. I didn't want to think about what had just happened. The previous two deaths I'd caused had been reflexes, accidents. This was nothing of the sort.

"What are we going to do Mara?" Burns asked.

I turned to him, frowning. "What do you mean?"

"About the body; we can't just leave it here. If the other men find out you shot Vincent, they'll kill you," he said.

I glanced over my shoulder to see the pack crowding at the gate, their eyes hungry, and their gazes not wavering off the warm, barely dead body of Vincent. I sought out Sebastian. He hung back, not looking at us or making eye contact with me. I swallowed hard. Twice now I'd stopped him from killing and yet I'd killed three men. Did it matter that I thought what I'd done was right? Did it make any difference in the end?

"I'm putting the body in with the pack," Burns said, picking up Vincent's legs. "Can you keep them away from the door, keep them off me?"

I nodded and opened the door, forcing the pack to make room for Burns and the body. I looked at where Vincent had died; a trail of blood followed from that spot into the rifle range. "They're going to know. They can follow the blood and see that he was shot outside," I said, my voice monotone and strange, even to my own ears.

Burns gave the body a last heave and the pack fell on it. As I turned to step out something snapped down on my calf, and I screamed as teeth sliced into my flesh.

With a roar Sebastian leapt forward, smashing my assailant on the head, knocking him unconscious. I whimpered and put a hand to my leg, the bite an open gash. Burns stepped up and put a hand under my arm. Sebastian growled and tensed; I put a hand on his arm, holding the baby awkwardly. "It's okay love. Burns is going to help me, that's all."

Sebastian stepped back and the pack slipped in around him, stealing the body and dragging it to the back of the rifle range. Bastian didn't move; he stared at me as Burns helped me out then shut the gate. "I'll be back," I said, and blew Sebastian a kiss. He nodded and sat down where he was, his back to the pack and their meal.

14

"We'll tell them that one of the pack members jumped out, bit through Vincent's throat, and then dragged him into the rifle range," Burns said, as we slowly made our way to the bunker.

"Will they believe that?" I asked.

"Similar stuff has happened; you saw on the way here the guy that got dragged out of the truck, and those Nevermores are quick bastards," he said.

As we came up to the bunker Burns stopped and faced me. "Marks will be in charge now."

"That's good though, isn't it?" I frowned and tightened my arms around her, my leg throbbing in time with my heart as it sped up. "What?"

"The kid's mom—the woman was Marks' ex-wife. He went back to find her once Vincent convinced him of a cure."

"You already told me that. Won't he be happy that I saved his daughter?" I asked, rocking the little girl in my arms.

"Marks wasn't sure the baby was his." I let out a groan. This was not going to be easy. Burns touched me on the shoulder. "How can you be sure the baby isn't one of them— that she's human?"

I stared down at the bundle I held, wrapped in Burns' jacket. Sound asleep, her body exhausted from lack of food and all the goings on, she looked like a perfect angel with her soft pink skin and downy blond hair. "I don't think she is. Burns, there are documented cases of women infected with AID's that don't pass the disease on to their children. I think maybe something like that has happened here. Her skin is normal; she isn't trying to eat us." I smiled up at him, but he didn't smile back.

The bunker opened up and it was just our luck. Marks stepped out, his brown hair rumpled and his eyes rimmed in red as if he'd been crying. My heart softened; I knew the pain of losing all you held dear.

"She's alright, she's human," I said, limping towards him. He froze, his jaw trembling as he held out his arms. I placed her in them and she whimpered in her sleep.

"She needs a name," I said.

Marks didn't say anything at first, just stared at his daughter with an intensity that only a new father could produce. I saw emotions flicker across his face: love, sadness and a fierceness that could only be his desire to protect her. "I don't know if she's mine."

"She's yours Marks. That is all there is to it," I said. She needed him and I thought that he needed her just as much.

"She looks like an angel," He whispered. I smiled, and then grimaced as my leg spasmed.

"I thought the same thing," I said.

"Seraphima. I think that would be a good name, it was my mother's name," Marks said, and went back down into the bunker, ignoring me and Burns, his attention solely on his little angel.

"He didn't even ask about Vincent," I said, surprise filtering through me. "Wouldn't they want to know where he is? Isn't he supposed to be the leader here?"

Burns shrugged. "We rarely ask questions when someone doesn't come back. The answer is always the same as to how they died."

He helped me down into the bunker and we made our way to a brightly lit area that I hadn't been in previously. It was clean with white walls and gleaming surfaces that highlighted the medical tools spread about.

"I don't know much about stitching wounds," Burns said, as he helped me onto a chair. "But I think we should clean it and wrap it tight."

I nodded and stared around the room, taking in the difference between here and the rest of the gloomy bunker. Burns noticed me looking and answered my unasked question as he prepared a tray of antiseptics and wraps.

"It's where Vincent worked on training the Nevermores. Torturing them for the most part, like you said."

I shivered. "Gives this place a whole new feeling when you know that."

It didn't take long for Burns to clean and wrap my leg up. Gritting my teeth through the worst of it (mostly the iodine), my body relaxed as he finished up the last layer. Burns stood and helped me to my feet.

"Thanks," I said, rubbing the back of my neck. I was exhausted, the mental and physical strain taking its toll on me.

We turned as Marks stepped into the room, Seraphima wrapped in a pink blanket from God only knows where.

"Mara, I need you to feed her, she isn't taking anything from me," he said, handing her over to me along with a bottle, also from God only knows where. I cradled her in my arms and stared down at her sweet little face, which was fading from the healthy pink of a newborn to a pale yellow. I sucked in a breath of air and looked up to see the concern on Marks' face.

Moving swiftly, I stripped her of her coverings and laid her out on one of the tables. Her body was indeed yellowing, but there was no hint of a marking like the broom flower, as the Nevermores carried.

"I think she's jaundiced," I said. Looking up I caught Marks' eyes. "I don't know what to do about it, but it's fatal if it isn't treated."

I wrapped Seraphima back up and held her tight, whispering to her. Marks stepped forward, everything about him vibrating with intensity. "Mara, I don't know how to help her, please do something."

"I'm not a doctor, or even a nurse," I snapped, fear coursing through me. "Isn't there anyone who has some medical training?"

Both men went very still and I looked from one to the other. "What? Is there someone else?"

Burns nodded slowly. "Donavan, he's a doctor. But he's crazy, gone over the deep edge when his wife took the Nevermore shot."

"I'm not willing to take the chance that he would hurt her," Marks growled.

"If he's her only hope, then what? You just watch her die?" I said, my anger growing. "Do you have any idea what I would do to see my own child saved? What I would give up, who I would beg?" I stepped towards him, Seraphima's slow breathing and her very, very deep sleep disconcerting. She should have been screaming bloody blue murder for food, something she'd not yet had since she'd been born.

"I'd do anything to save her," Marks snapped.

"Then talk with Donavan, beg him if you have to," I said. "I don't think she's got much time, she's too young and weak to fight this off." My throat closed at what I was saying, and I tucked my head down against Seraphima's to hide the tears.

Footsteps stomped away and when I looked up it was just me and Burns again.

"He'll do right by her. This baby is all he's got left," Burns said.

I nodded and crooned to the bundle in my arms. I could only hope Burns was right.

15

The next two days were hell. I'd barely slept, hardly eaten, couldn't do anything but hold Seraphima and pray she could fight this off. Worse, Donavan wouldn't parlay with Marks, no matter that a child's life hung in the balance. Apparently Donavan still believed that Vincent was alive, and refused to help us on those grounds alone.

We tried to feed Seraphima evaporated milk, water, and even a few mouthfuls of a box of baby formula one of the men found, but nothing stayed down. I begged God to let her live, to spare her life, to give us hope through her that all would be well.

Marks ranted and raved at Donavan, the world, and God, his shouts and anger not once disturbing the baby. I wanted to rant with him, but I knew it wouldn't help her.

The morning of the third day I startled awake, my arms numb from holding Seraphima all night long. I jiggled her softly and her head rolled. I sucked in a gasp of air. "Oh please, no," I whispered, my fingertips brushing against her cold skin.

The door creaked open and Marks stepped in, his uniform rumpled, his eyes tired and drawn. I couldn't say the words, I couldn't tell him, but my tears were enough.

He knelt in front of me and I slipped Seraphima into his arms as if she was still alive and he cradled her the same way.

"I'm so sorry baby girl," he whispered. "I'm so sorry." His shoulders began to shake and I did the only thing I could. I bent forward and wrapped my arms around him and held him as he grieved for his daughter.

We cried for I don't know how long, till the tears dried and the shudders racking us subsided.

"We need to bury her," Marks said, staring up into my face from only inches away. I blinked and took a deep breath. "Deep, it has to be deep." We both knew that a shallow grave would be quickly unearthed by one type of animal or another.

He leaned forward and pressed his lips to mine, softly, carefully with no lust or craving behind it. "Thank you, for loving her," He whispered. I bobbed my head, feeling the tears well again. "Thank you for letting me," I whispered back.

That day was silent as the men went about digging a ten foot hole, taking turns with the shovel and straight bar, the quiet only broken by a grunt here and there. All of us had lost loved ones, but to see a man bury his baby daughter was a pain we all seemed to feel. At the end of the day, as the sun began to set, we wrapped Seraphima in several blankets and lowered her in.

Burns held out a ratty old pink and purple teddy bear and put it in with her. "She might need it," he said, his eyes glassy with unshed tears as he stepped back and ducked his head. The entire troupe was there, their eyes and hearts melting with the loss of a child who wasn't even their own, the grief of their friend bringing home perhaps the losses they'd all had over the last few months.

Marks filled the hole himself, not once letting any of his men take a turn on the shovel. I couldn't stay any longer, not without losing my composure again. No longer a prisoner, I made my way to the rifle range. I hadn't seen Sebastian in the last three days as I fought for Seraphima's life, and my heart ached to be with him and to have him hold me.

The rifle range was strangely silent when I approached and my heart began to thunder. The last ten feet I ran to the gate. "Sebastian!" I screamed.

Nothing.

I ripped the door open and ran inside, spinning in a circle. They weren't here and I knew they weren't in the bunker. I let out a whistle, hoping that Scout would hear me, and waited. Again, nothing.

"Sebastian!"

"Marks let them go," Burns' voice turned me around. "He didn't want to kill them, he knew about Sebastian and the scrawny one. So he let them go."

I started to shake and slowly slid to the ground. "Sebastian wouldn't leave me."

Burns shrugged and crouched down to my level. "He took off with the rest of them, the minute the gate was open. Maybe he finally lost himself to the drug."

I hit the ground with my fist, the pain steadying my nerves. "No. It's been too long, if it was going to happen, if he was going to lose himself, it would have been before now."

Again Burns shrugged then held out a hand. "Come on, let's go back inside."

I stood on my own and brushed by him. The men here didn't care about Sebastian, he was just another mouth to feed, another monster.

Stomping my way into the bunker, I went to find Marks. He was in the war room with three other men. When he saw me, he waved them out. "We'll discuss this more tonight boys, I want to be very sure it's possible before we attempt anything."

The other men left, nodding to me as they stepped out the door. It clicked softly behind them, leaving Marks and me alone.

"Mara, we're going to attack Donavan's in three days time. I don't know what to do with you, I can't have you fighting, and I can't leave you behind." There was genuine concern in his voice and it slowed my anger, but only for a moment.

"Why'd you let the pack go? You knew Sebastian still had a connection to me." I folded my arms over my chest and glared at him. Marks nodded and scrubbed his hands over his face.

"I can't feed them and they were starving. I know they'll eat anything, grass, leaves, sticks, bugs. But I couldn't watch Diana live like an animal any more. And I couldn't watch her let the other monsters ride her."

I slumped into the nearest chair, my heart freezing over. "Please tell me Sebastian wasn't one of the men who . . ." I couldn't even say it.

Marks didn't move at first, and then slowly shook his head. "No, Sebastian never touched her, not as far as I know."

I let out a breath that turned into a sob and covered my face with my hands. I didn't want to believe that Sebastian would leave me, but it was more than obvious that he had finally forgotten me.

Marks walked over to me and crouched in front of me, taking my hands in his, baring my tear-streaked face.

"I'm sorry that this hurt you Mara. But believe me, it's better this way. The pain will ease. I promise."

He squeezed my fingers and then brushed a strand of hair from my face, his eyes never leaving mine. "You're a good woman Mara, faithful, one that I wish I'd met in another time."

"Don't do this Marks, as far as I'm concerned I'm still married." I tried to pull back, but the chair prevented me from doing anything but squirm.

His hands tightened on mine. "Tell me your heart isn't beating faster, that you don't want to be held by a man who won't turn on you, one that can keep you safe as well as love you and your child."

My throat started to ache and yes, my heart was beating faster, but it was from a strange mixture of fear and shame. What he was saying was true and not at the same time. Because I wanted Sebastian, not Marks; I wanted my husband to hold me and our child, not another man. I had to get out of here, I had to find Sebastian.

He stared into my eyes and I did my best to give nothing back. "I'm sorry Marks," I said. "I can't."

He surprised me by smiling. "It's okay Mara. We've got a lot of time." He lifted my hands and kissed the back of each one, then stood, changing gears completely.

"The last report we received was that Donavan was close to a breakthrough on finding a cure," he said.

My thoughts, which had only moments before centered on leaving to find Sebastian, stalled out. A cure. If there was truly a cure, I wanted it. I needed it for Sebastian. A small spark of hope flared where for so long there had been nothing but day to day survival.

Marks continued, "I've got to find a way into that compound. Perhaps a distraction, something that will keep Donavan's eyes on the front of his compound while we hit it from behind. Any thoughts?" He lifted an eyebrow at me and I frowned.

"What about a messenger?" I asked. Marks shook his head. A soft knock on the door and we turned in tandem to see Burns poke his head in.

"You said to come down here when I was finished," he said. Marks nodded and pointed to another chair.

"Have a seat. Mara and I were discussing a distraction for Donavan."

"Why exactly are you attacking him now that Vincent is gone?" I asked. "I know what he did to Seraphima is horrible, but to waste more lives on revenge is beyond me."

Marks took a deep breath. "I'd be lying if I said it wasn't somewhat about revenge. But more than that, he controls the harbour, the ships, and any chance we have of making it to the mainland. Not to mention if he *has* found a cure, we need to get it to those who can make it in large quantities and spread it around the world."

I frowned and rubbed at my cheek. "Why would he be the one to find the cure? And why wouldn't he share it?"

Marks and Burns both stared at me, eyes wide, but it was Marks who answered my question. "He won't share it because he is so far gone in his delusions, I don't think he even realizes there is a whole world out there waiting on him. As to why he would be the one to find the cure," Marks scrubbed his hand over his face before answering me. "He developed Nevermore. This is ground zero Mara."

16

It was finally decided that in three days I would go with Burns to the bluffs above the compound and set off explosives that had been set the night before. The explosives were mostly for show; there weren't any large enough for anything else, but the damage that would be done should keep Donavan's attention on the front gates. I only got to go along because I pointed out that Marks needed as many men as he could have to help him storm the back, and Burns would need back up. Reluctantly, Marks agreed.

The morning that we were to take the compound dawned with a coolness that reminded me fall was on its way. I made my way slowly up to the rifle range, as I had whenever I could find a moment, hoping for a sign that Sebastian was still, at least, close by.

I called for Sebastian, whistled for Scout, but there was no reply. Even the other packs in the area seemed to have faded into the background; maybe one of them had taken over Sebastian's pack. What if he was hurt, or worse, dead?

Shudders rippled through me and I circled my baby bump with my hands. The thought of being alone, pregnant, and then a single mom in this world was enough to give me anxiety attacks. I took a slow even breath and let it out. No, it would be all right. An image of Marks on his knees in front of me calmed me down, and that freaked me out all over again. I was becoming too dependent on the men in my life. I had to be strong now, not just for me, but for the baby.

Back down at the bunker Burns waited for me in a Jeep.

The drive to the bluffs was eerily quiet; no sign of any Nevermore packs in the area. That didn't seem right, not with this being such a large city. I asked Burns about it.

"Seemed that a lot of people thought they needed to get off the island when everything started to go wrong. I think a lot of them headed to the mainland, maybe in hopes of escape. I don't really know, but we could see them all from up on the base."

"But if this was ground zero, why wouldn't people stay? Why wouldn't they stay and try to fix things?"

Burns shrugged and didn't answer me. But the question stuck in my head like silly putty on a chalkboard, rolling around with me chasing it, trying to find the answer.

It didn't make sense, not unless there was some seriously powerful motivation to go to the mainland to deal with the trouble of fighting through hordes of infected and non-infected humans alike. What would drive them to the mainland?

A few short minutes later we rumbled to a stop. We were just on the outskirts of downtown, on the hill on top of Third street right next to the St. Peters Catholic Church.

"Donavan's compound is situated right on the harbour, in what was the Port Theatre," Burns said, as we drove slowly down the hill.

Burns, his eyes glued on the road said, "As soon as we set off the explosives, we'll get out of there and head back to the bunker. I still can't believe Marks let you come along."

I shrugged. "What if something goes wrong? You showed me how to set the explosives off in case something happened. You need a back up. End of story."

Glancing in the rear view mirror, I saw a flicker of movement. A body dashed between buildings, a distinct sheen of yellow on the skin. A shiver crawled up my spine as more bodies ducked and dived, stalking me and Burns in the Jeep. Shit. Double shit.

"Burns, I think we've got company," I said, as I continued to watch a very large pack make its way down Third St. using the buildings for cover. I tried to count them, but their scattered groupings made it difficult. "I think it's about twice the size of Sebastian's pack," I said.

Burns hit the gas and took a sharp right, a left, and then another right. I held on to the handle above my head, grateful for it as I grit my teeth against the swaying movement of the Jeep.

"Where are we going? I thought you said the compound was on the harbour?"

"It is, but we need some space between us and this pack, so I'm coming in at a different angle. It should throw them off."

It took us another fifteen minutes to circle around to the south and drive up a small hill and onto a bluff that overlooked the Port Theatre or, more accurately, Donavan's compound.

Burns pushed his mike tight against his head, a look of concentration coming over his face, some noise that could have been a voice barely audible to me.

"Got it." He nodded his head. "Okay, we'll get set here."

He turned to me, "Mara, they're all in place. Marks will wait on the first explosion before they move in."

His mike buzzed and he pushed it into his ear and his face quickly shaded red. Slipping it off, he handed it to me and got out of the Jeep. Curious, I slipped the headset on and adjusted it.

"Hello?" I asked, wondering what was going on.

Marks' voice came through loud and clear. "Be careful Mara. If at any point you think you and Burns have been seen, get the hell out of there. Understand?"

I nodded, forgetting that he couldn't see me for a moment. "Got it. Be safe Marks."

"You too, Beautiful."

The headset clicked and I took it off, tangling it in my hair. I cursed at it, using words I reserved for the very worst days of my life. My emotions were rioting left and right and I didn't know what to make of them. I'd never loved anyone like Sebastian, never been with anyone but him. But Marks, he was handsome and strong, and he hadn't taken the drug. He was right, it would be easy to fall for him, and that was what scared me. Just how quickly it could happen.

While Burns got the equipment ready, I stared at the theatre turned compound. The base of it was solid windows, good for a theatre I suppose, but not so good when it came to protecting what was inside. I could see many of them had been shattered, leaving dark holes into the interior. I suppressed a shiver. The gaping wounds in what had once been a place of music and laughter were disturbing. I blinked and shook the feeling off. The theatre was cylindrical in shape and it was at least four, maybe five stories high, surrounded by a large fence, like the kind you'd see around a construction site.

"You ready?" I turned to see Burns looking at me expectantly. I nodded and slipped some earplugs in. Burns nodded, opened a cover on a small black box and flicked a switch.

Nothing.

Burns frowned and flicked the switch back and forth several times. Still nothing.

Oh, this was not good.

Burns started to talk and I pulled out my earplugs.

". . . Check the wiring. They must have set it wrong."

"Isn't that just a tad bit dangerous? Haven't you already flicked the switch to set them off?" I put my hands on my hips. It was ridiculous to even think about climbing down there with live explosives. We'd just have to retreat and try something else another time.

"Marks is depending on me, Mara. There are only a few boats left in the harbour and we need access to them, as well as whatever cure Donavan has cooked up," Burns said, his young face looking as if he'd aged in mere moments.

Before I could say anything else, he brushed passed me and made his way down the ivy covered cliff, using the greenery for handholds and reaching the bottom with ease. I put my knuckles to my mouth as Burns crept along the outer of the fence, checking first one small package taped to the metal, and then a second.

It was then that the first of the explosives went off.

Burns dropped to the ground, the air shattering around him, and I bit down on my knuckles, swallowing a scream.

Metal twisted and screamed in protest, the explosives doing their job effectively.

Boom after boom rattled and then shouts and gunfire erupted from behind the theatre. All the explosives had gone off and Burns still lay on the ground, unmoving.

I couldn't just leave him there.

Following the same path he had taken, I made my way to the bottom of the cliff and ran to Burns' side. Placing a hand on his back, I let out a cry of relief when I felt him breathe.

Dropping to my knees, I turned his face to me. His eyes were closed, a trickle of blood dribbled from his nose. "Come on, Burns. Get up."

"You, what are you doing?"

I spun on my haunches to face the partially blasted gates and several large guns that were pointed at me.

"Please, he's hurt. I need to get him help," I said, hoping to appeal to their compassion. I couldn't see their faces behind the scopes of the guns, but they didn't seem that interested in helping.

"Lower your guns." A man stepped out around the others. He looked to be in his mid-forties, around the same age as Vincent. My gut told me I was looking at Donavan, the scientist who'd developed Nevermore.

Donavan smiled at me then made a waving motion with his hands and his men began to pull the gates back together. "I do believe that we will not need to shoot you after all."

Wiry thin hands grabbed my arms, veined in yellow, and I screamed as the Nevermore behind me roared. I twisted hard to the left, snapping myself out of its hands.

A second Nevermore launched itself at me and I swung my foot, connecting a solid blow to its left knee, dropping it to the ground. From the edges of the harbour crept the large pack that had been dodging me and Burns on our way here. At my feet, Burns began to stir. Crap this was bad timing on his part.

"Burns!" I screamed. He didn't answer with his voice but with his gun. The Nevermores nearest me dropped as he emptied his clip. There was still nowhere for me to run. The pack pushed me up against the tall fence, and Donavan and his men were on the other side, guns in hand, waiting for me to be eaten. Burns scrambled to his feet and ran in the opposite direction, back towards the cliff, his gait unsteady but keeping him upright.

I pressed my back into the hard wire, my heart galloping as gun fire went off in the distance. I hoped that Marks made it in to the compound, but even if he did there was no way he would make it to me in time.

The pack circled around, leaping in to push, poke and pinch me. I didn't understand at first why they weren't attacking me. I was on the ground now, my legs tucked under me as the pack continued to close ranks on me.

One young female came close enough that I was able to land a solid punch, catching her jaw and knocking her backwards. The pack stilled and removed their hands from me.

"What are you doing, eh? Or more importantly, what are you?"

I didn't answer Donavan, didn't have time to think about much of anything, when what I had to assume was the Alpha of this pack pushed his way through to me. He was at least as big as Sebastian, maybe even a bit taller, and easily as well muscled. With a single swift move he hauled me to my feet and stuck his nose against my neck, breathing deeply. I tried to think back to the last time I'd showered and knew it had been since before Seraphima came into the world, however brief her stay might have been.

I held perfectly still, but as the Alpha got more aggressive with his sniffing, and that turned into licking, I struck out, hitting him the chest. "No!" I snapped at him. He dropped me with a startled look.

Gunfire suddenly roared around us and two Jeeps came flying into view with men I didn't recognize in them. My heart sunk; Marks hadn't breached the compound and his Jeeps had been hijacked—that was the only answer to what I was seeing.

The Nevermores began to fall as Donavan's men shot them; I hit the ground, covering my head, a large body landing on top of me.

Soft, warm breath tickled on the back of my neck and my knees trembled. A large, very familiar pair of hands wrapped themselves around me and circled my belly, pulling me tight against a hard body I was intimately familiar with.

"Sebastian," I breathed.

"Love too," he rumbled at me, holding me close. I have no idea where he'd come from, or why he'd stayed away so long—and at that moment I didn't care. The Jeeps went roaring by and shot through an opening in the gate that was quickly closed by the men standing guard.

Sebastian jumped up and pulled me to my feet. He wasn't fast enough. The Alpha male roared a challenge that Bastian couldn't deny and he spun, placing me behind him, as they launched at one another.

Hands grabbed me and I spun to see Buck pulling at me. I followed him, dodging the bodies and using the smoke for cover as the sound of gunfire reached my ears. A bullet whizzed by, and then a few more for good measure.

Buck dragged me along until something bit into me and I stumbled, my left leg suddenly numb, followed by a brilliant haze of pain that forced me to my knees.

I buckled when my left leg touched the ground, the world around me fuzzing over, the noises dimming, and the lights flashing, but I felt nothing but the agony of fire in my leg.

I didn't realize I was screaming until hands slapped over my mouth and a pinch in my arm competed for my attention.

"Well, well, well. Beauty loves her Beast, but will the Beast follow her into the depths of hell?" Donavan leaned over me, his grin securely back in place.

It was at that point I knew I was caught and the world around me went black, silent, as I slid into unconsciousness.

17

I floated in a strange fog between wake and sleep for some time, trying to figure out where I was and why I was here. My eyelids flickered open and I found myself staring up at a chandelier that was swaying ever so slightly.

"I'm telling you she's infected and we should keep her with the rest of the animals downstairs. It's only a matter of time before she changes, you know that." I didn't recognize the voice.

"You don't understand Clint, the pack was trying to protect her, like she's one of them but she's obviously human. This could be the breakthrough in our research if she's taken the drug and her system has overcome it. This is what could save Juliana," Donavan said.

A shuffle of feet. "I still don't think it's a good idea. Either one of those big bastards might break in to get to her."

That made me groan and, though I didn't feel strong enough to sit up, I croaked out, "Sebastian, is he okay?"

A face came into view—Donavan's—and I got an up close look at his bright blue eyes. He smiled down at me, but the smile didn't reach anything but the edge of his lips. Marks had said Donavan was crazy and, staring into his face, I believed it. Donavan's eyelids twitched as he looked down on me; his eyes flicking first one way and then the other, seemingly unable to be still.

"I don't know a Sebastian. I'm glad to see you're awake. Do you have a name?" He asked, offering me his hand to help me sit up. I didn't take it, forcing myself into a sitting position with a hiss of pain, my leg protesting the movement.

"Mara. Do I have a bullet in me?" I touched the bandage wrapped around my upper thigh.

Donavan smiled at me. "No Mara, what hit you is a type of tranquilizer dart used to drop the Nevermores at a safe distance so that they can be brought in without damage to them."

"Will the drugs hurt my baby?" I asked, my hand going to my belly, my eyes searching his face, not trusting him to tell me the truth.

He tipped his head from side to side, his fingers flicking at unseen things. "They shouldn't. We will run some blood work and perhaps do an ultrasound." He twitched and his smile tightened. I swallowed hard. I was not safe here.

I knew that part of the blood work he wanted done was to see if I'd taken Nevermore, to see if my system had the antibodies or whatever it was he was looking for, but I didn't care. "That would be good, I'm about twelve weeks along now, I think," I said, as I started to get up. "I need to go see where my husband is, he was in the pack too."

Donavan shook his head. "No. There is no contact outside the gate. Lay back down and we'll bring the ultrasound in. Perhaps you could describe your husband to me. Maybe he's in the morgue already." Donavan patted the bed beside me as if that was some comfort, but otherwise didn't touch me. Chills swept through me but I refused to buckle under the possibility that Sebastian dead.

"Sebastian is 6'4, dark hair and built like a tank. He's was the new male fighting the Alpha of the pack." I watched his eyes and recognition filtered through the madness in them. "Yes, he's still alive and quite pissed the last time I saw him, circling the compound and pounding on the gate."

"Please don't hurt him," I whispered, remembering the explosion all too vividly, the spray of bodies on the ground. "He'll listen to me; I can bring him in. Please let me go get him."

Donavan's jaw twitched. "We brought most of the pack in; we don't shoot them like Vincent's crew does."

I frowned. "Then what was that explosion, all the smoke and the bodies everywhere?"

"A canister of tear gas, a light bomb and then a spray of fast acting sedative darts. The other explosions were from Vincent's crew."

"What do you want with the pack?" I asked.

Donavan bobbed his head while he smiled and steepled his fingers, a veritable Mr. Burns. "We'll run blood work on all of them, see if there are any anomalies. It's the only way we will be able to find a better cure. The sedatives are not working on the two big males, not at all." He grimaced, then his eyes brightened and I had a very bad feeling wash through me.

"If you think he will let you draw blood off him perhaps that could change things." He lifted an eyebrow at me. "Perhaps I could let you go if you were of enough help to me."

I frowned and thought quickly. I couldn't trust Donavan, that much was certain, but what if there was a cure? Something better than what Vincent had used on Adam and Eve. It was the best I could do at this point, and I would take it for what it was worth; at least Sebastian was alive. I nodded, my eyes glued to a dark stain on the floor.

Donavan and Clint stepped out of the room and a woman came in, the first I'd seen that wasn't a Nevermore. Her name tag on her starched white nurse's uniform said, "Lucy". She wrapped my arm with a plastic band and flicked at a vein until it came to the surface. I stared up at the ceiling and the sparkly chandelier, wincing as she jabbed me with the needle.

"You didn't take Nevermore?" I asked, just wanting to speak with another woman that wasn't pumped full of the supposed miracle drug, even if she was on Donavan's side.

She frowned down at me, her face a twist of unhappiness. "I hadn't put together enough money for it when the true nature of it reared its ugly head. Pure dumb luck. You?"

"I'm allergic to scotch broom. The doctor said it would kill me if I took it. Kind of squashed my plans of getting pregnant."

Lucy stared at me, and then pulled up a chair, all the blood drawn. "But you're pregnant now? That seems beyond stupid to get knocked up at a time like this."

I gave a half laugh that nearly tumbled into a sob. "My husband took the drug when the fertility tests came back that he was the problem, not me. I didn't know he took it. We were trying but not really." I didn't care that she was being rude to me; it was just nice to have someone to talk to.

She reached around me and grabbed another empty vile that she plunked on to the end of the needle. After three more vials full she pulled the needle out of my arm and pressed a cotton ball onto the open vein.

"Hold here for at least two minutes; I'll be back to put a bandage on in a few minutes." She stood to leave, her frazzled brunette hair tied into a messy bun.

"Can I ask you a question?"

"You can ask, I'll answer you if I can." She turned at the doorway, impatience highlighted in her hand on her hip, the arch of her eyebrow. I wondered if perhaps we were the only human women left on Vancouver Island. That was a horrible thought.

"Is Donavan as bad as Vincent made him out to be?"

"I don't know how Vincent made him out to be. But genius often comes in the guise of madness. Right now we need a genius to make this mess right again, to get our people back."

"Is there a cure?" I asked. Marks had thought so. I prayed he was right.

She shook her head. "He's close to a breakthrough, but that's all I know."

Lucy left the room, the door locking behind her. My eyes closed slowly, in what I thought was a blink, and when they opened, she was back in the room puttering.

"Mara, they're bringing the ultrasound in now. Drink this." She held out a glass to me and I took it, grateful for the cool clean liquid. "Was I asleep?"

Lucy grimaced. "You slept right through the night, didn't move a muscle, not even when I put a bandage on your arm. I should know, they made me sit in here and keep a watch on you."

I swallowed hard. A lot of things could happen in one night; I should know. "Is Sebastian still acting up?"

"The big boy? Donavan's tried to talk to him, see if he can get a response out of him like you said you could."

"How's it going?" I asked, as I sat up slowly, the room spinning slightly.

She shook her head, her earrings catching the light and throwing rainbow prisms around the room. "Not as well as he'd hoped, not as bad as he thought."

"That's enough now Lucy." Donavan stepped into the room and Lucy swallowed hard, her face blanching. What was it about him that kept people here helping? It couldn't just be the cause for the greater good, could it?

Donavan sat down in front of me, his eyes twitching, muscles in his face spasming. "Your Sebastian wouldn't talk to me, but last night when I said your name he calmed right down and stopped the rioting. Fascinating, really, very unusual for the species to behave in such a manner."

"I don't know if your Sebastian made it through the night." He lifted an eyebrow, watching my reaction as one would inspect a strange insect, a morbid mixture of curiosity and revulsion.

I closed my eyes and held my breath, letting it out slowly. I would not believe that Sebastian was gone until I saw the body myself; until then I chose to believe he was alive and well. Lucy came to stand over me, a tube in her hand. "I'm going to put some gel on you and then we can take a look at the baby."

Donavan held up his hand. "No. If you want to see your baby and make sure it's alright then you must go down and bring in your pet. I want to run tests on him and the sedative darts haven't worked. If he's dead, then call in the other big male, he seemed taken with you as well."

My stomach rolled at the thought of Sebastian being dead, the possibility higher than ever before with the matched size and strength of the other male. I licked my lips and nodded slowly. "Okay."

Donavan continued to smile and nodded as if he expected nothing else. Lucy let out an audible sigh of relief and I stared at her. What was her game in this anyway?

The two of them guided me out to the front door and all but shoved me forward.

"If you can't bring him in I will have him shot. If you try to run, I will have him shot. If you think to call your friends . . ."

"I get it," I said. "You'll shoot him. No need to spell it out Einstein."

Donavan laughed as if I'd hit the punch line in a joke. "No, no. I won't shoot him for that, your friends are all dead so there will be no need to try and call them. You are quite the tart aren't you?" He laughed as he shut the door, locking it behind me.

I started out across the tiled courtyard to the front gate, limping ever so slightly, the spot where the dart had stuck me throbbing in time with my blood pumping.

"Sebastian," I called out, my voice echoing down and out over the water, the ships moored there bobbing along with the gentle roll of the waves. It was peaceful considering how short a time ago it had been a freaking war zone.

I made it all the way to the fence without any movement. I called out again and waited. Nothing. My heart began to pound. What if he'd left me here, believing me safe, believing me better off without him? I didn't think I could go through that again.

"Sebastian!" I screamed, my fear giving me more decibels than normal.

I limped up along the fence line towards the bluffs Burns and I had stood on. I kept calling for Sebastian and still there was no response. As a last resort I let out a whistle.

There was a shift in the bushes at the base of the cliffs and my hopes rose. Scout pulled himself out of the shrubs and literally crawled to the fence. I crouched down and put my hands through, touching his face. It was obvious he was hurt badly, his left leg at an odd angle and his body a mass of bruises. Through his right bicep was a gunshot wound that had crusted over.

"I'm so sorry," I whispered, emotions clogging my throat. I stood and half ran to the nearest gate. I slipped through and locked it behind me, running to Scout's side. He grimaced when I helped him to sit up, propping him against the fence. "Sebastian, where is he?"

Scout shook his head and my throat tightened. No, he wasn't dead; I couldn't believe that was what Scout was trying to tell me. He pushed himself to stand and hobbled on his broken leg towards the water. I followed, trying to decipher what it was he was trying to show me. A shot rang out and a bullet ricoched off the pavement in front of me. Scout dove for cover behind the nearest bush and I held up my hands.

Apparently I wasn't to go towards the harbour.

Another shuffle of bush and Scout scuttled away down the water line, dragging his broken leg behind him. I scrubbed my face with my hands, emotions welling up hard and fast.

As my strength began to wane I turned and called for Sebastian again. I walked slowly, favouring my leg, back to the gate. A scan of the area nearly stopped my breath. There was a hand and arm sticking out from under one of the green hedges. I ran to where the body lay and let out a gasp of relief. It was the Alpha male; the one Sebastian had been fighting. His guts were ripped out of him, spread in a semi circle where the ravens and crows had made their feast.

Was this what happened to Sebastian? Had he died alone and in pain, keening for me? A sob ripped from my throat as I turned and familiar hands grabbed my arms.

Sebastian let out a low rumble, a wild look in his eye that I ignored as I threw myself at him, great gulping sobs of relief pouring out of me.

At first he didn't respond, and then slowly he slid his arms around me and buried his nose in the crook of my neck. Moist warmth slid down my skin and dripped into my shirt, leaving a burning tingle wherever the tears roved.

I clung to him, the razor edge of fear sharp on my heart leaving me more than a little needy. I was terrified to lose him again. "Sebastian, come with me, please," I said, as I took his hand and walked to the gate. He stared at the high fence and stopped dead in his tracks. I didn't blame him, the memory of Vincent and the captivity in that camp was too fresh. But we didn't have a choice. I knew that Donavan would shoot us both if we tried to run.

I didn't know how else to explain it so I took his hand and placed it on my belly. "Please."

He closed his eyes and a tremble rippled through him. I pulled on his hand and he stepped forward with me, slowly, but moving. A scuffle to our right snapped us both into high alert. It was Buck and he was watching us go inside the fence with a look of disbelief. Sebastian grunted at him and flung his hand as if tossing Buck something. Buck nodded and slipped back down the slope towards the water.

"You just made him Alpha, didn't you?" Sebastian nodded once and then touched my cheek with his hand. He had given up his leadership over a second pack to be with me, his love overriding the animal drive to be Alpha.

My eyes filled and we walked into Donavan's compound together, holding hands, ready to face whatever would come our way.

18

"I hope you're sure of this Donavan, bringing a Nevermore in here un-sedated," Lucy whispered to herself, as Sebastian and I walked past her. He glared at her but otherwise didn't make a single move in her direction. I clung to his hand, fear bubbling up in my throat. I had no illusions about what would happen to Sebastian if he went after one of the other people in this compound.

I headed back to the room that held the ultrasound machine and Donavan was still there. He didn't look up when we came in.

"No doubt your Sebastian wasn't as malleable as you'd hoped. Mara, it isn't your fault, my wife Juliana is the love of my life and she attacks the cage whenever I come ne . . ." His words stuttered to a stop as he lifted his eyes and saw us standing hand in hand in the doorway.

"This is Sebastian," I said, and smiled up at my scowling husband. I squeezed his hand. "Sebastian, this is Donavan; he's a son of a bitch, but may have a cure for Nevermore."

Sebastian's eyes narrowed, then he looked down at me and the wildness ebbed. He lowered his head and pressed it against mine.

Donavan cleared his throat, his smile gone, his eyes narrowed. "Ultrasound first then, as I am a man of my word, I will draw blood off the male." His voice was colder than it had been, even for him, and there was a sharp edge to it now.

I didn't let go of Sebastian, and he helped me on to the table. A few moments later Lucy came in, slightly pale, but still doing as Donavan wanted.

She said nothing and the silence was heavy and full of fear, the air around us seeming to thicken, clogging my throat.

The gel was cold and I sucked in a lungful of air. At Sebastian's concerned look I smiled, "Just cold."

He nodded, and then Lucy swirled the ultrasound on my little bump and a picture came up on the screen.

"There's the head," she said, and shifted the position. "And there's the heart."

A staccato not unlike the thrum of hummingbird wings came rushing over the ultrasound and I held my breath. Sebastian stared at the screen then looked at my belly and back again. Emotions filled me up and started to spill over. "That's our baby," I said.

"Love too," Sebastian strangled out, the words rough but I knew. "Love too," I whispered back.

Donavan stood, a strangled look on his face, and left the room, slamming the door behind him. Sebastian leapt to his feet, a growl on his lips at the sudden noise. I took his hand and pulled him gently back down to sit beside me. "It's okay Bastian. Just stay with me love."

He settled back down and Lucy blanched as she stared at me. "He really does love you doesn't he?"

I smiled back. "Yes, more than I ever imagined." I paused, took a breath, and asked a question that had been burning in the back of my mind. "Donavan is trying to bring his wife back, isn't he?"

Lucy stopped what she was doing and looked at me, finally giving me a slow nod. "Juliana is the whole reason he's doing this. They were married for nearly twenty years, childhood sweethearts. But she doesn't remember him at all. Just like the rest of them don't remember their family. It's why I'm here. To help him find the cure." There was more than sorrow in her voice; bitterness lay heavy on her words as she all but glared at me and Sebastian.

"Seeing me and Sebastian together hurts you, doesn't it?" I asked, my voice soft. Again she nodded. I closed my eyes and imagined what it would have been like if Bastian had forgotten me and stayed with Jessica. The pain at the mere thought was instantaneous and overwhelming. I understood why people resented us.

Lucy went back to the ultrasound and slid it across my belly. She stopped over a section that I thought might be the baby's tummy, but was hard for me to tell with the slight movement that continued through the whole session.

"Hmm," Lucy's eyes narrowed, and she slid the reader piece to the left.

"What? Is something wrong?" My heart started to speed up at the concern on Lucy's face. Sebastian picked up on my anxiety and started to stand, his face tight with worry.

"I don't know Mara. The baby is healthy, but I'm just not sure. I have to get Donavan back in here, I don't use this enough." She put the ultrasound down and left the room; I started to shake. Not again, I couldn't go through losing another baby. Please God, don't let this happen to us again.

I covered my face with my hands and Sebastian leaned over me, cradling my head to his chest, hiding me while I sobbed. I tried to pull myself together. When Bastian let out a low growl I knew that Donavan had come back in and I managed to stop the tears and hiccup back the last gulping sob that threatened to pop out of me.

"I'm sure it's nothing," he said, smiling at me and placing the ultrasound back on my belly. I grimaced as his fingertips brushed across my skin here and there. I was not comforted by him in the least.

He moved the ultrasound first to the left and then to the right and back again, his grin never slipping.

"What's wrong with the baby?" I asked, my anxiety getting the better of me.

Donavan turned the machine off and Lucy wiped my belly with a cloth. "The baby seems to have some deformities. It isn't apparent what exactly the final result will be, but I have no doubt they are a result of the Nevermore drug. You did conceive this child after Sebastian took the shot?"

I nodded, my heart numbing to what he was saying. I licked my lips, trying to work up the spit to ask the question. "But the baby is okay? I'm not going to lose the baby?"

Donavan shook his head slowly. "I don't think so. But it looks as if it has extra limbs. At least one extra arm for sure. Something I've seen on a few of the Nevermores. It's rare but does happen."

I let out a sigh and leaned back on the table. Sebastian stared from me to Donavan and back again. "It's okay, the baby is going to be okay." I had to trust in that, had to believe that I wouldn't lose this child, or my husband.

Donavan left the room and Sebastian and I were alone. He bent, laid his ear on my tummy and I put my hand on his head, running my fingers through his dark hair.

Moments later Lucy came in, needle and vial in her hand. "I need to draw blood and then I'll take you to your . . . room."

I got Sebastian to sit down and Lucy was able to draw blood quickly from him. He didn't even flinch when she had to jab the needle in. I glared at her and she staved off my words with a wave of her hand. "Their skin is thick like hide, there has to be some force or the needle won't go in, so no need to give me the stink eye girl."

I grit my teeth and contented myself with stroking Sebastian's other hand, tracing the veins and patterns under his skin.

"There," Lucy clapped her hands, making both me and Bastian jump. "We're all done."

I stood and she waved for us to follow her. I took Sebastian's hand, gripping it tight, as if by sheer force I could keep him here with me. I was deathly afraid to be separated from him and, even if it meant I would be caged like an animal, I didn't care.

Lucy led us upstairs, which surprised me. The theatre still had much of the local and native artwork up on the walls, but it didn't hide the fact that the theatre was utilitarian in looks. Everything was cement. Walls, floor, ceiling. Maybe it was for acoustics or maybe just a cost issue, but either way it was far from pretty. We stopped on the third level and took a door down a long hallway. It opened up into the Coast Bastion

Hotel and from there Lucy took us to a nice, clean room on the first floor.

"Don't know why you get this room, but here it is. The water works but don't expect it to be hot." We stepped inside and she shut the door, locking it behind her.

Alone with Sebastian, I stripped out of my clothes and walked to the bathroom. I didn't care if the water was cold; I just wanted to be clean. I think it had been nearly a week since my last bath in the bunker.

I cranked the water on, fully intending to have a bath. I could pretend I was camping at the lake or something.

As the tub filled I peeked back into the main room to see Sebastian sitting on the floor, his back against the wall so he could stare at the bedroom door. His breathing was rapid, his chest rising and falling so fast I thought for a moment he might be having a heart attack.

"Bastian?" I ran to his side and dropped to my knees. His arms circled me and he held on to me as he gulped down great gasps of air. It took me a moment to realize that he was crying, sobbing so hard he could barely get air in to breath past the emotions.

I closed my eyes and held him, instinctively knowing the reason. Somehow, despite the fact that what Donavan had said was beyond simple instructions or words, Sebastian understood that something was wrong with the baby. That the deformation the child now had was because Sebastian took the Nevermore shot.

"Babe," I took his face in my hands, stared into his yellow eyes, and stroked my fingers across the skin that was becoming as familiar to me as its human counterpart. "It doesn't matter. The baby will be alive and will be with us. And we will love him no matter how he looks."

Tears streamed from his eyes as his chest continued to heave and he shook his head, hiccupping hard enough to shake his body. I fought the tears that wanted to join him, he needed me to be strong for him and I could do that much at least. He'd given up so much for me, fought so hard, the least I could do was be his rock now.

19

"Babe," I whispered. It was the third morning of our stay in the compound. Sebastian grunted and rolled over in his sleep, giving me his back. I traced the yellow lines that made up the shadowy tattoos, the tingle in my fingertips not solely from the scotch broom he carried. I followed the lines down to his hips, swirling my finger over each whirl. Donavan had Lucy take blood from both of us every day, morning and night. I don't know if it was helping his research, but for the moment we were useful to him and that kept us alive.

Sebastian grunted and scooted away from me. I slapped him hard on the hip, snapping him awake. He rolled over and frowned at me; I glared at him.

"I'm allowed to touch you."

His frown deepened and he got out of bed.

"I mean it Sebastian."

Ignoring me he walked to the window and stared out, the view over the harbour something he would watch for hours on end, hardly moving a muscle. I got up and went to stand beside him, to see what it was he was looking at.

What was left of the pack milled about, scavenging for food amongst the docks, staying far from the water. They screamed if even a single small wave splashed against them, which I thought was strange, but was the least of my worries.

I swallowed hard. "Do you miss them?" Sebastian shook his head, then nodded and shrugged his shoulders. I wondered what it was like for him, living between the two worlds, not really human, not really a Nevermore. I had a feeling that if it took much longer for the cure I would lose him, the pull of his instincts strengthening every day. The call of the pack and the wildness in him was more than apparent as it battled against the love he held on to for me.

I slipped on my clothes and banged on the bedroom door till Lucy came and opened it. Her bedroom was two doors down from ours, so she could keep an eye on us. "What is it?" She asked, her hair dishevelled and her eyes at half mast.

"I need to speak to Donavan," I said, as I pushed my way past her and ran down, through the long hallway and down the three flights of stairs.

The basement was where the lab had been set up. It was easy to find, even though I'd never been there. Despite the early hour, Donavan was already up tinkering away at his tests.

I began to pace the room. "He's slipping further away Donavan. I don't want to wait to see him completely transformed. How soon before you have something ready?"

Donavan smiled, tucked his hands behind him, and paced a small circle around me. "Do you think you're the only one who's lost a loved one to Nevermore?" He snapped at me, his grin never slipping, though his tone was far from congenial.

I flushed. "Of course not."

"Then what the hell makes you think I would go to the ends of the earth for your precious Sebastian? I'm doing this for Juliana, to bring her back to me. If the antibodies he carries can help me find a cure, then he is valuable to me, and only then," he snapped.

He walked up to me, his face twisted with the jealousy and frustration that must have been simmering for the entire time we'd been here. "The only reason you and Sebastian are being treated as well as you are is that you are my only hope for some sort of breakthrough. If Sebastian is slipping away then he is no more use to me than any of the other Nevermores."

"What are you saying?" I asked, a whisper of foreboding passing over me.

"If Sebastian is not the link I need to find the cure, then I'll dispose of him as I have all the other Nevermores. We don't feed the monsters, Mara."

"You feed Juliana," I said, though in fact I didn't know that, I'd never seen his wife.

"She's different."

"So is Sebastian."

We stared at each other, only a foot between us. I wouldn't back down; I owed it to Bastian to fight for him.

"We'll draw more blood today and see if the cell count is different. Perhaps he's not changing at all; perhaps he's just giving up on being human," Donavan said, as he turned and slipped on a lab coat and safety glasses, ending our conversation.

I ran back up to our bedroom; Lucy was waiting to see me in. She pointed and I went in to find Sebastian pacing. God, if I could only know what he was thinking! I shut the door behind me and leaned against it, as Lucy locked it once more. Sebastian stopped his movement and stared at me, his bare chest rising and falling evenly with each breath. I couldn't lift my eyes to him so I stared at the hollow of his throat. If Sebastian didn't hold the key to the cure, Donavan would kill him and I couldn't let that happen.

"Sebastian," I whispered. "We have to go; we have to find a way to escape."

He walked over to me and put a hand on either side of the door, effectively caging me with his body. He let out a low growl and placed his lips on the side of my neck, nipping at the skin lightly, and then, bringing his hands in to touch my shoulders, he ran them down to my fingertips. Pressing his body against mine he put his lips to my ear.

"Love."

I couldn't hold the tears back and I wrapped my arms around his neck, clinging to him. I wouldn't lose him, not when we'd both fought so hard to be together.

We tumbled backwards into the bed, clothes disappearing in a rush of desperation to touch one another. For a moment the intimacy pushed the fear back, leaving only a blazing fire of love and desire to scare away the dark that was coming.

I lay in his arms, body tingling, heart racing, and I knew what I had to do.

Lucy was my only hope. I'd seen how she stared at Donavan, her eyes soft and full of emotion. Maybe she could convince him to change his mind, to help me keep Sebastian safe.

"I need to speak to Lucy," I whispered into his ear, kissing the edge. He reached up and stroked my face, his other hand pressed against my breast, distracting me. Most effectively. I smiled, and then moaned as he began to work my body over, his gaze never leaving mine. "Sebastian, I have to . . ."

I gave up and surrendered to his touch, the whisper of his lips on mine, the brush of skin tingling with passion.

When I was finally able to untangle myself from Sebastian the sun was high and I had the beginnings of a plan. Body still humming with Sebastian's caresses, I banged on the door until it opened. "What now?" Lucy grumbled.

"Can I talk to you?" I asked.

"We are talking. You look a little flushed," she said, her eyes roving over my reddened skin, reactions to Sebastian's touch and saliva breaking out all over my body. Ah, what I wouldn't give for a dose of Benadryl.

"Yeah, I'm okay," I cleared my throat. "I need to talk to you about Donavan."

Lucy blinked and her eyes widened. "Why?"

"He's going to kill Sebastian if the key to the cure isn't in the next round of blood work."

Lucy stepped back to let me through. "I'm not surprised, it's what he does."

I fell into step beside her as we walked down the circular hallway. "I know, but I made the mistake of saying that I was worried about Sebastian slipping. It was a moment I can't take back, even though it isn't true."

Lucy shook her head, messy bun bobbing slightly. "What do you want me to do about it?"

I took a deep breath. "I know how you feel about Donavan; I see it in your eyes. Keep him distracted while we try to get away."

She flushed, her face going bright pink; then she let out a strangled laugh. "You think I haven't been trying honey?

There was only one time and he was plastered. It was right after Juliana tried to kill him. Donavan's as devoted to her as you are to Sebastian. You think someone could seduce you away from your man?"

I thought of Marks and slowly shook my head. "No. I suppose you're right."

I stopped and rubbed my face, burying my hands into my hair. What the hell were we going to do?

"I didn't say I wouldn't help you. I just don't think I can seduce him. Here," she handed me a key. "This will get you outside, but from there you're on your own."

I tucked the key into my jeans pocket. "I don't know when, but we'll leave as quickly as we can; I don't want to test Donavan's patience, or his sanity."

I walked back upstairs to our room to find it empty, the door wide open. My heart pounding, I searched the room. There was no way Sebastian could have opened the door, he didn't have the motor skills.

Donavan.

I turned and ran back down the stairs, scrambling at each landing to pick up speed. As I reached the bottom floor I could hear raised voices, and then a roar of anger from Sebastian.

"Please, please, please," I whispered under my breath, not entirely sure if I was pleading for more speed or to make it to the lab before Donavan did anything crazy.

The door to the lab was open and I ran through, skidding to a halt at the scene before me. Sebastian was strapped to a metal table, an IV hooked up to his left arm.

Donavan stepped out from behind a several IV's. "Ah Mara. I thought about what you'd said and decided that the next batch of remedy I whipped up would be perfect to try

258

out on Sebastian. Then you can't say you didn't try to save him."

"No," I gasped. Stumbling to the metal table, I reached for the IV.

"I wouldn't do that. A half dose would turn him into a vegetable for sure. A full dose is the only chance he's got."

I lowered my hand and placed it on Sebastian's chest. His eyelids flickered, the iris' wobbling, and I swallowed hard on the bile rose in my throat.

Donavan stepped up and put his hands on the table. "It will take a week to ten days for the full effects to be known. Then we can decide whether to put him out of his misery, or of course, if he comes around we will administer the same treatment to the others."

"You mean Juliana."

"One of which will be Juliana," he nodded, and I felt something inside me snap, a cruel streak I hadn't known existed until that moment rearing its ugly, vicious head.

"She'll never come around. She didn't love you enough to hang on, that's the reality, and you're just prolonging her agony and yours by believing you can still be together."

Donavan slammed his hands on the edge of Sebastian's table, his face a storm cloud of fury barely contained. I glared back at him, not backing down for an instant.

"You've doomed him to be nothing more than a shell of a man," I hissed. "Don't expect me to play nice anymore. Maybe instead of Juliana coming back, you should take the Nevermore shot and go to her."

Donavan's eyes widened then narrowed. "You know nothing Mara; you're a desperate, foolish little girl who thinks love can conquer all. It can't. I should know."

He turned to walk out of the room, but I stopped him with a single phrase, something I remembered from a silly little calendar. "Love is something eternal; the aspect may change, but not the essence."

Donavan paused, but didn't look back. "You know nothing."

I didn't answer him, only pressed my hands to Sebastian's slowly rising and falling chest, praying that the remedy would work.

Donavan left, flicking the overhead lights off and plunging Sebastian and me into a semi-darkness, lit only by beeping machines, the silence filled by the steady drip of the IV.

I whispered into that gray light, holding onto my husband for all that I was worth.

"Come back to me Sebastian, my love, my heart. Come back to me."

PART III

DAUNTLESS

Love makes everything that is heavy light.
— *Thomas P Kempis, German Monk*

1

Belief in that which you cannot see, touch, taste or smell is called faith by some and foolishness by others. I don't know which I would say is more painful, to have faith and trust in an impossibility or to succumb to the reality of the world and let a dream die.

I wanted to believe that Sebastian was becoming human once more; I wanted to believe that the "cure" Donavan forced on him would do what it should and bring him back to me. But the trembling muscles under my hands and the flickering eyelids that gave me only brief glimpses into yellowed irises stole what hope I had. Three days Sebastian had lain on the gurney, his every move monitored—as was mine.

"I don't know why you even bother to stay here," Lucy said on one of her hourly checks on us.

"I can't leave him, besides, it's not like I can just walk out of the compound. I'd be shot, you know that." I didn't bother to look up, just sat in my chair and continued to watch Bastian for any sign of movement other than the muscle tremors. The scent of antiseptic and sickness hung heavy in the air, clinging to the back of my throat.

"Listen," she paused and took a deep breath; I finally looked up at her. She gave me a weak smile. "You aren't safe here. Donavan's losing his mind and it's going faster every day."

Lucy bent down to me, her face full of concern. "The rest of us are going to make a run for it and if you're still here, you'll take the brunt of his anger."

"Why are you telling me this?" I asked. Lucy was one of Donavan's supporters; she believed in him and his work.

The door creaked and Donavan strode in. "Lucy. Out," he snapped.

Lucy left the room, her face pale and her eyes wide. Behind Donavan's back she mouthed something to me. I couldn't be sure, but I think it was Vancouver. My eyebrows crunched up. Why would she mouth the name of a city to me?

"I see Sebastian is still unconscious," Donavan said.

"Well done Captain Obvious," I said. "Perhaps you'd like to point out that I'm awake?"

Donavan stared at me, his eyes empty of emotion. That blank expression was almost worse than if he had gotten angry. I swallowed hard but refused to lower my eyes.

"Sebastian doesn't seem to be improving. It looks as if I will be back to the drawing board tomorrow." He flicked his finger against Sebastian's cheek. "By tonight I'll have to have him removed," Donavan said.

"What do you mean remove him? He's sick, it's your fault. You can't move him right now," I said, standing up and putting myself between Donavan and Bastian.

"I didn't say I'd move him somewhere else. I said I'd have him removed. Those are two very different statements," Donavan said.

My skin twitched over my back as what Donavan was saying sunk in. He didn't believe that Sebastian was improving. I struggled for my next breath of air as the muscles in my body constricted, my hope shrivelling up. Where would that leave him—a vegetable? Or would he just go back to being a Nevermore? If I had to choose, I'd take him being a Nevermore, but it wouldn't be my choice. Sebastian gave a shudder, his body trembling with the "cure" that coursed through his veins. I placed my hand over his, gripping his fingers.

The rest of Donavan's words sunk into my mind. Donavan had every intention of having Sebastian removed tonight. Killed. Eliminated.

No, I couldn't let that happen. Sebastian and I'd come too far, worked too hard to have this maniacal, twisted individual end our journey together. Without thinking I swung my fist at Donavan, catching him by surprise. His head snapped back in a perfect arc and his teeth gave a loud crack as they snapped together.

Those unblinking eyes rolled back in his head and he dropped to the floor, his head hitting a side cart on the way down. Blood burst out of the wound, just above his right temple, and quickly covered the floor.

I stared at the unconscious man at my feet and then rubbed the knuckles of the hand I'd hit him with. I really hadn't expected that to go as well as it had. Now what? I rubbed my knuckle again, and then rubbed at my eyes. I was exhausted and wasn't thinking straight.

The door opened and Lucy stepped in. "Donavan, I was . . ." She trailed off at the sight of the body and blood on the floor.

"I hit him harder than I thought and he hit his head on the table on his way down…" I rushed the words out.

"Either way, let's get him secured," she said, bending down and picking Donavan up by the arms. "Help me get him on to the other gurney."

I stood there just looking at her until she snapped at me. "He's going to wake up soon, help me Mara."

I made myself move and did as she asked, picking up Donavan's feet. We hauled him to the second gurney, breathing hard as we lifted him onto it awkwardly. He let out a low groan and lifted his hand to his face as we plunked him onto the table.

With a speed that surprised me, Lucy went to work securing Donavan to the gurney using the crazy straps. By the time he started to fully come around he was completely secured to the flat, steel gurney.

"Just lay there Donavan and everything will be fine," Lucy said, her voice the perfect, calm voice you'd expect out of a nurse.

I stepped away, putting distance between myself and the crazy man I'd just laid out. I didn't think he was going to be that happy with me and Lucy. I was right.

As he came to scream after scream ripped out of his mouth. We focused on the noise, trying to get a gag into his mouth. What we should have been noticing was how he worked his hand into his pocket and pulled out a small remote. But like any good magician, he distracted us with his theatrics, leaving us gasping when the first boom sounded outside the theatre walls. The world swayed, the structure above us groaned and I crouched beside Sebastian's gurney. I stared at Lucy over Donavan's body and she pointed to the remote in his hand. I made a grab for it, snatching it just as his finger depressed another button.

Another boom and Lucy gripped the edge of the gurney. "He just unlocked the cells."

"What?" I was afraid I knew the answer, but I needed to be sure.

"Where he kept all the test subjects, all the Nevermores. He threatened us with releasing them all the time."

A piece of the puzzle slipped into place. Crap. That was why they all stayed. Fear of having a horde of Nevermores unleashed on them.

Equipment beeped and buzzed, flickered and went out, plunging us into complete darkness. I gripped Sebastian's hand and was surprised when he squeezed back.

"Sebastian?" I whispered. He let out a groan, and Lucy let out a squeak.

"The sedative wears off quick. We need to get out of here," Lucy said, and her fingers found my arm and started to pull.

"No!" I snapped as another boom sounded and the world around us swayed once more.

"You don't know that he'll recognize you, the cure could have wiped his memory or even made him more aggressive!" Apparently, I hadn't been informed of all the possible side effects. Great, just freaking great. What was going to happen to him? Would this "cure" allow him any of himself back or would he . . . I shook off the negative thoughts. I didn't have time to dwell on them; I had to get us out of here.

The only sound for a brief moment was tinkling glass and equipment tumbling to the floor; then the squeak of the gurney as Sebastian shifted his weight.

"Fine, stay here with your monster then," Lucy yelled, as she let go of my arm and shuffled her way to the door. I held perfectly still, the darkness covering Sebastian's every move though his breathing was loud and laboured. A rumble of falling cement echoed through the basement and something smashed against the door. That did not bode well for us.

A more distant boom and I put my hand out to steady myself. My fingertips brushed against a hard belly and smooth skin. He grunted and his hand covered mine, squeezing it painfully.

"Sebastian, not so hard," I said.

The squeezing intensified and I yelped; tried to pull my hand out of his, fear escalating quickly. He was huge, way stronger than me, and full of a drug that made him animalistic at best. Did it matter that I loved him if he tried to hurt me? I yanked my hand hard and he followed, not letting go; he stumbled on something and crashed into me. Unable to see or even begin to brace our fall, we rolled in midair and I ended up on top of him.

He let out a moan and released my hand. I slid off him and felt my way to the door, hoping to get us both out of here in one piece—though our odds weren't looking good at the moment. The handle turned easily but the door was stuck on something. I put my shoulder against it and shoved hard, opening the door a very small fraction. I let out a breath and the world shook around us again. We had to get out of here. We were on the bottom floor of a very large building. There would be no rescue crew if the place collapsed on top of us.

Again, I put my shoulder to the door and threw my weight against it. The door creaked, the wood giving before whatever it was stuck on would move. The darkness was starting to feel claustrophobic, the idea of being buried alive singing through my brain like an unwanted theme as I struggled to keep myself under control.

Slowing my breathing down, I leaned my head against the door. There had to be a better way; I couldn't keep throwing my body against the door.

"Mara?"

My head snapped up at the sound of Marks' voice. He hadn't been killed!

"Here!" I yelled, "We're here!"

More voices and now the shuffling of feet and large objects were right outside the door. A beam of light filtered through the crack and Sebastian grumbled something unintelligible.

"Mara, we have to move some debris, but we'll have you out of there in no time," Marks said through the doorway.

"Okay." I paused, feeling the need to say something more, but somehow feeling disloyal to Sebastian if I voiced the words. I swallowed hard.

"Marks."

"Here, I'm here," he said, his voice muffled.

I put my hand on the door, my heart breaking a little. "Thank you, for coming to find me."

He chuckled. "You didn't think I'd leave you in the compound did you?"

I shook my head, forgetting for a moment that he couldn't see me. The fact of the matter was, I didn't think any of the boys were alive. I'd believed that Sebastian and I were on our own again.

Thank God I was wrong.

2

The boom of explosions continued the entire time that Marks and his boys extricated me and Sebastian from the lower level of the compound. I managed to get Sebastian out the door without the men having to come in, then turned my back, shut the door and walked away, knowing that I was sentencing Donavan to death. But I couldn't find it in me to care, not when he'd been ready to kill Sebastian with far too little reason. I didn't tell them that Donavan was still inside the medical room.

Sunlight streamed in through the frames where windows had once circled the theatre-turned-compound. Shattered glass lay strewn everywhere and the smell of sulphur and burning wood filled the air.

"A transmission came through on the radio," Marks said. "The government has set up rendezvous points to fly out survivors. The Vancouver Airport is a sanctioned area that is set up for testing people as they come through. We just have to get there." I stumbled to a stop, disbelief making my feet clumsy and my already pounding heart stutter. I grabbed

Marks' arm. He glanced down at me and nodded. I couldn't even pull the words out of my mind. There was a place that we could go . . . that we could be safe. My mind tried to wrap itself around the concept of safety, but it was a hard task; I quickly gave up and focused back on the here and now.

He paused and checked around a corner before waving the rest of us forward. I glanced back to see Sebastian unmoving on the gurney, a man on either side pushing it along. It hadn't been much of a fight to convince the boys he had to come; they'd seen me fight for Sebastian already and knew I wouldn't be dissuaded.

Marks tapped me on the shoulder to get my attention. "Listen, Mara, I'm going to put you, Burns and Sebastian into the Jeep and send you up island. We need a boat, something that can get us across the strait safely."

I frowned and shook my head. "What about the harbour, wasn't it was full of boats?"

Marks gave me a pointed look and the sound of the explosions rippling through the building suddenly made horrible sense.

"He knew, knew it would be our only way off the island," I whispered.

Marks lifted an eyebrow at me. "Donavan?"

I nodded.

He shrugged, re adjusting his rifle strap across his shoulder. "Once a few boats blew up and some caught fire the rest followed, the oil and gas setting the whole harbour ablaze."

We started to walk again, making our way through the debris to the far side of the theatre, avoiding the worst of the rubble. I stumbled over a piece of rebar and Marks caught my arm, helping me get my balance back. He stared into my eyes, continuing to hold onto my arm too long for my comfort, the intensity behind his gaze anything but neutral.

"What happened here then?" I said, wanting to divert his thoughts back to the business at hand. I didn't want to encourage him in a romantic way, had never wanting his feelings for me to spill over in that direction.

"We hit the compound as soon as we saw the harbour start exploding, but most everyone had already scattered. No sign of Donavan either," he said. I said nothing as to the whereabouts of the man who'd run this compound.

As we rounded the corner I saw the Jeep, Burns already waiting for us with a grin on his face. I smiled and waved, feeling a small ember of hope start deep inside of me. Maybe we could get out of here okay after all.

"Where are all the Nevermores?" I asked, suddenly acutely aware that we hadn't been mobbed once.

"The explosions are drawing them like moths to a flame. It will give us a window to get the three of you out," he said, his hand brushing my arm yet again, his fingers hot against my skin. Before I could pull away he dropped his hand.

"Okay boys, we need to lift Sebastian into the back of the Jeep." Marks said already two steps ahead of me.

It took three of them to lift Sebastian; not only was he tall, he was a solid mass of muscle. They got him in to the Jeep, laying him across the back seat, his legs scrunched up. Other than his initial rousing from the sedative, he had given us no trouble.

Marks started to bark orders and the men ran in all different directions. Then he turned back to me. "We have to find Donavan," he said.

I shook my head. "No, you don't have to Marks. You can leave this place and he'll die or the Nevermores will find him. Either way he's done." No one needed to go back into the compound. I knew for a fact Donavan wasn't going to make it out.

Marks directed me into the passenger seat and I let him guide me.

"You're probably right Mara. But I can't take the chance he'll slip through my fingers. Not when he's so close. There's also the possibility of a cure. We don't have a lot of time, so we'll do a sweep and clear out the compound. One way or the other we'll find Donovan and whatever he's cooked up." He pointed a finger at Burns and then me. "You keep her safe." Burns nodded and gave a salute, his eyes solemn.

Marks bent and kissed me on the cheek and I put a hand out to stop him.

"There is no cure, Marks. Donavan said so this morning. The last batch of whatever he used on Sebastian is a failure. He was going to be killed tonight." Marks' face fell and he nodded once, his mouth turning into a thin hard line. I had no doubt that he would still look for Donavan; there was no point in trying to stop him. Without another word, Marks turned on his heel and jogged back around the compound. I put my hand to where his lips had brushed my skin and willed my heart to settle back down. I wasn't encouraging him, but I wasn't discouraging him either. Guilt made me flush. Though I'd done nothing wrong, for a moment I'd not thought about Sebastian or that fact that he was still my husband; I was still married. That scared me as much as the thought of losing Sebastian.

Burns started the Jeep and we sped out of the downtown area, dodging stalled and abandoned vehicles with ease. I held on to the edges of my seat, my mind whirling with what if's, now that I had nothing else to do but think. What if Sebastian didn't come out of this? What if Marks didn't come back? What if we couldn't find a boat?

I reached back for Sebastian, needing to touch him, to feel his heartbeat under my skin, wishing he could comfort me. I had no illusions about what was coming. Whatever Donavan had given Bastian would be the end of him one way or the other. There were two possibilities, either he would end up a drooling shell of a man with not even as much personality as the Nevermores had or . . . I pinched my eyes shut and swallowed hard.

"Will he survive do you think?" Burns asked me, breaking the silence. I let out a shaky breath.

"I don't know. That's what scares me the most, Burns. All along I thought we'd make it, somehow, but now..." I ran my fingers through my hair, the heat from Sebastian's skin making my own skin feel unnaturally hot. "Now, I just don't know. He's so sick, his fever is so high. I don't know." I was repeating myself, but there was nothing else to say. I didn't want to give in to the hopelessness that was welling up within me. If I let it loose, I would never be able to hide it away again. And for the sake of our child, I needed to be strong, to fight my way through this.

Again, I reached back to brush my fingers against Sebastian's skin, in spite of the way it seemed to scorch my finger tips with the heat that radiated off him.

"Do you love him?" I spun in my seat to see Sebastian sitting up, his eyes unfocused and still yellow, but the iris was almost normal, nearly round again.

"Sebastian!" I yelped, my fingers brushing his jaw as his eyes rolled back into his head and he slumped into the seat, unconscious again. "Stop the Jeep Burns!"

Burns slammed on the brakes, the jeep sliding sideways and shuddering to a stop. I turned towards Burns, my own eyes feeling as if they might fall out of my head.

"The cure. Donavan might have actually given him the cure," I whispered. "We have to go back for it. I know there were more vials, all marked the same as the one Donavan gave Sebastian."

"Marks told us to leave, we can't go back. If we go back with the Jeep, I don't think we'll have enough fuel to get to the rendezvous point."

I shook my head. "This changes everything, what if Sebastian has been given the cure? We need to have the other vials, to be able to give them to the doctors, the real ones, when we get to safety." I said it all as if it was to be, as if we were all going to make it.

"Okay, you stay here." Burn's got out of the Jeep, his back to the road. "I'll go back on foot, catch up with Marks and be back here in no time." Shutting the door he leaned in through the Jeep's window. "If I don't get back to you, if something goes wrong, the rendezvous point is…" Burns never got to finish his sentence. He'd committed the cardinal sin when it came to the Nevermores. He turned his back on them.

3

Burns was seized from behind, yellowed hands grabbing him all over. In a split second, before I could even reach for him, he was snatched from the side of the Jeep and hauled away, the gurgle of blood overwhelming his screams.

The pack barely dragged his body ten feet away before they started to feast. The only thing I could be thankful for was that he was dead before they ripped at his flesh, his neck severed by bites. I swallowed down tears, hiccupped back a sob and very slowly leaned forward to pull the Jeep's door shut, doing my best to not draw their attention to us.

I crawled into the back seat, scrunching myself between the passenger's seat and Sebastian, laying my head against his chest. His heartbeat was erratic, thumping at an elevated rate then going silent for nearly a minute before picking up speed again. Tears slipped down my cheeks and onto his bare chest. I wanted to curl up in a safe, warm place where I could sleep for days and wake knowing that there was nothing wrong with the world.

His big hand lifted up and he placed it on my head. I stared up into his face, his eyes at half mast. "No tears," he rumbled, then closed his eyes and slid back into unconsciousness.

I hiccupped back another sob and the tears slipped down my cheeks faster.

I lay there with Sebastian, my heart heavy and my mind frozen. I didn't know what to do. Did I go back for the cure, or hope that Marks found it? Of course he wouldn't know what it was, or which bottle to take. This could literally be what the world was waiting for and I didn't think I had it in me to just walk away. Finally, somewhere between waking and dreaming, I made my decision.

Sliding back into the front, I shimmied into the driver's seat, my eyes scanning the area. There was some movement on the edge of the brush, but nothing else. I clipped on my seatbelt and reached for the walkie talkie.

I flicked the dial on and scrolled through the channels until I heard a voice. It sounded like Marks.

"Marks, it's Mara. Burns is dead. I was wrong. The cure, there might be one," I said, huddling over the speaker, try-ing to muffle the noise. The pack was still eating but, after a quick glance that turned my stomach, I could see that there wasn't much left of Burns to keep them occupied.

His voice was scratchy as it came through. "Mara . . . bunker cleared out . . . wait for me . . . explosions are worse . . ." Marks voice faded in and out and I cursed. I tried to adjust the dial, turning it ever so slightly counter clockwise.

The walkie talkie squawked, letting out a screech that lifted the hairs on the back of my neck. One glance out the side window confirmed what I already knew. I wasn't the only one who'd heard it.

The local pack rushed the Jeep and I fumbled the keys, dropping them on the floor. I bent, my seatbelt stopping me from reaching the keys over my ever expanding baby belly.

"Son of a bitch," I snapped, unbuckling myself as the Jeep rocked, the pack pushing it as they screamed out their hunger.

My hand grabbed the keys and a handful of dirt from the floor, and I sat back up, doing my best to ignore the open mouths and scratching nails on the metal. Heart pounding, I focused on getting the keys in the ignition and starting the Jeep. Again, the vehicle rocked hard and I held my breath as we teetered on two tires for a split second. Miracle of miracles, the Jeep dropped back down on the ground.

I turned the key and the Jeep fired up. Slamming it into reverse, I hit the gas pedal and cranked the wheel hard. The frame shuddered as we spun into the pack, thumps and screams of pain filling the air. I bit down on the remorse that tried to surface. They'd eaten Burns, torn him apart, and they'd do the same to me.

I threw the gears into first, shifting as we picked up speed; the Jeep lurched each time—I was out of practice driving a manual, but we quickly left the pack behind. A groan from came the back seat and I checked the rear-view mirror. Sebastian was twitching, his body shivering and jerking as if he were some strange marionette. I swallowed, my heart beating so hard I could feel it against the walls of my chest.

"Please let him be cured. Please let him be cured..." Became my mantra as I drove.

The drive back to the compound didn't take long, at least not long enough for me to come up with any sort of a plan— just that I had to get the vials I knew were in the basement. I pulled into the underground parking lot of the Coast Bastion Hotel and put the Jeep in park. I would walk from here and at least Sebastian would be out of sight and, hopefully, safe.

I dug through the Jeep and found a flashlight and what I thought was a Billy club. That, or a fish bonker. Gripping the two-foot-long dark wooden shaft did not make me feel particularly safe, but it was all I had. I slid into the back with Sebastian.

"Love, I've got to go for a bit. Stay here. I'll be back." I kissed him, his lips unmoving under mine. A tear slipped down my cheek and dripped onto his face. With the heat that radiated off his body, I almost expected the liquid to sizzle. Stroking his hair and giving him another kiss, I knew I was stalling. I didn't want to have to go back in the compound, but I knew that if Sebastian was cured and found out I'd run away from bringing the cure to others I'd never be able to look him in the face again.

I closed the Jeep's door softly, only a light click, but in the darkness and the vast emptiness of the underground lot it sounded like a shotgun to my oversensitive ears. The shuffle of bare feet on concrete, on the far side of the lot, snapped my head around. I dropped to the ground beside the Jeep, peeking under it.

Feet so dirty I could see the filth, even in the dim light, scuttled into view. The distinct tones of yellow with the broom pattern underneath the skin confirmed what I already suspected. I held my breath and waited for the Nevermore to either pass the Jeep by or make a move closer to me and Sebastian. I prayed it would pass by. My hands were clammy clutching the club, and I knew that if it was a big Nevermore

I was going to have a hard time killing it with an over-sized fish bonker.

The Jeep rocked suddenly, and Sebastian let out a howl, startling both me and the feet on the other side. The Nevermore let out a growl and fingernails scratched down the metal doors.

Shit.

I wasn't going to have a choice about this. I pushed myself to a crouch and plastered my back up against the Jeep. One more deep breath, a prayer whispered with words I weren't sure were going to help, and I stood to face the Nevermore.

Compared to Sebastian he was small, scrawny and had minor injuries all over his body. It would have made it easy to kill him or, at least, easier. But I wouldn't have too. I let out a shuddering breath and lowered the club. It was Scout.

4

"Scout," I said.

His head snapped up, a grimace on his face, then he lowered his eyes. I snapped my fingers and let out a low whistle and he scooted to my side, pressing his face into my thigh as his fingers dug into my calf. I patted the top of his head and tried not to think about how dirty he was.

I opened the Jeep door to show Sebastian to Scout. "You stay here. You need to guard him," I said. Sebastian took the moment to let out another groan as he rolled, the Jeep's shocks protesting.

Scout cocked his head and started to lean in to sniff Sebastian, the intensity in his body changing ever so slightly. I didn't understand at first, but as Scout snuffled the air and his eyes dilated I saw the hunger creep in, the tell tale sign he was about to bite. I saw it and smacked him on the nose, startling him and sending him backwards. "No," I snarled, putting my body between Sebastian and the Nevermore. Scout had been with us from the beginning, but it was obvious that

Sebastian no longer smelled right. Scout never would have tried to take a bite out of an Alpha male.

"Stay. Guard Sebastian," I said, and closed the Jeep door. "You protect him, Scout. I mean it. No biting. You stay with him, no matter what, and keep him safe."

Scout stared at me, and I wasn't sure he understood. Sometimes it looked as though he did; other times I doubted his ability to still comprehend English. Slowly he nodded and tucked himself into the shadow of the Jeep. This time I was lucky; he seemed to grasp what I'd said.

Not wanting to waste anymore time, I headed out at a slow jog, through the parking bay and out into the streets of downtown. The theatre-turned-compound that I was headed for wasn't far—it was less than a block away—but between me and it lay a lot of open space. At the edge of the parking bay I peeked out, surveying the area, my heart pumping with adrenaline. If I ran, I could probably make it all the way to the theatre in less than five minutes. But that could attract more attention than I wanted.

"Come on Mara, you've got to move," I whispered. I stepped out and jogged to the edge of the next building, using it for cover. Blood pumping far faster than it should have been, I took a moment to calm my breathing and looked around again. It was so quiet, but I knew that there was a full-sized pack of about 30 Nevermores ranging through here, not to mention Marks and his men.

Yet, there was no gunfire, no howling, no snarling. I was close enough to the theatre that if humans and Nevermores were fighting I should have been able to hear them. While I stood, watching for signs of movement, the hairs on the back of my neck began to stand up and the pit of my stomach fell to the ground. Ever so slowly, I turned my head to look behind me. There at the entrance to the underground parking lot were three Nevermores, two males and a female. They were staring into the darkness, seemingly deciding whether or not to go in.

"Don't. Just turn around, walk away," I said softly. To my dismay, the bigger of the two males started in, his body quickly disappearing from sight. The other male followed. There was no way Scout could protect Sebastian from all three of them and a good chance he might join in when they attacked the Jeep.

I didn't think, I just acted, knowing I could draw them away. "Hey! Over here!" I yelled. The female spun and I waved at her, watched her eyes widen before I leapt into a run towards the compound. Arms pumping, I focused on the fence that was still sort of up around the building where the cure was. I ignored the shrieking and howling behind me, the slap of bare feet on the pavement and the heavy breathing as they drew closer. I reached an open gap in the fencing and grabbed the edge of it, swinging myself into the compound. I didn't slow down though; I knew I couldn't take on the three of them.

Breathing hard, sweat running down my face and back, I sprinted the last few strides to the theatre door. Yanking it open, I leapt through the glass door and it shut with a swoosh behind me. The three Nevermores banged up against the glass, their fists drumming at it with an alarming amount of force. I backed away, unable to take my eyes from them as they attacked the wall with increasing ferocity.

In short, they were pissed.

I turned and started to run towards the lower levels. If the Nevermores broke in, I would be hunted down for sure and

I had a feeling it was only a matter of time. As if on cue, the sound of glass shattering reached my ears.

"Great, just freaking great," I muttered. The interior of the theatre-turned-compound was dim but not dark. Chandeliers had fallen, paintings were hanging askew or completely off their hooks, dust and rubble lay everywhere. I made my way through the debris to the far side where I knew the stairs to the lower levels were. Moving as quickly as I could, I stumbled when I came to a body on the floor. It was one of Donavan's men. I thought his name was Clint. He had a huge gash in his forehead and a hunk of concrete with a matching blood splatter lay beside him.

I tried to feel sorry for his death, but all I truly saw was a way to keep the Nevermores busy. I bent and grabbed Clint's arm, dragging him closer to the centre of the room, away from all the doors.

"Thanks Clint, you have no idea how much I appreciate this," I said. I stood beside the body and even I could smell the fresh blood, the coppery tang on the air and the faint scent of a bladder let loose in death.

Only moments passed and the three Nevermores stepped into the room; they saw me, let out a combined howl and ran towards me. I stepped back and they leapt as one unit, dropping to the ground right in front of Clint's body. If there was one thing I'd learned about Nevermores it was that they were opportunists. They'd rather eat something already dead or immobilized than chase down a potential meal.

They tore into his body as I backed away. Only once did the female lift her eyes to me, the yellow iris and square pupils offset in her otherwise human face. We stared at one another, and if I didn't know better, I'd say there was a flicker of human emotion there.

Leaving the feasting Nevermores to their meal, I made my way into the stairwell. I flicked on the flashlight and carefully headed down the stairs. There was no telling what kind of structural damage had been done by all the explosions.

At the bottom of the stairs I paused, recalling which way I had to turn to get to the lab. The decision was almost taken from me when a hand reached out and grabbed my arm. I snapped the club down on the yellowed wrist, the flashlight throwing its beam everywhere in the scuffle giving me only a brief impression of a petite female Nevermore.

She let out a howl and I ran to the left, jumping over the chunks of concrete that were everywhere. Concrete dust flew up and tickled my nose, the dry powder nearly odour free, but it still coated my mouth and throat, making me cough, which slowed my steps.

The doorway to the lab was in front of me and I yanked it open, jumped through and slammed it behind me. The rattle of a body being thrown against the frame shook me, but only for a moment. She was small and I thought I could take her if it came to that. But really, did I want to try?

I heard a groan off to my left and I snapped the flashlight up, the beam centering on a figure still strapped to the gurney where I'd left him.

Donavan turned his face to me. "You came back, Juliana, my love you came back."

5

"No, it's not . . ." I paused and thought through what I was about to say. If Donavan thought I was Juliana, he'd be more inclined to help me. I wanted to make sure I had the right vials; the right version of the cure.

"Donavan, which vials have the cure in them? Which one did you give to Seb . . . the big Nevermore?" I asked, keeping the beam of light in his eyes so he couldn't see me clearly.

"Oh Juliana, I missed you so. You have no idea how badly I feel for letting you take Nevermore. Can you ever forgive me my love?" His voice was weak and he let out a sob. I steeled myself against the compassion that was rising through me. He'd been ready to kill Sebastian, he wasn't a good man.

I licked my lips, tasted concrete and said, "Honey, I need the cure. I have friends I need to give it to." The door rattled again and I glanced back at it. Donavan didn't seem to notice the noise at all.

"Help me get up, help me out of these straps and I will get the cure for you my love," he said, blinking hard, his eyes watering. I lowered the flashlight and stepped closer to him.

His words made me think he was gone, his mind slipped fully into the madness that started when he lost Juliana.

Holding the flashlight under my armpit and the club between my knees, I undid the bindings that held him down. Donavan let out a groan and sat up, rubbing his wrists. "My love, thank you. Let's go, we need to be free of this place. There's a wicked woman here, she doesn't understand how important you are to me. She forced me to help her first."

A bubble of hysterical laughter tried to work its way out of me but I bit down on it. "I'm sure she's gone. Now, the cure. Which vials?"

"Oh, yes. You have a friend, who is it?" He asked. His body was barely indistinct against the darkness as he shuffled carefully towards the shelving unit where the various chemical concoctions were kept. I tracked his movements with my flashlight. His hand was on a vial with a red sticker and a large black S on it.

I rubbed my hand over my face. "Lucy, my friend Lucy." I thought using a name he was familiar would appease him. I forgot that he might not have such fond thoughts about Lucy.

"That bitch won't be getting ANY of my cures!" He roared. "She helped the other one tie me down. They left me here to die."

I cringed, guilt washing over me. I had left him here to die. There were no two ways about it.

"Juliana, my love, we must leave this place. The bombs will be bringing it down in very little time." He reached for me in the darkness, my light picking up the edge of his movements.

I stepped sideways, avoiding his hand. "What bomb? Donavan, they all went off already." Please God let that be the case.

Donavan shook his head. "No, no. I rigged the boats and a few bombs around the theatre to go off together. But there was a time delay on a few more explosives. Ones that will bring down the entire downtown core."

My mouth went dry. The core was a huge section of the city; it took close to ten minutes to *drive* out of it, never mind if you were on foot. I had to get back to the Jeep and get us the hell out of here. Like now.

"How long before it goes off Donavan?" I asked.

Another rattle of the door and several things happened before he could answer me. The lights overhead flickered on, illuminating the room. Donavan saw me, his face contorted with rage and then the Nevermore burst through the door, shards of wood flying everywhere, her obviously red hair wild about her face. She was petite and pretty for her age; I could see that, despite the yellowed skin and animal eyes.

Something hit me from behind and I dropped to all fours on the ground, the breath knocked out of me.

"You bitch; I'm going to feed you to Juliana," Donavan snarled.

I dragged in a lung full of air, my hand gripping my club as I glanced over my shoulder. I was between the two of them, a snarling Nevermore and a madman bent on blowing up the freaking world. I kicked out with a foot, surprising Donavan, catching him in the knee and dropping him to the floor along with me. On three limbs, I lost my balance and fell to my side.

With a scream of rage he lunged at me, his weight rolling me onto my back on the cold cement floor. I dropped the club and wrapped my hands around his throat, squeezing for all I was worth. I was not going to die in the basement of this theatre. He let out a hiss, spittle hitting me in the face, the rank smell of teeth gone too long without a cleaning filling my nostrils.

The Nevermore, Juliana, screamed and jumped on the doggy pile, crushing Donavan to me and making me lose my grip.

"You see," he gasped. "She does love me; she is saving me from you."

Juliana reared up, her mouth open wide, ready to strike.

"I don't think she's saving you from anything but a clean death," I said. Her teeth snapped down on the back of his neck with the speed of a striking rattlesnake.

"Juliana!" He screamed. She growled around the mouthful of flesh and ripped him off of me; the lights flickered and went out, plunging us into total darkness.

His screams filled the tiny room, the darkness making it even more claustrophobic. I lay on the floor and put my fist to my mouth to keep from sobbing. I wasn't sad about Donavan; he got to be with his Juliana in the end after all. The horror though, it was just too much in one day for me. Too many deaths and close calls. The worst part of it was that the day wasn't even near being over.

Donavan's screams suddenly cut off and I stood shaking in the darkness; my flashlight trembled in my hand as I flicked it on and trained it on the floor at my feet. Ever so slowly, I turned and aimed the light at the shelving unit. There was only one vial with the red label and the S on it. I took it down and tucked it into my bra, the vial cool against my flushed skin.

The flashlight's beam guiding me, I made my way through the room. I had to push the gurney aside to step around Juliana and Donavan—I didn't want to get too close and have my leg mistaken for a drumstick. Again the laughter inside me tried to bubble up, but I shoved it back. I could see how Donavan would crack. I could feel the hysteria inside myself, my mind dealing with too many horrors, too close together. It wasn't good for the psyche.

My beam caught Juliana as she ripped a piece of flesh upwards, her face smeared with the blood and intestine of her husband. My gorge rose and I gagged on the stench of opened bowels that suddenly filled my nostrils. I stumbled past them, retching and dry heaving as I all but threw myself into the hallway.

The trek up through the stairwell was a blur of darkness and scattered light. The Nevermores were still eating where I'd left them, feasting in the main parlour. Again, I gagged. I had to get back to Sebastian, I had to put some distance between me and all this death. I didn't know when the other bombs would go off and I didn't want to be around to find out.

I ran to the door and slipped through, the Nevermores completely focused on filling themselves. The streets were eerily empty and I walked slowly back to the underground parking lot, my adrenaline gone, my heart sore from the culmination of events and my body exhausted.

As the darkness of the parking lot covered me, I let out a sigh of relief. My shoes made only the slightest of sounds on the smooth concrete as I quickly made my way back to the Jeep.

One swift look around showed me that Scout was missing. That wasn't necessarily a bad thing. At some point we were going to have to say goodbye to him. I doubted that I would be able to take him on any plane, no matter how I cajoled them into seeing what a well behaved Nevermore he was.

I opened the door of the Jeep and slid into the driver's seat. "Okay Bastion. We've got the vial, let's get out of here." I turned in the seat and let out a low moan. It was all I had left to give.

Sebastian was gone.

6

At first I just sat and stared at the empty space where he should have been. How had he gotten out? The Nevermores didn't have the motor skills to open things. My heart caught in my throat. It had to be the trial cure that Donavan had given him. It really *was* working and he was getting some of his human abilities back.

Then I got out of the Jeep and looked around. The parking lot was empty. I let out a low whistle hoping Scout would hear and come back to me. Not this time.

Shit.

There hadn't been any sign of Nevermores out the south side where I'd come in from, so maybe they'd headed up the streets, back into town. But that wouldn't make any sense. I wracked my brain. Where the hell would they go? And why?

I snapped my fingers and threw the flashlight into the Jeep. The waterfront. Sebastian had been fascinated by the waterfront the entire time we'd been confined in Donavan's compound.

Slipping back into the streets, one ear listening for the sound of Nevermores, I ran as fast as I could across Front Street then looked down over the edge of the rise that overlooked the Georgia Strait. The ground sloped down in a steep angle and I found myself on my butt, surfing the brown grass all the way to the bottom where a walkway took over. The walkways spread all around the harbour, through a lagoon and out to the far North side of the waterfront. When Sebastian and I first came to the island to hunt for real estate we walked the whole loop during a break from viewing houses. Then it had taken nearly 45 minutes to walk from one end of the walkway to the other. I took a deep breath and the salty tang of the ocean filled my lungs, the crisp air reviving my senses.

I could feel the time ticking away inside my head. I had to find Sebastian and find him fast. Looking first one way, then the other I decided on heading North. There was more ground to cover that way, but there was also easy access to the water. I jogged down the wide walkway. The pressed concrete was smooth and the hand railings looked as if they were freshly painted, a brilliant clean white. I kept my eyes peeled for anything that would give me a hint of where Sebastian might have gone.

After a few minutes my anxiety began to grow. What if I was wrong? What if he hadn't come down here?

I didn't have the time to search the whole downtown core for him. We had to get out of here. Tears began to burn at the back of my eyes and my throat tightened. I didn't want to think about the conclusion I was coming to.

If I couldn't find him in the next few minutes, I would have to turn around and leave, go on without him.

The sudden, sharp, pain in my chest wasn't from the exertion of jogging; it was from my heart trying to break. I ran up a slight rise in the walkway and looked down over the lagoon. It was fenced in by cement barriers that rose five or six feet in the air over the water and a beautiful white bridge that arched over where the lagoon met the ocean.

The sound of splashing and a squeal of fear moved me towards the beach access for the lagoon. For some reason my mind tried to come up with the name of the place. It was a strange one, a real mouth full. Swinging longa, or something like that. Distantly, I recognized that my mind was scattering in all directions, that I was tired, hungry and afraid. All of which was not helping my mental process.

I rounded a corner and there on the lagoon's beach was Scout, having a complete and utter meltdown, his hands flapping and eyes wild as he jumped all over the place, unable to make himself go in the water.

Sebastian was in the lagoon, up to his neck and still walking out deeper.

I ran along the paved boardwalk and skidded down the stairs to the sandy beach and into the water.

It wasn't too cold, but to be fair, I barely noticed it as Vincent's words echoed in my head.

"Genistin increases the calcium content in bones and prevents more bone mass loss. This also increases the bodies overall mass, making them heavier and less buoyant."

Sebastian was almost up over his mouth.

"Bastian! Stop!" I yelled, as I floundered through the first few feet of water to the point where I could start to swim out to him. My clothes dragged at me and I struggled to keep my own head above water. I reached him as his nose dipped and he snorted in some salt water.

I did the only thing I could think of. I grabbed the back of his head and pulled a handful of hair, yanking him back to shore. He grunted but didn't fight me; he didn't have too. His body was solid and he only stumbled back far enough to literally give him some breathing room.

I kicked hard, pulling him off balance, which spun him to face the shoreline.

"Come on! Help me Bastian," I snapped, getting a mouthful of salt water.

"I'm no good Mara; I don't think I can control the monster in me," he said, his words, the fact that he was speaking in full sentences, jarring me. Treading water, I turned to face him and really looked at him.

His skin was clear, the yellow tones gone; his eyes were human in shape, though they had retained the golden irises. More than that though, I could *see* Sebastian in his eyes, with no hint of the Nevermore that had raged through his system.

I reached for him and he stood still, let me touch his face. "You're back," I whispered, the waves rippling around us. A piece of sea weed floated by and Sebastian shook his head.

"I don't know that I am."

From the beach Scout let out a squeal. Treading water, I slowly spun to see a group of Nevermores approaching the beach. This day was not improving.

The Nevermores circled Scout who cringed and tried to scuttle away from them. A single blow from one of the males and Scout was on the ground, whimpering and put in his place.

Still treading water, my mind raced to solve this new set of problems. I couldn't come up with anything. I could see that we were safe, but only as long as we were in the water. And once the bombs sunk the downtown core, we were in serious trouble. I shuddered, the water rippling out around me.

"You aren't safe," Sebastian said.

"Neither are you. You don't smell right to them anymore. Scout would have attacked you if I hadn't stopped him," I said over my shoulder.

"I can't protect you from them anymore. You shouldn't have tried to bring me back."

A ringing went off in my ears, the world around me flickering and swaying, and I thought for a brief moment that the explosions had started—but it was just his words that made me feel as if a piece of me was dying.

He kept talking, ignoring the tears that started to trickle down my face. "At least as one of them, I could keep you safe, could keep the baby safe. Now, I can't do that. I have nothing to offer you. I'm a liability, sick and you would be better off . . ."

"But the sickness will pass, Bastian," I said, believing the words and hoping I could make him believe them too.

With the Nevermores in the backdrop, the sounds of the waves lapping at the shoreline and a lead weight in my heart, I understood that he didn't want to live anymore. That this trek into the water wasn't some misfire of the chemicals in his brain as he came back to me.

Sebastian was back and he didn't want to be.

Tears streaked down my face, an uncontrollable fount of pain escaping me. "Please, I've fought so hard to have you with me. Please don't leave me now."

"I will always love you Mara." He turned away from me and started his death walk into the depths of the lagoon.

I stared at his back and the pain slowly turned to anger, a burn that began in my belly and fired its way all through my body until it erupted out of my mouth.

"You selfish son of a bitch! You think that this was easy? You think that I had a good time watching you become one of them? You know what Bastian, grow the hell up. This is our life and I don't care how bad it gets, how hard it gets, we both have to live it. Period."

He froze in his tracks but didn't turn to face me.

"That's right, walk away, run away from all the fear and pain and sorrow that you are leaving to me and our child. You think that I'll have it easier without you here? That's just your excuse so you don't feel bad about leaving me in the biggest lurch of my FREAKING LIFE!"

I started to swim to the edge of the lagoon; the man-made waterfalls were dried up now but still tiered in order to make the cement barriers look more aesthetically pleasing. I looked along the edge and sized up my route. It looked as though I could pull myself along the edge of the barriers, under the bridge and then continue on around the seawall, back to the spot where I'd slid down the grass. Hopefully, the Nevermores would have forgotten about me by then.

Hopefully by then I'd have forgotten about Sebastian's betrayal, though I doubted it. I reached the first tier and something tugged at my shirt. I slowly turned to see Sebastian standing neck deep in the water, his eyes full of pain.

"I'll come with you. For now."

I nodded but didn't say anything, still too angry to give him anything more than that.

The Nevermores ran to the edge of the lagoon and reached over the chain hand railing, howling at us, screaming their hunger. We were well out in the lagoon now where the water was deep and dark, but we clung to the edge, pulling ourselves along. A deep rumble in the distance slowed me for a brief second.

"We have to hurry," I said, and re-doubled my efforts, the muscles in my upper body burning from the extended exertion. We reached the bridge and paused for a breath underneath it, the Nevermores above us growling and snarling. We were just out of reach and they were pissed. The water here was shallow, only a few inches deep. I took a breath and surveyed where we were in relation to where we needed to be.

"We'll hug the seawall all the way back to the harbour. It parallels the walkway, but the Nevermores won't be able to reach us."

Sebastian nodded but said nothing.

One of the Nevermores made a lunge for us over the edge of the bridge as we stepped on to the cement breakers on the far side. He fell with a scream, hitting the hard ground with only a minor splash. It seemed to stun him, and he lay there for a moment.

Sebastian jumped at him, grabbed him by the scruff of his neck and flung him out into the deep water of the lagoon. A single splash, a few bubbles and the Nevermore was gone. But it cost Sebastian precious energy as he swayed, leaning perilously close to the edge of that deep water himself. I grabbed his hand and pulled him with me.

We slogged through water that reached our knees, the Nevermores tracking us the whole way, the high sea wall separating us from them. It was like a three story circus. We were on the bottom level in the water, the Nevermores were on the walkway a good five feet above Sebastian's head and then the boulevard I'd slid down was another level above the walkway. The trek, which had taken me a mere matter of minutes before, took much longer on the way back, but every step brought us closer to the Jeep, closer to escaping this place.

We reached the spot where I'd slid down to the boulevard, but the sea wall was even higher here, a good 4 or 5 feet above Sebastian's head.

He didn't offer any solutions, and I stood there staring at the seemingly insurmountable rock wall in front of me. I put my hand against the wall and curled my fingers around the stone, digging them into a groove that was barely perceptible.

We could climb the wall. It wasn't too high, and there were spots that we could use as handholds. "How are your hands?" I asked.

Sebastian came up beside me. "You mean to climb this?"

I nodded. He flexed his fingers and gripped an edge. "I think I could manage. If there wasn't a pack standing above our heads."

I glanced up and the Nevermores stared down, their faces twisted with hunger, their eyes wide and greedy. Yes, that was going to be a problem. The ground below us shook as the explosion from another bomb rocked the harbour. I swayed on my feet, placing the palms of my hands on the wall for support. Barnacles pressed into my skin, their sharp shells digging in to the soft flesh. We were in trouble. I could see no way out of this.

A scuffle to the left, back the way we came caught my attention. Scout was making his way along the boulevard, his eyes searching for us. I gave a wave and he brightened; a lopsided grin stretching across his face as blood trickled down from a slice in his cheek, but otherwise he looked to be no worse the wear from his earlier scuffle.

I let out a low whistle and he crept forward, coming as close as he could without disturbing the rest of the pack, who crouched at the edge of the wall. They were all on the same level, the pack crouched right in front of us; Scout fifteen feet down the boulevard and peering at us with concern.

Sebastian touched my arm. "If Scout were to challenge the entire group, it would be enough to distract them. There is only one thing more important to a Nevermore than food." He paused and glanced upwards at the milling group. "Loyalty to the pack."

I closed my eyes, grief filling me. I knew what Sebastian was saying. There was a way out of here, but it would depend on Scout and his loyalty to me. And it would most likely cost him his life. Swallowing the lump in my throat, I lifted my eyes and smiled at him.

"You've been a good friend Scout. I need you to do one last thing for me," I said, my voice catching on the tears that threatened.

He grunted, gave me a sharp nod and tapped his chest with his hand.

"I need you to start a fight; I need you to take the pack away from here so we can climb out. Can you do that?" I asked.

Scout cocked his head, a quizzical expression on his face. A faint glimmer of understanding passed over his eyes. He nodded slowly, sorrow filling his face; my eyes filled with tears.

"Be ready to climb," I whispered, placing my hands on the rock wall, getting a good hand hold. Scout touched his chest again and then motioned at me with the same hand. Sebastian let out a choking sob and I forced myself to keep my composure.

Scout was saying goodbye.

7

With a screech Scout threw himself towards the pack, hands and feet flailing, taking all of them by surprise and startling them into spreading out a little. Scout grabbed the smallest pack member and wrestled with the petite male. Scout snarled and ripped the male's throat out with his teeth then threw him out into the water. The rest of the pack shrieked, panicked and ran as a group back down the sea wall towards the lagoon. It gave us the opening we needed. I gripped the stones, the barnacles slicing into my skin as I put all my weight into my hands and tips of my feet, climbing as fast as I could. Blood curdling howls and screams reached my ears, but I dared not look up.

In moments, I'd scaled the wall and was pulling myself over the lip, scraping my hands and knees but thankful to be on this side of the sea wall. Sebastian was right behind me, breathing hard, his head low.

A high pitched shriek snapped my head around to see Scout held between three Nevermores, his belly bare to the sky.

"Oh God please no," I whispered. Scout's eyes found mine as I stumbled to my feet, and for a moment I was unsure of whether to run or help him. Scout blew a raspberry at me as one of the female Nevermores struck, her face and teeth burying into his exposed flesh.

Scout let out a howl of pain, and I reached down for Sebastian, pulling him to his feet and hustling him up the slippery slope of grass, scrambling to the top.

The screams continued, striking my heart through with the reality of what I'd done. It was taking so long—usually when a Nevermore killed, it was over quickly, and in a way, mercifully.

"He challenged them," Sebastian said as if reading my mind, answering the question I hadn't voiced. I glanced at him, his face hard and drawn. I doubted I looked any better at this point.

"Why does that matter?" We skirted between buildings, Sebastian mimicking my movements, always just a step behind.

"He challenged them and defended us, proving he was no longer loyal to the pack. They will keep him alive a long time; they'll all participate, even though it means letting us go. They'll all want a piece of him," he said. "Literally."

I snapped my mouth shut. I didn't want to know the ins and outs of a Nevermore pack. I had enough fodder for the nightmares that would haunt me for the rest of my life. I didn't need to add to it.

As we entered the underground parking lot, I let out a sigh of relief. We'd made it; the Jeep was in view, we had a vial of the cure, and Sebastian was with me. The cool, dim interior echoed our footsteps back to us as we walked to the

Jeep. Sebastian didn't seem to be able to do more than that, his body wrung out from fighting with the cure for the last few days.

I leaned my head against the Jeep and took a deep breath, one hand holding the keys tight, the other cradling my belly. For just a moment I needed to pause, to slow down. It felt like I was forgetting something, or if that wasn't the case, that I *would* forget something vital, and important. Everything was happening so fast, I barely had time to think, I could only react.

I hiccupped back a sob that started to well up. Scout had just died for us and I didn't even have time to grieve for him properly. His loyalty had saved us and all we could do was run away. Scrubbing away tears, I pushed the grief back down. Later, I had to believe that there would *be* a later to say good-bye to Scout, to be grateful for his sacrifice. Right now, we had to go, there was no more time to waste on wondering and thinking how things could be, or might have been, different.

I opened the door to the Jeep and slid into the driver's seat. Sebastian was still making his way around the vehicle, his every step laboured and stumbling. I turned the key, the engine coming to life easily, and leaned across to open the passenger side door for Bastian. Taking his hand I balanced him as he struggled to make his body do as he wanted.

A sudden and thunderous boom filled the parking lot, and Sebastian was only halfway in the Jeep.

"Get in!" I screamed at him as I revved the engine. There was a second boom and then an answering groan from the twenty plus story hotel above us. Shit.

Sebastian slid the rest of the way in, and promptly closed his eyes. I reached across and slammed his door shut then hit the gas pedal. The tires squealed on the slick pavement as we tore out of the underground parking lot. My foot hammered on the gas as we sped back out into the bright sunlight and the building began to collapse behind us, dust flying up everywhere. As if on cue, other buildings began to explode, the noise deafening, the smoke that flooded out making it hard to see.

I wrenched the wheel, dodging a large chunk of concrete that appeared out of the smoke, clipping the edge of the Jeep. My grip tightened as the vehicle rocked, but all four wheels came back down to touch the pavement. I let out a breath and stared at the road, using all my miniscule talent in driving to get us out of the war zone.

At the top of the hill, next to St. Peters Catholic Church once more, I slowed the Jeep and stared in the review mirror. A black cloud of smoke filled the sky, buildings enveloped by a massive roil of dust. That is, if there were any buildings still standing. Had Marks and his men gotten out? I didn't dare go to the bunker, I was low on fuel as it was and any side trips would only suck the tank dry faster. I picked up the walkie talkie and flicked it on. A low thrum of static was all I got, no matter where I set the dial.

"Damn it," I said, shoving the walkie talkie into the glove compartment. So much for that idea.

I looked over at Sebastian, his eyes still closed, his breathing far from even. I put a hand to his forehead and winced. His fever was still raging—that was not a good sign. He moaned and shifted in his seat, raising his hands to fend off an invisible enemy.

I shifted the Jeep back into gear and headed down the Third street connector and back on to the Inland Island

Highway, the Parkway. I would have to leave the Parkway and get on to the Old Highway that ran along the water's edge to see about finding a boat. Only, the gas tank was less than a quarter full and that would barely get us home, without any detours—and the Old Highway was "scenic." Which translates to extra long and winding.

But, it had to be done; we had to find a way across to Vancouver.

My eye half on the tank of gas and half on the surrounding areas, I banked off the Parkway as soon as we were far enough from the downtown core and started up the Old Highway.

My mind began to wander as I drove, and it was a bloody miracle I didn't run over the woman who ran into the road in front of me. I jerked the steering wheel hard to the right and swerved around her, jarring Sebastian and nearly tipping the Jeep over. Sebastian didn't wake; he just lay there as I hit the brakes and sat there panting with adrenaline. I gripped the wheel and willed my heart to slow down. I took slow even breaths and tried not think about splattering the young woman all over the front of the Jeep. It had been that close.

The woman jogged up to my window. She looked to be in her mid twenties; was an average build, a little on the slim side, and had blond hair with purple streaks and a diamond nose piercing. She peered in and I got a good look at her hazel eyes, weary and drawn around the edges. I wasn't the only one struggling to keep moving, to survive.

"I'm sorry. I just was so excited to see you and thought you saw me, too. You looked right at me," she said, her voice light and airy.

I let out breath before answering. "Are you okay?"

309

She nodded. "My name is Annie, my brother Dustin is just over there, I was wondering . . ." She trailed off as she got a good look at Sebastian. No, his skin wasn't as yellow as it had been, nor were there broom outlines under his skin as apparent. But, they were still there.

She backed away from me, her eyes wide, her mouth an open "O." "You're crazy. He's going to eat you!" She yelped as she spun on her heel and sprinted away from me. I shook my head and got the Jeep going again. I tried not to think about her reaction; tried not to think about what it would mean when we got to Vancouver. Would there be blood tests? I couldn't remember, the details were foggy in my brain, but I had to assume that there would be some sort of test. The officials there were unlikely to just allow *anyone* to get on a plane.

As we drove North, the number of Nevermores was drastically reduced. At first it seemed like every corner I turned there was a pack waiting for me. Then it was every other corner and then the population of Nevermores thinned, and I was able to drive for ten minutes at a stretch before seeing any of them at all.

We passed several harbours, but none proved fruitful. Either there were no boats or there were too many Nevermores to risk trying to even see if there were boats. Anxiety started to make itself known, my nerves fluttering with each passing mile. I glanced at the gas gauge and tapped it to make sure I was seeing it right. The indicator was lower than the E.

"Okay Bastian, we can't look anymore, we have to try and make it all the way home," I said, not expecting an answer.

"Why?" He asked, startling me.

I thought for a minute before answering and gave him the best truth I could.

"Because I feel safe there. Because it's home. Because I don't know where else to go."

"It isn't that safe," he said, his words slurred as if he'd been drinking.

"Well, we did fine until Vincent showed up. And, Dan is still there. He can help us," I said, the sign for Bowser flashing by us. We were almost there; another ten minutes and we'd be in Fanny Bay.

Sebastian didn't answer. The Jeep gave a cough and I grit my teeth.

"Come on baby, don't fail me now," I whispered.

I slipped the Jeep out of gear and coasted down a long hill, letting the engine have a break and hopefully use less gas. At the bottom of the hill, when the Jeep lost momentum, I put it back in gear and pushed on the gas pedal.

Again it coughed and sputtered, the engine running on fumes and hope. If we could just get over this next rise, we could coast almost all the way into Fanny Bay. It wouldn't be a long walk from there.

On what must have been the last drops squeezed from the tank, the Jeep lurched past Rosewall Creek, up the hill and crested the top. I popped it out of gear again and the engine died.

We coasted down the road, past the Oyster operation and the gas bar and made it maybe another half mile on momentum. But, the Jeep only had so much to give and as it rolled to a stop I put the brake on and looked over at Sebastian.

"This is it," I said. "We walk from here."

8

We were about a five minute drive from home. Walking was going to take at least four times that long, maybe more with Sebastian lagging. With his arm over my shoulders and me taking as much weight from him as I could, we made our way down the side of the road.

Ten minutes later we weren't even half way to the house, but at least we hadn't run into any Nevermores. My ears strained for the telltale sounds of a pack bare feet running on the hard ground, the snap of a branch or any other noise that would give them away.

"You have to leave me Mara," Sebastian said, his words slurred as if he'd had too much beer.

"I'm not leaving you so don't bother. We'll make it. We're more than halfway there," I said, keeping my voice low and soft.

"Liar," He whispered into my ear.

I smiled and tightened my grip on him. "You calling me out? Want to take this outside?"

He grunted. "You don't lie well and we're outside so what do you want to do about it?"

I glanced up into his golden yellow eyes and lifted my left eyebrow. "When we get home, we're going to discuss this liar business. I'll probably have to beat you some. Maybe with a large stick."

Sebastian let out a laugh and I found myself laughing too, if only for a brief moment. I snapped my mouth shut when I saw a shadow up ahead, a flicker of movement that stepped sideways and disappeared into the underbrush.

I pulled Sebastian into the ditch on the side of the road, making him crouch beside me. We were as hidden as we could be, though it wasn't much.

"What is it?" He asked, his voice gaining clarity with each passing minute.

"Something up ahead. I don't know if it's a human or a Nevermore," I said, keeping my voice low.

Sebastian stiffened in my embrace, his body going rigid under my hands. I glanced at him. "What is it, are you in pain?"

"You didn't think of me as human?" His eyes betrayed the calm words, anger flickering through them.

My jaw tightened and my own anger began to burn. "What, you have a better way of identifying one from the other?"

He said nothing, just stared down the road at where I'd seen the shadow. This was not the time or place for an argument, much as I wanted to grab Bastian and shake him till he saw sense. I didn't mean it in a derogatory way, but what else was I supposed to say?

We crouched in the shadows, not touching one another, the anger burning off both of us making it an uncomfortable silence.

"I think we should move on," he said, moving to stand up. I didn't stop him.

A loud, sharp crack and a bullet whizzed by us. Sebastian dropped back to the ground, his eyes wide and his mouth open.

"What the hell!" I yelled. "We're human, stop shooting!" I reached to Sebastian and gripped his hand.

I didn't realize until the animals were quiet just how much noise they were making. The birds around us had gone silent and even the crickets had stopped their late summer songs. I couldn't hear anything, no running feet and no more gunshots.

Sweat trickled down the center of my face and dripped off the end of my nose. I scrubbed at it and dared to make my way to the top of the ditch and peek out, making sure Sebastian stayed put where he was.

My eyes scanned the area taking in the broom plants, no longer bright with yellow flowers but covered in seed pods, the distant cry of the ocean gulls and a figure of a man, half in, half out of the shadows. He stood about ten feet away with his gun pointed at me. The rough army clothes, the grizzled cigar hanging out of his down-turned mouth and the body covered in ammo. Dan.

The skin around my mouth was stretched into a grin I couldn't repress. "Dan!" I said, waving my arm. "It's me, Mara."

He didn't lower the gun but I stood up anyway, confident he wouldn't shoot me. A crack, a puff of dust and a spray of pebbles all over me stopped my forward momentum.

"Dan. Please don't shoot me," I said, my voice cracking. "Remember I made you cookies?"

"They were burnt," he said.

"I'd never used a wood stove for cooking Dan. I explained that when I brought them to you." I kept my hands at my sides, not moving an inch. I had a feeling that if I did anything rash or tried to dive for cover, he would open fire on me.

"Dan, why are you shooting at me?"

"I'm not shooting at you. I'm shooting at them," he said, gesturing with his gun behind me. Turning slowly I spun until I could see what exactly was behind us.

The pack had crept up, silent in their hunting techniques. At first I wondered at why they held back and then I saw them eyeing Dan. They seemed to understand what the gun meant, what it could do. My heart began to race as I counted the pack. There were twenty one Nevermores and instead of an Alpha male, they seemed to be following the lead of one of the females.

My breath caught in my throat at her dishevelled appearance, the beautiful Caribbean eyes gone under the Nevermore drug's influence. Her body had hardened, no longer the soft teenager I'd met when we'd first moved to Fanny Bay.

Jessica snarled; I stepped forward. Sebastian was between us and I wasn't about to let her have him.

"Woman, you can't take the whole pack on," Dan said.

"They can't have Sebastian," I replied, my mind trying to come up with a solution that would get us all out of here alive.

Sebastian, hearing his name perhaps, pulled himself up to the top of the ditch. Jessica snarled again, her body leaning towards us, and the pack shifted with her, their bodies pressing forward in a mass of yellow skin and hunger filled faces.

Sebastian's eyes were hazy and I could see that he was sliding back under another round of with the fever. Crap.

"Sebastian. I need you to come to me," I said, my voice low.

The pack started forward and Dan shot at them but didn't hit any of them.

"Dan…" I started to say.

"If I shoot any of them they will attack. They're protective of each other," Dan said.

I nodded. Of course they were. Look at what Scout had done for us.

Sebastian started to crawl towards me, his movements slow and laboured. Jessica, and another female I didn't recognize from the original pack, lunged forward.

I did the only thing I could think of. I jumped towards them, mimicking their movements, startling them both with my scream.

I landed next to Sebastian and yanked him to his feet, no longer trying to be careful—just trying to keep him from being eaten.

Jessica saw him clearly, perhaps for the first time, and I saw the recognition flicker over her face. She grimaced, sniffed the air and then a smile spread over her thin lips. This was not going to be good.

9

Dragging Sebastian with me, we half stumbled, half ran towards Dan. Our jerky movements set the pack off and they clamoured through the ditch and were after us in less time than it took to breathe out a curse.

Dan shoved us on ahead of him while he kept the pack at bay with well aimed shots at the ground.

"Up the driveway on your left woman," Dan yelled; I didn't dispute his directions, just turned to the left and pulled Sebastian along with me.

We ran as best we could, the trees hanging low over us creating a natural archway. The birds were singing once more, as if this was now just a part of everyday life. Breathing hard, Sebastian and I barely made it to the top of the driveway. There were two options: the house, which had been partially burned down—the thick smell of char still lingered in the air—and the barn.

"The barn woman, get to the damn barn!" Dan yelled, and again I obeyed.

We crashed through the large outer door. Dan followed and slammed a large bar into place, locking us in and the pack out. From there he hustled us up a ladder into the loft. The ladder was the hardest for Sebastian. The whole barn was on a weird slant and the ladder was no different. Instead of being straight up and down it leaned towards us at a sharp angle, forcing Sebastian to use his hands to grip the rungs. Although his hands had gotten better as his fine motor skills improved, it was still hard for him to hang on to the thin rungs…Not to mention he seemed light headed with fever, and swayed at each step.

"Up, get up there!" Dan continued to bark orders at us.

"Going as fast as we can," I said through gritted teeth.

The door of the barn groaned as Sebastian pulled himself into the loft and I looked down to see the pack burst through the old wooden slats as if they were made of popcorn, bits and pieces flying every which way.

"Move your ass woman!"

This time I didn't sass him. I scrambled up the last few rungs and found myself in a haze of gold. The light streamed through the cracks in the roof, and the piles of old straw and hay—even the specks of dust floating through the air—seemed to glow golden. There was Sebastian, laying in a pile of hay, fitting right in, his skin still a dusky yellow even though the color had faded quite a bit. I shook my head and turned to find Dan taking in the same scene, his gun slowly lifting.

I put myself between the two men. "He's not one of them Dan. Not anymore." The sounds of the Nevermores trashing the barn below made it so I nearly had to shout to be heard.

"He looks enough like them for me to shoot him and not feel bad," he said around the stub of his cigar. "Now help me pull up the ladder."

We yanked and pulled, freeing the ladder and laying it out on the floor. That should be enough to keep the pack away from us.

"You should put that out while we're here," I said, motioning at the smoking cigar.

He grunted, spit on the floor and shook his head. "There is no cure, so how can he not be one of them?"

I quickly filled Dan in on what had been happening to us, Vincent, Donavan and the possibility of a cure. I pulled the vial out of my bra and showed it to him.

"This could change things Dan. This could bring people back."

"Might. Might not." He sat down on a bale of hay and leaned back against the wall.

"What do you mean? You weren't there; look at Sebastian, he's getting better," I said. Something crashed below us and I tried to see through the cracks in the floor, but other than the hint of movement, I couldn't see anything.

"Well, I don't think he's getting better. I'm inclined to believe in his current state he's more likely to die than get up and shake my hand." Dan's words crashed in my brain, causing a complete malfunction of all thought processes.

In lurches and fits, I started to look at Sebastian's condition as an outsider would. Sure, he might be showing signs of humanity, but everything else was falling apart. Fever, loss of muscle control, balance issues, sleeping whenever he could, erratic heart rhythms. Even now he lay on a bundle of straw and hay, his chest heaving for a few moments and then falling silent before picking up again.

I tightened my jaw. "No, he's going to make it. I won't let him die."

Dan tapped his nose with a thick finger. "You might not get a choice woman. He might just die on you."

The back of my throat was tight, but it was hard to be mad at Dan. I'd thought the very same things myself, but didn't dare voice them. I didn't want Sebastian to think I'd given up.

In desperation, I changed topics. "How long do you think we'll be stuck up here?"

Dan shrugged. "Most likely overnight, the Nevermores seem to sleep right at dawn so we should be able to get out of here then."

He stood and went over to a large tack trunk, flipped a horseshoe off the lid and opened it up. Inside was a variety of foodstuffs, several blankets, two milk jugs full of water and a pile of ammo.

"Did you put this all in here?" I asked, reaching in for a package of beef jerky, my mouth watering at the thought of salty meat.

"Got caught out hunting this way twice. So, I decided to set up some safe houses. Enough food here for a day or so," he said, taking a swig of water before handing the jug to me. I drank down the tepid, slightly bleachy water. I turned and tried to pour a small amount into Sebastian's mouth. He coughed and spit but it didn't look like anything went down.

I put the jug on the floor and shook Bastian. "Come on babe. I need you to wake up. You need to drink."

He let out a growl in his sleep, his lips pulling back over his teeth. I stared at him, my heart aching for what he was going through, for the simple fact he might not pull out of it.

Dan reached and took the jug back, had another swig, and then capped it. "Might as well settle down for the night. They aren't leaving anytime soon." He pointed downstairs and I nodded. Then he pulled a length of rope out of the box and started towards Sebastian.

"What are you doing?" I asked, standing up between the two men.

"You don't know he's cured woman. The last thing I want is to wake up with the big boy on top of one of us, having a midnight snack." He shoved past me and set to tying Sebastian's hands. A few knots later, Bastian was tied to one of the beams, his hands clasped as if in prayer. Through the whole thing he hadn't stirred once. I didn't try and stop Dan; he needed to feel safe, and I had to admit, he could be right. Sebastian could very well revert.

The daylight began to fade and the golden haze that filled the barn slowly dissipated. I lay beside Sebastian, staring at the cracks in the roof, the distant twinkling of stars caught here and there. Dan was snoring within minutes of closing his eyes and the Nevermores below us seemed to have calmed down. I took in a deep breath, the tang of ocean, the distinct smell of the old hay and dust vying for my senses. I ran a hand over my face, my thoughts too tangled to sleep.

I sat up, hay poking at me through my clothes, and pulled the vial out of my bra. This one little jar could save the world from this madness we plunged ourselves into. Was I really so naive as to believe that it really was a cure?

Sebastian lay on his side, his breathing irregular. I ran my fingers through his lovely dark hair and for a moment I let myself believe it would be okay. That we would make it out of here, to the mainland.

Shaking those unrealistic thoughts away, I let myself see the true reality of our situation for the first time. We would have to cross the Georgia Strait, somehow navigate our way close to the airport, and then go overland to get there. The sheer number of people surrounding, and within, Vancouver would mean that the Nevermore population would be massive, nothing like our single pack here in Fanny Bay, or the few packs in Nanaimo.

No, Vancouver would be a bloody death trap. But, I had to try. I had to be able to say that we'd done our best; we'd made all the effort we could.

Tears trickled down my face at the enormity of the task ahead of me because, who was I kidding, in Sebastian's current condition he was just along for the ride.

I lay back down and stared up at the sky again. Sleep didn't take me that night, despite my desire to escape the waking world, if even for only a few hours.

So I lay there, thinking of all the obstacles, the challenges and the impossibilities until my mind was numb and I stared in a blank haze at the night sky.

Just before dawn, when I could see the miniscule light change within the barn and the morning birds began to sing in the trees next to the barn, the Nevermores began to jabber at one another. Grunting and snarling. A low growl here and there. I rolled onto my side and peeked down between the floor slats to see the pack split into three groups, each group positioned against one of the support columns that held the loft up.

"Oh shit." I leapt to my feet. "Dan, up, we've got problems."

The barn swayed underneath us and Dan let out a curse as he rolled out of bed, hay in his hair.

"Wondered when we were going to get to this point." He strode over to Sebastian and sliced through the ropes with his knife.

I crouched on the floor, nothing to hold on to, my body swaying with the rocking of the building. "What do you mean?"

"They seem to be getting smarter. Figuring things out," he said, as he loaded his gun and shimmied towards me.

The barn groaned and the loft slipped sideways as one support beam went out, sending us all to one corner of the rickety old building. Sebastian sprawled out, limbs flopping as if lifeless.

I grabbed at his arm and felt the smallest flutter of a heartbeat under my fingertips, just as another column gave way, smashing the loft into the trees that grew beside the barn, slowing our fall. The floor of the loft slipped further towards the ground, but it was still held up on one end by the remaining column. It groaned as the pack pushed it and, finally giving way, the loft collapsed down with it.

I think I screamed, but the noise of the building coming down around us muffled any noises coming out of our mouths. Dust flew up everywhere and boards smacked me all over. I curled around my stomach, protecting the baby as best I could. I tumbled, but not as far as I thought I should have, landing against some loose bales of hay. There was a sharp sting across my back and warmth trickled down my side.

The silence was the first thing I noticed. I thought the Nevermores would have been on us in a flash. But the silence held, and then a few groans. From underneath us. I looked around to see Sebastian curled in a tight ball and let out a sigh of relief when his chest rose and fell in a decent rhythm.

"Stupid bastards pulled the damn barn down right on top of their own heads," Dan grumbled, as he pulled himself up out of a pile of boards and debris. He had a gash over one eye, blood trickling down his face, and his right arm was hanging limply. That was going to make it difficult for him to shoot to say the least. Crap.

We started to stand and the barn groaned again. The floor was busted up, humps and bumps from the fall leaving it a land mine of rusted nails and splintered wood. Loose hay made the footing even more treacherous, our feet slipping in it as we slowly made our way to a window opening and peeked out. No movement, no sign of the pack. I flexed my back, feeling the sting of a deep cut. Probably a rusty nail with the luck we'd been having. I did my best to ignore the pain; for the moment there was nothing I could do about it.

"We've got an opening, woman. We've got to go now." Dan's voice was sharp and I knew he was right.

"Sebastian." I ran to his side. He groaned and rolled away from me. I didn't have time for this; I couldn't baby him if we were going to get out of here alive.

I slipped and skidded my way to the trunk and pulled out the jug of water. Un-screwing the cap I poured it all over Sebastian. He was slow to respond, but at least he opened his eyes.

I grabbed his hands and started to pull. "Up. Now."

Sebastian's movements were stiff, more like that of a ninety-year-old man than that of one in his prime. He shuffled, his feet kicking up dust and hay, but he was moving.

We were able to step out of the barn and onto solid ground, which was a blessing. I didn't think Sebastian could do anything more than the shuffling gait he was managing.

"Come on woman, get him moving!" Dan snapped, his face pale, his teeth clamped hard over his cigar. I pulled at Sebastian, forcing him to move faster, but to no avail.

"This is it Dan I can't make him go any faster. Besides, the pack is under the barn, remember?" I hoped this was still true.

"You think they were the only pack around here?" He leaned in and grabbed Sebastian's other arm with his good one, helping me half drag, half carry my husband.

We made our way back out onto the street where there were the least amount of obstacles for our feet. No words between us, we just forged ahead, ears and eyes scanning the area, waiting for the moment we'd have to run.

I forced my exhausted muscles to keep working, made my mind stay away from the pain in my back and focused on one thing: Getting to our farm.

10

It took us over an hour to make it the rest of the way to our farm. Twice the three of us fell to the ground, stumbling over something; maybe just our own tired feet. We slid inside the gate and Sebastian dropped to his knees. Though he hadn't done much of the actual work, he was covered in sweat head to toe and his skin was a nasty pallor.

I sat on the hard packed dirt and stared around me. The grass had gone brown, the weeds had grown tall and the house's doors and windows were hanging open. I knew that Marks and the other men hadn't left it in this disarray.

"Did you ransack our place Dan?" I wasn't upset, not really. I would have done the same, only I would have shut the doors and windows.

He sat across from me and shook his head. "Nope, somebody else beat me to it."

I nodded. It was the way of our world now. I stood, my body protesting every step. Everything hurt from the muscles in my neck down to the arches of my feet.

"Help me shut the gate." I motioned at the massive wrought iron panels.

"It won't keep them out. It's not tall enough," Dan said, pulling himself to his feet.

"What?" My brain didn't like that; neither did my heart, as the words sunk in. I could feel my breathing escalate. I thought we'd be safe here, that we could heal up and then try and find a boat. That we would have time.

"You saw how the pack took down the barn? They've started to work together, as one unit, to get at food. To get at us." Dan walked over to me, his face in a twisted grimace, no doubt from the pain of his broken arm.

"I still think we should shut it. Why give them an open invitation?" I asked. Together we pushed the gates shut and I slid the bar that locked them into place.

Feeling totally exposed, I forced Sebastian to his feet once more and prodded him until I had him inside the house. Dan followed and I began to wonder why he was still here. He made himself at home on the couch as I put Sebastian in the guest room on the ground floor. There was no way I was going to try and get him upstairs to the master bedroom.

I went through the house, locking doors and shutting windows, not really caring about the rising temperature. I just wanted to feel safe and secure for a little while. The cupboards were bare, dirt and dust floated everywhere, but overall the house was still in good shape. A few broken windows; that was the extent of the damage. Anything of value had been taken by Vincent and his men, but that was to be expected. As I walked through, I collected what was left of our personal items—my journal, our wedding photos and scrapbooks—and carried them with me upstairs. Our bedroom was musty smelling and, after putting the memorabilia on the dresser, I opened the window to air the room out. Unless the Nevermores learned how to fly, it was safe to open the upstairs windows.

I checked in on Dan who was attempting to make a splint and a sling. I helped him until we had his arm strapped close to his chest. Sweat beaded his upper lip and the scent of sour smoke drifted out of his mouth. I wrinkled my nose and blurted out a question before I thought better of it.

"Why are you helping us Dan? The first time you were here, you couldn't brush us off fast enough and now…" I waved around my head as if to encompass everything. "You've risked your life to help us. I don't get it."

Dan leaned back on the couch and closed his eyes. For a minute I thought he was going to sleep, that he wouldn't answer me.

Without opening his eyes he spoke. "There are some people in this world Mara who can make it through anything. The odds seem to be in their favour; they make good choices, but more than that, they have an instinct for survival." Now he did open his eyes and lean in towards me. I stared at his craggy face, breathed in his smoke-ridden breath and held my ground. He smiled, yellowed teeth peeking out at me.

"You are one of those people. I saw it when that first Nevermore jumped you." He tapped my head with a thick finger. "No matter what this world throws at you, you fight back for yourself and your man."

He leaned back and closed his eyes once more.

"You are *dauntless* Mara. That's why I helped you."

I sat on my heels and absorbed what he'd said. High praise from a man who seemed to have nothing but critiscm for everyone else.

Dan let out a cough. "And, I need a place to stay. My house burned to the ground."

I let out a laugh and he laughed with me. But I had a feeling that what he'd said earlier really was how he felt. He wouldn't say those things if he didn't mean them. It wasn't his style.

"How?" I managed to get out.

For the first time, I watched the colour rise in his neck and cheeks.

"Fell asleep with my cigar lit," he mumbled.

I tried to bite back the grin, but it slipped through despite my efforts. I changed the subject.

"We need to find a boat Dan. We have to get to the airport in Vancouver," I paused, then went on. "Have you been down to Deep Bay?" That was where all the local boats were kept, if there were any left.

"Nope. Didn't go that far. You got any painkillers? This arm is aching like a bitch in heat."

I grimaced at his expression. He could be so foul. But, I said nothing. It was hard to think of nagging at a man who'd saved us from the Nevermores. I stood and walked out into the kitchen and opened the small cupboard where I'd kept my medicine, not really thinking there would be any left. To my utter amazement, it was all still there.

It must have been their placement; the painkillers and antihistamines were on the same shelf as my bowls. Most likely whoever was looking was going fast and saw only the white and blue designs on the bowls and not what was in them.

I grabbed the bottle of extra strength Tylenol and popped three tablets into my hand. Scrounging around I found a decently clean container and went outside to fill it from the well.

Drawing water took some time and I looked around our property. It really didn't look all that different then when we were taken by Vincent and his army. The garden was actually doing not too badly. Even at this distance I could see that some of the veggies had come up in our absence.

I took the water back in the house, gave three Tylenol to Dan along with a glass of water, then took the same to Sebastian.

He was on his back, panting, though it wasn't that hot in here.

"Sebastian, sit up love. I need you to take this medicine," I said.

He struggled to get upright and ended up slumping against the headboard. I put the pills into his mouth and encouraged him to drink the water down with them. As soon as he swallowed, he slid back down.

"I think Dan's right," he said.

I stroked his hair with one hand, the other cradling my ever growing baby bump. My heart constricted with what I knew he was going to say.

"Shhh. Don't say anything," I whispered, tears clogging up my throat.

"I think I'm dying Mara."

I shook my head, though he couldn't see me. "No, that isn't what's happening at all."

Sebastian said nothing more; just lay quietly, his breathing evening out as I stroked his hair. Tears slid down my cheeks as I cried silently. I lowered my chin to my chest and bit back the sobs that threatened.

So much pain, fear and loss had dodged my ever footstep. I made myself consider the question that haunted my dreams.

Could I go on without Sebastian, if it came to that? I looked down on my belly, thought of the child I carried and the love I already had for him or her. Of how, even as a Nevermore, Sebastian's love for the baby helped him stay true to who he was, how he remembered me though the drug's haze. That love would continue, no matter if Sebastian was there beside me or not.

Resolve flickered through me, slowly hardening to a solid belief that I could do this, that I could finish this frightening journey we started together.

If Sebastian died, I could go on. It seemed that Dan might have been right about me after all.

11

The next few days passed in a blur of picking up old routines. Checking fences, bringing in water, finding food. There were a few peas on the vine, some baby carrots and the start of some squash, though they seemed to be behind in their growth. So the garden hadn't been a total waste of our time.

The blackberries had come in on a heavy crop; Dan and I spent the mornings picking enough to go with whatever else we managed to put together for meals. Sebastian seemed to improve with the steady diet of Tylenol, cool compresses and mashed berries. Though still weak, his conversations with me were longer and more cohesive.

Picking berries next to the front gate on the second morning, I broached the subject of the boat again to Dan.

"Woman, I don't know what you're thinking. Sure there might be boats, but you've got not one but two invalids to deal with. We have to wait until at least one of us is more capable."

I yelped as I pricked a finger on a thorn. My yelp was echoed back to me from the other side of the fence.

My head snapped around and Dan spun slowly.

"You heard that too?" I asked, keeping my voice low.

Dan nodded.

Another whimper and now I recognized it, though the shock nearly brought me to my knees.

Nero.

I was running along the fence line, struggling with the gate before Dan could stop me.

Shoving the one panel open, I let out a whistle. A sharp bark answered me and I ran to the right, the direction of the noise.

I pushed my way into the bush; I was ten feet in when I found him, lying on his side. He was skinny and scabbed over, dull-coated and wide-eyed with fear, but he was my Nero.

I dropped to my knees and reached for him, then paused. He was pinned to the ground by two sticks jammed through the loose skin on his flank and under his front legs. Blood oozed out of the wounds and he whimpered again.

"Who would do this?" I said.

Dan came up behind me, breathing hard. "We've got to get back inside the property woman."

"I have to get him out of here without making the wounds worse," I said, my hands brushing the sticks.

"Remember when I said the Nevermores were learning?" Dan asked me, his voice getting softer as he spoke.

I looked over my shoulder at him and took in the wide eyes, the tight line of his lips. I tried to swallow but couldn't get past the fear clogging my throat.

"Yes. I remember," I said, also keeping my voice soft.

"Why do you think they did this to your dog Mara?" He asked me.

Jaw clenched, I already knew; I didn't have to say it and neither did Dan.

They'd used him as bait.

Dan nodded and a crack of a branch off to my left slowly brought my head around. Three Nevermores crouched in the shadows, watching us watch them. Their hunting strategies were changing. In the past they would have jumped us immediately, now they seemed to be stalking us. Dan was right, they were learning, getting smarter. It was a terrifying notion, one that left me feeling sick to my stomach.

I knew that if Dan, Nero and I were going to make it out of this mess we'd have to move fast.

"Dan. I can't leave him."

He let out a grunt and the Nevermores shifted. "Then it's going to be on you to get him out of here."

I nodded. "On three."

Dan counted. "One." The Nevermores shifted towards us, their mouths open, their eyes wild.

"Two." I put my hands on the tops of the two sticks.

"Three." Dan leaped back the way we'd come and I ripped the sticks out of Nero's side. He let out a howl and I scooped him up and turned, already in a flat out run. Though we were only ten feet in, the bush was thick and slapped at my face, forcing me to duck my head. Instinctively, I closed my eyes to protect them from the branches rushing at me. That was a mistake.

I was all turned around; I didn't know which way we'd come in and I could hear the Nevermores in the bush around me. Were they herding me? My breath was coming fast and sharp and Nero quickly became a weight in my arms.

Fingers grabbed at my hair and some of my long brown locks were ripped out of my head. I kept running, the pain only spurring me on. They would do far worse than pull my hair if I was caught.

The bush clawed at me, and I gave a final burst of energy and stumbled out onto the open road. I'd come out about twenty feet south of the gate; between me and safety was the pack. I backed up as fast as I could, angling towards the fence line while still keeping an eye on the stalking pack. I could toss Nero over the fence and then climb it, but I wasn't sure I could make it in time. The pack was advancing steadily and I held Nero tight. Tears started to trickle down my cheeks as the realization hit me. I couldn't save us both. I'd been stupid to run out of the safety of the farm, right into the Nevermore's trap. Either way, Nero was going to die. I kissed the top of his once downy head, my tears dripping onto his fur.

"I'm so sorry Nero," I whispered.

12

I started to put him down on the road, his big brown eyes staring up at me. Dark pools filled with trust that broke my heart.

"Get over the fence woman!" Dan yelled. I looked up to see him inside the gate, his gun propped up on the top rail. I clutched Nero to me, spun and ran for the fence.

The pack screamed and howled as Dan fired into them, their attention completely diverted away from me and Nero. I stumbled through the ditch and found myself at the old barbed wire fence first, the nice, clean, easy-to-climb page wire another 6 inches in.

Holding Nero by the scruff of his neck, I reached over as far as I could and only had to drop him two feet instead of four. Then it was my turn. I started up the barbed wire, the rusty points digging into my hands, my back crawling with the fact that I couldn't see how close the pack was behind me.

I didn't need to.

A mouth clamped onto my upper thigh, my jeans the only thing to keep them from slicing into my flesh. I couldn't stop the cry that slipped out past my lips. Her teeth cut clamped on tight and the pain rocketed through me. I was caught with one leg on the farm side of the fence and one leg in the mouth of a Nevermore.

I pulled, but the Nevermore (one of the women) growled around her mouthful of my leg. I rode the edge of the two fences. The barbed wire bit into my inner thigh while I pulled on the brace that ran along the top of the page wire, trying to free myself. It was no use; there was no way I could pull my leg out of her mouth. I steadied myself with my left hand and cocked my right arm.

"Let go!" I yelled, snapped my arm forward and landed a solid blow, hitting her square on the nose.

The moment slowed as cartilage crunched under my fist, blood flew from her nose and a howl erupted out of her mouth. Unbalanced, I rocked in my precarious position and found myself thrown forward.

A breath, then another, as I struggled to keep myself from falling between the two fences. The Nevermore had stumbled away from me, shaking her head, dirty blond hair splattered with blood.

"I've got you."

Sebastian.

He helped me down from the fence and, though my legs were wobbly, I managed to stay upright.

Bending down, he picked up Nero and cradled him in his arms. "I heard the screaming. It woke me up." His eyes were fuzzy and I could tell he was uncertain. Did he wonder if he was still asleep, caught in some strange fever dream?

Words caught in my throat and I gave up trying to speak. I reached up and touched his cheek, the hollows so prominent from the sickness the cure brought on. His skin was clear of any hint of yellow and the images of broom plants under his skin were gone.

His eyes, though, remained golden, giving evidence to the fact that he had indeed been a Nevermore.

"I'm sorry Mara," he whispered, and I slid my fingers over his lips. The Nevermores continued to rant at the fence, but we ignored them.

"You don't need to apologize," I said. A glance over my shoulder at the pack as I reached for Bastian's hand. "Let's go inside."

We took a few steps and he stopped. "I do need to apologize. For giving up, for making you carry me and you both through this."

I closed my eyes and bit my bottom lip, pausing for a moment before answering. "Would you have acted any different if the roles had been reversed?"

"Of course not, but I'm supposed to take care of you, it's my job," he said.

I laughed and shook my head. "Bastian, that is a two way street."

With a gentle tug, I got him moving again.

Once inside, I tended to Nero's wounds first. They weren't life threatening, but they were going to take a long time to heal. Dan came stomping in as I was cleaning out the holes the sticks had made.

"Damn it to hell and back. Woman, you nearly got us both killed over a dog," he snarled, throwing himself into a chair, a grimace on his face. Nero lifted his head, saw Dan and wagged his tail.

A sneaking suspicion crept over me. "You know what I was trying to figure out Dan?" I asked.

"What?"

"How a small puppy like this could have survived for so long and only just now got caught by the pack," I said, rubbing a small amount of polysporin on the open wounds.

I glanced over at Sebastian who was sitting quietly at my side, his hands working at a burr on the back of Nero's leg.

I looked back to Dan and he flushed bright red for the second time that day.

"Ok, so I took care of him while you were gone. He took off when the house burned down," he grumbled.

I smiled and reached out to touch his arm. "Thank you Dan." There *were* cracks in the tough guy veneer after all.

Sebastian leaned forward. "We can't stay here."

"We've already discussed that Sleeping Beauty." Dan snapped his cigar, barely even recognizable now he'd chewed it so much.

I rubbed at my eyebrows, an ache beginning to form. "We need to get a boat and get across the straight. They're still evacuating people out of the Vancouver airport. It isn't much, but it's all we've got."

Sebastian nodded slowly. "Then tomorrow, that's what I'll do. I'll find us a boat."

"It isn't like before," I said, sitting down beside him. "You won't be able to sneak past the Nevermores. You aren't one of them."

"I'm not going to sit here and let you and Dan do this on your own. You especially, Mara. Have you even thought of the baby with everything you're doing? Do you even realize how many risks you've taken?" he asked.

The blood drained from my face; I could feel it disappear. I spoke in clipped words so I wouldn't start screaming at him.

"Everything I've done has been in an attempt to keep not only the baby safe, but you, too."

"Like taking the bait and going after Nero?" he asked.

I glared at him. "Like going into a pack of Nevermores to keep you close, like fighting off Donavan to get the cure, like hauling your sorry ass all the way back here to make sure you would live!"

Silence weighed the room down and it was Dan who broke it.

"With all you've been doing Mara, he's right. Let us find the boat."

I stared at him in disbelief. Only a short time ago we'd been discussing Deep Bay and how we were going to acquire a boat.

"Fine," I said. I bent and pulled Nero into my arms and stomped my way upstairs. Dragging out a laundry basket, I made a bed in it for the pup and put it beside the door. Then I all but threw myself on our old bed, the covers a little dusty but otherwise relatively clean.

Footsteps echoed up the stairway and I rolled to keep my back to the door. It gave out a little creak, and I closed my eyes.

A weight on the other side of the bed, which I also ignored, rolled me a way to the middle.

"I'm sorry if I upset you, babe. It's not that I don't think you can do it," Sebastian said.

"Then why are you trying to make it sound like I have been deliberately putting the baby in danger?" I asked, still not turning to look at him.

He was silent a long time before he answered. "This whole time, you've had to take care of yourself, even though

I was with you, I really . . . I wasn't. You had to be strong for all three of us. Let me take some of that now; let me help."

Now I did roll over on to my side, propping my head on my hand. "I don't want to lose you Bastian. Four times now I've thought you were gone forever." I ticked them off on my fingers. "When you told me you'd taken the Nevermore shot, when you went off with Jessica,"—he tried to interrupt me there but I rolled over him. "The water in the lagoon and now dealing with a cure that we aren't entirely sure of. One that seemed determined to fry you from the inside out. I refuse to think about losing you anymore. It's too hard on me, on my heart."

He turned and stared down at me. "You won't lose me."

"I've fought for you Bastian. I've learned that I was stronger than I ever knew before. Don't try to strip me of that because you feel like your manhood is threatened," I said.

His jaw tightened and the muscle under it twitched. I'd hit the nail on the head and we both knew it.

"We all go together or we don't go at all," I said. "It's safer that way. More weapons at hand, more eyes to scan for trouble."

He couldn't argue with that. Standing up, he kept his back to me. "Have we changed so much that you can't even tell me you love me anymore?"

Emotion caught in my throat. "Don't turn this into a game, Sebastian. We'll both lose."

He turned slowly and looked down at me, tears streaming down his cheeks. "I didn't think we'd ever be here again, not together. And, I am making a complete ass of myself."

Lips trembling, I smiled at him. "It's one of things I love you about you."

"That I make an ass of myself?" he asked, his eyebrows lifting. I nodded and bit down on a smile that was creeping out the edges of my lips.

Two steps and he was on the bed with me, his hands stroking my face, our foreheads pressed together. "Please Mara; forget everything I've said except this. I love you; I will do anything to keep you and the baby safe, to keep us a family."

"That's all I want, too," I whispered.

His lips found mine, teasing a groan out of me, the soft whisper of a love thought lost. His hands worked me out of my clothes and his quickly followed. No matter what else went on in our lives, the fear and uncertainty ended when it came to the love we had for each other and the passion that sealed the bond between us.

13

It was decided that we would go together, with all the supplies we could muster in the backpacks. Nero couldn't walk yet, so we made a sling out of an old sheet to wrap him in, and then hung him from Sebastian's chest.

Everything else would have fit in the bottom of one pack if it hadn't been for the blackberries.

"This isn't much," I said. The medicine cupboard went into the bottom of the pack and we'd harvested the last of the veggies from the garden. Blackberries were stuffed into plastic containers and filled the rest of the bag. A few bottles of water when into a second pack, then that bag, too, was filled with blackberries.

"It won't take long to get across the strait," Dan said. "A few hours at most."

"What if there aren't any boats with engines? Can we row across?" Sebastian asked. It was the same question hovering in my mind. There was no guarantee of a boat at all, never mind one with a running engine.

Dan let out a grunt and stuck a toothpick in his mouth. He'd had to convert once he finally gave up the cigar he'd chewed to near non-existence.

"I've got a boat down there, inside the bay but anchored off shore. Fuelled up and ready to go," Dan said.

I started to smile and then frowned. "Why didn't you say so before?"

"Didn't want you leaving without me," he said.

Sebastian slipped one of the packs on. "Maybe that's something you would do old man, but at the very least, you've got to realize Mara would never do that. Hell, she ran straight into danger for a mutt." He gave me a wink to soften the words and I slapped him on the shoulder, our old camaraderie securely back in place after our talk and lovemaking the previous night.

"Let's go boys," I said, securing my own pack. Dan handed a gun to each of us with his good arm. I didn't know what kind it was, only that the safety was off and I knew how to pull the trigger.

Sebastian led the way out the front door, his broad back a comforting presence as we started on what I hoped was the last leg of this journey.

The gate creaked as we opened it, and as we stepped through, I turned around to stare at out little farm, our sanctuary in this world that had turned upside down. The farmhouse, the woodpile, our garden. We would never see any of it again; of that I had no doubt.

"Let's go woman, before the wildlife shows back up," Dan said.

I took a deep breath and turned my back on our farm, prepared this time to leave it behind.

We headed down the dirt road until we hit pavement and then hung a left. We planned to stay on the main roads as much as possible, avoiding the bush and all it might hold.

The birds were singing, a good sign, and the heat was starting to fade as summer slipped away from us. We hadn't gone very far when Dan, who was in the lead, put his hand up to stop us. Finger to his lips, he crouched into the shadows, Sebastian and I following suit.

Adrenaline filled me, prepping me for a flight or fight situation. Keeping as low as we could, ducked into a small cluster of huckleberry bushes, I peeked through the leaves to see why Dan had stopped us.

The sweet scent of the tiny orange berries filled my nose as I scanned the road in front of us. A large black bear trundled out onto the road, his nose lifted in our direction. Bob wasn't looking so good though. My heart started to slow its pace; I feared Bob far less than I feared the pack of Nevermores. We may have taken their numbers down between the barn and Dan's shooting, but there were still at least fifteen left.

"Stay low. Bob isn't as friendly as he once was. Soon as I wasn't able to feed him, he turned on me," Dan said in a low whisper.

Bob made his way to a large apple tree that was hanging low over the road. There weren't many apples left, maybe a half dozen in the higher branches. He stood on his back feet and wobbled closer, his reach just enough that he could pull an apple down.

With a heavy sigh he plunked down on the ground and bit into the apple, seeming quite content.

"We're going to back through the bush and come out onto the road a ways down," Dan said.

Sebastian and I nodded our agreement, but the second we rose to go deeper into the bush, Bob let out a roar, freezing us in our tracks.

With great trepidation I turned, fully expecting Bob to be bearing down on us. In some ways, it was worse than that. The Nevermore pack had him surrounded, Jessica once more taking the lead.

As a single unit they leapt at Bob, two of them latching on to his back, their teeth burrowing into the flesh on his neck. I clenched my hands into fists. "Get them Bob!" I urged, still keeping my voice low.

A hand on my arm turned me. "We have to go Mara, this is our chance," Sebastian said. I let him lead me away as Bob's roars echoed through the neighbourhood. They went on for some time before a single howl went up from the pack, quickly joined by the rest.

"They killed him," Sebastian said, his voice soft.

"You can't be sure. He could've gotten away," I said, pushing a branch aside.

He glanced down at me. "I do know Mara. I still understand their language, even if I'm not one of them anymore."

"It's just one more reason for us to keep going," Dan said. He sped up the pace and even with his broken arm and the fact that he had twenty years on me, I found myself panting to keep up.

The rest of the day was uneventful; the pack presumably had enough food to last them a while and we took advantage of the respite. We stopped briefly for water and some berries twice, but that was it. By the time night fell, we had just made it into Deep Bay and Dan led us to a small house on the water front.

"We'll stay here tonight. I've got supplies stocked in the pantry and we can get to the boat tomorrow. If there was more light, we'd go now, but in the dark it would be treacherous. It's all trails through deep brush, perfect for an ambush," he said. Sebastian stared at him a full minute before asking the question that was on my mind.

"How long have you been planning this, Dan?"

Dan shrugged, then grimaced as his sling shifted. "Soon as that shot came on the market."

Sebastian grunted.

I was too exhausted to argue, my body aching and my feet swollen from walking on pavement most of the day. I wanted nothing more than to sit down for longer than five minutes.

The two men worked at opening tins of spaghetti-o's, which we ate cold, for dinner. Nero wiggled free of his sling and Sebastian set him on the ground. The pup got his own tin of pasta and red sauce, which stained the blond hair around his mouth. The image invoked one of the Nevermores devouring their feasts, and I quickly wiped the pup's face clean.

None of us talked much as we settled in for the night. Tomorrow was the day we got out of here, the day I could finally let my guard down and say goodbye to some of my fears as we left the pack behind.

Unfortunately for me, tomorrow was a day too far away.

14

A shattering of glass brought me bolt upright out of the nightmares I'd been reliving in my fitful sleep. Leaping to my feet in the semi-darkness, I grabbed my pack and had Nero in his sling before either of the two men were on their feet.

"The pack found us," I said.

"You sure?" Sebastian asked.

"Who else is going to be throwing rocks at us and breaking windows?" I asked, handing him his pack. No doubt that they were learning the longer the drug was in their systems.

The moon wasn't high but the reflection on the water gave us enough light to see by. Sebastian slipped the pack on and then went to the window. Chills rippled through me as Sebastian let out a low growl and then a sharp yip. Nero whimpered in the sling and I stroked his head to soothe him and me.

In answer, a chorus of howls and snarls went up all around the house. We were surrounded.

"Son of a pack of bitches," Dan cursed. He slung his own backpack on with his good arm then picked up his gun. "Come on children, we've got to get the hell out of here."

"They just want Mara." Sebastian's words rooted me to the spot.

"What?" I whispered.

He swallowed and put his hands on my shoulders. "They can't have you babe, we won't let them."

"But why?" I asked.

"I can only guess, but with Jessica leading the pack . . ." He trailed off.

I knew though. She'd seen me as a rival the minute the drug kicked in and Sebastian was a part of the pack, but more than that, he'd been their Alpha. I'd taken him from her, from the pack. It was my fault they were without a strong Alpha male.

"Out the back, it's closest to the docks," Dan barked out, no longer trying to be quiet. It didn't matter now; the pack knew we were here.

"Wait!" I said. I shrugged out of my pack and opened up two of the containers of berries. "What else is here Dan?" His eyes widened, but he caught on quick.

Within moments we had a five gallon bucket full of berries, canned goods and anything else edible we could find.

Hefting the bucket high, Sebastian took the lead. "This won't give us much time."

"Enough to get to the water?" I said.

He shook his head. "I don't know babe."

"Why the water? Why not the boat?" Dan asked.

"Nevermores are heavy, they sink, they don't float," I said. We stood at the back door, closest to the water. The waves were still a good hundred feet away and the docks even further than that.

At a nod from Dan, his face pale even in the dim light, Sebastian stepped out first and started to pour a line of slop. Food splashed out in a horrid mess of liquids and solids; the smell of beans and sweet fruit mixing with each other made my stomach roll. I gagged and swallowed hard to keep my own food where it needed to stay.

The Nevermores came bursting out of the surrounding trees and bush, falling on the food. It was hard not to stare and even though I knew we should be running for it, I couldn't pull my eyes away. Nero whimpered and I tucked his head into the sling.

A hand gripped my wrist and suddenly I was running full out, as fast as I could, Sebastian and Dan herding me along.

And then there was just Sebastian and me.

"Where's Dan?" I yelped as we dodged a large rock and raced out onto the upper reaches of the beach.

"Covering us." A large boom rattled and a chorus of screeches and howls ripped through the night air.

"No! They'll kill him!" I said.

Sebastian said nothing, just kept pressure on me to move forward as we ran straight towards the ocean. We reached the edge of the water and he pointed up the shoreline to the docks. There, moored a ways out in the bay, was a bobbing boat.

"That's Dan's," Sebastian said.

Three more sharp retorts of the rifle from behind us and then the night went silent once more. We slowed our pace; we had to. I was completely out of breath and Sebastian wasn't much better.

The silence was punctuated by the lapping of the waves across the rocks and the distant call of an owl. Nero panted heavily, the heat from our two bodies creating far more warmth then was necessary on a summer night.

"We have to hurry," I whispered, very aware at how our voices travelled out here in the open.

Sebastian nodded and we managed a slow jog all the way to the wharfs, down the half-rusted-out metal gangplank and onto the dock proper.

Dan's boat was not tied to the dock, but instead was anchored ten or fifteen yards out.

"Why would he do that?" I muttered.

"He said it was so no one would steal it. It's harder to get to and with all the other options available . . ."

We stared around us. There wasn't a single boat left, not even a row boat.

I slipped off my pack and handed Nero and his sling to Sebastian, then gave him the vial from inside my bra. "Can't have this floating away if I'm going for a swim."

"I can do it," Sebastian said.

"I don't think it's a good idea, Bastian. Are you sure you'd float?" I doubted if he'd lost the additional weight of his Nevermore created bones so quickly.

His jaw tightened and his lips thinned. "You're right."

I slipped out of my shirt and pants, the cool late summer air raising gooseflesh on my arms and legs. Sitting on the edge of the dock, I slid into the water with only a short gasp. Sebastian handed me a key.

"Did you and Dan plan this?" I asked.

He shrugged. "Dan slipped me the key last night. Figured I had the best chance at getting to the docks."

I took the key and Sebastian bent forward, pressing his lips to mine. "Be careful love."

"Always," I said.

Something cool and slimy brushed across my legs, slowly wrapping itself up my calf and I bit down a on a scream.

"What is it?" Bastian asked me, his hand already outstretched to pull me from the water.

"Seaweed," I hissed. "I hate the stuff, feels like it's going to pull me under." I started to doggy paddle away from the dock, each stroke of my hands or kick of my feet pushing through the bed of weeds.

Halfway to the boat, I spun onto my back so I could see Sebastian and maybe at least keep my hands out of the green sticky seaweed that seemed to be so attracted to me. On my back, Sebastian stood out on the dock, his tall figure silhouetted in the light of the crescent moon. But it was what crept towards him from the edge of the dock that had my complete attention.

Damn it, I should have waited. But, I was too close to the boat now to turn back. "Behind you," I called out. He turned to face her. Sebastian would have to deal with Jessica on his own.

15

The boat's hull was cold and had a lot of barnacles on it. On the side of the boat were deep indents that created a ladder of sorts that I used to pull myself up, handhold by agonizing handhold. My hip bumped into one of the bright orange fishing balls that hung off the side, swaying with each wave that rocked the boat.

Finally, I flipped over the railing, landing in a rather undignified heap, limbs akimbo. The key was in a death grip in my right hand and it was hard to loosen my frozen fingers.

Shaking from the cold water, and now seemingly colder night air, I fumbled with the ignition on the boat. A screech rent the air and my head snapped up to see Jessica and Sebastian at the edge of the dock, hands locked as he kept her from attacking him.

I turned the key and the engine rumbled smoothly to life. "Thank you, God," I breathed. Knowing that steering would be tricky, I manoeuvred slowly towards the docks, flicking through all the buttons, trying to find the lights. If I could shine them on the dock, I could see how the fight was progressing. As it was, all I could catch was movement and the occasional grunt. Finally, I found the right switch and flicked it on.

Sebastian was on his knees, slumping to the side and Jessica stood over him, one foot on his chest and a wicked smile on her face. Fear and anger warred within me, slamming against my heart so hard they took my breath away. My fingers clenched on the steering wheel as Jessica bent close to his face, her mouth open to strike.

"Get away from him you bitch!" I yelled as the boat slid into one of the parking bays and bumped around before settling to a stop. I flicked the engine off and scrambled out of the boat. There was blood around Sebastian's head, and I noted that one of the dock pylons had a dark smear on it where she'd smashed him. The only good thing was I could see the steady rise and fall of his chest. He was unconscious, but alive.

Jessica hissed at me, her eyes narrowing, her nostrils flaring as she took in my scent.

"Come on then, this is between you and me," I snarled. She lunged at me and I caught her hands, the same as Sebastian had. She was immensely strong for such a small girl and I remembered everything that Vincent has spoken of, that I'd seen so often in the last few months.

The Nevermore's speed, strength and ability to heal. The density of their bones and their intense fertility. As that thought bubbled forth, I looked down. Jessica *was* pregnant, her little belly protruding ever so slightly. But, I didn't have time to feel sympathetic. It was me or her.

With a grunt I stomped the heel of my foot on the top of her foot; she let out a howl and snapped forward, her teeth latching on to my collarbone.

I couldn't repress the scream that erupted out of my lips as she gnawed at my bone like a rabid dog. I forced my fingers underneath her jaw and gave a short, sharp jab. Jessica gasped and let go, shaking her head as her hands went to her jaw. I didn't give her a second respite.

I grabbed her hands, and with a twist, spun her, using her momentum to drop her to her knees, precariously close to the edge of the dock. She whimpered as I held her wrists, holding her out over the open water.

"We are done," I growled, bending her wrists to keep her in place. I was going to have to push her into the water if I was to end this.

She cried out and tears trembled on the edge of her eyelids, her yellow eyes with the strange rectangle irises full of more than hunger for once. They were full of fear. I felt my own eyes begin to well up. She was a Nevermore, but still, somewhere inside of her was the young girl with the beautiful blue eyes that danced when she smiled. Could I truly watch her drown knowing that perhaps she could be cured?

Jessica lowered her eyes, but I continued to hold her.

I took her hands and held them with my own, rubbing my fingers over her knuckles. If she were my daughter, my child, I would want her to have this last moment of humanity, touching one of her own kind before she forgot everything she was and could have been.

"I wish we could've done more."

Frozen in place, some of my last words to Jessica rolling over and over in my mind, I think I would have stayed there indefinitely if it hadn't been for Dan.

"What the hell woman? What were you thinking ram-
ming my boat into the dock?" he grumbled as he stepped
onto the wharf. He was covered in bites and scrapes, was
limping slightly and his gun had a chunk out of the stock,
but otherwise he was unscathed.

"You didn't leave instructions on how to drive it. Now
would you mind getting me some rope?" I said, trying not to
smile too much. It wasn't often you saw a friend come back
from the dead.

"You don't really want to bring her along do you?" he
asked, even as he uncoiled a length of rope with his good
hand and helped me to bind Jessica's arms and legs.

I nodded, my decision made, and helped him tie her up
as, while she didn't lunge at me, she snapped at Dan more
than once.

"If the cure is a fluke, we can let her go, or put her out
of her misery. But if it isn't a fluke and there's a chance for
her . . ." I trailed off and found myself flashing back to the
moment at our farm gate, thought of how I'd said goodbye to
Jessica at our home, through the fence. How I knew if she'd
been my daughter, I would've hoped someone looked out for
her. I let out a sigh. She couldn't be held responsible for the
things she'd done as a Nevermore. I knew that, as much as a
part of me wanted to hate her for coming on to Sebastian as
she'd done when he first turned or how she targeted me even
tonight.

Dan grunted and grabbed the rope around her ankles
with his good hand and helped me lift her into the boat. "By
the way," Dan said. "Nice gitch."

I looked down at my bra and panties, the once bright
pink fading to a dull colour that was covered in what had

once been hot pink lips with wings on them. I hadn't even noticed till now how awful they were. Laughing, I pulled on my clothes while Dan bent and roused Sebastian.

He was groggy; the gash in his forehead didn't seem that deep but was still bleeding. I started to get a strip of cloth to bandage it when there was rustling in the bush.

"Time to go kiddos," Dan said. Sebastian didn't answer; he was strangely mute as we helped him into the boat along with Nero and the rest of our packs.

Dan was able to navigate easily, if for nothing else than the fact that there were no other boats in the harbour. It didn't hurt that he had a massive set of floodlights on the top of his boat that lit his path as well as if it were daylight. His boat was about twenty feet long and had a full cab that the four of us huddled in. The cold air whipped around us as he pushed the throttle slowly up, the boat quickly skimming over the waves. Even with a broken arm he got us out of the harbour in no time flat.

I held Sebastian's head against my chest and whispered into his ear. "What happened back there?"

"I don't want to talk about it Mara. Maybe later?" he mumbled, as he wrapped his arms around me and held me tight. Nero wriggled out of his sling and wobbled over to us, nosing his way in between our bodies.

Jessica lay across the cab and she stared at us, a blank look in her eyes. I got to my feet and wobbled over to her, the waves rocking my every step. Now that she was still and not trying to attack and eat us, I could see that she had been battered and bruised, her ribs showing every minor detail as the yellowed skin was pulled tight across them. Her eyes were sunk deep into her head and as she stared up at me, panting,

I could see that several of her teeth had been broken off and one knocked out completely.

An old blanket lay bundled up in the corner of the cab. Though the wool was musty, it was at least dry. I draped it over her shivering body, the shreds of clothes she had left barely covering her. I shook my head. Even if I got her to the airport, they wouldn't let her on the plane. Then I'd be forced to let her go into a new area, with a new pack that she didn't know. Who's to say that the new pack wouldn't just kill her outright, as an intruder?

"You did the right thing." Sebastian came up beside me, holding the railing for balance with one hand and pressing the cut on his head with the other.

"You shouldn't be up and about," I said, reaching out to touch his arm.

"If the cure works as well on the others as it has on me, you never would have forgiven yourself if you'd left her behind when you could have brought her with us. So stop fussing about the what ifs," he said. Once again I was struck by how well he knew me, and I smiled, just the corners of my lips lifting up. A wave hit the side of the boat, sending a spray of salt water up and over the cab. I steadied myself on the railing, the tang of the ocean filling my nostrils.

"Thanks. Let me take a look at that gash. It may need to be stitched if we can stop and use the first aid kit, there's no way I'm using a needle on you with the swells like this." I glanced over at Dan at the wheel to see if he took note of my words. Nope. He stared straight ahead, a cigar clamped firmly once more in his mouth, a curl of smoke trailing out behind him. He must have had a stash on the boat.

Sebastian sat and leaned his head back while I gingerly pulled the cloth away. I didn't want the bleeding to start again, but I would have to take this off at some point to see just how bad the wound was.

The bandage stuck and he winced as I had to work it off his skin. "The bleeding seems to have slowed down. That's good," I said.

With the bandage off, I cleaned all around the gash, before starting to work on the wound itself. I too a deep breath, waiting for a calm between waves. Sebastian held stoic underneath my hands.

"How's it look?" He asked.

I swallowed hard as the blood disappeared under the cloth, revealing shiny, pink new skin where his body had healed the injury. In less than half an hour. I closed my eyes and bit down on the inside of my cheek.

Sebastian was still healing like a Nevermore.

16

"What is it? Mara?" His voice cut through my fear and I snapped my eyes open. Sebastian stared at me, his brows pinched with concern. "Is it that bad?"

I slowly shook my head, then picked up his hand and placed his fingers where the gash has been.

His eyes widened as his fingers probed and slid over the new, healed skin.

"You're still healing fast. Too fast," I said.

He shrugged. "It's probably just a hangover from the drugs. No doubt it will fade too, like the rest of the symptoms."

I nodded and he pulled me into his arms, kissing the top of my head. He was right, I was sure of it. But, in the back of my mind I wondered.

I fell into a fitful sleep, nightmares and fear chasing me through dreamland. Every time I startled awake Bastian was there, soothing my anxieties, holding me close. I finally fell into a heavy sleep, one that took me too deep for dreams and allowed me a measure of peace.

As dawn crept over the horizon and the rays of light settled on my face, I slowly woke up. Sebastian was snoring lightly, his chin on his chest. I unravelled my limbs from his without disturbing him and went to stand next to Dan, who was guiding the boat down the coast.

"How long before we have to disembark?" I asked, knuckling my back and suppressing a yawn.

"We got company," Dan said, jerking his head to the right.

I turned to see a small row boat making its way towards us, two people waving like mad at us.

"What do you think? Should we help them?" Dan asked.

I frowned. "What do you mean? Of course we should help them!" I snapped. How could he think we would just walk away from someone in need?

Dan grunted and spun the wheel with one hand, taking us out towards what I realized now was a floundering boat. As we drew closer, I saw, with great surprise, a young woman I recognized.

"Annie?" I called out, dredging her name up out of my memory banks.

Her blond head snapped up, purple highlights catching the morning sun. She frowned and then her eyes widened with recognition. "You didn't get eaten!" she cried out. I smiled and then the smile faded as I recalled how afraid she'd been when she'd seen Sebastian passed out in the Jeep.

What would she think when she saw a fully fledged Nevermore tied up in the bottom of the boat?

We helped Annie and her brother on to the boat just as the wooden dingy they'd been in began to truly sink, water swelling over the sides and up through the bottom. The young man, he looked to be about thirteen or fourteen, cried out as we hauled him into our boat.

"I can't swim," he whispered, his blue eyes wide, beads of sweat popping out on his forehead.

I racked my brain. "You're Dustin, right?" I asked. He nodded and I helped him into the cab and settled him into one of the seats. He glanced down at Jessica, looked away and then back again, letting out a scream as he scrambled to get away from her.

"Shhh. She's tied up. She won't hurt you," I said, trying to calm the suddenly frantic and terrified boy.

Nero started to bark while Jessica let out a growl and attempted to lunge at Dustin.

Dustin threw his body back, right into the controls. The boat lurched into action and I heard Dan yelp, but I didn't look back. I grabbed at Dustin and all but threw him out of the cab, shoving him out past Jessica and into the waiting arms of his sister.

Dan rushed past me. "What the hell!" he snarled, as he grappled with the controls. One look up through the window and I knew why he was scrambling. We were headed for a sharp out cropping of rocks that were scattered through this section of water—and we were a long ways from shore.

"Brace yourselves!" Dan hollered, and I reached for one of the railings just as we hit the first rock. The boat shuddered, the hull groaning, and water started to roll in through the hole.

Jessica let out a howl as the water splashed in around her. Of course; she would sink and she knew it. "Sebastian!" I yelped, as I pulled Jessica to a sitting position. She was chattering at me, her teeth clacking together, her yellow eyes wide with fear. I worked at her knots furiously until a hand tried to pull me away.

"She'll attack us!" Annie yelled at me, while Dustin muttered "I'm sorry." Over and over again.

I ignored him and answered Annie. "No, I won't let her attack anyone. Besides, she's more afraid of the water than anything else right now," I said.

Once she was free of the ropes, Jessica flung herself at me, clinging to me like a child. Her entire body was trembling, her breathing erratic and her clutch so tight it was almost unbearable. I turned to see where the others were. Dustin and Annie clung to one another; Dan had picked up Nero and Sebastian stood at the railing, staring out at the sky. At first I was angry—why hadn't he helped me with Jessica? Why the hell was he just standing there?

Very slowly my mind grasped what he must be going through. Both his father and his brother were killed in a boating accident, before we'd met. It had been a freak storm that swamped the boat and the bodies were never found. And here we were, in a sinking boat. I couldn't count on him right now to help me; for now I would have to make do with Dan.

Of the group, I knew that Dan and I *might* be able to swim the distance to shore. Annie probably could too and maybe, between the three of us, we could drag Dustin. But Jessica would sink for sure and Sebastian . . .

"This ain't going to turn out well," Dan muttered. "I only got one life jacket." He held up an ancient looking orange rag, mold growing down one side of it, which appeared to be one of the forerunners to the modern life jacket. He handed it to me and I stared at the limp hunk of material.

"You're kidding me, right?" I asked, my eyebrows climbing into my hairline. He snatched it back and tied it on to Dustin himself. The boat had a foot of water in it now and Jessica was crying as she clung to me.

Sebastian continued to stare out at the distant sky and ocean. "You got a flare gun, Dan?" he asked. We all went silent and looked out in the same direction he was. In the distance was tiny black speck in the sky. A helicopter.

Scrambling, Dan had to duck his head under water to get to the flare gun buried in a pile of his junk. The water had risen another foot and was almost to my knees now. Dustin was whimpering and Annie was attempting to soothe him. I couldn't blame him for panicking when he saw Jessica. No doubt what the two kids had to survive to get to this point would have been horrendous.

Sputtering up to the surface, Dan stood. He set the flare gun and pulled the trigger. For a brief second I thought it was a dud and then a brilliant red streak of light leaped out of the barrel and into the sky.

The boat lurched; Annie and Dustin screamed and clung to one another. I held Jessica on her feet and Sebastian continued to stare out at the helicopter. They had to have seen that flare, there was no way they could've missed it. Even as the thought crossed my mind, the helicopter turned and flew down the coastline away from us.

Our mismatched group let out a collective groan. There was no one coming to save us.

17

"What are we going to do?" Annie whispered, her voice easily carrying over the water.

"We're going to get to shore and set up camp," I said, prying Jessica's fingers off of me. Dan's eyebrows lifted and he spit out his soggy stump of a cigar.

"Just how do you plan to do that? One can't swim, one'll sink like a rock, I got a broken arm and . . ." He trailed off and looked over to Sebastian's broad back.

Sebastian turned his head towards us. ". . . And you don't know yet whether I will be able to keep my head above water."

I slogged through the knee deep water and looked over the side of the boat. The fishing buoys were still hanging off the edge. There were four of them. "We'll use those. Annie and Dustin can use one, Dan and Sebastian can each have one, and I'll help Jessica."

In under a minute, we had the floaters cut free. They wouldn't be perfect, but they would do the job.

"I don't want to do this," Dustin whimpered.

Before I could say anything, Annie grabbed his shoulders and gave him a shake. "Hey, you've faced down scarier things than this. So grab the floater and let's go." She turned him, her face drawn and looking far older than her years. But, she got Dustin in the water and they started towards the shore.

Dan went in next, his gun slung across his chest, taking Nero with him too. We tied the puppy to the buoy so once he tired he wouldn't drown or get swept away.

The water was up to my waist now and Sebastian and I watched the two groups swim out into the ocean with no difficulty, other than Nero making an attempt to catch the seaweed as it floated by him.

"What if we tied the last two buoys together? Would that make it easier?" I asked.

Sebastian shook his head. "Yes, then if I sink, you can easily get to shore with two buoys."

His words hit me hard and I swayed where I stood, telling myself that it was the waves, not my emotions. "You aren't going to sink," I managed.

"Just the same. I don't want to be separated from you, especially if these are the last minutes we have." He reached out and smoothed my hair, tucking it behind my ear.

We'd said goodbye so many times before, I just didn't have the heart to do it again. "No, I won't say it, so get your ass in gear and let's get out of here."

He smiled at me, a whisper of the cheeky man he'd once been. He opened his mouth, then froze.

The boat groaned and we sunk another few inches. Jessica let out a yelp, her fingers digging into my arm as she shivered and clung to me. "We have to go," I said, my throat tightening with fear.

Sebastian swiftly tied the two floats together and he beck-oned me over. Jessica made it difficult, but we managed the few steps. I tried to get Jessica to hang on to the float and a very large flaw in our plan became apparent. She couldn't grip anything; she didn't have any fine motor skills.

I pinched the bridge of my nose. "Shit."

"Now what?" Bastian asked.

The water was past my belly button and I let out gasp as the water lapped even higher. Jessica stood tight against me, her whole body quivering, her eyes shut tight and her lips parted as she panted for air. Sebastian stood quietly, his eyes not giving any indication of fear or any other emotion.

"We'll have to tie her to the floats."

She didn't resist us as we rushed to tie her between the two floats. Once secured, Sebastian took the float on the left, I took the one on the right and we went to step out into the open water.

"Wait!" Sebastian said, our feet on the lip of the boat. I jumped, startled, as he turned back and dove down into the cab of the boat. I sucked in a lungful of salty air, my heart struggling to catch up with my racing thoughts. What was he doing? There was nothing in there of any value. Bubbles floated to the surface as I started to count in my head. When he'd been down for forty-five seconds I started towards where he'd gone in.

"Come on babe," I whispered, my hands clenched around a cold, wet length of rope.

A sudden rush of bubbles and he broke the surface, gasp-ing for air. I struggled towards him, grabbed his hands and helped pull him upright. Gripped in his teeth was a large knife.

"You went back for that?" I asked. He nodded and I shook my head as the boat suddenly shifted, groaned, and began to sink in earnest, the water rising at an alarming rate. Jessica let out a howl and I swam—it was easier than walking at that point—to her side. The water was to her chin. I tightened the ropes and tucked her between the two floats. Taking a deep breath I looked over to Sebastian. He had the knife in his left hand, the right on the ropes attached to the float closest to him. He gave me a smile and a wink and my heart lifted a little. For now, he was with me, 100%.

With a small push, we were out in open water, the floats sagging under the weight of the three of us, but holding. Jessica whimpered, her eyes still shut, her body limp in the ropes.

"This isn't so bad," I said, as we started to swim for shore.

"It's a long ways in, love. I wouldn't get too cocky, yet," Bastian said. I rolled in the water to face him and saw that he was struggling to keep his head above water. He was still heavy with the effects of Nevermore, the density in his bones dragging him down.

There was nothing I could do except swim harder and hope, to all that was holy, that we would make it.

Halfway to shore was when the quiet calm that had settled over us evaporated in the hot mid-afternoon sun. My mind and body were numb from the constant push. I could see Sebastian out the corner of my eye still struggling, but keeping it together. Jessica was still pretty much a rag doll in between us, her breathing rapid, but her body still.

And then she opened her eyes. Letting out a screech that startled me right off the float, I was pushed under by a wave. The water was cool and soothing on a sunburn I hadn't realized I'd been getting. For a moment I let the water hold me and I floated in an empty spot, my mind revolting at the thought of something else going wrong. Only a few seconds passed, but it felt longer, like I could let myself float there forever.

One stroke and I broke the surface of the water to see Jessica flailing, her body only held up by the floats. "Stop it!" I yelled at her as I swam closer. She flung out her arms, catching me in the side of the face, stunning me with its force.

"We have to cut her loose!" Sebastian yelled, already hacking at the ropes.

"No! She'll drown!" I yelled.

"It's us or her, we can't all make it to shore," he shouted, as one of the ropes broke free, plunging Jessica under water, her howls muffled and the bubbles from her last breath quickly rising to the surface.

"Mara, don't come so close, I'm afraid she'll . . ."

I didn't hear the rest. A hand clamped onto my calf, nails digging into my skin, yanking me under water before I could even take a breath.

I opened my eyes to see Jessica staring up at me, her eyes wide and pleading. She wasn't trying to hurt me; she was terrified.

Reaching down I pried her fingers off my leg and held her hand as I swam upwards, pulling her with me. It was no use. She was too heavy and I watched in horror as the rest of the ropes trailed down around us, like streamers thrown at a party.

I flashbacked to the last time I'd seen Jessica as a human. The final words I'd said to her, how impossible my plea had been considering what we both knew she was becoming. My tears were swept away by the ocean. I squeezed her fingers and her eyes softened as she gave me the slightest of nods, her hand opening in mine.

As she sank into the darkness, her eyes never left mine and I mouthed the words I'd said to her once before.

"Be safe, sweetheart."

18

My head broke the surface and Sebastian pulled me into his arms, a sob rippling out past his lips.

"I thought I'd lost you," he said, body shaking as he held me.

I wanted to cling to him, wrap myself in his warmth, but we still had a long way to go. Minutes rolled by as we swam for the beach, Dan, Annie and Dustin urging us on, Nero barking at their feet.

A quick glance at Sebastian, who with the help of the float was keeping his head well above water, eased my mind. Stroke after stroke we cut through the water, the swell of the waves occasionally lifting us and propelling us forward.

When my feet brushed against the sand, I started out of the daze I'd settled in. My muscles screamed at me, the fatigue I'd been ignoring finally crashing down over me. Sebastian slogged through the water and wrapped an arm around me, kissing me on top of my head.

"We made it," he whispered, the disbelief in his voice surprising me.

I smiled up at him, then let the smile fall, as I once more in my mind saw Jessica float down into the depths of the ocean, her eyes wide and trusting. I burst into tears and Sebastian held me close. Then another set of arms and another and another wrapped around me, until I was cocooned within them. The sobs trailed off into hiccups that left me shaky. Dan patted my back and left the group hug first, his sling gone and his broken arm tucked into his shirt.

"You did the right thing, Mara," he said, his voice gruff as he waded back to shore.

Annie gave me a last squeeze and Dustin followed her lead as they too headed back to shore. Sebastian and I linked hands and stumbled the rest of the way in, our legs weak.

Once we were all on the beach, it was decided we would camp there for the night, building a fire and sticking close to the water in case any Nevermores showed up. That way we had an easy escape.

I sat down, my back against a large piece of driftwood, the tiny pebbles that made up the beach shifting underneath me as I settled my weight. The small rocks were hot and warmed up underneath me. Nero trotted over to me, his limp improving already, and flopped down in the rocks by my side.

Letting my hand rest on his still damp back, I watched Annie take charge and direct the boys to get firewood as she started on building the pit a few feet away from me.

She glanced up, her blue eyes tired. "My dad used to take us to the beach all the time. He showed us how to start a fire and we'd roast marshmallows. . ." Her voice was suddenly thick with tears.

"We're almost there, Annie," I said, reaching out to touch her purple and blond hair. Somewhere along the way she'd lost her diamond nose ring. I didn't think now was the time to tell her.

She nodded, swallowed down the tears and went back to piling rocks in a circle to make a barrier for the fire.

I lay back on the rocky beach, my right hand on my belly, the sun warm on my face and drifted in and out of sleep. Something rolled under my right hand and my eyes opened wide. The baby.

"I felt the baby move!" I shouted and everyone froze what they were doing. I pressed my hands against my stomach and . . . there is was. Like a butterfly fluttering around in there, only bigger—maybe a bird would be more accurate.

Annie was the first to crouch beside me. "Can I feel?"

I nodded and she placed her hands on my belly. "I don't feel . . . wait, there!" She lit up, her smile stretching across her face.

I looked around to see Sebastian staring down at us, his face grim. I smiled up at him, refused to be pulled into his worries, and fears about this child.

"Sebastian," I called to him, keeping my voice soft. He closed his eyes and his chest lifted as he took a deep breath. Like going into battle, he strode over to my side and dropped to his knees.

His big hands pressed gingerly into my stomach and Annie snorted. "You have to press real hard, you aren't going to break her."

I gave Annie a wink and put my hands over Sebastian's, pressing them in to my belly.

He didn't seem to feel the first flutter of movement; he kept his eyes closed and his mouth tight. Annie, perhaps sensing this was not a moment for her to be a part of, stood and went to help the others gather wood.

Alone, I whispered to him. "No matter what, we will love this baby Sebastian. No matter what."

Tears trickled down his cheeks. "It's my fault, Mara."

"That I'm pregnant? Yes, that is your fault. Nothing else is though," I said.

He opened his eyes and I drew in a big breath. It would take me a long time to get used to him having golden eyes. I didn't mind though, he was with me; that was all that mattered.

"That the baby is deformed." He took a breath and let it out in a shuddering sigh.

I shook my head and took his face in my hands. "We have not come all this way to give up now. You are going to make it with me to that airport, we are going to get on a plane and we are going to get the hell out of here. Got it?" I rubbed the tear tracks off his face with my thumbs.

He leaned in and kissed me, softly at first and then deeper, wrapping his arms around me and pulling me into his lap. If only we'd been alone… but of course, it was at that moment that Dustin came running around the corner, out of breath, his eyes wide and his words barely intelligible. It took three tries to get him to spit it out. And as the seconds passed, I could only imagine what it was going to be. Nevermores? Marauders? A forest fire that would burn all the way to the beach? I was betting on one of the first two, though I would rule out nothing at this point.

Dustin took a big gulp of air and finally spit it out.

"A boat! There's a big boat coming this way!"

19

We scrambled to our feet as Annie and Dan came around the corner. "We've got to get that fire going. Now!" Dan shouted.

The five of us threw the firewood on, Annie and Dan fighting over the best way to light it. Dan finally produced the flare gun. "Get the kindling ready, we'll shoot into it and that should light it."

Annie had her hands on her hips, her head shaking, her twenty-something attitude showing. "I don't think it will work."

"Have you got a better idea, pipsqueak?" Dan growled at her.

We all stepped back as Dan lined up the gun and squeezed the trigger. Again, there was a delay and then a puff of smoke and a red streak flew right into the pit. Of course, Annie was right too, and kindling and burning wood burst out of the pit. We all ran to get the pieces and get them back on the pile and within a few short moments, we had a blazing fire going, the tinder-dry wood lighting easily.

But there was no smoke.

"We need some wet wood," I said, casting my eyes around. Up the slope was a small stand of alder trees, their leaves still green. That would work. I made my way up the slope and started to break off branches, throwing them down to Dustin who ran them over and threw them on the fire.

The green wood produced a large cloud of smoke that curled up into the sky.

I smiled, one hand on the closest alder tree for balance, the other pumped into the air. "It worked!"

From the higher ground, I could see a large freighter cruising into the harbour, avoiding the rocks that we crashed into and anchoring just off shore. A rowboat was lowered into the water and two men jumped aboard. We waved and hollered, making damn sure they could see us. I mean really, how could they miss us? But, still we waved.

One of the two men's heads snapped up and with it a gun, aimed straight at me. What the hell? I ducked and slid as the boom of the rifle ripped through the air and a squeal of rage erupted from behind me. I didn't turn around, I knew what was there.

I slipped and slid down the slope and into Sebastian's waiting arms where he held Nero tight. Dan stumbled, cursed, and rolled to his back as a Nevermore leaped onto him. The Nevermore's head exploded in a shower of blood and bone, the marksmen covering us.

Annie bent and grabbed Dan's arm, Dustin grabbed the other, well above the break. Sebastian and I were steps away from the water when I was suddenly standing by myself. I spun as Sebastian dropped Nero and was yanked into the fray by three large Nevermores.

I scooped up Nero as one of the Nevermores attacking Sebastian dropped to the ground, a bullet wound appearing in his neck. I hadn't even heard the rifle shot over the howling and high-pitched screaming.

"Get in the water, Mara!" Sebastian yelled, as he slugged a Nevermore in the jaw. I did as he said, sloshing into the water, the waves up to my knees in a few brief heartbeats. One of the men jumped out of the boat and slogged his way over to me. I handed him Nero and ignored the surprised look on his face. "Take him. I'll help the others."

He grunted, and I spun back to face the blood bath that only moments before had been a quiet sanctuary. Sebastian was in the water, blood trickling from a bite wound on his collarbone and a split lip, but otherwise he was okay. Annie stood in the water, also up to her knees, breathing hard, Dustin clinging to her—No, he wasn't clinging to her, *she* was clinging to him.

"Annie..." I called out.

She turned towards me, her eyes streaming with tears. Dustin was limp in her arms, his neck no longer whole. I could see the white of his spine as his head flopped with each effort she made to hold him upright. I ran to Annie as she started to scream, her head tipped back to the sky, peal after peal of anguish ripping out of her. I didn't try to hush her, just wrapped my arms around her body and held her until her voice ran ragged and her breathing slowed.

"I won't leave him," she whispered.

"Of course not," I said. I motioned and Sebastian came and lifted Dustin up into his arms, so carefully, as if the boy was only sleeping and not gone forever. Annie followed them, her hand holding one of Dustin's.

Again, I turned to the beach.

Dan, where was Dan?

I couldn't see the crotchety old man and my heart constricted. I pushed hard and was ankle deep in a few seconds. There was blood everywhere, and no sign of Dan. The Nevermores pulled back, opening up a corridor of yellow skin, where at the back of the beach lay Dan.

"Dan!" I yelled.

"They didn't kill me that easily," he said, hawking a wad of blood on the ground beside him.

I tried to see a way around this; we couldn't just leave him there.

"Don't you dare even think about coming for me. They struck me a killing blow, a nice slow one to draw you in. You remember this, Mara. They're getting smarter, they're learning our weaknesses." He coughed and groaned as I stood helpless on the edge of the beach, the water now just deep enough to cover the tops of my feet. This couldn't be happening, not when we were so close to safety.

"Dan, we can't leave you here. The men have guns, they can . . ."

He interrupted me. "Not enough to kill the pack quick-like so you can get me out. Even if you did," he coughed and spit blood again. "I don't think I'd make it. So, I have only one thing left to say."

Tears started to creep down my face and I dashed them away. Dan wouldn't appreciate tears, not at his expense.

He let out a low moan as he slid himself into a sitting position, just as Sebastian came up beside me, slipping an arm around my waist.

"Dan?" Bastian said his voice heavy with sorrow.

Dan grunted. "This is what I got to say to the two of you."

We waited while he caught his breath. "I'm proud to say you were my friends, and..."

Sebastian's arm tightened painfully around me, and I bit the inside of my cheek to keep from crying out.

"You make a damn fine cookie, considering they were burnt." He gave me a wink and slid his hand behind him. I heard the rifle click and buried my head against Sebastian's chest.

The boom of the gun and the ensuing squeal of the Nevermores was enough for me; I didn't need to see what was left of Dan. We turned in the water and swam out to the boat where the men helped us in, my tears disappearing into the waves.

One of the men, who later told us his name was Pete, grunted with the strain. "Damn, you don't look that big man."

Sebastian grunted, but said nothing as the men hauled him over the side. Once in the boat, I held Annie, our grief binding us as nothing else could. I tried to keep her eyes on things other than her little brother's lifeless body, but it was impossible. The men lifted Dustin's body in and wrapped it in a tarp.

"I can't believe he's gone. I thought we'd made it together, we were so close," Annie said, the highlights in her hair looking duller, the brilliant hue of her eyes clouded with grief. She couldn't seem to stop staring at his wrapped body.

There was nothing I could say to ease the pain for her, so I said nothing, only held her, turning her head away from him and holding her tight. It wasn't much, but it was the only comfort I could give.

We were lifted up, boat and all onto the larger freighter; no, it was one of the old ferries. No wonder it took them so long to get to us. The old clunkers were not known for their speed.

"Here we are," Pete said. "We'll be back in Vancouver in an hour or so. We came as quick as we could."

Pete continued as our tour guide. "We did see your flare, but the helicopter was running out of fuel, so they sent the boat after all of yous." He smiled, showing us missing teeth and one gold capped tooth that sparkled in the sunlight.

"Thank you." Sebastian reached out and shook Pete's hand.

I kept Annie tight to my side and we went in under cover, sitting down in one of the green faux leather seats that filled the ferry. Leaning my head back, I closed my eyes, Annie's head dropping to my shoulder, Sebastian on my other side holding Nero, one of his hands tucked into mine. I let out a deep breath.

We were finally safe.

20

The ferry, The Queen of Saanich to be exact, docked at the Tsawwassen ferry terminal where we disembarked. Walking through the terminal with its empty booths and empty lanes for vehicles was spooky. Our footsteps echoed through the hallways, feet slapping on the tiled stairways that took us down to where armoured vehicles—that at one point in their lives had been Brinks Security trucks—waited for us. I sat quietly between Sebastian and Annie, Nero asleep in my arms. None of us spoke a word for the first few minutes. It was me who finally broke the silence.

"I didn't get the chance to thank Dan for taking Nero in when we were taken away," I said.

Sebastian scrubbed Nero's head, messing up his fur. "I bet the little beggar whined at Dan's door till he let him in." Though I doubted that very much, I smiled at the image it put in my head, no doubt Sebastian's intent.

In under an hour, we were at the airport and taken into one of the waiting rooms. Our names and information were taken down and were then sent to the medical teams for blood work and a general health evaluation.

Annie went in first, Sebastian and I held back. This was the moment of truth, when we found out how well the cure really worked.

"We should go in together," I said. Sebastian nodded, and I led the way when my name was called.

There was a doctor and a nurse, both women. "Hello, I'm Dr. Stanwell. This is nurse Allton." Dr. Stanwell looked to be in her late forties, early fifties and her blond hair had grown out, showing the grey roots beneath. Sharp, intelligent green eyes met mine and I swallowed hard.

I reached inside my bra and pulled out the vial I'd stolen, what seemed so long ago, from Donavan's compound. "My name is Mara Wilson, this is my husband Sebastian. We were held captive by a man named Donavan, and he had what he thought was a cure for Nevermore."

The two women stared at me, their mouths hanging open as I quickly spun out our story, albeit missing the parts where Sebastian was a Nevermore. I wasn't telling them anything I didn't have too. I finished by explaining how Marks and his men had broken into the compound, had saved Sebastian and me, and how I'd gone back for the cure.

"Why didn't Sebastian go instead?" Dr. Stanwell's eyes narrowed. I swallowed and took a shallow breath.

"He was sick, running a high fever. He could barely walk," I said, as Sebastian nodded in agreement.

"And that's it. That's how we got here." I handed the vial over to her. "I don't know if it needed to be cold or what, but at least we got it here."

"That you did, Mara," Dr. Stanwell whispered. She handed the vial to the nurse with instructions to take it to the lab immediately. Nurse Allton rushed out of the room.

"You have brought us hope, you and Sebastian. But," she held up a finger, "if either of your blood work doesn't come up clear, I can't guarantee you will be leaving Vancouver." Again, her eyes narrowed. "I find your eye colour fascinating Sebastian. So much like that of the Nevermores."

I had to give Bastian credit. He just shrugged and gave her a lopsided smile. "These eyes have drawn many a woman into my lair." He wriggled his eyebrows at her as I slapped him on the arm.

"Quit that you lech," I said, a nervous laugh escaping my lips.

Dr. Stanwell's lips didn't twitch. Apparently we weren't that good at lying because she seemed suspicious.

I tried a different tactic, cleared my throat and asked, "Have you had anyone tested that didn't pass?"

Dr. Stanwell shook her head. "No. You either are a Nevermore or you are not. I don't think either of you have anything to worry about. The blood work is just a precaution."

I thought Sebastian blew it when he asked. "But what if you found someone who was trying to sneak through, what would happen to them?"

She blinked several times as if trying to process his question. Taking in a short sharp breath she answered. "I suppose we would have to decide that at the time it happened. Most likely we would have to eject them from the airport, at the very least. More likely, they would be executed as there is no cure and the last thing we need is more Nevermores." She paused and leaned over the desk. "Is there something you'd like to tell me Mr. Wilson?"

I froze and felt Sebastian do the same beside me. He let out a laugh and shook his head. "No, I was just curious that's all. We've been out of touch with the world for weeks and have no idea what's going on out here."

She slowly stood, pushing her chair out behind her and changed the subject.

"I think there are people here you would like to see. You mentioned a "Marks" in your story, correct?"

The words sank slowly in and I blinked several times. "Yes, that's right. Why? Did you hear something? Did he make it out alive?"

Now she did smile. "I think I'll just send you down to the barracks and you can see for yourself."

She drew my blood first, and then Sebastian's.

Bastian didn't look so fine by the time the needle was prepped and ready. He was positively green as Dr. Stanwell drew blood from him.

"Is there anything else you need me to attend to?" She asked as she labelled the vials.

"I'm pregnant," I said.

She nodded. "I can see that."

"We had an ultrasound that showed the baby might have deformities. I would like a second opinion," I said. My heart-beat picking up. I hadn't believed Donavan when he'd said the baby was deformed. That was the only thing that got me through, but now I had to know the truth.

She nodded, and called out to another nurse who brought in an ultrasound machine. I lay on my back on the sterile, white paper-covered gurney, sucking in a breath as they spread the cool gel on my protruding belly.

The machine beeped to life and Dr. Stanwell rolled the sensor over my skin. "You look to be about four months along." At my nod she continued. "Everything looks good so far. I see fingers and toes. Heads, arms, legs. Yes, everything looks just fine."

A loud buzzing rushed through my ears. "Heads?" I squeaked out. Donavan was right then. What kind of deformities did our baby have?

Dr. Stanwell smiled and nodded as Sebastian gripped my hand so hard I thought the bones would pop.

"Yes, heads. You knew you were having twins didn't you?" She asked.

Silence reigned for a brief second and then Sebastian let out shout that made everyone jump, including me. His hands were in the air and his eyes filled with tears, as did mine. Twins. We had TWO babies. That's what Donavan had been seeing, not three arms on one baby, but two babies with only some parts showing.

Dr. Stanwell left us as they put the machine away; Sebastian sat beside me, his hands over our babies.

"I didn't ruin this at least," he whispered.

"You didn't ruin anything my love," I whispered back, my hand grazing his cheek.

We were assigned rooms that had once been offices and then were encouraged to go down to the main hall to see when the next flight was and where it was going.

On our way, we bumped into Annie, her hair and face clean; she'd even put on fresh clothes and a light dusting of makeup. But, her eyes were haunted. I knew that it would take a long time before the shadows disappeared.

"We're going to the barracks, Annie, do you want to come with us?" I asked. She shook her head.

"No, I'll wait for you here."

I nodded, and we struck out for the barracks. We made our way out to one of the small airstrips where it was practically a tent city.

"I guess they need to be close to where the fighting would be, huh?" I said

"Probably," Sebastian answered.

We were met at the front tent, the large green canvas flaps rustling in the wind, by a young man in well-worn uniform.

"I'm looking for Marks," I said.

The man—boy really—nodded. I was reminded of Burns and a sudden lump rose in my throat. He ran into the camp, motioning for us to wait for him. Only a few minutes passed and a familiar figure jogged into view.

I lifted a hand, "Marks!"

"Good to see you beautiful. I knew you'd make it. Give me minute, I need to check out and then I'll walk you to the command center." He flashed me a smile and ducked into the tent.

Sebastian put his hands on my shoulders and spun me slowly to face him. "I have to know, was there anything between the two of you?"

I blushed and Sebastian's mouth tightened into a thin hard line. "No. Marks . . . he wanted more than friendship. Sebastian, I have never looked at another man, never loved another man the way I love you. I would never break our wedding vow, not even . . ."

"Not even while I was a Nevermore," he said. I shook my head and he pulled me tight against his chest. "I'm sorry I doubted you."

I shrugged. "I doubted you too, with Jessica, and I know that nothing happened there."

He leaned down and kissed me lightly. "Forgiven?"

"Of course."

Marks popped back out of the tent and all but glared at us as we held each other loosely.

I could feel Bastian's muscles tighten as he and Marks glared at one another until I let out a cough. "Marks, this is Sebastian. Sebastian, this is Marks. If you two boys don't play nice together you're going to see a very ugly side of me. Got it?"

They turned to stare at me, giving almost identical looks of shock. I lifted one finger and pointed it first at Marks and then my husband. "I mean it."

Marks gave a sharp nod and Sebastian tightened his arms around me. "I don't want him calling you pet names," he said, loud enough for Marks to hear and go bright red.

"Sebastian, Marks looked out for me while I was stuck with Vincent. Perhaps instead of being an ass, you could thank him for looking after your wife while you were incapacitated," I said, loosened my grip on him and pulled away. That made it easier to give him the dirty look he deserved.

The young man let out a chuckle. "Damn, if you didn't already have two men at your feet, I'd be down there, too. Always did love me a fiery woman." Both Marks and Sebastian glared at the young kid till he swallowed hard and backed away.

395

Sebastian surprised me by holding out his hand to Marks. "She's right. Again. Thank you, for looking out for Mara. . . When . . . I . . . couldn't." He seemed to have some difficulty getting the words out but he managed.

Marks took his hand and gave it a single shake. "I would do it again. Only I wish the outcome were different."

Nope, that was not okay and this infatuation with me had to end now. I reached out and slapped Marks, stunning the men into stillness.

"Do not ever say that again. You are my friend, and I though you understood that was all there was between us, all there ever would be. If you can't get that through your thick skull then we can't even be that," I snapped, my voice hard and cold even to my own ears.

I linked hands with Sebastian. "We are going to the command centre."

Marks' cheek had a brilliant red hand print, but he nodded. "I'll show you the way." Setting a sharp pace; he led, and we followed.

Back into the terminal, the "command centre" was what had once been gate 9. It had the best view of the airstrip and the chairs and tables had been set up accordingly.

Annie was already there, waiting quietly in a corner. She saw us and stood, her eyes widening as they lit on Marks.

"I know you," she said, a soft blush creeping up her neck and into her cheeks. Well this was interesting.

Marks walked over to her. "You were the girl in the window."

"I'm hardly a girl. I'm almost twenty six," she said, a small spark of her fire showing itself. Interesting indeed. We left Marks and Annie to speak alone, and we made our way across the room.

"Where do you think they're going to fly us?" Sebastian asked.

I shrugged. "I don't know. I guess it really doesn't matter as long as there aren't any Nevermores."

On the far side of the main hall was a large world map, big black X's through several of the continents. In fact there was only one continent without an X through it and my breath caught in my throat. They couldn't be serious, could they? Marks caught up with us, Annie at his side.

A brief explanation from him quickly revealed that, indeed, they were serious. It was the only continent that didn't dive into the Nevermore revolution, weight wasn't an issue for the people there. The tribes had killed off the Nevermores who had appeared, and as a whole, the continent was the only one left pretty much intact.

We were going to Africa.

21

The next week while we waited for the test results allowed us some semblance of normality.

Annie and Marks became almost inseparable, their shared grief at losing loved ones tying them together as much as some chance encounter they'd had. For the most part Sebastian and I stayed in our own quarters, making up for lost time, revelling in the facts that not only were we together, but the babies would be fine.

We learned there were small pockets of humans living on each continent, surviving amongst the Nevermores, fighting them off as we had. But while most groups had decided to head to Africa to start again, a few had decided to stay where they were and try to make a go of it. I personally didn't think that was a good idea, but then, going to Africa had started to freak me out, too. Either way, the world had a major re-set when Nevermore was released on us all, like someone had pushed a button and thrown us all back five hundred years. Now the trick was not who could make the most money, or have the biggest house, but who could survive the best. Those would be the ones who helped to re-make the world. Dan had been right; it was survival of the fittest on the grandest scale possible.

The best news of all was that the vial we'd brought from Donavan's labs looked good. The initial tests were showing signs in the affirmative and the medical staff was ecstatic. We may have, with Donavan's mad genius, helped to bring the world back to some semblance of order.

Finally, the three of us were called down to the medical labs to get our results. Just inside the door stood two guards with guns, their faces giving away no emotion. I didn't like this. No one else had guards in attendance when they got their blood work results.

I reached for Sebastian and he took my hand, rubbing his thumb over my knuckles. Again, Annie went first and came out, if not smiling, then not frowning either. She was clean.

Then it was our turn.

We walked in and Dr. Stanwell motioned for us to sit in the ripped leather chairs opposite her.

"I'd really rather stand," Sebastian said.

"I think you'd better sit for the results," she said, her tone sombre.

He sat, his face losing colour as fast as he could plant his butt in the chair. This was not good.

She took a deep breath. "Sebastian. You aren't human anymore."

I couldn't bite down on the gulping sob that leaped out of my mouth. I put my fist into the offending orifice and bit down. No, this could not be happening! I stood up fast, tipping my chair over backwards. I wouldn't let them kill him.

"Give us a little time, we'll leave, the both of us," I said, leaning across the desk. "Please, he isn't like the other Nevermores, I don't care what the results are!"

Dr. Stanwell's green eyes widened behind her glasses. "Sit down Mara. I'm not finished."

Shaking, I did as she asked, my whole being torn apart by this news.

She took off her glasses and laid them on the desk. "You aren't human, but neither are you a Nevermore. We tested your blood several times, but they all came out the same. You are not a Nevermore. You will be free to go with Mara to the colony in Africa."

Stunned silence held sway, but before either Bastian or I could say anything she went on.

"Mara, your results were abnormal as well."

"What?" Sebastian asked. "She didn't take the shot! How is that possible?"

I put my hands to my belly, to the twins growing inside of me. "The babies," I whispered.

Dr. Stanwell nodded. "Exactly. I believe they have helped you with your allergy to the components. Not unlike an allergy sufferer that becomes immune to their local allergens. The children, I believe they will have many of the beneficial qualities of the Nevermore drug, not unlike Sebastian here. Those qualities and their being inside of you have spread some of those traits to you."

I thought about the last night in the cabin, as the Nevermores attacked, how easy it had been for me to see. How quickly I was healing from every nick and cut I received in the last four months, how my hunger seemed to have lessened, and yet I was no less able to go on.

I lifted my eyes. "What will happen to us when the colony finds out about this?"

She shook her head. "They won't. These papers will be shredded."

"Won't that get you in trouble?" I asked.

She laughed. "With who? The government, what is left of it, has far more pressing matters than the two of you. If there are things that people don't need to know, this is the time to put them aside. Sebastian is not a monster any more than you or I. I believe he deserves to be left in peace for what remains of your lives together. Though I am not impressed you tried to slip through, I understand why you did not say anything. I would have done the same for my husband, rest his soul."

My eyes welled. "Thank you, thank you so much."

She clapped her hands together.

"Now, you two have a flight to catch."

We left, hand in hand, all but floating our way back to the small office that had been our home for the last week.

"What does this mean for us?" Sebastian asked, as we packed our meagre belongings. I lay down on the bed and rested a moment, the roller coaster ride of emotions having drained me.

"All I know is that I can finally breathe and not be afraid of taking the next breath, I don't have to wonder if there will be a next breath. For you or me," I said. I reached a hand out for Sebastian and he lay down beside me; I rested my head on his chest. The beat of his heart was a steady drum in my ear. It was hard to fathom, after all we'd been through, that we'd both made it out alive and whole. Together. I held him tight while we waited for the announcement that the flight was ready.

"I love you, Sebastian."

He ran his fingers through my hair. "I love you too, more than anything, more than all the stars in the sky, more than the countless drops of water in the ocean . . ."

I slapped his arm. "Stop being such a drama queen."

"I'll show you drama queen!" He growled as he wrestled me around, our laughter filling the room.

He finally pinned me below him, his gaze darkening with desire. Leaning in, he kissed me, his lips working their way from my mouth along my jaw to the lobe of my ear.

That was about when the announcement came on that our flight was boarding.

Grabbing our small packs, we put a leash on Nero and were loaded onto the plane along with twenty five other people. Annie was already there and she gave us a smile.

The last person on board truly surprised me, but it made sense when he went and took a seat close to Annie. I gave Marks a wink and a thumbs up. It seemed to be a good match. I was happy for them.

The engines started up and we started to taxi down the runway. I thought about the people we were leaving behind, alive and dead. But, mostly those that had lost the battle to live. Burns and his earnest nature, Seraphima and her innocence, Scout and his loyalty, Jessica and all the world should have offered her. Dan and his pragmatic, gruff nature, Annie's little brother Dustin. Tears started in the corner of my eyes and quickly slid down my face as I was finally able to grieve for those who would travel with us no more. The safety had settled on me over the last week, but I hadn't truly trusted it until now.

"They're still with us, love," Sebastian said into my ear, again showing me how we were bound, not only by marriage, but deep inside our souls. I tipped my head and pressed it into his shoulder.

"They gave their lives, and because of them, we made it through," I said, my voice catching on the words. He wrapped his arm around me and pulled me tight. "We won't forget them, babe."

I nodded and the plane started to speed up, the force pushing us into our seats. I wiped away my tears. "Thank you, all of you," I whispered. For a moment, so brief I wasn't sure I hadn't imagined it, there was pressure on my leg and I looked down, expecting to see that Scout had somehow survived, and had hidden away on the plane.

Sebastian was right, they would always be with us, and we would carry their memories until we met them on the other side, hopefully years from now. But, for this moment, we were safe; I had Sebastian, a few friends and a new life ahead of us filled even with that elusive dream of children.

As we took to the air, the plane erupted with cheers and whistles, all of us headed to our new home.

One could only hope it wouldn't be quite as dangerous as our last move, to Fanny Bay.

Then again, it *was* Africa.

Turn the page for an excerpt from Shannon

Mayer's exciting new book,

"Dark Waters, Celtic Legacy Book 1"

The cool, wet sand slid through my toes as I scrunched them up. A rolling wave splashed up around my ankles; the wetsuit I was wearing only came to mid-calf and was hardly a protection against the cold water. Chesterman Beach was beautiful, everything the package had promoted it to be and then some, and I hoped that Ashling appreciated what it took for me to be here; to face my fears for her. She didn't seem any worse for the wear after our short, and my nightmare filled night. I on the other hand found myself stifling yawns; daydreaming of sleeping the afternoon away.

I fingered the small sheath on my upper thigh, the knife that Grandpa had given me right before he went into the institution. I'd wondered at the gift at the time, he'd really never bothered with me before. But when I'd told him that I was going diving, he'd been frantic for me to have the knife.

"Here, here. Take it." He'd said, nearly slicing me with his eagerness to give the knife to me. It had a bone handle and the blade was about eight inches long, intricate engravings swirling down the back of the blade, the edge honed razor sharp.

"Always take it with you when you go in the water. Promise me. That's when the monsters come." Grandpa had said.

I'd taken the knife and given him my promise. It was always the same with him. The monsters he saw, her feared they would come for the rest of us. So even if I wasn't his favourite, it was better, according to him, that I survive and the monsters die. Yup, he did say that to my face. I shook my head, scattering the thoughts.

I hated to admit it, but I took comfort in the knife, and did indeed take it with me diving. It had saved me once already. I grit my teeth as memories rushed through my mind and threatened to suck me into a panic attack. Using slow even breaths I managed to get my heart rate to a normal level. Okay, almost normal. Those memories needed to stay in the past, where they belonged. If only it was that easy.

Though this was what Ashling wanted, surfing was not my idea of a good time. Surfing on the west coast of Vancouver Island was even less of a good idea, at least to me. The water was cold even through the heat of the summer and was known for its riptides and jagged rocks as much as its waves. And yet, here we were. I shook my head, curls catching in the wind that stirred up the waves.

"Come on, Quinn, that water is great and the waves are bitch'n!" Ashling yelled. I stared at her, out in the water sitting on her surf board, unruly strawberry blond curls escaping her ponytail and dancing in the wind.

I waved at her and forced a smile to my lips. I wouldn't ruin this day for her; this was her moment, her celebration.

"I hate this." I muttered under my breath.

"Then why are you here?" A strong male voice asked me. It was our instructor, Luke. Damn, the voice I'd heard on the phone more than matched the man it was attached to. Rich and sensual.

I had a hard time looking at him. Drop dead gorgeous wouldn't even begin to describe the man in front of me. Not too tall, maybe 5'10, blond hair that seemed to shimmer in the sunlight and blue eyes that I couldn't look away from. I swallowed hard and stared at the sand at my feet. Far too pretty, far too dangerous with his silky voice that made me forget my own name. Ashling had been, to say the least, delighted when she saw him and realized he was our surfing instructor. Flirting and prancing in her little red bikini, she'd been determined to get his attention. But while he was kind to her, he didn't fall into her arms as she'd been hoping. Secretly, I was laughing. She was so pretty, petite and feminine, she wasn't used to men turning her down.

I fingered the cuffs on my wetsuit, anxiety starting to build. "I promised her we could do anything she wanted for her graduation gift."

We were the only ones here on this part of the beach, the early morning enough to scare many of the tourists away as well as the die- hard locals by the looks of it. From what the brochure had said, usually the beach was flooded, despite the cooler water, and the mist that wouldn't burn off till afternoon. In the distance I could see a few surfers riding the waves, black specks on the water.

"You must care for her a great deal." Luke said. He sounded surprised.

I frowned at him. "She's my baby sister man, of course I care about her."

"That's too bad." He said his voice soft. My frown deepened and a thrill of alarm started at the base of my spine.

"What the hell is that supposed to mean?" I asked, frowning at him.

He didn't have a chance to answer me.

"Quinn!" Ashling's call was sharp and far too high pitched. Not her usual light, airy tones. I spun to see her in the water with only her head above the waves as she gripped the surf board. Even from this distance, her pale green eyes were wide and full of fear. I didn't hesitate- though my body quailed with remembered fear and pain- didn't think about anything except getting her out of the water.

I took one step and arms circled around me, holding me tight and stopping me from diving into the water. "She'll be fine. Let her be."

"Let me go!" I yelled, jerking my body left and right, trying to free myself. Luke's grip only tightened; his arms like vices around my middle. Damn he was strong.

"Quinn!" Ashling's voice went up another octave and I stared in horror as her head bobbed down on the last bit of my name turning into a gurgle. Something large and black, skin shiny with slime breached in the water next to her then slid back under the waves. My heart constricted with fear, my body thundering with adrenaline. It had to be a killer whale, even though I didn't see a fin. That was the only thing out here that could be attacking her. We didn't have sharks on the west coast. At least, not that I knew of. God, I hoped not. I couldn't face that again.

Luke held me tight. "Quinn, please believe me, she'll be fine." His voice caressed my skin, his words reverberating inside my skull until I believed them. I relaxed into his arms, my head leaning back into his chest as a wave of fatigue swept over me. I slumped as my blood slowed and the fear left me. Luke was right, Ashling would be okay. She was a strong swimmer and this, his arms around me, felt so nice. Maybe she was just playing with me again. Like humming the theme to "Jaws". He turned me to face him, my back facing the ocean and the distant cries of the gulls. His hand came up and stroked my face; brushed an errant curl back and tucked it behind my ear.

"Ah, Quinn, let her go. It will be better for you to let her go now, rather than later. I know that's hard to hear, but you must trust me that I know what's best for you." He leaned down, holding my face in his hands as his thumbs rubbed intricate designs on my cheeks; his lips pressing into mine.

It was if I was kissing sunlight, golden warmth rushed through my veins, waking parts of me I had no idea were even there. The heat stirred some long dormant piece of me. The empty pieces that had left me hollow my whole life filled my body, sealing the broken bits together.

Quickened.

Pushing up against Luke's energy, my own power rippled through me, answering his kiss, my nerve endings flashing, and clearing my mind. Tingling from head to toe, I pulled away, tried to untangle my limbs from his. Though I didn't understand it, I felt the power and knew it for what it was. Magic.

Magic that gave me the strength to fight what Luke was trying to do to me.

"Ashling." I gasped out. Luke pulled back, a frown slipping over his beautiful face, marring it, taking the glamour away.

I slid my hand down my thigh to the knife sheath. "Let me go!" I said, again trying to pull myself out of his arms to no avail.

"Trust me Quinn; I'm saving your life right now. If you go into that water, you'll not come back out. You have to trust me." He said, the power in his voice sweeping over me again. I bit down on the inside of my cheek, the pain keeping my mind from dissolving under his words. But more than that, my own power seemed to buck under his attempts to sway me. I clung to it for all I was worth.

"I don't *have* to do anything!" I yelled.

I flicked the neoprene knife sheath open, and grasped the smooth bone handle. Jerking it out I plunged it into Luke's thigh. He let out a howl and stumbled backwards as I turned and sprinted into the surf, slipping my knife back in its sheath as I ran.

"Ashling!" I shouted, fear for my baby sister rolling over me; stronger than the fear I had of the water and what lay beneath it, though just barely. The ocean was not warm, and it stole what heat the kiss had infused me with. I dove in, slicing underneath the surf as a wave rolled over me.

Memories of the last time I'd swum, over three years ago, nipped at my heels; I did my very best to ignore them. But, they caught me between diving under the waves and surfacing. The bite of a shark on my leg, the fear as my respirator slipped off at forty feet below the surface, the panic at not being able to breathe.

Breaking the surface, I gasped for air; nearly turned back as I imagined all the things that swam below me. Paralyzed by my past, I couldn't move forward; I couldn't go back. Treading water, I trembled, my breath coming in short, sharp gasps. Heart hammering, my vision blurred as I struggled to get enough air, my body shutting down as the panic set in full force.

A wave rolled and in the valley of it was a flash of white and in my mind all I could see was the white belly of the shark as it rolled with me in its mouth.

Nothing but fear filled my mind, I couldn't think, couldn't hardly breathe as I swam back to shore. I was waist deep, scrambling for dry land, Luke reaching out for me when something grabbed me around my left ankle.

411

I let out a cry as I was dragged down; Luke stopped at the edge of the water his hands in his hair and a look of pure agony on his face.

Eyes closed tight, I fought like a wild thing, thrashing and punching at whatever it was that had me in its grip. And, then, for no reason I could see, it let go; I swam for the surface. Gasping for air I looked around; I'd been pulled out to sea. Way out.

I spun and something bumped me in the back. A shark, it was testing me out for a meal. My heart about to burst I spun to face Ashling's surfboard. One of her hands gripped the edge of it, white knuckles bobbing in and out of the water, the surfboard actually getting pulled under with her; the sight broke my paralysis. Her head was submerged except for the ends of her hair which floated on the surface. Something cold and slimy brushed against my legs and I bit down on a scream that made it all the way to my lips before I caught it. Salt water slipped inside my mouth; I spit it out and slid around the side of the board, but not before she lost her grip and disappeared under the water.

"Ashling!" I screamed. My voice echoed out over the water but the only answer I got was the gulls crying over head.

Looking down, I couldn't see anything below me; I could barely see my feet. Breathing deep, I prepped myself to dive, but on the second gulp of air, the choice was taken from me.

Teeth latched onto my calf yanking me under the water, my hands slipping from the surfboard. The bite was all too familiar. Apparently, I'd been wrong; there *were* sharks in these waters. Serrated teeth sliced through my flesh, biting all the way through the muscle, my foot clamped inside a powerful set of jaws.

My first thought was that mom couldn't be upset with me now for losing Ashling, not if we were both gone. My second thought as I rolled in the water- the pain drawing my eyes to the source of it- was that I'd lost my mind. It was no shark on my leg, but a monster, human in appearance with a single eye set high in the middle of its forehead; a massive mouth filled with sharp, shark-like teeth. The thing smiled as its hands, hooked like claws, rose up to dig into the waist of my neoprene wetsuit. The jagged tips brushed against my bare skin inside the suit and I trembled with fear, a new fear. What the hell was it?

"Can you hear me little Tuatha? I wonder if you know me deep in your soul? We are coming for you. All of you."

I blinked and stared into the huge, soulless eye, felt the keen edge of years behind it and much as I wanted to deny what I was hearing, acknowledged that the voice in my head wasn't my own. It was his.

What are you? I mouthed into the water, salty brine washing over my taste buds, morbid curiosity overcoming rational sense.

"I am your enemy, the one that will strip your flesh from your bones and bathe in your blood."

It, he, rumbled and rolled in the water, taking me with him, end over end until I no longer knew which way was up. Finally, he stopped and began to pull me into the depths of the ocean, the water getting colder with each inch we moved deeper, away from the sun and air.

Air. How could I still be under the water and not need to breathe? I didn't have time to think about that, as strange as it seemed.

Movement further below and to the right brought my attention off my own situation. It was Ashling, fighting with a monster very much like the one on my own leg. They were tumbling in the water, her hair floating about like tentacles as she fought the thing off. How could she be in this deep, for this long? How could I? Again that once hollow piece of me responded. This was why we'd never fit in, these abilities, this magic, these monsters. Though my head said that none of this was real, my heart and soul spoke louder.

This was real, this was happening and if I was to save Ashling I had to move now. That thought broke through the last of my fear, its hold dissolving under the reality I had accepted.

I grabbed my knife out of the sheath and slashed at the monster that held me in his mouth, slicing through the bulbous eye, white fluid pouring out of it. He jerked away from me, releasing my leg- a spray of blood clouding out around me- as he writhed in the water

He screamed, wordlessly, the echo of his pain reverberating in my skull.

Turning my back on him, I swam hard towards Ashling, holding the knife in my mouth. Twenty feet, fifteen, ten. I was nearly to her before she looked up.

She saw me coming and kicked the monster that held her tight, sending it into a spin away from her. Ashling swam for me, her lips tight, eyes wide and dilated. Five feet. Three. I reached for her, my hand wrapping around her slender wrist.

I didn't pause, just turned and started to swim for the surface. She swam hard beside me, but I refused to let go of her.

"She is ours, you will not have her!"

We were yanked to a stop in mid stroke, the surface only a few feet away, the sunlight streaming down through the waves with tantalizing nearness. I turned in the water and looked down. Ashling had a sea monster on each leg. Her pale green eyes were so wide they seemed to fill her face as they jerked her from my hands, speeding into the depths faster than a rock sinking. Her hands reached for me, futilely.

Hands grabbed me and pulled me upwards, away from Ashling, out of the water.

"No!" I screamed as I broke the surface, the last of my air erupting in denial. There were people all over the water; rescuers dove after Ashling. But, I knew what they didn't. They would never find her, somehow I knew that not only had my sister been stolen away, but my world had just shattered beyond repair.

And, it was all my fault.

Made in the USA
Charleston, SC
11 July 2014